"Ashley Herring Blake knocks it out of the park again with a rivals-to-lovers story with a big beating heart! She has a knack for writing characters who feel like they could be your friends—flawed women with complex inner lives who leap off the page with personality."

—Alison Cochrun, author of *The Charm Offensive*

"As only she can, Ashley Herring Blake weaves magic through each corner of her work, transporting readers to an inclusive haven they'll never want to leave." —Courtney Kae, author of *In the Event of Love*

"If you've read the first in this series, you wouldn't think this could be even better, but somehow it is! Blake has outdone herself. She's truly a romance powerhouse and an auto-buy author."

—Meryl Wilsner, author of *Mistakes Were Made*

"Returning readers will be delighted to revisit Bright Falls and any romance fan will thrill at the sexual and emotional gratification on offer here." —*Publishers Weekly*

"Blake tenderly explores Astrid's journey to becoming more herself—which involves interrogating her career dreams and realizing that she's bisexual. Astrid and Jordan are both appealing characters, and Astrid's boisterous and endearing group of queer friends will make Bright Falls a town readers won't want to leave. A steamy, emotional, and charming romance about defining success on your own terms."

—*Kirkus Reviews*

"The characters and relationship feel balanced and fresh. . . . Blake's second 'Bright Falls' novel (after *Delilah Green Doesn't Care*) is a good fit for readers looking for stories involving thirtysomething characters, bisexuality, strong friendships, and character growth."

—*Library Journal*

"Ashley Herring Blake's follow-up to *Delilah Green Doesn't Care* is a hot and hopeful renovation romance." —*BookPage*

PRAISE FOR
DELILAH GREEN DOESN'T CARE

"Blake captures all the complications of family, friendship, and romance with humor and heart." —*Kirkus Reviews*

"A fun hometown romance, planned as the start of a series of Bright Falls–set queer romances." —*Library Journal* (starred review)

"There's family drama, trauma, childhood memories, love, romance, diverse relationships between not just the main couple, but everyone in the book, that'll have you on the edge of your seat. The novel also does a great job of inputting a queer love story in the middle of an enticing read." —*USA Today*

"A hot, frothy rom-com with a relatable heart beating at its center. I loved every hilarious character, every outrageous shenanigan—and most of all, I loved Delilah Green. I can't wait for the rest of the series!"

—Talia Hibbert, *New York Times* bestselling author of *Act Your Age, Eve Brown*

"A truly exquisite romance about second chances, new beginnings, and the fragile joy of letting people in. I can't even count the number of gorgeous lines I highlighted. The setting, the scheming, the spice—Ashley Herring Blake paints every scene with a lyrical, tender brush. I'm wildly in love with this book."

—Rachel Lynn Solomon, author of *Weather Girl*

"A classic in the making, Ashley's adult debut is a warm welcome home from the first page. A swoon-worthy, laugh-out-loud romp of a romance, this rom-com deserves to be amongst romantic titans like *You've Got Mail, Breakfast at Tiffany's,* and *Sleepless in Seattle.*"

—Kosoko Jackson, author of *I'm So Not Over You*

"A spectacular debut brimming with yearning, swooning, and healing. *Delilah Green Doesn't Care* reads the way realizing your crush likes you back feels. Ashley Herring Blake is a romance star on the rise."

—Rosie Danan, national bestselling author of *The Intimacy Experiment*

"Ashley Herring Blake draws her characters with such beautiful, loving depth, and infinite compassion for the many ways relatives and friends can both hurt and heal each other."

—Lana Harper, *New York Times* bestselling author of *From Bad to Cursed*

"Snarky, steamy, and swoony in equal measure, I never wanted this book to end, but there's an easy momentum to Blake's writing that made it impossible to put down."

—Meryl Wilsner, author of *Mistakes Were Made*

"Charming and entertaining.... *Delilah Green Doesn't Care* entrances the reader with the redemptive power of love.... Blake's masterful blend of sexual tension and growing affection will have readers swooning." —Karelia Stetz-Waters, author of *Satisfaction Guaranteed*

BERKLEY TITLES BY ASHLEY HERRING BLAKE

Delilah Green Doesn't Care
Astrid Parker Doesn't Fail
Iris Kelly Doesn't Date

IRIS KELLY DOESN'T DATE

Ashley Herring Blake

BERKLEY ROMANCE
NEW YORK

BERKLEY ROMANCE
Published by Berkley
An imprint of Penguin Random House LLC
penguinrandomhouse.com

Copyright © 2023 by Ashley Herring Blake
Readers Guide copyright © 2023 by Penguin Random House LLC
Excerpt from *Make the Season Bright* copyright © 2023 by Ashley Herring Blake
Penguin Random House supports copyright. Copyright fuels creativity, encourages diverse
voices, promotes free speech, and creates a vibrant culture. Thank you for buying an authorized
edition of this book and for complying with copyright laws by not reproducing, scanning, or
distributing any part of it in any form without permission. You are supporting writers and
allowing Penguin Random House to continue to publish books for every reader.

BERKLEY and the BERKLEY & B colophon are registered trademarks of
Penguin Random House LLC.

Library of Congress Cataloging-in-Publication Data

Names: Blake, Ashley Herring, author.
Title: Iris Kelly doesn't date / Ashley Herring Blake.
Other titles: Iris Kelly does not date
Description: First edition. | New York: Berkley Romance, 2023.
Identifiers: LCCN 2023007812 (print) | LCCN 2023007813 (ebook) |
ISBN 9780593550571 (trade paperback) | ISBN 9780593550588 (ebook)
Subjects: LCGFT: Romance fiction. | Novels.
Classification: LCC PS3602.L3413 I75 2023 (print) |
LCC PS3602.L3413 (ebook) | DDC 813/.6—dc23/eng/20230224
LC record available at https://lccn.loc.gov/2023007812
LC ebook record available at https://lccn.loc.gov/2023007813

First Edition: October 2023

Printed in the United States of America
1st Printing

Book design by Alison Cnockaert

This is a work of fiction. Names, characters, places, and incidents either are the product
of the author's imagination or are used fictitiously, and any resemblance to actual persons,
living or dead, business establishments, events, or locales is entirely coincidental.

For Meryl and Brooke

IRIS
KELLY
DOESN'T DATE

CHAPTER

ONE

IRIS KELLY WAS desperate.

She paused on her parents' front porch steps, the June sun feathering evening light over the blue-painted wood, and took her phone out of her pocket.

Tegan McKee was desperate.

She typed the words into her Notes app, staring at the blinking cursor.

"Desperate for what, you little minx?" she asked out loud, waiting for something—anything that didn't feel overdone and trite—to spill into her brain, but nothing did. Her mind was a terrifying blank slate, nothing but white noise. She deleted everything except the name.

Because that was all she had for her book. A name. A name she loved. A name that felt right. A name that Tegan's best friends shortened to *Tea*, because of course they did, but a solitary name nonetheless. Which meant, in terms of her second full-length romance novel—the very one her literary agent was already up her ass about, that her publisher had already bought and paid for, that her editor was expecting to land into her inbox in two months' time—Iris had nothing.

Which meant Iris Kelly was the one who was desperate.

She glanced up at her parents' front door, dread clouding into her belly and replacing the creative panic. Inside that house, she knew what awaited her, and it wasn't pretty. Her mother's dentist, perhaps? No, no, her gynecologist more likely. Or, maybe, if Iris was really lucky, some poor sap who wanted to be there even less than Iris— because Maeve Kelly was nearly impossible to resist once she set her mind on something—and Iris and the aforementioned sap could commiserate over the absurdity of their situation.

Hell, maybe Iris could get some content out of it.

Tegan McKee was on a date. She hadn't planned the date, nor did she recall being asked out.

Iris froze with one foot on the step and opened up her Notes app again. That actually wasn't too bad . . .

"Honey?"

Iris dragged her eyes from that infernal blinking cursor—*Why the hell don't you want to go on a date, Tegan?*—and smiled at her mother and father, now standing in the open doorway, arms around each other, marital bliss causing their faces to glow in the summer light.

"Hey," she said, tucking her phone away. "Happy birthday, Mom."

"Thanks, sweetheart," Maeve said, red and gray-streaked curls bouncing into her face. She was a round woman, with soft arms and hips, and a hefty bosom Iris herself had inherited.

"More gorgeous every year, she is," Iris's dad said, kissing his wife on the cheek. Liam was tall and lithe, pale red hair ringing the shiny bald spot on top of his head.

Maeve giggled, and then Iris watched as her parents started

full-on making out, which included a flash of Liam's tongue and the definite, not-so-surreptitious slide of his hand down Maeve's ass.

"Jesus, you two," Iris said, stomping up the stairs and averting her eyes. "Can you give it a rest at least until I get in the house?"

They pulled away from each other but kept the obnoxious grins.

"What can I say, love?" Liam said, his Irish accent still fully in place even after forty years in the States. "I can't keep my hands off the woman!"

More kissing noises commenced, but Iris was already past them and heading into the house. Her younger sister, Emma, appeared with her four-month-old, Christopher, hidden under a nursing wrap, which Iris assumed meant the baby was attached to one of Emma's boobs.

"God, are they at it again?" Emma asked, chin-nodding toward the front door, where Maeve and Liam whispered sweet nothings in each other's ears.

"Are they ever not?" Iris said, hanging her bag on the hook in the foyer. "But at least it's distracting Mom from—"

"Oh, Iris!" Maeve called, pulling her husband into the house by the hand. "I have someone I want you to meet."

"Fuck my life," Iris said, and Emma grinned.

"Language," Maeve said, then hooked her arm through Iris's.

"Isn't there a dirty diaper in need of changing?" Iris asked as her mother dragged her toward the back door. "A filthy toilet I could scour? Oh, wait, I just remembered I'm late for a pap smear—"

"Stop that," Maeve said, still tugging. "Zach is perfectly nice."

"Well, if he's *nice*," Iris said.

"He's my spin class instructor."

"Oh, fuckity fuck."

"Iris Erin!"

Maeve shoved her onto the back deck, which was how she found herself sitting next to Zach, who, thirty minutes later, was busy extolling the virtues of CrossFit training.

"You never really know how far your body can go, what it can do, until you push it to the edge," he was saying.

"Mm," was all Iris had to say back. She sipped a Diet Coke, cursing her mother's habit of saving the wine for the meal, and looked around for a savior.

Liam was silent at the grill, a stalwart of *That's none of my business*, so he'd be absolutely no help. She loved her father, but the man was complete trash for his wife, bending heaven and earth for the woman whenever possible. Which meant Maeve sprung these "dates" on Iris nearly every time the family got together, and Liam would simply smile, kiss Maeve on the cheek—or make out for ten minutes as the case may be—and ask what she wanted him to grill for said blissful occasion.

Emma was currently sitting across from Iris at the redwood patio table, her red hair cut into a sensible, advertising executive bob, smirking at the whole situation. Emma thought her mother's setups were hilarious, and she also knew Iris would never, in a million years, go for someone Maeve dragged home.

Mostly because Iris hadn't gone for anyone at all in over a year.

"Have you ever done HIIT?" Zach asked now. "Feels like you're going to die while you're in the throes, but whew, what a rush!"

Emma snorted a laugh, then covered it by patting her newborn on the back.

Iris scratched her cheek with her middle finger.

Meanwhile, Aiden, Iris's brother and the eldest of the three Kelly siblings, was running around in the backyard growling like a bear, chasing his twin seven-year-old daughters, Ava and Ainsley, through the dusky golden light. Iris seriously considered joining them—a good game of tag seemed like a better way to spend an evening than this tenth circle of hell.

Of course, Iris had expected this. Just last month, at a gathering to celebrate Aiden's move from San Francisco to Portland, Iris had found herself seated next to her mother's hairstylist at dinner, a lovely lavender-haired woman named Hilda who led off the conversation by asking if Iris was a fan of guinea pigs. Iris then spent the next week wasting at least five thousand words on her novel as Tegan wandered around looking for a meet-cute in a PetSmart. She'd ended up scrapping the whole thing, then promptly blamed her mother for the horrible inspiration.

"You know that stuff will kill you," Zach said, nodding toward her soda and smiling wryly, showing all of his perfect teeth. He was a white guy—blond hair, blue eyes—but he was also vaguely . . . orange. Iris had to bite back a reply about tanning beds and skin cancer.

"Oh, see if you can get her to drink more water, Zach," Maeve said as she came outside with a tray of homemade veggie burgers for the grill.

"Water is really the only thing I drink," he said, leaning his elbows on his knees, admittedly impressive biceps flexing. "That and the occasional cup of green tea."

"Jesus Christ," Iris said, chugging back some more soda.

"What was that?" Zach said, leaning closer to her. His salty-piney cologne washed over her—a tsunami rather than a gentle wave—and she coughed a little.

"I said cheese and crackers," she said, slapping the table and standing up. She tugged at her cropped green sweater, which just barely covered her midriff. "I think we need some."

"Cheese and crackers, cheese and crackers!" Ava and Ainsley both chanted in between giggles and squeals from the yard, where Aiden had them both hoisted over his broad shoulders. Their long auburn hair nearly brushed the grass.

Aiden deposited the girls on the top porch step, and Iris immediately pounced, grabbing their tiny hands with her own. She moved so fast, she imagined she looked like a vulture descending from the sky, but honestly, she didn't care. She would one hundred percent use her adorable nieces to get her out of this situation.

"I can get it, honey," her mother said, depositing the platter of burgers into her husband's hands and moving back toward the door.

"No!" Iris yelled. She slapped on a smile and softened her voice. "I can do it, Mom, you take a load off."

And with that, she pulled Ava and Ainsley into the house, walking so fast their gangly legs nearly tangled with hers. She managed to get all three of them inside without ending up in a heap on the floor and bustled the two little girls into the kitchen through some carefully curated tickles.

Aromas of baking bread and sugar greeted them. Emma's husband, Charlie, was mashing potatoes in a giant blue ceramic bowl, forearms flexing, while Aiden's wife, Addison—resplendent in a belted shirt dress and ruffly apron—laid strips of pastry over what looked like a rhubarb and strawberry pie. It was like a fucking Norman Rockwell painting in here.

Iris waved at her siblings-in-law, then quickly located the charcuterie platter on the butcher block island her mother had already prepared. She immediately stuffed a rectangle of cheddar in her mouth, then spread a smear of brie onto a sesame seed cracker before dipping the whole thing into a tiny stainless steel cup full of locally sourced honey.

"Easy," Addison said as the twins reached for their own snacks. "Don't ruin your appetites."

Iris stuffed another delectable, meal-ruining square of bliss into her mouth. Addison was nice, and she and Iris had always gotten along okay, but the woman still dressed the twins in matching outfits, braided their hair in the same styles, and ran a mommy blog about how to balance style with efficiency in the home. She also had a tiny long-haired chihuahua named Apple, cementing their *only A-names allowed* household.

Not that there was anything wrong with any of that, but Iris, whose apartment was an amalgam of mismatched furniture and housed a drawerful of various sex toys in both of her nightstands, was never quite sure how to bond with her sister-in-law. Especially when Addison said shit like *Don't ruin your appetites* to kids eating tiny cubes of cheese.

Iris made a point to slather the honey extra thick onto her next cracker. Conveniently, this also meant her mouth was practically glued shut when her mother bustled into the kitchen, eyes aglow and fixed on Iris.

"So?" Maeve said. "What do you think?" Behind her, both Aiden and Emma, along with baby Christopher, spilled into the room.

"Yeah, Iris, what do you think?" Aiden said with a smirk, popping a square of pepper jack into his mouth.

Iris glared at him. Growing up, she and Aiden had been pretty close. He was only two years older than she was, and he worked as a designer at Google. He and Iris were both creative, both prone to dreaming, but ever since he married Addison and became a dad, they hardly ever talked except at family events like this one.

Not that Iris didn't understand—he was busy. He had a family, kids to feed and mold into responsible human beings, a spouse. He was *needed*, while Iris spent most of her time lately staring up at her dust-covered ceiling fan wondering why the hell she ever thought *writing* was the correct career choice after she closed her paper shop last summer.

"What do I think about what?" Iris said, playing ignorant.

"I think he's cute," Emma said, swaying while Christopher dozed in her arms. He squirmed a little, wrinkled eyes closed, mouth a tiny adorable rosebud.

"You would," Iris said to Emma. Emma was . . . well, she had her shit together. Always had. Three years younger than Iris, she'd married the perfect man at twenty-four, already worked her way to junior executive at a lucrative advertising agency in Portland by twenty-six, and popped out a kid at twenty-seven. Incidentally, this timetable had always been her plan, from age sixteen when she skipped her sophomore year and made a perfect 1600 on her SATs.

"There's nothing wrong with being health conscious," Emma said. "I think someone like that would be good for you."

"I can feed myself, Em," Iris said.

"Barely," she said. "What did you have for dinner last night? Potato chips? A Lean Cuisine?"

Needless to say, Emma and Addison were BFFs and co-chairs of the Perfect-Women-Who-Have-It-All club. Iris imagined it as an elite group that probably met in an opulent, password-guarded penthouse apartment, where all the members brushed each other's gleaming hair and called one another names like Bunny and Miffy and Bitsy.

"Actually," Iris said, popping a green olive into her mouth, "I fed on the repressed tears of uptight women who need to get laid, thanks very much." She eyed Charlie. "No offense."

He just laughed, cutting cubes of butter into the potatoes, while Emma's mouth puckered up in distaste. Iris felt a twinge of guilt. Unlike Aiden, she and Emma had never been close at all. As a kid, Iris had relished the idea of being a big sister, and there were myriad pictures of the precious Emma—the youngest, the surprise blessing, the completing jewel in the Kelly family crown—cuddled in Iris's arms. As the years passed, their roles shifted, the line between older and younger sister blurring, as Emma always seemed to know the answer, the right behavior, the correct choice, a split second before Iris did.

If Iris figured it out at all.

"Iris, really," her mother said, taking Christopher from Emma and patting his back. "Your father and I worry about you," Maeve went on. "All alone in your apartment, no roommate, no steady job, no boyfriend—"

"Partner."

Her mother winced. Maeve and Liam Kelly, both survivors of Irish Catholic upbringings, had always accepted Iris's bisexuality with open arms and hearts—even going so far as to set her up with Maeve's queer, guinea pig–loving hairstylist—but they still got trapped in heteronormative language sometimes, particularly when all of Iris's siblings were straight as fucking arrows.

"Sorry, honey," Maeve said. "Partner."

"And I have a job," Iris said.

"Writing those SEAs or whatever you call them that you don't even experience?" Maeve said.

Iris gritted her teeth. No one in her family had read her first novel yet. It wasn't out until the fall, and Iris's family members weren't exactly the romance-reading types. *Fantasy*, her mom called the genre back when Iris first fell in love with the books as a teenager. "Real romance takes work," Maeve had said, then promptly stuck her tongue down Liam's throat.

"*HEAs*, Mom," Iris said. "Happily Ever After."

Maeve waved a hand.

"Shittily Ever After," Aiden said, getting a couple of beers out of the fridge and handing one over to Charlie.

"Daddy said shit!" Ava said.

Aiden winced while Addison glared.

"Syphilis-ly Ever After," Charlie said, popping his beer open.

"What's syphilis?" Avery asked.

Aiden guffawed. "Septically Ever After."

"Aiden," Addison said.

"Fuck you both very much," Iris said.

"Iris!" Addison said, her tone like a middle school teacher, then promptly ushered her daughters out of the kitchen.

"Barn animals, all of you," Maeve said, covering one of Christopher's tiny ears. "Iris, all we're saying is that we worry about you being all alone."

"I'm fine," Iris said. Her voice shook a little, belying her words, but that's what a family ambush will do to a person. She *was* fine. Sure, she'd had to close her paper shop last year—she still designed and sold her digital planners out of her Etsy shop, but no one bought paper enough these days. Once Iris started offering digital planners, the brick-and-mortar aspect of her business suffered. It was a difficult call, but it was also exciting. After a few months of feeling a bit adrift, Iris decided to try her hand at writing romance. She'd always loved reading and had long dreamed of penning a book of her own. Turns out, she was a pretty decent writer. She banged out a story about a down-on-her-luck queer woman, who had a life-changing encounter with a stranger on a New York subway, then kept running into the same woman all over the city in the unlikeliest of places. She got several offers from agents and went with Fiona, who was the perfect blend of ruthless and nurturing, and sold *Until We Meet Again* to a major romance publisher in a two-book deal. Granted, she didn't sell it for a killing or anything, but Iris had enough money in savings to keep her afloat, and her Etsy sales brought in a steady stream of cash.

But of course, the dissolution of her business only made her mother freak out even more about her *future*, and Maeve considered writing a hobby more than a stable job. The fact that Iris hadn't dated anyone seriously in over a year didn't help. Iris imagined Maeve dedicated many hours a day to envisioning Iris dying poor and alone.

For Iris, the blatant lack of romance in her life was wonderful.

No drama.

No heartbreaks from partners who couldn't deal with the fact that Iris didn't want to get married or have kids.

No lies from people who claimed Iris was the most wonderful creature they'd ever met, only to find out from their sobbing spouse that they were fucking *married with children.*

Iris shook off the memory of the lying, cheating, asshole Jillian, the last person she'd let into her heart, thirteen months ago. Since then, she'd contented herself with writing about romance and had simply removed dating from the equation, along with conversation, phone number exchanges, and any sort of scenario that left room for *I'd like to see you again.*

There was no *again.* No second date. Hell, what Iris had been doing with people she met on apps and in bars for the last several months wouldn't even qualify as a first date.

Which was exactly the way Iris wanted it.

Because, if she was being honest, romance novels *were* a fantasy. Not that she'd ever admit that to her mother, but that was what she loved about them. They were an escape. A vacation from the harsh reality that only zero-point-one percent of people in the world actually got a for-real HEA. Stories like her mom and dad's, romances that lasted forty years, meet-cutes where the couple accidentally picked up the other person's luggage after an international flight to Paris—that shit wasn't *real.*

At least, it wasn't real for Iris Kelly.

For Tegan McKee however . . .

"Iris!" Maeve screeched, jolting Iris out of her brainstorming and startling poor Christopher awake.

"Sorry, Jesus," Iris said, then took Christopher from her mother and kissed his bald head. He reached a hand toward her, yanking on her long hair. Iris smiled down at him. He *was* fucking cute.

"See?" Maeve said, beaming at Iris. "Isn't it wonderful to hold a baby in your arms? Now just imagine your own—"

"Oh my god, Mom, stop," Iris said, then handed Christopher back to Emma.

"I'm sorry, sweetie," Maeve said. "But all I'm saying is that someone who's ready to settle down might be good for you. Zach told me he's *tired of dating*." She widened her eyes like she'd just revealed government secrets. "So are you!"

Iris rubbed her forehead. As usual, her well-meaning mother hit the mark just left of the bull's-eye. "I'm doing fine by myself, Mom."

"Oh, honey," Maeve said, looking at her with big *you poor thing* eyes. "No one is fine by themselves. Look at Claire and Astrid. They're happy now, aren't they?"

Iris frowned. "Just because they both have partners who make them happy doesn't mean they weren't happy before."

"That's exactly what it means," Maeve said, and Emma nodded, because of course she did. "Since she and Jordan got together, I've never seen Astrid Parker smile so much in the twenty years that I've known her."

"That's just Astrid," Iris said. "She was born with resting bitch face."

"Point," Aiden said, jutting a carrot stick into the air before biting off half. He was well acquainted with Astrid Parker's fierceness, as she'd eviscerated him on their high school debate team when he was a junior and she a mere freshman.

"And *my* point," Maeve said, grabbing the second half of the carrot stick out of her son's hand and throwing it at him before fixing her Concerned Catholic Mother eyes back on Iris, "is that all this gallivanting around, seeing a new person every week, avoiding adulthood, isn't healthy. It's time to get serious."

Silence filled the kitchen.

Get serious.

Iris had grown up hearing one version or another of that very phrase. *Get serious* when she got suspended her junior year of high school for getting into a verbal match with the assistant principal in the middle of a packed cafeteria about the archaic dress code. *Get serious* when she told her parents she wanted to study visual art in college. *Get serious* when Iris dreamed of turning the doodles in her journals and notebooks into a custom planner business. *Get serious* for the entirety of her three-year relationship with Grant, enduring constant questions about marriage and babies.

See, Iris liked sex. A lot. In her family's minds, she was *promiscuous*, which, even with her parents' best efforts at progressive thinking, still made her mother's mouth pinch and her father's fair Irish cheeks burn as red as his hair. Not that she shared many details with them about her personal life, but Iris was never very good at keeping her feelings or opinions to herself.

"Honey," Maeve said, sensing Iris's hurt. "I only want you to be happy. We all do, and—"

"Here's where you're all hiding," Zach said, his blond head appearing in the doorway. He stuffed his hands in his jeans pockets, which were so tight, Iris was amazed he could fit one finger in there, much less five. "Can I help with anything? Liam said the burgers are nearly there."

"Wonderful," Maeve said, brightening and clapping her hands together once. She eyed Iris meaningfully. "Iris, will you and Zach set the table for us?"

Another thing Iris wasn't very good at? Subtlety. Call it the product of a childhood as the quintessential middle child, call it a flair for drama, call it an inability to be *serious*, but if Maeve wanted Iris and Zach to couple up, then who was she to deny the woman her dearest wish on her birthday?

"Oh, we absolutely will," Iris said. "But first, I have a very important question for Zach."

He lifted a blond brow, a sly grin on his face. "Yeah? What's that?"

Iris smoothed a hand over her hair, tugging on one of the tiny braids plaited through her dark red locks like she did when she was nervous, a tick her mother knew full well.

Maeve tilted her head.

Iris took a deep breath.

Then she yanked the moonstone ring from her left index finger and went down on one knee, presenting the ring to Zach with both hands.

"Here we go," Aiden said.

"Oh no," Emma said, pressing her eyes closed.

"Zach . . . whatever your last name is that I will happily take as my own upon our union," Iris said, "will you marry me?"

"Iris, for god's sake," Maeve said, dropping her head into her hands.

"Um . . ." Zach said, backing up one step, then another. "Wait, what?"

"Don't break my heart, Zachie," Iris said, making her eyes as wide as possible, lifting the ring into the light.

"Iris, come on," Emma said.

Behind her, Iris heard Charlie snort-laugh.

"I . . . well . . ." Zach continued to splutter, his orange-toned skin deepening into russet. He took another step toward the living room and fished his phone out of his back pocket, squinting at the screen. "Oh. Wow. You know what?"

"Early meeting tomorrow?" Iris asked from her place on the hardwood floor. She stuck out her lower lip in a pout. "Family emergency?"

"Yes," he said, pointing at her. "Yes, exactly. I'm . . . this has been . . . yeah." Then he turned and bolted out the front door so fast, a cologne-soaked breeze fluttered the ferns in the entryway.

The sound of the door slamming shut echoed through the kitchen as Iris got to her feet and calmly slipped her ring back into place.

Her family watched her with partly amused, partly annoyed expressions on their faces, which was pretty much her childhood captured in a single scene. Wild-haired, nail-bitten Iris, up to her usual antics.

Despite this familiarity, Iris's cheeks went a little warm, but she simply shrugged and reached for another cube of cheese. "I guess he wasn't ready to settle down after all."

Her mother just threw her hands into the air and finally—dear god, finally—opened a bottle of wine.

CHAPTER TWO

ADRI AND VANESSA were making out.

Not that anyone else sitting in Bitch's Brew in the middle of downtown Portland would notice—the two were hiding behind a battered edition of *Much Ado About Nothing*—but Stevie knew the signs. Adri's pale fingers were grasping the orange cover just a little too tightly, and her mermaid-green hair, just visible over the top of their barricade, bobbed ever so slightly with the motion of her . . . well.

Anyway.

Stevie eyed the happy couple from her spot behind the espresso machine, black apron tied around her waist, batting a rainbow-hued streamer out of her face while she finished up a flat white. She and Adri used to do the exact same thing—up until about a year ago— giggling and kissing like teenagers in a coffee shop behind whatever screenplay they were studying at the time.

"Didn't she come here to talk to you?" Ren asked. They were sitting at the bar, two different cell phones lying in front of them, along with a sleek silver laptop and a large glass of cold brew.

Stevie shrugged. "I think that's what she said."

Stevie didn't think—she knew. Adri had definitely texted her this morning and asked if she could stop by Bitch's on one of Stevie's breaks so they could chat. Granted, this wasn't exactly out of the ordinary. She and Adri were still friends. Best friends. Vanessa was Adri's new girlfriend as of a month ago and, incidentally, also one of Stevie's best friends. Ren, the fourth member of their little queer crew that had bonded together during freshman orientation at Reed College and hadn't let go in the ten years since, worked remotely at Bitch's nearly every afternoon.

Stevie knew this situation wasn't unusual in queer communities. With such tight-knit groups, cemented together because of sheer numbers and shared experiences, it was pretty common for friends to have slept with each other once or twice, or at least engaged in a kiss or two. Still, Stevie and Adri had been together for six years— from senior year of college to . . . well, six months ago—and while Stevie had agreed when Adri instigated their breakup and everything had been mutual and mature and all that adult shit, Stevie wasn't quite prepared for Adri to jump into bed with one of the very people on whose couch Stevie slept when she first moved out of Adri's apartment.

She should've chosen Ren's couch.

But Ren, god bless them, lived in a luxury apartment in Portland's most expensive neighborhood, which also meant their place was the size of a toaster. It was immaculately decorated, all the finest linens and furniture, but their king-size bed took up the entire bedroom—for real, they didn't even have a nightstand—and a single love seat and coffee table made up the whole living space. It was all very Ren, who either invested in high-end stuff or went without.

But this was fine, because Stevie had found her own place, just a block from Bitch's where, yes, at twenty-eight, she still worked in between auditions and any roles she actually managed to land.

Which, lately, wasn't many. Her most recent acting job had been nearly a year ago, a modernized remake of *The Importance of Being Earnest* in Seattle, where she played Gwendolen and got decent reviews, resulting in absolutely zero interest from other directors.

Needless to say, she was in a bit of a rut. Ren, a publicist for an ethical clothing company, said she simply needed to remake her brand. Whatever the hell that meant. If Stevie had a brand, it was an underwhelming amalgam of anxiety and childish dreams she couldn't seem to relinquish.

How very inspiring.

"They're extremely unclassy," Ren said, glancing at Adri and Vanessa with a white stylus pressed to their cheek, head tilted elegantly. Ren's apartment wasn't the only thing that was immaculate. They were dressed in a three-piece gray suit, purple-and-green paisley tie, and three-inch purple heels. Their hair—black, short on the sides and long on top—coiffed and swirled upward in a way that would make Johnny Weir jealous. Their makeup was also perfect, silvery-purple eyeshadow, winged liner, shimmery lavender lip. Ren was Japanese American, nonbinary, pansexual, and the single coolest person Stevie knew.

Stevie laughed, shaking her curly fringe out of her face. She knew Ren loved Adri and Vanessa just as much as she did, but, yeah, she wouldn't mind if they took their little midday make-out sesh elsewhere. She had a feeling that the Shakespearean fortress was for her benefit—don't show PDA in front of the ex—but it wasn't exactly successful.

"They're fine," Stevie said, even as she thought the opposite. Ren eyed her, their quintessential *I'm calling bullshit* expression firmly in place. Stevie waved a hand and loaded the hopper with more glossy espresso beans. "It's fine, Ren."

"Okay, sure, whatever you say, Stefania."

"Oh, bringing out the full name, I see," Stevie said. "I must be in trouble."

Ren shrugged. "I'll bring out your middle name too if you don't grow more of a goddamn backbone."

Stevie's stomach pinched and she looked away. She knew Ren didn't mean to be harsh. They understood—better than anyone, lately—that Stevie's struggles with Generalized Anxiety Disorder were very real, but Ren tended to have a tough love approach to things, which, sometimes, made Stevie even more anxious.

Not that she'd ever tell Ren that.

"They're dating, Ren, what do you want me to do?" she asked.

"I want you to bring someone into the Empress and stick your tongue down their throat in front of Adri," Ren said calmly, tapping at something on their phone. "That's what I fucking want you to do."

The idea was so preposterous, Stevie couldn't help but laugh. The Empress was Adri's theater and they all loved it dearly—small, all-queer right down to the gaffer. Stevie had acted in nearly every production when Adri was first getting it off the ground, but about a year ago, she'd sworn off community theater. Adri hadn't been happy, but she'd understood—if Stevie was ever going to make a living off of acting, she had to go for bigger roles, bigger theaters, bigger exposure.

Lot of good that had done her lately.

"Who would I even make out with?" Stevie asked. She couldn't decide what was more unbearable—thinking about her flailing career or her nonexistent love life.

"Ever heard of a dating app?" Ren asked, a smirk on their face.

Stevie shuddered.

"A bar?" Ren said.

Stevie pretended to nearly throw up.

Ren laughed. They both knew Stevie was horrible at talking to people she didn't know, bordering on disastrous. Extreme anxiety made her literally nauseous, and nothing triggered that lovely symptom more than trying to charm a beautiful stranger.

"Okay, fine," Ren said, picking up their cold brew, "but something's got to give, or else you'll end up watching former lovers metaphorically bang in your place of employment for the rest of your life." They jutted their thumb toward Adri and Vanessa, who were now making out with such gusto, the screenplay had fallen and Adri's hands were tangled in Vanessa's lustrous hair.

Stevie's stomach, jerk that it was, leaped into her throat and set up shop. It wasn't that she wanted Adri back. She didn't. They had fizzled out long before they officially broke up, and deep down—*way* the hell deep down—she was happy for her two best friends if they wanted to be together.

But goddamn.

Just once, she'd love to be the one *doing*, instead of the one *watching*.

"Oh, for fuck's sake."

Stevie startled as Bitch's Brew's owner, Effie, came up next to her. She was dressed all in black, as usual, and her thick Cockney accent always seemed to make her sound pissed off.

Granted, this time, she was pissed off.

"Oi!" she yelled in Adri and Vanessa's direction. "This ain't a fucking brothel, you two."

Adri and Vanessa sprang apart. Vanessa fumbled with the screenplay, which she'd clearly only just realized had fallen from her fingers, and opened it back up to a random page. Adri just laughed and ran a hand over her chin-length hair, that dimple Stevie used to kiss at night before bed pressing into her pale skin. Her lipstick was bright red, as always, but now it was smeared all around her mouth.

Stevie mimed wiping her lips with the back of her hand.

"Sorry, Effie," Adri said, taking Stevie's cue and pressing a napkin to her mouth. "You know how it is."

"The fuck I do," Effie muttered, then went back to the tangled string of rainbow-colored lights in her hands. Bitch's Brew's normal decor was dark and cozy—shelves full of colorful bottles and jars, lots of potted plants scattered about, vintage posters depicting recipes for home remedies using mugwort and sage and feverfew. But now, with Pride month officially begun, Effie brought out her full queer witch, dousing the place in rainbow flags and lights. She also offered seasonal drinks like Pansexual Pistachio Cold Brew, which Ren was currently enjoying.

"Get these untangled, will you?" Effie said, thrusting the lights into Stevie's arms. "And handle your mates. I'll take over the bar."

"Sure," Stevie said while Ren narrowed their eyes at her. Stevie gave them a befuddled look and came out from behind the counter. Effie was her boss—what did Ren expect her to do, refuse to comply with a hearty *fuck you*? Easy for Ren to say—they already had their dream job that paid six figures and included a wardrobe allowance.

"Hey," Adri said as Stevie approached.

"Is now a good time to talk?" Stevie asked.

"Yes, absolutely," Adri said, except there were only two chairs at this table, and Vanessa was in one of them.

Silence reigned for a split second.

An awkward, fuck-Stevie's-life kind of silence.

She adjusted her simple black tee, feeling suddenly plain and underdressed. Vanessa Rivero-Domínguez was the single most beautiful person Stevie—or most people—had ever seen. She had dark, impossibly shiny hair, high cheekbones, a mouth that looked like it was designed for pouting, Disney-princess eyes, and a voluptuous figure she knew how to dress. Stevie once witnessed a middle-aged white man run headfirst into a lamppost on the street because he was checking her out.

Needless to say, the fact that Adri's first girlfriend after Stevie— whose wardrobe consisted mostly of youth-sized thrift store T-shirts with things like *Oak Elementary Believes Kindness Counts* printed on them—ended up being their goddess-like best friend didn't do much for Stevie's self-esteem.

Stevie cleared her throat.

"Oh shit, sorry," Vanessa said, standing up and gathering a pile of papers she seemed to be grading before she'd locked mouths with her girlfriend. She taught Latin American literature at Reed, so she was yet another full-blown adult in their foursome, and a literary genius at that. "I need to get back to campus anyway."

"Bye, babe," Adri said, lifting her chin for yet another kiss.

Vanessa complied—Stevie tried not to notice Adri's pierced tongue briefly getting into the mix, she really did—then whispered, "Let me know how it goes."

"I will," Adri whispered back.

"Go easy on her," Vanessa said to Stevie as she slung her messenger bag over one shoulder. Her long wavy hair got caught in the strap, and it seemed like everyone in the café watched, open-mouthed, as Vanessa worked the glossy tresses free. "She's desperate."

"What?" Stevie frowned, glancing between her two friends.

"Van," Adri said. "I was going to try and butter her up with a scone or something first."

"Stevie can get her scones for free," Vanessa said, leaning in to kiss Stevie's cheek. "Good to see you. Like I said, go easy on her."

And with that declaration, Vanessa squeezed Ren's shoulder in farewell, then all but flounced her way out the door and into the cloudy June afternoon, Bitch's patrons' eyes trailing her as she went.

Stevie looked at Adri.

Adri smiled.

"So," Stevie said.

Adri waved toward the now-vacant chair. "Sit down, will you?"

"As long as you help me untangle these lights, or I may have to sic Effie on you."

"God, anything but that," Adri said, lifting her coffee mug to her lips. The drink had to be cold by now, but Adri never minded cold coffee.

Stevie slid the chair around to the opposite side of the table—no way was she same-siding it with her ex, best friends or not—and plopped the lights onto the table. Adri leaned forward and grabbed a knot, working the wires with her long fingers.

"How's it going lately?" she asked, eyes on the lights. "Had any auditions?"

Stevie hated this question. The answer was always yes. She was a relentless auditioner, constantly spanning Portland all the way up to Seattle. She'd even driven to Vancouver two months ago. The real question was not whether she'd auditioned, but whether she was landing parts.

Which was a definitive and depressing no. Granted, she didn't really cast her net very widely. She knew she needed to expand, maybe even get the hell out of the Pacific Northwest, go to LA, New York, Chicago, but the thought of taking those trips alone, much less *moving*, made her stomach feel like it just might take up permanent residence outside of her body.

"Here and there," she said, keeping her gaze on the colorful bulbs. A perfectly satisfying, if vague, answer.

"So you're not working a show right now?" Adri asked.

Jesus. Adri always did like to say it plain. Stevie never knew how to say anything plain.

"Um, well, no, not right now. I'm—"

"Oh thank god," Adri said, blowing out a breath and sort of crumpling onto the tabletop for a second. Then she sat up, posture totally straight. "Sorry. Van's right. I'm a little desperate here."

Dread filled Stevie's gut. Auditions. Roles. She knew where this was going.

"Adri," she started, but Adri leaned forward and grabbed her hands.

"Please," she said. "I need you."

"I told you, I'm done with community theater."

"I know, I know, and I get it, Stevie. I really do, but the Empress . . . she's in trouble."

Stevie paused. "What?"

Adri pressed her eyes closed. "*I'm* in trouble. Rent has skyrocketed, I can barely pay my staff, and with inflation, people aren't going out to shows as much anymore. All that on top of our somewhat niche take on things, the Empress is suffering."

Adri Euler was the only female theater owner in the city, not to mention the only lesbian theater owner. For the last several years, she'd worked hard to get the Empress off the ground, a tiny venue just south of downtown, and had managed to staff a few regular actors while leaving room for community roles in every production. The Empress specialized in queer interpretations of classics—gender-bent, swapped, and inverted, as well as trans, lesbian, gay, bi, pan, ace, and aro character arcs woven into familiar cishet plots.

The Empress was a queer institution in Portland. A safe space, a community. A home for many.

"I had no idea," Stevie said.

"Because I've only told Vanessa," Adri said.

Stevie nodded, but she couldn't help feeling a pang of loss. She was no longer Adri's confidante. And while Vanessa and Adri had always been close, it still stung to hear Stevie was now an outsider when it came to Adri's emotions.

"Right," Stevie said.

"But I've decided to turn this next production into a fundraiser. We're doing *Much Ado*."

Stevie tilted her head, smiling. Adri smiled back and, for a second, the last six months hadn't happened. The last six years, even. Instead, they were best friends who hadn't yet crossed into romance, sitting in that crappy apartment with the ant problem that the four of them shared senior year. Stevie and Adri were sprawled on the plaid couch they'd found on the street and doused in three bottles of Febreze, reading through *Much Ado* in order to "reimagine" the iconic play for their senior thesis.

"This would be so much better if everyone was queer," Stevie had said, reading yet another of Beatrice's diatribes at Benedick. "Take out the toxic masculinity, add a little good old-fashioned gay yearning, and—"

Adri had slapped her hand onto Stevie's leg. They looked at each other, both of their eyes wide, and that was it. Adri kissed her—*really* kissed her, for the first time—and they spent the weekend huddled together, nitpicking every line, blocking out every scene, and noting facial expressions to turn the play into something funny and familiar, yet entirely new.

A few years later, the Empress was born.

"Always a crowd-pleaser," Stevie said now.

"Exactly," Adri said softly, squeezing Stevie's fingers. "And we're going all out—a sit-down dinner on closing night after the final performance, a silent auction, you name it. Except . . . I need butts in the seats for this to work. I need people to buy tickets to even be able to put it on."

Stevie pulled her hands free. She couldn't think straight while being touched. Never could.

"And?" she said, going back to a particularly stubborn knot in the wires.

"And," Adri said, "I need you to play Benedick."

Stevie closed her eyes. She fucking loved Benedick. He was an asshole, sure, but playing him as a queer person, opposite a queer Beatrice . . . well, there was no doubt that would be quite a show.

"You'll bring in our supporters," Adri said. "The community

loves you and, fine, go ahead and deny it, but Stevie Scott is a name
in this town."

Stevie scoffed. If she was a name in Portland's theater world, she
wouldn't be sitting in a coffee shop with a potentially degrading
swear word in the name, untangling rainbow twinkle lights for a
cranky practicing witch from Liverpool.

"You are," Adri said firmly. "You're an amazing actor, you've done
dozens of shows all over this town, ninety percent of them to rave
reviews. With you on the bill, we could pull the crowd we need."

Stevie didn't look at her. Couldn't. She knew if she did, she'd cave
and say yes, and hell, who was she kidding? She was going to say yes
anyway. *No* was never a very easy word for Stevie when it came to
Adri, when it came to anyone, really. She could handle the little
stuff—*do you want a soda, have you seen this movie, do you like onions on
your pizza*—but the big stuff, the stuff that caused disappointed expressions and down-turned mouths . . . yeah, she sucked at that part.
Her anxiety would flare, and she'd spend the next week convinced
her friends hated her, she'd die alone and miserable, and wasn't worth
a damn to anyone. Then, when said friend or family member eventually got ahold of her to tell her that, no, of course they didn't hate her,
why in the world would she think that, her anxiety would crest once
again, convincing her that she was terrible at understanding people
and could never trust her own brain to make heads or tails of any
social situation.

Easier to simply say yes.

So that's exactly what she did.

"Oh my god, thank you," Adri said as soon as the "Okay" was
out of Stevie's mouth. She leaped out of her chair, nearly knocking
over her mug, and launched across the table to gather Stevie into
a hug.

And Stevie found herself sort of . . . melting into the embrace.
Adri still smelled the same—the rainwater lotion she used, cinna-

mon from her toothpaste—and the smoothness of her cheek against Stevie's was almost too much. Stevie very nearly *nuzzled* her, for god's sake, and it wasn't because she was still in love with her ex.

She simply hadn't been touched in so long. Ren wasn't much of a hugger. Their comfort usually came in the form a slap on the back, along with an admonition to suck it up. And while Stevie had told Adri and Vanessa she was one hundred percent fine with their blessed union—she *was*, goddammit—she hadn't really touched either of them since they started dating. She hadn't touched *anyone*, and now, with Adri's cinnamony breath in her ear, her skin sort of . . . woke up.

She turned her head, just a little, ready to give in to the urge to press closer. She just needed—

"Hey, hi, wow, what's going on here?"

At the sound of Ren's voice, Adri pulled back, laughing awkwardly even as she held on to Stevie's hand. Stevie blinked the café back into focus, winced as Ren glared down at her.

"Stevie here has agreed to be my Benedick," Adri said, totally oblivious to Ren's dagger eyes.

"Has she now?" Ren said, their voice dripping with sarcasm.

The glaring continued.

Adri, however, remained clueless. She gathered her things together, tossing the copy of *Much Ado* into Stevie's space. "I need to get going." She stood and slung her bag over her shoulder. "Stevie, auditions for the other roles start next week. Let's get together soon and talk about some logistics?"

"Yeah," Stevie said, still slightly dazed. "Okay."

"I'll text you," Adri said, then headed for the door. As soon she stepped outside, she nodded and said something to someone off to the left. Suddenly, Vanessa appeared, launching herself into Adri's arms. The two kissed, linked arms, and disappeared down the street, Adri gesticulating wildly in that way she did when she was excited.

Guess Vanessa didn't need to get back to campus all that soon after all.

"Holy shit, did *you* just get played," Ren said, falling into Adri's now-empty chair, lifting their drink to their mouth.

Stevie turned back to look at her friend. "You heard all that, did you?"

"Oh, I did. Hearing like a bat," Ren said, gesturing to their ears, which were loaded with tiny studs and hoops.

Stevie sighed. "It's not like I have anything better to do right now."

"You keep telling yourself that."

"It's a play," Stevie said. "It's exposure."

"Same town, same stage. What's it been? Ten years?"

Stevie shook her head. She and Ren had had this conversation many times—Ren wanted Stevie to branch out, move to a bigger theater city. Stevie was terrified to do so. Etcetera, etcetera.

"Okay," Ren said, waving a hand, short nails painted black as always. "Fine. You're doing the play. Save the Empress. Great. None of us want it to go under. What I'm more concerned with is . . . what the fuck was that? A cuddle? A snuggle?"

Stevie groaned and dropped her head into her hands. "I know. It was bad." She looked up abruptly. "Did Adri notice? Do you think she could tell?"

Ren winced. "I mean . . . I could see her face and she didn't look like she was ready to nuzzle back, I'll say that."

"Shit," Stevie said. "Fuck, fuck, fuck."

"It's fine," Ren said. "She was too distracted by roping you into yet another career-stalling role to be too concerned."

"That's not what she's doing."

"I know she doesn't *mean* to do it, but it's still what she's doing."

Stevie rubbed her forehead. "I'm just a little lonely. Like for physical stuff."

"You mean horny."

Stevie blushed. "Call it whatever you want, but that's all this is. I haven't been out with anyone since Adri and I—"

"Hold up." Ren presented a hand. "No one?"

"You know I haven't, Ren."

"I mean, yeah, I know you haven't dated anyone, but I didn't realize you hadn't even, like, had a dating app hookup or anything."

Stevie gave them a look. "Really? You do know who you're talking to, right?"

Ren grinned. "Okay, by *hookup* I mean sharing a nice meal and going for a walk through the park, followed by a cuddle on the couch while watching *While You Were Sleeping*, possibly concluding with a little French kissing. You know, a Stevie-style hookup."

Stevie plunged her head back into her hands. "God, I'm fucking pathetic."

Ren laughed, pulled down Stevie's hands. "You're not. You're just terrible at one-night stands. There are worse things to be."

Stevie nodded. Ren was right. She *was* awful at one-night stands, but she wanted to be different, even if just once, to prove that she could. That she wasn't the friend left behind sniffing her ex's neck at the first sign of physical affection. That she could meet a stranger she liked, talk to them without embarrassing herself, kiss them, fuck them, and say goodbye. She liked sex. A lot. That was never the problem. It was building up to that point with someone she barely knew that she could never handle.

But she wanted to.

"Okay, so help me," she said.

Ren lifted a perfectly sculpted brow. "Help you do what?"

"Have a one-night stand."

Ren's eyes widened. "I'm not exactly an expert."

This was true. Ren had certainly had their share of hookups, but they preferred an actual dating relationship as opposed to fevered one timers.

"Yeah, but you know how to talk to strangers," Stevie said. "Charm them. How to act like a person who knows how sex works."

Ren laughed. "Okay, well, when two people like each other, sometimes, they'll take off their clothes and—"

Stevie threw an empty straw wrapper at them. "You know what I mean. Come on, even my therapist thinks I need to do this," she said.

"Keisha told you to go have a random hookup?"

"Not in so many words. She said I should take a friend with me and ask someone out in a bar. To, you know, get more comfortable in that atmosphere."

Ren's brows popped at that. "How long ago did she issue that prescription?"

Stevie winced. "Four months?"

"Jesus." Ren sighed, looking at Stevie through narrowed eyes. "All right. I'll help you. But let's do it tonight before you lose your nerve. Knowing you, you'll get a good night's sleep and come to your senses."

Stevie nodded, nerves sparkling through her belly. "Okay. Fine. Tonight."

Ren lifted their glass to seal the deal. Stevie clinked Adri's coffee cup against Ren's but didn't drink it. No way in hell was she toasting her impending one-night stand with her ex's cold coffee.

CHAPTER

THREE

BY THE TIME Iris escaped the birthday dinner from hell, it was nearly ten o'clock. The meal had dragged on and on, and her mother insisted that everyone play at least one round of Scrabble before leaving, which turned into three, because Aiden couldn't handle the fact that Emma was incapable of losing a word game and kept calling for rematches.

Iris endured it all, particularly after her *theatrics*, as Emma called them, had caused her mother to drink not one, but two glasses of Pinot Noir at dinner. Iris had never known her mother to consume more than a sip or two of alcohol in a single sitting, and the resulting hiccups were both comic and worrying.

Still, when Maeve brought up Grant's impending wedding as soon as Emma's final letter tile hit the triple word score, bringing game three to a merciful end, Iris had had just about enough.

"Yes, Mother, I got the invitation," she said, scooping tiny wooden letters off the dining room table and into the velvet bag while her siblings gathered their sleeping children from the living room. She'd always known her ex, Grant, would get married eventually. He'd dreamed of a big family, wanted to grow old on a front porch, snapping peas at twilight surrounded by grandchildren, so it wasn't like Iris was all that surprised to receive the thick ivory invitation in the mail a few weeks ago.

"Her name is Elora," Maeve said, taking a sleeping Christopher in her arms so Emma and Charlie could collect the amalgam of shit needed to keep a baby alive for an evening. "What kind of name is that?"

"A nice one," Iris said brusquely, packing everything away in the Scrabble box and jamming on the lid.

"Odd, if you ask me," Maeve said. "Not as nice as *Iris.*"

"Mom," Iris said, pushing her fingers into her temples. "Please don't."

"I'm just saying, you two were great together," Maeve said.

Iris pressed her mouth flat. More and more lately, coming over to her parents' house felt like undergoing a root canal—she felt exposed, judged for her choices, and left with a fierce need for some self-medication.

"You talking about Grant?" Aiden said, a passed-out Ava propped on his hip and probably drooling on his shoulder. "God, I miss him."

"We all do," Maeve said. "I felt like I lost a son when he and Iris broke up."

"Thanks, Mom," Aiden said, rolling his eyes.

She swatted at his arm. "Oh, you know what I mean. He was a keeper, that one."

Iris slipped the game into the sideboard, alongside several other board games, and tried not to scream.

"I wonder what his fiancée is like," Aiden said. "Bet she's hot."

"Who's hot?" Addison said, appearing in the doorway, holding Ainsley's hand. The little girl was nearly asleep on her feet.

"Um," Aiden said, and their mother grinned.

"Grant's fiancée," Iris said, smirking at Aiden's betrayed look.

Addison barely batted an eye though. "Oh, she is. I Instagram-stalked her when we got their wedding invitation."

"You did?" Maeve said. "What's she like?"

"Here, I'll show you," she said, pulling her phone out of her pink cashmere coat. "She's gorgeous. And Grant looks *so* happy."

The family huddled around Addison, quickly joined by Emma and Charlie, all of them oohing and aahing over Grant's perfect new life in Portland with his perfect new dream woman.

Iris stood alone and wished for an asteroid to collide with earth.

"My god, these two will have such beautiful babies," her mother cooed, clasping her hands to her chest as she ogled the screen.

And that was the last goddamn straw.

Without a word to anyone—her father had long disappeared into his study for some peace and quiet and, honestly, fuck the rest of them—Iris grabbed her coat and bag from the rack in the foyer and slipped out the front door. She didn't dare slow down but headed straight for her Subaru parked on the curb, started the engine, and peeled down the street so fast, she was positive she left tire marks on the asphalt.

At this time of night, the two whole stoplights in Bright Falls were blinking yellow, so she didn't stop until she parked outside her apartment building in downtown. She shut off her engine, but then flopped her head against her seat instead of getting out. She glanced up at her unit's window on the second floor—she hadn't left any lights on. She always forgot to do that when she left for the evening, but tonight, for some reason, the idea of walking into her place in the dark, alone . . . it all felt like a bit too much.

She dug her phone out of her bag and texted the group chat.

Iris: You won't believe what my mother did tonight

She waited for someone to respond. The chat's name was currently *I've Got a Queery*, but it changed on the regular, usually because Iris was bored or sitting at home alone while everyone else participated in their domestic bliss and—she could admit it—she was vying for some attention.

She stared at the screen.

Nothing.

She tried again.

Iris: Actually you probably would believe it

Iris: I think I might be engaged to a fitness icon. It's unclear

She added a bicycle emoji, followed by a diamond ring, still to no avail.

There was a time when their group chat was on a constant stream, hardly quiet for even an hour. Iris knew it was to be expected for things to take a little longer these days—everyone was coupled up, living together.

Everyone but Iris.

Her throat went a little tight and she gave herself a mental slap, then set her thumbs to work again.

Iris: ALL RIGHT LOVERS, CODE RED OVER HERE!

Then, finally, a response. Iris ignored the way her heart literally fluttered in her chest with relief.

Astrid: Stop yelling

Iris: I am most certainly not yelling. I'm cajoling

Delilah: You're yelling

Iris: Astrid and Delilah agreeing, well, my my

Delilah: 👆

Claire: Were they cute, at least? Your mom's setup?

Iris: He was orange. And hated Diet Coke

Jordan: That stuff will kill you

Iris: Wait, Jordan . . . are YOU actually a spin instructor named Zach?

Astrid: I sure as hell hope not

Jordan: I have a confession . . .

Iris smiled, then started tapping out her next pithy reply when an email notification from Fiona popped onto her screen.

"Shit," Iris said, wincing as she tapped on her email app. She shouldn't even read it. While her agent worked at all hours of the day, Iris knew it was perfectly acceptable for her to delay her own work until the morning, but she was a glutton for punishment.

Hey Iris, Fiona's email started, I wanted to check in and see how the novel was coming along. Are we still working through the ornithologist on a Caribbean island idea?

Oh, Jesus, no, they were most definitely not still working through that idea. While a hot bisexual scientist who studied birds was appealing, Iris knew zilch about poultry and, honestly, didn't give a shit about the mating habits of parrots.

I'm here for brainstorming if you need it, but a gentle reminder that getting this book in on time will be the best bet for building your brand. We want book two to release no later than a year after your debut.

Iris stared at the screen. She'd heard all of this before. The romance world moved fast, the fans hungry for more and more, and while Fiona had assured her that they could ask her editor, Elizabeth, for an extension, it really behooved Iris's career to keep things moving.

Simon—Jordan's twin brother and a literary fiction writer—had been absolutely appalled at the timeline. His lot took years to pump out a single two-hundred-page novel that then won them Booker prizes and spots on the National Book Award longlist.

If you're struggling, Fiona's email went on, I'll tell you what I tell all my clients dealing with a block—take a break. Do something creative that has nothing to do with writing. Take a pottery class or learn how to make sushi. Anything that's low stakes and gives your brain the space to come up with something brilliant!

Iris glared at that hopeful exclamation point, but Fiona's idea wasn't all that bad. She could think of a few low-stakes creative activities she'd like to engage in right now, though none of them involved a class. After the dating ambush tonight, followed by the shaming of Iris's way of life that seemed to be a new family tradition, Iris would welcome a distraction.

A human-shaped, no-strings-attached distraction.

Iris: Anyone up for an impromptu night out?

Astrid: It's ten-thirty

Iris: So that's a no for Astrid

Jordan: I go where my woman goes

Iris: Thrilling life you two lead

Claire: I've got to open the store in the morning—my manager's on vacation

Iris: I assume that means you're also out, D?

Delilah: Look, I'm VERY comfortable with my current situation, as Claire is . . . never mind

Claire: BABE

Delilah: 😏

Iris: No, please, keep going. Fodder for my dead-on-arrival novel

Delilah: I swear to god, if my admittedly mind-blowing love story ends up in one of your books, Iris, I will connect all of your freckles with a Sharpie while you're sleeping. I have a key to your place, I'm not afraid to use it

Iris: "Delilah Green didn't care about anyone and consistently forgot the names of the women she slept with. Until she met Claire Sutherland." I like it. Catchy

Astrid: Laugh out loud!

Delilah: Astrid, use a damn emoji, and Iris, I'm buying a fresh pack of markers

Claire: Babe, she would never

Iris laughed. It was true, she would never, but she did find it extremely unfair that Astrid and Claire, her best friends of twenty years, both had fairy-tale love stories. She was happy for them, of course, but Jesus, what amazing rom-coms both of their lives would make.

Iris: Fine. Go to sleep, you geriatric romantics

She swiped out of the chat and tapped on Simon's name, forgoing texts altogether.

"You'd better be dying." His voice was languid, like he was either asleep or tipsy.

"I'm alive and well," Iris said. "Sorry to disappoint."

"Stranded?"

"Nope."

"Being held at gunpoint?"

"I kicked him in the balls and got away."

"Then to what do I owe the horror?"

"Wow, you sure know how to make a gal feel special."

Simon grunted. "Sorry. What's up?"

"Are you in the city?" she asked.

"Yeah," he said cautiously. "Why? Or do I even want to know?"

Iris smiled. "I need a wingman. Are you up for it? Please say you're up for it, because if you're not, I'm going to show up at Emery's apartment with a suitcase and a pillow and a whole hell of a lot of comfort food, and you know how Emery likes to keep their place nice and tidy."

He laughed. "I guess I'm playing wingman tonight, then."

"Good answer, my darling," Iris said, starting up her car, then plugged in her phone so the call came through the speakers.

"You doing okay?" Simon asked.

Her throat went suddenly tight. Simon had this way about him, a tender manner of speaking that seemed to cut through all of Iris's jokes and make her question everything—*was* she actually okay?

"Yeah," she said. "I'm great."

"Uh-huh."

She sighed. "Just family shit. I need to blow off some steam."

"And by steam, you mean . . ."

"Yes, Simon, I want to have sex with someone, okay? Happy?"

He laughed. "I mean, I already had sex tonight, so, you know, you get yours."

"Okay, brag."

She ended the call, thinking about how she was a mere half hour from getting lost in a crowd of people in a club. She could let the music propel her around a dance floor, the dim lights making everyone and everything look beautiful and dreamy. Hopefully, she'd meet someone who'd help her forget about her novel, her family, the creeping loneliness she sometimes felt when her friends were all coupled up and tucked in for the night.

She gripped the wheel as she sped down Main Street toward the state roads that would lead her to I-205. And when she'd told Simon she was fine, she was great even, it didn't even feel like a lie.

CHAPTER

FOUR

THERE WAS A reason Stevie didn't often go out to bars, especially ones like Lush. The club was dimly lit, featured neon lights blinking through the room in nauseating patterns, music loud enough to incinerate her eardrums, and a crush of bodies that made her feel the need to take a shower.

Immediately.

"This was a bad idea," she said as Ren kept a clawlike grip on her hand and dragged her toward the bar.

"Nonsense," Ren said. "You just need a drink."

Stevie climbed onto a stool. The pleather top was sticky, so Stevie dived into her bag for some hand sanitizer.

"Jesus H, what are you doing?" Ren said, yanking the little bottle from Stevie's hands and tossing it onto the bar.

"I'm—"

"Rhetorical question," Ren said. "Okay, rule number one? No one wants to hook up with a germophobe."

"I'm not a germophobe. I'm practicing basic personal hygiene."

Ren didn't respond to this and flagged down the bartender, a person with hot pink hair and tattoos of elegant birds soaring around their neck. The effect was stunning.

"Tequila," Ren said. "Two. And a club soda."

"Oh god, Ren, even if I could drink on my meds, I'm really bad with tequila," Stevie said, recalling the one time in college she'd gotten drunk on too-strong margaritas at a house party and proceeded to sing Fleetwood Mac songs on top of a pool table.

Where people were trying to play pool.

If it hadn't been for Ren pulling her off and plying her with water and stale pretzels, she probably would've stripped naked.

"I remember," Ren said. "Viscerally. But it's not for you, it's for me. I have a feeling I'm going to need it."

The bartender set two liquid-filled shots in front of them, along with a glass of club soda. Ren scooped up the liquor, handing the soda to Stevie.

"To finding you a good time," Ren said, holding up their shot.

Stevie clinked her glass with Ren's before knocking back a few cold gulps. The bubbles burned her nose, and she pretended it was alcohol lubricating her senses a bit.

"Okay," she said, nodding. "Okay, let's do this." But the second she turned around to face the room, all the colors and bodies blurred together. The music felt like it was coming from inside her head, and she couldn't focus on one person more than any other.

"Yeah, it's busy," Ren said, reading Stevie's facial expression. "But we can do this. Let's just take it slow. Rule number two to hooking up—don't rush it. Take your time and find someone whose vibe you really like."

They both leaned their backs against the bar and surveyed the dance floor. Lush was a queer bar, so that alone set Stevie at ease. Everyone here was at least a little bit like her, and while not everyone who identified as a woman was necessarily into women like Stevie was, the chances of feeling a pull toward a straight girl was significantly less.

Since coming out as a lesbian at age thirteen, falling for someone who was cishet had always been a huge fear of hers, particularly after crushing on one of her theater friends in high school, making out with her on multiple occasions, and then listening as this friend explained that she was straight. Not exactly a great moment for Stevie's already heightened social anxiety, and she'd never forgotten how small and stupid she'd felt.

So, Lush was a good choice. But even as she watched the amalgam of people swirling through the room, spotting a pretty face here, an intriguing glance there, she still couldn't imagine actually walking up to someone and starting a conversation.

"I can't do this," she said.

"Just breathe," Ren said. "If we don't find anyone tonight, we don't find anyone. It'll be fine. Stop putting so much pressure on yourself and just *be*."

"Just be," Stevie said and tried to mirror her friend's relaxed position. But Ren was pretty much social royalty and could charm anyone into doing anything they wanted them to do with a single glance. She knew Ren had had their share of hardships—being a queer person of color was never going to be a smooth journey through life, especially in the small, midwestern town where Ren grew up. But Ren had flourished in college and beyond, finding their place, their style, their confidence, and fuck anyone who didn't like it.

All Stevie had found was a failed relationship and a propensity to dress like a twelve-year-old boy.

"How do I look?" she asked, rolling her shoulders back.

"Hot," Ren said, fluffing Stevie's fringe. She needed a haircut, as her shaggy curls were attempting to go full-on mullet, but somehow, the look worked for her. "Hotter once you take that jacket off."

Stevie smoothed her hands down her legs, clad in the high-waisted plaid pants Ren had insisted she wear. She'd paired them with a sleeveless mustard-and-cream-striped crop top, high-necked and showing most of her rib cage, all of which was still hidden by her gray jacket. She'd picked the top, feeling bold and desperate after her humiliating near-nuzzle with Adri, but now, here, she wasn't sure she could—

"You can," Ren said calmly, surveying the room casually. Stevie smiled at them. She yanked off her jacket before she could triple-think it, and slung it over the barstool, shoving the sticky texture out of her mind.

The humid air hit her midriff and she was tempted to cover herself, but she forced her arms to her sides.

"Badass," Ren said, winking at Stevie without even looking at her, which was probably the most badass thing Ren could do.

"Okay," Stevie said. "Who do we see?"

"Who do *you* see," Ren said. "I already see . . . several."

Stevie followed Ren's gaze toward a group of people by the pool table, a few of them just Ren's type. One femme-presenting person in particular, a zaftig brunette, was already smiling at Ren from underneath long lashes.

"You should go for it," Stevie said.

Ren waved a hand. "Maybe later. I'm here for you first and foremost. What do you think?"

Stevie concentrated. It wasn't easy, but as her senses acclimated to the lights and sounds, she was able to make out individuals, details and colors and shapes.

"All right, what about them?" Ren said pointing to a white woman with long blond hair and glasses—Stevie did love glasses—and a pool stick in her hands. Tight jeans. Toned arms. Very nice mouth . . .

. . . which was now attached to a Latinx person with leather pants and hot pink fingernails.

"Okay, never mind," Ren said.

"I guess that's the tricky thing about a queer bar," Stevie said. "Everyone could be into everyone."

"True. But also, a bonus." Ren waggled their eyebrows and Stevie laughed. Ren was a huge advocate for everyone having at least one threesome in their lifetime. Stevie had a hard enough time with one person—the idea of two made her brain feel the need to leave her head via her ears.

"All right, what about her?" Ren said, motioning toward a lovely Indian woman with several ear piercings by the hall that led to the bathroom. "She's—"

"Making out with two people at once," Stevie said. Sure enough, a blink after Ren spotted her, a dude with blond hair licked a stripe up the woman's neck, while another person nibbled on her ear.

"Damn, good on her," Ren said softly. "See, she knows how to make the queer bar dynamic work for her."

Stevie smiled and shook her head, crossing her arms as she continued to look around the room. Everyone she noticed seemed to already be coupled up, dancing and making out and laughing like old friends. Her shoulders slumped a bit as she wondered how people did this all the time. Every night of the week, strangers met strangers, hooked up, fell in lust, fell in love.

Some days, Stevie spent an hour wondering if that customer whose order she'd screwed up at Bitch's was going to sue the entire business and shut everything down, destroying all of Effie's hard work and putting Stevie out of a job. An irrational thought, she knew, but that didn't keep her brain from latching onto it like a sloth around a tree limb.

Acting was the only part of her life where she was free from this crippling second-guessing of every move she made. When her therapist first suggested she try theater in middle school, shortly after coming out and getting diagnosed with Generalized Anxiety Disorder, her mother was terrified. Stevie could barely answer a question in class—how was she ever going to get up in front of an audience and rattle off lines?

But Stevie wasn't Stevie when she was on stage. She was Gwendolen Fairfax. She was Amanda Winfield. She was Ophelia and Rosalind and Bianca. Assuming a character's identity, their dreams and fears and quirks, had always come so naturally for Stevie. Stepping into being someone else . . . well, it was a relief, if she was being honest.

As she stood in the middle of Lush, looking for a stranger to talk to, her stomach clenching with anxiety, she realized all she needed to do was step into a character. She wasn't Stevie, twenty-eight-year-old barista and struggling actor. She was Stefania, a sought-after, New York- or Chicago- or LA-bound, midriff-baring theatrical badass.

She straightened her posture—Stefania would never cower from nerves—determined to find someone to approach. But seconds turned into minutes, and she was just about to say fuck it, order a tequila for herself, and force Ren to go talk to that curvy goddess by the pool table, when she saw her.

A redhead.

Standing by the jukebox, talking to a white guy with glasses and a trimmed beard. Stevie watched them for a moment, looking for signs that they were together, but the guy looked a bit rumpled, like he'd just gotten out of bed, and the woman was definitely looking out at the crowd with a tilt to her head.

Stevie recognized that tilt. The *I'm interested* tilt. The *What have we here* tilt. Not that she was such a genius at reading body language. She simply had a feeling that the guy was sort of like Stevie's Ren— a wingperson, moral support.

"Ren," she said out of the corner of her mouth, like it was a secret. "The redhead by the jukebox. What do you think?"

Ren straightened and gazed through the crowd, eyes widening when they landed on their mark. "Nice."

"You think she's here with him?" Stevie asked.

"Nah," Ren said. "She looks hungry."

Stevie smiled, thrilled she'd actually gotten that one right. Now all she had to do was . . .

Shit.

She actually had to do this.

She took a few deep breaths, observing the woman as she let Stefania, Sexy Wonder-Thespian, seep into her bones. The redhead was white, her skin so pale it looked nearly blue underneath the dim lighting. She had little braids plaited throughout her long hair, freckles over much of her face. She wore a cropped green sweater and tight jeans, but only about an inch of her stomach was showing. Stevie started to feel self-conscious about her shirt again but forced herself back into character.

Stefania wasn't self-conscious.

Stefania was a queer marvel.

A gift to sapphics everywhere.

A genius in bed.

A—

"You're doing that thing again, aren't you?" Ren asked.

Stevie blinked her reality back into focus. "Huh?"

"You're pretending you're someone else." Ren narrowed their eyes.

"I'm . . . I'm just doing a little mental exercise to boost my courage," Stevie said. She knew it was weird, trying to become a fictional character off the stage, but it worked for her. Besides, her name *was* Stefania. She *was* an actor. "Do you want me to go hit on that woman or not?"

Ren presented their hands in surrender. "Fine. Do what you gotta do, I guess."

Stevie frowned at Ren's disapproving tone, but she shook it off. She needed this. Needed a night free of being . . . well, herself.

She cleared her throat. Fiddled with her fringe. She took a deep, calming breath. She took one step toward the redhead and froze.

Because the redhead was already walking across the room, her eyes fixed on Stevie.

CHAPTER

FIVE

SIMON WAS BEING a terrible wingman. On the phone, he'd failed to mention that Iris had in fact woken him up and, while he'd dutifully gotten dressed, and Emery hadn't complained when Simon left them in their bed to come out to a queer club with Iris—Emery knew Iris well enough by now to think nothing of it—Simon was less than energetic once they'd arrived at Lush.

Luckily, Iris didn't need much help finding someone she liked.

"Okay, one o'clock," she said. "The person with the shaggy curls and plaid pants."

"Lovely," Simon said, yawning.

"Jesus, Simon, seriously?"

"I'm sorry," he said. "I've been up late the past week working on my book, and—"

"Oh, you poor *New York Times* bestseller."

Simon had written a book a few years ago, *The Remembrances*, that had done extremely well, earning him enough to write full-time and be an insufferable, if loveable, ass about it. He'd finally turned in his second novel to his editor—a year after the first one debuted—

and he was currently hard at work on his third. Bisexual himself, his stories were chock-full of queer characters, and Iris, despite her general disdain for literary fiction, really loved his writing.

"If it makes you feel any better, it's going horribly," he said.

"A bit," she said, grinning. "And same."

"Still no ideas?" he asked.

"Nothing I'd pull off a shelf. I think I spent all the romance from my past relationships on my first book. I've got nothing, feel nothing. Maybe I should write horror."

"Okay, calm down," Simon said. "You're *good* at romance. Your writing is funny and sexy and emotional. You just need . . . I don't know. Have you considered going on an actual date? Getting some real romance into the mix?"

"Hell no."

"Iris. Jesus. You're like the Scrooge of true love."

"Bah humbug."

"Scrooge caved in the end, you know. His heart grew three sizes or whatever."

Iris laughed. "That's the Grinch."

"Potatoes, potahtoes," Simon said, sliding his glasses down his nose so he could properly glare at her.

Iris sighed and motioned toward the writhing bodies on the dance floor. "This works for me, okay? I don't want to complicate things."

"And by *things*, you mean your heart."

She ignored that. "Fiona thinks I need to do something else to get some space from my book. Like a pottery class or some shit, I don't know."

"That's actually solid advice."

"I know. Which is exactly why I'm here."

"So . . . random sex with a stranger is creative?"

"It is the way I do it," Iris said.

Simon laughed, his cheeks going a bit red. "Anyway," he said, nodding toward Shaggy Curls. "She's cute. Go for it."

Iris nodded and had just started to turn away when he grabbed her hand.

"One question," he said, his tone soft, concerned, and Iris knew exactly what was coming.

"I'm fine," she said.

He lifted his brows, hazel eyes doubtful from behind his glasses.

"I am," she said. "I just . . . my mom tried to set me up again. With a health fanatic."

"Yikes," Simon said. "Is your mother aware of how many bags of salt and vinegar chips you consume a week?"

"Exactly," she said. "Not exactly my type. And then . . ." She inhaled, steadied her voice. "My ex, Grant, is getting married, which is totally fine and I'm happy for him, but my family . . . well, they just . . . they're . . ."

"They're being assholes about it," he said.

She nodded. "They really loved Grant."

He squeezed her shoulder and she leaned into him for a second.

"Hence," she said, straightening up and nodding toward the woman, who was talking to an Asian person in a flawless gray suit and heels Iris had to remember to tell Astrid about. "I just need to let off a little steam."

"Okay," Simon said. "Understandable. But you know there are other ways, right? Ice cream? Watching rom-coms? A manicure?"

Iris laughed. "I'll do all of that tomorrow."

Simon nodded, but his brow remained creased. Iris knew her friends would never slut shame her—her choice to limit her romantic life to casual hookups was her own and they respected it—but lately, she got the distinct feeling that they agreed with her mother. Just a little. None of them ever said that they wanted to see Iris settled like they were. It was just a vibe she got, but it always made her want to fuck the next willing person she came across. If she was being honest.

She didn't need to be settled to be happy. Sometimes, happiness meant the opposite of settled. Sometimes, happiness meant a cute, curly-haired person in a crop top whose name Iris was completely okay never knowing.

"You good?" she asked Simon.

"I'm good," he said. "I'll hang around for a few minutes. Just shoot me a thumbs-up or something if you're okay. And text me when you get home, no exceptions."

"So chivalrous," she said, leaning up and kissing him on the cheek. Then she turned and started walking toward the woman, her shoulders back to show off her boobs, which, honestly, were usually the first things people noticed about her. Well, that, and her red hair—a thrilling combination for most.

Always good for a nice fuck, that Iris Kelly.

Iris's steady stride faltered, just for a second. She shook off the words she remembered guys laughing over in high school and college, words she'd felt afresh when everything with Jillian went down over a year ago. Because honestly, she *was* good for a nice fuck.

And she was just fine with that.

She was halfway across the dance floor when the woman turned away from her friend and started walking toward Iris as well. She didn't get far, freezing as soon as their eyes met.

Iris smiled and kept walking, not slowing down until she reached her target.

"Hi there," she said when she reached the woman who, for her part, looked like a deer staring down the end of a barrel.

Maybe Iris had read this wrong.

"H-h-hi," the woman said.

Iris tilted her head, smiled slowly. "You want to dance?"

The woman's throat worked. She nodded but didn't budge. Her

eyes were as wide as Frisbees, and so light brown they looked almost amber. "I'm Stevie. Shit. I mean, I'm Stefania."

Oh. She was nervous. That's what this was and, honestly, it was more than a little adorable.

"Hi, Stevie-Shit-Stefania," Iris said. "I'm Iris."

The woman laughed, her cheeks a dusky pink. "Sorry. It's Stefania."

"Pretty," Iris said.

"You . . . you too."

Iris laughed. Fucking. Adorable. "I meant your name, but I'll take that compliment."

Stefania rubbed her forehead. "God. I'm terrible at this."

"Maybe," Iris said. "But it's working for me."

"Yeah?" Stefania looked so hopeful, Iris's heart gave a little flutter.

"Yeah. So what about that dance?"

"Sure. I mean, yeah. Yes. Let's do it."

"Great." Iris held out her hand. "This song is—"

"I mean, not *do it* do it," Stefania said, twisting her own fingers into a knot.

Iris dropped her arm back to her side.

"I didn't mean that," Stefania went on. "I just meant dance. Let's dance. Not that I'm opposed to *doing it* doing it, I just. Didn't want to assume."

Iris blinked.

Behind Stefania, her friend had both hands over their mouth, watching the interaction in horror.

"Wow," Iris said. "You really are bad at this."

"Fuck," Stefania said quietly, closing her eyes. "I know. I'm so sorry. I tend to babble when I'm nervous and . . . yeah. I'm sure you're really glad you walked over here."

Iris pressed her mouth together to keep from laughing. "Weirdly, I am." Granted, this encounter wasn't the pheromone-fueled interaction Iris had planned, but she still found herself intrigued. Stefania was beautiful and sexy and a complete disaster. Iris couldn't walk away now if she tried.

"Luckily," she said, stepping closer and lacing her fingers with Stefania's. "I'm very, very good at this."

Stefania's eyes widened, a small smile settling on her full mouth.

"Still in?" Iris asked.

"If you don't say yes, I'm going to shave your head in your sleep," Stefania's friend piped up from behind her.

Stefania laughed, then rolled her shoulders back like she was getting ready for battle. "I'm still in."

Iris didn't wait for anyone to say anything else. She wanted this woman on the dance floor immediately, so she wove them through the melee toward the back, where it was a little less crowded. She had a feeling Stefania wouldn't want to be in the spotlight, and Iris didn't care where they danced.

When they reached a shadowy spot at the edge of the dance floor, Iris spun Stefania around and settled her hands on her hips, pulling her close. For a split second, Stefania froze, but then she inhaled deeply and looked right at Iris.

Smiled.

She looped her arms around Iris's neck and pushed even closer. Their hips aligned and Iris got a whiff of coffee and something a little cooler—orange blossom maybe. The blend was oddly intoxicating, as were Stefania's bare arms, the way her hair kept tickling Iris's cheeks as they moved to the fast-paced song.

Stefania seemed to unlock, throwing her head back, exposing her lovely throat, lifting one arm in the air. Her hips were magic, swirling against Iris's in a way that made Iris feel the need to either clench her legs together or get this woman alone as quickly as possible. She didn't want to push Stefania too far—she seemed easily spooked—so she let her take the lead.

And Stefania did. She laughed, her body moving like water as she spun Iris around so she was behind her, front aligned to Iris's back for a second, before twirling her around again.

"You're certainly not terrible at this part," Iris said, tightening her grip around Stefania's waist.

"No?" Stefania said.

Iris shook her head. "Quite the opposite."

"It's easy with music," Stefania said. Her arms were draped over Iris's shoulders again, fingers playing with a braid. "I have a context. A purpose. Move your body to the rhythm, that's it."

"Are you as adept in bed?" Iris asked, a coy grin on her face. She couldn't resist. "That has a purpose, doesn't it?"

Stefania's mouth dropped open. "Do you usually say exactly what you're thinking?"

"Hell yes. Life's too short not to, and everyone will judge you, leave you, or tell you to go fuck yourself either way. So why not?"

Stefania narrowed her eyes at this, studying Iris closely. Then she shook her head. "I'm not really sure."

Stefania's breath ghosted across Iris's skin, and goose bumps broke out along her arms. "You're not sure what?"

Stefania just shook her head, looking away. Iris wasn't sure if her cheeks were red from the exertion or from shyness—probably a little bit of both.

"Tell me," Iris said, shaking Stefania's hips a little.

Stefania laughed, ducked her head. Definitely from shyness, then. "I'm not sure if I'm adept in bed. How's that for a turn-on?"

Iris's brows popped up.

"I was with one person for a long time," Stefania said, biting her lower lip. "It's hard to tell, I think."

Iris found the brutal honesty refreshing, to be honest. "Okay, what about kissing?"

Stefania met her eyes, then let her gaze fall to Iris's mouth. Iris didn't let her answer. She simply leaned in close . . . closer . . . until her bottom lip brushed Stefania's.

Then she stopped.

Stefania had to come the rest of the way.

CHAPTER
SIX

STEVIE COULDN'T BELIEVE this was happening. She couldn't believe she'd actually done it. Granted, Iris's first impression of Stevie was probably less than ideal, but it certainly didn't seem to be putting the woman off. After getting past Stevie's embarrassing nervous babbling, Stefania had taken over.

And with gusto.

Stefania was confident. Sexy. Alluring, even. Stefania *was* adept in bed. She was a goddamn genius.

Iris's mouth brushed against hers but didn't press further. Stevie knew she was waiting for her, and god, Stevie wanted to push into those last couple of centimeters between them.

And she would.

Just as soon as she got her stomach to stop flipping around like a gymnast.

She slid her hands down Iris's arms, just to give her a second to get Stefania back in control. She felt alarmingly like Stevie in this moment—nervous, unsure. What if she sucked at kissing? What if, in their six years together, Adri had simply tolerated Stevie's kissing, and that was actually the secret reason Adri had wanted to break up?

Stevie closed her eyes to shut out the intrusive thought. She knew it wasn't true. She felt like she was a pretty good kisser, and she and Adri had always had a good time in bed, even if Adri did call most of the shots. Still, Stevie knew how to make Adri happy, how to make her come and then come again.

That was real.

But that was also after years of knowing Adri as a friend, a *best* friend, and Iris was . . . well, Iris wasn't Adri.

"You okay?" Iris said, backing up a little. "We don't have to—"

But before Iris could finish her sentence, Stevie grabbed her hips and yanked her closer, silencing all of her doubts. Like Iris had, she stopped a millimeter from Iris's lips, but only long enough for Iris to smile. After that, Stevie closed her mouth around Iris's bottom lip, tugging ever so slightly with her teeth before settling into something softer. Stevie kept her tongue to herself, using her lips to play with Iris so they could both settle in.

Iris, however, didn't seem to want soft. She buried her hands in Stevie's hair and opened her mouth wider. Her tongue sought Stevie's, tangling them together as a moan slipped from her throat. It made Stevie feel wild. Soon, she had Iris pressed against a wall, her hands roaming her bare waist.

Iris's own fingers explored too, sliding over Stevie's rib cage, then down her backside, then up and around toward her breasts. Stevie felt dizzy, her breath coming so fast she worried she'd pass out.

"Do you live nearby?" Iris said, her teeth scraping against Stevie's neck.

"Um . . . yeah . . . I . . . a few blocks."

"How many is a few?"

"Um . . ." Iris sucked Stevie's earlobe into her mouth. "Fuck."

Iris laughed, then pulled back a little. "Sounds doable. Want to get out of here?"

Stevie nodded, her lust-addled brain screaming *yes* in a thousand languages.

Before she could even process what was really happening—what it *meant*—Iris was pulling her through the crowd and toward the door. Stevie looked around frantically, finding Ren still standing by the bar, the curvy person from the pool table pressed close against their side. Ren caught Stevie's eye and gave her a chin nod, and the two-second interaction gave Stevie the courage to keep going.

She could do this.

Clearly, Iris liked her.

Clearly, Iris *wanted* her.

Stevie could goddamn do this.

IRIS HAD A forest green Subaru. And she drove fast.

After managing to put her address into Iris's phone, Stevie found herself facing the door of her third-floor apartment within fifteen minutes of leaving the club. She barely remembered the drive over. Everything felt like she was underwater, blurry and dreamlike.

"Nice place," Iris said as they stepped into the apartment.

She was being kind. Stevie's studio apartment had a rust-covered stove and plumbing that squeaked every time she flushed the toilet. Still, she'd made it hers and had coated one wall with chalkboard paint where she scribbled out her thoughts most nights—the evening brain dump, her therapist called it—used high-quality dove-gray bed linens Ren had helped her find on sale, and covered her pink velvet thrift store couch with a blanket she crocheted herself the week she and Adri broke up.

"You want something to drink?" Stevie said, heading to the kitchen area and opening the fridge. "I don't have much. Water. Some tomato juice I think might be expired."

Iris just shook her head and sauntered—yes, fucking sauntered—toward Stevie.

"I think we can skip the pleasantries," she said, hooking her arm around Stevie's waist and pulling her close.

"Oh," Stevie said, a nervous laugh bubbling up from her gut. Iris pressed her mouth against Stevie's throat, then slid down to her collarbone. "Okay. Wow."

Iris froze. Looked at Stevie. "You still want to do this?"

"Yes," Stevie said, even as her stomach gave a worrying lurch. Fuck this anxiety. "Absolutely."

She took Iris's hand and led her toward her neatly made bed, which was centered on the chalkboard wall. A single lamp on the nightstand was on, casting a calming golden glow over the small space.

She kissed Iris. She tried to kiss her like she'd kissed her in Lush, but it was so quiet, all Stevie could hear was the sound of her own blood rushing through her ears.

"Maybe if we had some music," she said.

Iris smiled. "Sure."

Stevie plucked her phone from her pocket and selected something slow and languid. Calming, yet sexy.

It helped. She breathed in . . . breathed out. Looked at Iris who, fuck, was really, really beautiful. In the clearer light, Stevie could see that Iris had bottle green eyes and her hair was an even deeper red than Stevie originally thought, almost ruby in tone. She was a little shorter than Stevie and curvy, with a small waist and breasts that filled her sweater, thighs that pushed the limits of her tight jeans. Stevie felt ravenous looking at her. Desperate.

She also felt terrified. Because Iris was way out of her league. And

Iris had been right—she *was* good at this. She'd probably gone home with a stranger dozens of times before, knew exactly how to smile, how to touch, how to fuck like it was nothing more than bodies coming together.

Stevie wanted that. She wanted to be like that, like Iris. Sexy and strong and sure.

So she dug deep for Stefania. She closed her eyes, cupped Iris's face in her hands, and kissed her. Not soft and slow, but hard and hungry. Iris responded, opening to Stevie, tugging at Stevie's belt loops. She moaned into Stevie's mouth, and Stevie knew she was already wet—that they both were—and it gave her the confidence to pull at Iris's sweater.

Iris took the hint, yanking the green garment over her head and tossing it behind her. Stevie had to stop and stare. Had to. Iris's bra was a dusky pink and completely sheer, her nipples already hard and straining against the fabric.

"God," Stevie said, and Iris laughed.

"Yeah?" Iris said.

Stevie nodded. "You're gorgeous."

Iris smiled, but Stevie could swear a little blush swept over her cheeks. "So are you."

Stevie closed her eyes. She couldn't imagine getting undressed in front of this woman. Suddenly, she was thirteen years old again, standing in her middle school's locker room the week after she came out, feeling every eighth grade girl's eyes on her back as she undressed. A few of them wouldn't even change in front of her—they insisted on going into a bathroom stall.

She shook her head to clear it. No idea why that memory popped into her head, but now that it had, she couldn't seem to get it to go away. That feeling—self-conscious and lonely and, even though she knew it wasn't true, like she was somehow *wrong*—lodged its claws into her heart, her chest, her stomach.

"Hey," Iris said, setting soft hands on her waist. "We really don't have to do this."

"No," Stevie said a little too loudly. She softened her voice. "No, I want to. I really, really do." She kissed Iris again, putting all she had into it. Iris was sweet. Iris wouldn't hurt her or make fun of her. Yes, she would leave her, but she was supposed to. That's what a one-night stand was, by definition. Stevie just needed to get out of her head. She needed to listen to her body instead of her brain.

Iris's hands drifted over Stevie's ribs. "This top?" she said, mouth on Stevie's jaw. "Has been driving me crazy all night."

"Really?" Stevie asked. "M-maybe we should take it off."

"Maybe we should." Iris's hands roamed over the fabric, over Stevie's breasts. She released a little groan. "No bra. Fuck, that's hot."

Stevie froze. Shit. She'd forgotten this shirt was tight enough that she didn't need a bra. Her chest wasn't anything impressive. Half the time, she went braless even in T-shirts, but tonight, she was cursing the decision.

Because as soon as her top was off, she'd be naked from the waist up.

In front of Iris.

Iris, whose last name Stevie didn't even know.

Not that she should.

Not that Stevie hadn't known a hookup usually involved some degree of nakedness.

Not that any of those facts were helping quell the panic rising in Stevie's gut right now.

She could hear herself breathing, air huffing through her nostrils, and not in a sexy way. Her stomach roiled, her mouth watering in warning.

Breathe, she told herself. *Just fucking breathe.*

"Are you okay?" Iris asked. She'd stepped back again, and Stevie nodded, reaching for her once again to convince them both. Instead of coming into her embrace, however, Iris gripped Stevie's forearms and peered into her face.

"You look a little . . ."

But before Iris could finish her sentence, Stevie's stomach had finally had enough. It rebelled, full and utter mutiny. Stevie leaned over and threw up all over the scuffed oak floor. It wasn't much—her extreme anxiety pukes never were—but it was enough to splash a little on Iris's jeans, her bare feet.

For a second, neither of them moved. Stevie stood there, still breathing heavily, and waited for some monster of the underworld to burst through her floor and swallow her whole.

Unfortunately, no such creature appeared.

Iris still held on to Stevie's arms.

She must be in shock.

"Okay, then," Iris finally said, breaking the horrible, vomit-covered spell. "Well."

"I'm so sorry," Stevie managed to say. Tears had sprung into her eyes. In these moments when Stevie didn't pay attention to the signs that her anxiety level was reaching a fever pitch and do a little triage—take her as-needed meds on top of her regular Lexapro, slow down, remove herself from the anxiety-inducing situation if possible—and she ended up hurling, she always followed that delightful experience with a hearty round of sobbing.

"It's okay," Iris said, but her voice sounded tight, uncomfortable. Unsurprising, considering she'd just been vomited all over by someone she was trying to seduce. How very sexy.

The thought made the tears overflow, running down Stevie's cheeks and stealing her breath.

"Oh god," Iris said, noticing the tears. "Okay, it's all right."

"It's not. Shit, I'm so, so sorry," Stevie managed to say between hiccups. "You can go. Please."

Iris released Stevie's arms and guided her backward, careful to avoid the puddle of sick on the floor. She sat Stevie down at the end of the bed, then headed toward the kitchen. Stevie heard some cabinets opening and closing, and then Iris returned with a roll of paper towels and a bottle of cleaner.

"No. Iris, oh my god. Don't."

But Iris kneeled down and wiped up the puke with a few swipes, then sprayed the floor with cleaner and wiped that up too. Stevie knew she needed to get up, kick Iris out, and clean up her own mess, but she felt glued to the bed, tears still on a runaway train down her face.

"Iris," she said, but Iris kept ignoring her, wiping at her feet and jeans, and then taking everything back to the kitchen. She ran the tap for what seemed like an hour—undoubtedly scouring a stranger's vomit from her hands—before she returned to the bedroom with a glass of water.

"Here," she said, handing it to Stevie. Then she pulled the covers down on the bed, literally fluffing Stevie's pillow. Stevie watched in half horror, half fascination. She drank her water dutifully, but the cool liquid did little to assuage her humiliation.

"Iris," she tried again, but Iris still didn't respond. Instead, she took Stevie's half-empty water glass and set it on the nightstand, then pulled Stevie up by her arms and guided her under the covers.

She tucked Stevie in.

After that, she went into the bathroom and found Stevie's tiny trash can, setting it next to the bed. Stevie just watched her, her chest so tight she could hardly breathe.

"Okay," Iris said, hands on her hips. She was still shirtless, beautiful. "You need me to call anyone for you?"

Stevie could only shake her head.

Iris nodded, then looked around for her sweater. She found it by the couch, slipped it on, and hoisted her bag over her shoulder. "Well. Good night. I hope you feel better."

Stevie offered a weak wave. She wanted to explain—because what if, after all of this, Iris was worried about catching some horrible bug from Stevie—but she couldn't seem to get any words to form. Her head was fuzzy, her tongue a useless lump in her mouth.

It didn't matter anyway. Iris barely waited for a response, turning quickly and finding her shoes by the front door. She didn't even slow down to put them on. She simply slipped out the door, clicking it softly shut behind her.

Stevie stared at the ceiling, hoping, as she laid in bed, that she'd realize this whole shitshow of a night was a dream. The music she'd put on to calm her down still played through her phone, so she grabbed it off her nightstand and silenced the sultry tones. She was just about to toss her device on the floor when it buzzed with a text.

It was from Ren, sent to their group chat that included Adri and Vanessa. A group chat that had been pretty quiet lately.

Stevie tapped on the message. It took her a few seconds to realize that she was looking at a photo of herself and Iris, dancing at Lush in a way that could've been a deleted scene from a queer version of *Dirty Dancing*.

> **Ren:** Stevie and Ren, on the fucking town. Look at our girl go!

"Oh my god," Stevie said.

Ren sent a few other pics—one of themself with the curvy brunette, followed by a line of empty shot glasses on the bar.

But Stevie knew what Ren was doing.

They wanted Adri and Vanessa to see Stevie with someone else. That was the whole goal of tonight anyway—someone different, someone new. The other photos were simply a cover, so it all seemed less pointed and more casual.

And it worked.

Because a split second later, Adri texted back. And she didn't say anything about Ren's zaftig or the copious amount of alcohol.

Adri: Wow, Stevie, she's gorgeous

Vanessa: Way to go, Stevie 🔥 🔥 🔥

Adri: What's her name?

"Shit, shit, shit," Stevie said, dropping her face into her hands. She couldn't answer. She could barely even think about Iris's name right now.

Her phone buzzed again, and this time, Ren had texted only her.

Ren: You fucking badass you

Ren: Also you'd better be engaging in some truly scandalous sex acts right now

Stevie turned off her phone, pulled the covers over her head, and hoped to god or whoever that the end of the world was nigh.

CHAPTER SEVEN

"SO?" SIMON SAID as he and Iris settled at a table on the Everwood Inn's patio. The trees surrounding the property blazed green in the summer sun. "How was it?"

Iris huffed a laugh and took a long sip from the ice water already set out at their table, chewing on the end of her biodegradable rainbow straw the inn was using for Pride month. "I'm going to need to be very drunk to talk about that."

Simon winced. "Bad? She looked so nice."

"Oh, she was," Iris said. "Nice and sweet and grateful, especially when I was cleaning up her puke."

Simon's eyes went wide. "What."

"You heard me." Iris shuddered at the memory.

"Wait, wait, wait," he said, waving his hands and leaning forward in his wrought iron chair. "She threw up?"

Iris nodded. "Indeed. One look at me in my bra and up it came."

A laugh burst out of Simon. He slapped a hand over his mouth. "I'm sorry," he said through his fingers. "It's just . . . wow. Talk about a hell of a meet-cute."

"I didn't mind the puke," Iris said. "I mean, don't get me wrong, it wasn't the best of times, but she couldn't help it. She was clearly mortified, and I was happy to help. But yeah, it wasn't the greatest hookup I've ever had."

"Yeah, but now you've got an amazing start to your novel," Simon said, then spread his hands out like he was displaying a title. "*Tegan McKee Doesn't Vomit.*"

"You know, sometimes I wonder why we're friends."

He just laughed even harder.

Iris tried to laugh too, but the memory was still too visceral. She had no idea where she and Stefania had gone wrong. Maybe the woman really had been sick, but two days after tangling tongues, Iris still felt fine. The real conclusion to draw here was that Stefania couldn't stomach sleeping with Iris.

Literally.

"It's fine," Iris said, waving a hand. "It is funny, I guess. Maybe in about twenty years, when my pride has recovered and I learn how to use my tits for good and not evil, I'll laugh too."

That just made Simon laugh harder.

"What's this about your evil tits?" Delilah said. She and Claire approached the table, holding hands and looking like they just spent a weekend under the spell of a forty-eight-hour orgasm.

Then again, they probably had.

"Oh, nothing," Iris said. "Just a hookup gone bad."

"Jesus, I'm so glad those days are over," Delilah said, settling one ankle on her gray-jeaned knee and leaning back as she perused the menu. Her dark curly hair was particularly voluminous today. "I used to hate leaving in the middle of the night. That was the worst."

"You? I'm shocked you didn't stay and cuddle," Iris said.

Delilah flipped her off.

"I don't see how you do it, Ris," Claire said, sipping on her water.

She had on a sky-blue sundress and cognac sandals. "I was always terrible at one-night stands."

"Because you're so good at forever-night stands," Delilah said, leaning over to kiss Claire's neck.

Claire giggled, and the two commenced whispering to each other and kissing.

Iris caught Simon's eye and he made a face like he was going to puke.

"Don't," Iris said. "I've had enough of that."

He busted up laughing again. Meanwhile, Claire and Delilah remained oblivious. Iris couldn't help but smile at them, despite their saccharine display of affection.

"Hey, we're here, we're here," Astrid said, hurrying toward the table in a pair of wide-legged linen pants and a loose black tank top, pulling Jordan Everwood by the hand behind her. Jordan, as usual, was clad in a printed button-up shirt, this one featuring tiny yellow suns. "Sorry we're late. Explosion in the kitchen."

"A food explosion while trying out a sauce recipe," Jordan said, sitting down and smoothing a hand down Astrid's arm. "Our new intern turned on the blender without the lid."

"Yikes," Simon said.

"Pumpkin puree everywhere," Astrid said. "Even on the ceiling."

"And in your hair," Iris said, reaching over and plucking a piece of soggy pumpkin from Astrid's shaggy blond locks.

"Oh god," Astrid said, raking a hand over her head.

Jordan laughed. "It's okay, baby, we'll get it out in the shower later."

Astrid blushed, twining her fingers with Jordan's. Iris, for her part, was quite proud that she refrained from teasing her cotillion-trained best friend about bathing with another person.

"Let's order, shall we?" she said instead.

"Yes, let's," Simon said brightly, probably eager to get off the topic of his twin sister's sex life.

The server—a woman named Bria with a gold hoop in her nose—took their order for a pitcher of Bloody Marys, duck confit eggs Benedict, mixed fruit, and a basket of Astrid's freshly baked blueberry oat muffins.

"So," Claire said lightly after Bria left. "We have some news." She looked at Delilah, her cheeks going red.

"Oh?" Astrid said, but something about the way she said that one syllable word made Iris think she already knew.

And Iris realized that she knew too. Her gut did, at least. Of course, they had all talked about Delilah and Claire getting married. Everyone knew it was going to happen. Iris had even conspired with Delilah about what sort of ring Claire would want—vintage yellow diamond surrounded by smaller stones, platinum band—but Iris had no idea Delilah was actually planning to pop the question.

Her throat went all achy and her chest felt suddenly tight like she was about to cry. She reached under the table and grabbed Simon's hand. It was the only thing she could think to do, the only person she could hold on to right now so she didn't float away.

He tilted his head at her, but she just smiled.

Smile, smile, smile.

"Well," Claire said. She took Delilah's hand, kissed her fingers. Iris could swear Delilah's eyes were actually glistening. The whole scene was so sweet, Iris felt a surge of affection for all of them, even as her grip on Simon tightened.

"I asked Delilah to marry me," Claire said, her eyes on her fiancée, "and she said yes."

The table erupted in shouts and cheers. Astrid clapped and leaned over to kiss Claire's cheek. Jordan squeezed Delilah's shoulder. And Iris . . .

Iris promptly burst into tears.

"Oh, honey," Claire said, getting up and hurrying over to Iris.

Simon tried to squeeze her hand tighter, but she yanked it out of his grasp. "Shit," she said, grabbing a napkin and pressing it to her eyes.

"Sweetie, are you all right?" Claire asked, now kneeling next to her.

Iris fluttered her napkin around. Everyone was staring at her, eyes wide, mouths open. "I'm fine. I'm just happy!" She hooked her arm around Claire's neck and pulled her in for a tight hug, forcing herself to get her shit together.

Iris had never been that little girl who dreamed of her wedding day. She'd never played with dolls as a kid, rocking tiny bald plastic babies to sleep. She'd never envisioned wearing white and walking down the aisle. Of course, she knew how monumental the Marriage Equality Act was, that people like her weren't always able to spend the rest of their lives with their partner, legally speaking, anyway. And she wanted that for every queer person in her life who wanted it for themselves.

She wanted it for Delilah and Claire.

And while Iris prided herself on being the best kind of friend, she couldn't help but feel a tiny swell of fear at how everything was changing. How her two best friends were experiencing something—and were going to continue to experience all sorts of things with marriage and family and kids—that Iris wasn't going to be a part of.

She was the single friend.

And she always would be.

Iris wasn't built for long-term. She'd been with Grant, her ex, for three years. She'd loved him and he'd loved her, but in the end, they'd broken it off because Grant wanted kids. Lots of them. He wanted a wedding in a church and matching Christmas sweaters for holiday pictures and a front porch crawling with grandkids someday.

Iris didn't.

And while their parting was amicable and she'd agreed whole-heartedly as he explained that they wanted different things, that he needed to follow his own dream, there was a part of the whole experience that left her feeling like there was something inherently wrong with her.

Like she wasn't the *right* kind of woman.

Then there was Jillian, who ended up being married—and not in an ethically nonmonogamous sort of way—a fact Iris only discovered when their phones had gotten mixed up and Lucy, Jillian's wife, had called trying to locate her. A call Iris had answered. Jillian had used Iris, lied to her, and while none of that was Iris's fault, she'd had a hard time shaking off the aftereffects of being an unwitting mistress.

After that shitshow, Iris decided to lay off dating, because it wasn't just about Grant and Jillian. Throughout her sexual history, she'd always been the good lay, the one-night fuck. Even when she did date someone for a while, it always ended with very little fanfare, a ho-hum parting of the ways.

Because Iris . . . well, she was good at sex.

She wasn't all that good at love.

She could get shit done. Plan a hell of a party. Coach her friends to chase their dreams or true loves or whatever the hell, but when it came down to it, Iris wasn't marriage material. And after Jillian, she also didn't want to risk getting all infatuated with someone who only saw her as a side piece of ass. Hence, her relationship moratorium, which had been working just fine for the last year. She was fine being the fifth or seventh wheel. She was fine being the single friend, the fun Aunt Iris.

She was fine.

She just needed to get her stupid, childish heart on board here, that was all.

"I love the hell out of you," she said to Claire now, then pulled back and beamed at Delilah. "Both of you."

"I'm touched, Kelly," Delilah said wryly, but she was smiling.

"Show us the ring!" Astrid said as she got up and came over to Iris's other side, settling on the arm of the wooden chair. Iris leaned into her.

Delilah scowled. "We're really going to do all the squealing over the rings?"

"Hell yes, we are," Jordan said. "Cough it up, Green."

Delilah pursed her lips, then winked at Claire in a way that made Claire audibly sigh.

Jesus, these two. Iris kissed Claire's temple.

Delilah finally displayed a very important finger, upon which sat a square black diamond with a black rhodium band that swirled over the centerpiece stone. Very Delilah.

"Wait, so you asked Delilah?" Iris asked Claire.

Claire nodded. "It just sort of happened. I was in Portland this past Tuesday night for a reading at Graydon Books—that queer romance author I really want to do some events with you at River Wild, Ris—and I stopped by this little curiosity shop afterward. I found this ring and it was like . . . I don't know. I just knew I wanted the ring, and I wanted Delilah to wear it."

"I'll never take it off again," Delilah said, and Iris didn't even think she was being sarcastic.

"How's Ruby?" Astrid asked. "Is she excited?"

"She was actually with me when I got the ring," Claire said. "She spotted it first. And, yeah, she's really excited."

"Who wouldn't want me as their super awesome, cool-as-hell stepmom?" Delilah said. "Show them yours, babe."

Claire brandished her own hand, which was now sporting a gorgeous vintage yellow diamond, the very same style Iris and Delilah had discussed about a month ago.

"Luckily, I had it on hand," Delilah said.

"For months," Claire said, stretching out her fingers. "You've had my ring since Christmas."

"That's gorgeous," Simon said, inspecting Claire's ring.

"Okay, let's talk details," Astrid said, clapping her hands. "At the Everwood, next summer. Or maybe spring? I'm thinking outside, with a gauzy tent that—"

"Shit, Claire, we're eloping," Delilah said.

Claire laughed. "Ruby would never forgive us."

"Oh my god, Ruby as your maid of honor," Iris said, then her tears started flowing again, because apparently, she was a fucking mess, a status she was not enjoying.

So Iris did what she did best.

She got loud and funny and opinionated.

"A toast!" she said, grabbing her glass of champagne Bria had placed on the table in lieu of their actual order, and climbing onto one of the wrought iron chairs. Eyes followed her like bugs to a blue light, even those brunching at the inn who weren't with her party. She felt the attention, felt it soak into her bones, making her feel strong and invincible.

"Here she goes," Delilah said, but she was smiling, and Iris smiled back, a coy little grin over her shoulder as she flourished the hem of her floral dress over her knees. Claire had joined Delilah, their arms around each other, and all five of her dear friends were beaming up at her.

This was the Iris they knew.

This was the Iris they loved.

"Damn right," she said. "Now, a toast. To the most nauseatingly beautiful couple the Pacific Northwest has ever seen."

"Should we be offended?" Jordan said to Astrid, who just laughed and kissed her girlfriend's cheek.

"And to," Iris went on, "a lifetime of happiness, joy, and enough great sex to keep Delilah from lighting the world on fire."

"I'll cheers to that," Claire said, blushing.

Delilah just shook her head, but she tipped her glass to Iris.

Iris laughed, then drained her entire drink in three, nose-burning gulps.

⁓

AN HOUR LATER, Iris ran across the inn's gravel parking lot back to her car. She'd started to feel better during talks of venues and dates, smiling and laughing about how she was going to throw the happy couple a sex toy shower—she absolutely was—but now her chest ached.

She found out why when she fell into her Subaru's driver's seat and immediately burst into tears again.

She wiped furiously at her face, berating herself for acting like such a baby. She was *happy* for Claire and Delilah.

"I'm fucking happy!" she yelled and banged her fists on her steering wheel.

"Sure looks like it."

She yelped at the deep voice, jumping so high, her head brushed the roof of her car.

Simon Everwood peered down at her through the window.

She exhaled, clutching at her chest. She should play this off, she knew. No good could come from her whining about being *single*, for god's sake, but her face was already a mascara-streaked, blotchy mess, and she didn't have the fucking energy.

She lifted her hands and let them slap back down into her lap, sniffing snot back into her runny nose.

Simon rounded the car, opened the passenger door, and slid inside. Then he turned to face Iris and proceeded to simply stare at her with this expectant expression that made her want to smack his glasses off his face.

"I'm fine," she said, wiping at her face again. "I'll *be* fine."

"I know you will," he said so softly, she nearly started boo-hooing again.

"I'm just . . . I'm restless." She pressed her puffy eyes closed. "My book is a disaster, my mom is up my ass to fall in love and pop out a million babies."

"Sounds like something you'd do."

Iris snorted, but somewhere under the laughter, there was a sting of hurt. Even her best friends knew she wasn't falling-in-love material.

"I just need to focus on my book," she said. "But I'm totally locked up."

"You sure that's all this is?" he asked. "Writer's block?"

"Yeah."

"You know, I don't believe in writer's block. If you can't figure out what to write about, it's because you've gone wrong somewhere earlier in the book."

She rolled her eyes. "Thank you, Iowa Writer's Workshop."

"Oh, I'm just naturally this brilliant."

She flipped him off and he laughed, nudging her shoulder.

"Well, your theory doesn't hold up," she said, "because there is no *earlier* in my book. I don't even have a first sentence."

"You need some space to *get* a first sentence, then. Your agent's right—you need to do something low stakes, something creative that's not writing, to clear your head."

"I hate that I tell you things."

"Actually," he said, drawing out each syllable.

Iris smirked. "Don't you know that no white cis dude should ever speak that word?"

He laughed, taking out his phone and tapping on the screen. "*Actually,* after you told me what Fiona said, I did some digging. Because honestly, I could use a creative distraction myself." He presented his phone, and she took it, scanning the screen.

"A play?" she asked.

"A *queer* play," he said. "A gender-bent version of *Much Ado About Nothing*. It's at that queer community theater in Portland, the Empress."

She scrolled through the page, eyes skimming over information about open call auditions happening this coming week, how the play would open at the end of August for a fall run. "I've heard of this place."

"I went to one of their plays a while back," Simon said. "I want to say it was another Shakespeare. Maybe *Taming of the Shrew*? Anyway, it was amazing. The lead was a trans guy playing opposite a gay man, the whole cast was queer, and I'm pretty sure I cried at the end."

"You would," she said.

"Look who's talking," he said, wiping a bit of mascara off her cheek.

She sighed and handed his phone back to him. "It looks fun. You should do it."

He grinned. "I think you mean *we* should do it."

She pressed a hand to her chest. "I'm sorry, did you actually just include me in the elusive, all-powerful *we*?"

He rolled his eyes but kept smiling. "I did. What do you think?"

"I think you're high."

"I didn't even drink. Champagne tastes like carbonated puke."

"I thought I told you never to bring up puke again."

He nudged her shoulder. "Come on."

"Are you serious?" she asked. "You want me to do a community play with you?"

"I do."

"Hell no."

"Why not?"

"Because I don't act."

He scoffed.

Literally *scoffed*.

She lifted her brows at him. "And what, pray tell, good sir, was that for?"

He circled a finger at her face. "You can't even tell me off without being dramatic about it."

She grabbed his finger and twisted it. Softly, but enough to make him yelp.

"You're sort of making my point here," he said.

She stopped twisting but kept a hold on his finger.

"Think about it," he said. "You'd get to meet a ton of queer people. You'd get to do something new, which is, my darling, what you were just complaining about."

She opened her mouth to protest, but snapped it shut. He had her there.

"And it's in Portland," he said, "so you'd get out of town at least a few times a week."

"I can already do that."

"Yeah, but this outing doesn't come with the possibility of an STI."

She dropped his finger, and he had the decency to look a little abashed.

"I'm sorry," he said. "That was out of line."

"I'm always safe, Simon," she said, but her voice wobbled a bit more than she'd like. She cleared her throat. "And I get tested regularly."

"I know," he said, rubbing her forearm. "Like I said, I'm sorry."

"Delilah used to sleep around a lot, you know," she said. "In fucking New York City. And now that she's monogamous, no one thinks twice about it."

Simon sighed. "I know."

"So, then, what?" she asked, her voice rising. "What the hell is so wrong with me having sex when I want to, with whomever I want, if that's what makes me happy? What?"

She felt the tears rising again. There it was again, this feeling that deep down, her friends thought she was a little *too* free. A little *too* wild. That she wasn't what a grown-ass adult of thirty-two should be.

"Nothing," Simon said, squeezing her arm. "I promise you, nothing is wrong with that."

She shook her head, only half convinced.

"But, sweetie, does it?" he asked.

She sniffed, turned to frown at him. "Does it what?"

"Make you happy?"

For the second time, she opened her mouth, but no words came out. At least, not at first. She let her jaw hang wide for a second or two while she found the right answer.

"Yes," she said, but even to her, her voice sounded a bit robotic. She tried again. "Yeah. Of course it does."

Simon's gaze narrowed, just a little, but then he nodded. "Okay. I still think you should do this play with me. It would be fun. And I think they're turning this one into some sort of fundraiser to keep the theater going, so it'd be for a good cause."

"You and me singing 'Sigh No More, Ladies' in period clothing is going to save the Empress?"

He laughed. "Hell yes. Who else?"

She laughed too. She couldn't help it. Simon was so . . . hopeful. He had been since the day she met him. And he had a point—the play actually sounded like it could be fun. Portland. New faces. She had actually taken a theater class in high school, during which even the teacher—Mr. Bristow, who Iris always felt was staring at her boobs—said she was a bit too dramatic.

In drama class.

She nearly laughed at the thought, but honestly, doing this play with Simon sounded like exactly what she needed, not that she'd ever admit that to him.

"Fine," she said. "But if we get cast, you're picking me up for every rehearsal in a Bentley filled with caviar and champagne."

He tapped his chin. "How's a 2018 Honda Accord and some donuts?"

"Deal."

CHAPTER

EIGHT

WHEN STEVIE WALKED into the Empress on Tuesday morning, she expected Adri to smile at her, maybe ask about the woman in the photo Ren had sent to everyone on Friday night, and then move on to shop talk. A little light teasing, and that would be it.

But that is not what she did.

At all.

First off, Vanessa was here, which was a surprise. She had a day job, after all, but she didn't have Tuesday classes, so she'd blocked off the day to help with auditions.

Second of all, Ren was also in attendance. They did this now and again—took off a morning or worked remotely in order to help out with costumes or some aesthetic aspect of the current play. All four of them had been involved with theater at Reed, studying under the thrall of Thayer Calloway—their theater professor they were all half in love with, who was now directing in New York—and Ren even had a minor in costume design.

Therefore, when Stevie entered the small theater, all three of her best friends looked up from where they were sitting on the stage, grinned, and kept their eyes glued to her reddening face as she walked to meet them.

She slowed her steps. Maybe if she delayed her arrival, someone else would show up—Julian, the Empress's assistant director, or maybe Dev, the gaffer.

But as she trailed her fingers along the plush purple chairs Adri had spent a fortune for, glancing at the exposed brick walls, no one else swooped in to save her.

When she stopped in front of the stage—a short walk from the entrance, unfortunately—her friends kept staring and grinning.

"Um," she said. "Good morning?"

"Indeed," Ren said, swinging their legs, which were hanging off the slightly raised stage. They were wearing sleek black pants, a white button-down under an aubergine vest. No tie. This was casual for Ren. "You never texted me back this weekend." They waggled their perfect eyebrows.

Stevie winced. She hadn't texted Ren back when they inquired about how her evening with the redhead had gone, and that was one hundred percent on purpose, as was her decision to ignore Adri's question about Iris's name. She had zero plans to divulge what had happened.

"Yeah, sorry," Stevie said.

"I take it Iris stayed over, then?" Ren said when Stevie remained silent.

"Iris?" Adri said, glancing at Stevie. She had on her clear-framed glasses, which Stevie had always loved, and had a heavily annotated script in her hand. "So that's her name."

Stevie just nodded.

"She was hot, Stevie," Vanessa said, wrapping her arms around one leg. Her long dark hair tumbled down her back, so shiny under the house lights, Stevie had to squint.

She nodded again.

That, at least, wasn't a lie. Iris *was* hot. So much so, that when

Stevie thought about her pre-vomit, her belly swooped pleasantly. But then her memory would catch up to the puke and the nausea swelled once again.

"Are you seeing her again?" Ren said.

"I sure hope so," Vanessa said, "She was too gorgeous to let go."

"Babe," Adri said, eyeing her girlfriend.

"Is this the part where I say *Not as gorgeous as you, sweetie?*" Vanessa asked, batting her impossibly long lashes.

Adri hesitated for a split second, then laughed, pulling Vanessa in for a kiss.

Stevie wrinkled her nose. She couldn't remember the last time she and Adri had joked around like that when they were together. They lacked a playfulness toward the end, the ability to take a joke. If Adri had made a comment about the attractiveness of one of Ren's or Vanessa's hookups, Stevie probably would've quietly fallen apart, then sobbed in the bathroom for a good half hour.

Which was probably part of her and Adri's problem.

She swallowed hard, trying to shake off the thought and smile. Then, as she met each of her friends' eyes, she felt her shoulders straightening, her chest expanding just a little. She breathed a bit easier than she had the last time they were all together. Her smile felt a little less forced. For the first time in months, her friends were looking at her like they used to. Like she had a life plan, a damn good one. Like her dream of the stage wasn't childish and played out.

As she smiled back at them, she even caught a bit of admiration in their eyes. She supposed a person who could attract a woman like Iris would be at least a little intriguing, and god, it had been so long since Stevie had felt interesting to anyone. Her short stint with Iris didn't even count, as any intrigue Iris might have felt for Stevie was completely ruined by the ending.

"So?" Adri pressed. She tilted her head, eyes slightly narrowed. "Are you going out again?"

Vanessa mouthed *yes* over and over, her eyes gleaming.

Ren just watched Stevie with their brows lifted.

There was really only one right answer. The only one that would make Stevie feel like she wasn't a complete disaster, the one that would make Ren believe they'd actually helped Stevie out, make Adri and Vanessa feel a little less guilty about their newfound love.

And *no* was not that answer. Stevie couldn't even imagine speaking it right now, the way everyone's expressions would fall, disappointment filling their eyes. Or worse, they wouldn't be shocked at all, because . . . well, because this was Stevie.

"Yeah," she said before she could overthink it. She inhaled quietly, thinking about Stefania from Friday night, the woman who'd kissed Iris first before everything went to hell. "Of course I am."

Vanessa held up her fists in victory and Ren grinned at Stevie like she'd just found the cure to cancer. Adri smiled, no teeth, just that soft gaze that Stevie knew meant she was thinking. Stevie wasn't sure she wanted to know the specific thoughts.

"That's my girl," Ren said, hopping off the stage and taking Stevie by the shoulders. "See? I knew you could do it."

Stevie just nodded, her brain whirling already at how long she could keep up this lie. Knowing Vanessa, it was only a matter of time before she suggested a double date, triple if Ren could find someone to bring, which they undoubtedly could.

Right now, though, Stevie shoved those thoughts away. Right now, she reveled in *this*—the feeling of being okay, of being someone other people might desire. Even if it was all a lie, the way her friends were looking at her right now—the way they were making her feel— that was real.

⌒

"OKAY," ADRI SAID after Ren brought up the picture of Stevie and Iris again at the club and Vanessa had nearly passed out from Iris's hotness, "time to get down to business. Auditions start at eleven, and I need to go over some things with the crew before then."

"I'm going to go talk to Phoebe," Ren said. "See what she has in mind."

Adri nodded as Ren headed off backstage. Phoebe was a trans woman, a brilliant artist, and had been the Empress's lead costume designer since day one. She was one of the very few staff members with a full-time salary, and Adri pretty much did anything she had to do to keep her.

"I'll head out to the lobby to set up the sign-in table," Vanessa said. "Company auditions are with Julian, right?"

"Yeah, in the back hall. He's already there, I believe. Thank you, baby," Adri said, then the two kissed once . . . twice . . . three times before they finally unlocked, and Vanessa hopped off the stage.

"I can't wait to meet Iris," she said as she passed Stevie, squeezing her arm.

Stevie just nodded. Pretty soon, her head was going to lop off her neck from overuse.

"Come on up," Adri said, motioning Stevie toward the stage.

Stevie took her time climbing the stairs on stage left, preparing herself to be alone with Adri, particularly after the way Stevie had nearly nuzzled her neck at Bitch's on Friday.

She settled next to her ex, took out her copy of *Much Ado* from her bag.

"So," Adri said, flipping through her script. "You're really dating her?"

Stevie blinked. Adri always did know when Stevie was bullshitting her, which was why Stevie rarely bullshitted her. Still, Stevie wasn't going for honesty, here, no matter how much Adri pressed.

"Yeah," Stevie said.

Adri nodded, finally meeting Stevie's eyes. "She looks . . . fun."

Stevie frowned. "What does that mean?"

Adri waved a hand, laughed. "Nothing. I don't know. She seems . . . different."

"Different how?"

"Just . . ." Adri shook her head, looking up as she pondered. "She seems wild. Has that air about her, you know? Party girl."

Stevie bristled. "You got all that from one picture in a dim bar?"

Adri smiled and shook her head. "You're right. That was a stupid thing to say. I'm happy for you. Let's get to work, okay?"

Stevie took a surreptitious deep breath. She hated when Adri did shit like this, saying something that made Stevie feel small and un-sure, then immediately apologizing so Stevie couldn't even be mad about it.

"Fine," Stevie said. "Yeah."

"Okay. Our first priority is finding our Beatrice."

"What about Tori?"

"Pregnant," Adri said, smiling. "Nearly six months and due in September, so she can't do it."

"Oh my god, really?" Stevie said. "That's great for her." Tori was a Black lesbian who'd been with the same woman, Lakshmi, since they were fifteen and baby queers in Arkansas. They'd been trying to get pregnant for years and had gone through a couple miscar-riages, so Stevie was delighted to hear this.

Tori was also their best lead actress.

"There's no one else?" Stevie asked.

Adri shook her head. "No one good enough. Molly hates Shake-speare and Cassandra can't do comedy to save her life. I've already cast Jasper as Hero. We've got to find someone new. Someone amazing."

"Should be easy enough," Stevie said wryly. Like all directors, Adri was picky, critical, and demanding. Double that when it came to Shakespeare, so finding a brand-new Beatrice with whom Stevie had onstage chemistry and who satisfied Adri's standard of perfection?

Well. It was going to be a long day.

SEVEN POTENTIAL BEATRICES later, Stevie was ready to fling herself into the sea.

Too bubbly.

Not enough energy.

No intuition.

They're trying too hard.

I don't believe you want to bang them, Stevie.

That last one was a real zinger, as this comment from Adri felt like it was more about Stevie's acting than the hopeful thespian with whom she was sharing the stage. Still, Stevie didn't take it personally—acting was the one area in her life where she could take direction and not immediately feel the need to breathe into a paper bag. This was the game, the show, and if you wanted to get better, to *shine*, you had to be willing to suck every now and then.

Still, Adri was particularly brutal today and Stevie's exhaustion level was climbing.

"What, my dear Lady Disdain!" Stevie said as Benedick. A terrified-looking white person named Candice stood opposite her, ears full of piercings, short hair dyed lavender, eyes wide as saucers as they looked at the script.

"Are you yet living?" Stevie went on, motioning toward Candice.

"Um, oh, right." Candice peered at the script before speaking robotically. *"Is it possible disdain should die while she hath such meet food to feed it as Signior Benedick? Courtesy itself—"*

"Thank you," Adri said, forefinger and thumb rubbing at her temples. Then she smiled beatifically. "Wonderful, Candice, we'll be in touch."

Candice skulked away, and Stevie collapsed onto the stage, limbs flailing out like a starfish.

"Oh, don't be so dramatic," Adri said, but she was laughing.

"I thought that was the point," Stevie said, staring up into the lights and wires.

Adri sighed. "I can't help it if these people can't act."

"You didn't even let the poor soul finish the line!" Stevie sat up and rubbed her face. "I need a break."

"Okay, yeah," Adri said, plopping down into one of the velvet seats. "It's past lunchtime anyway. Maybe we could get something delivered."

"No," Stevie said, getting to her feet. "I'll go pick something up. I need some air."

Adri nodded. "Sushi?"

"Sushi," Stevie said, coming down from stage right and grabbing her bag from the first row. "You want your usual?"

Adri's eyes went soft, her smile small and a little sad. "You still remember it?"

Stevie didn't answer at first. Of course she fucking remembered it. Spicy tuna. Philly roll, but with avocado added and fresh salmon instead of smoked. Steamed gyoza. Six months couldn't erase six years, no matter how much Adri sometimes made Stevie feel like it could.

Stevie nodded, clearing her throat as she dug into her bag for her phone. "Okay, I'll be back," she said after she put the order in at their favorite place, then started heading up the aisle.

"Stevie," Adri said, grabbing her hand as she passed.

Stevie froze, her breath locked in her chest. Before she could stop herself, her eyes went to a tiny tattoo at the base of Adri's throat—a solid black heart, inked five years ago. Stevie had a matching one just like it, an ill-conceived romantic gesture on their one-year anniversary she couldn't bring herself to get removed.

She didn't want Adri back. She knew she didn't. Toward the end, they were practically roommates—no kissing, no sex, just quiet nights and sleeping back-to-back.

But.

She missed being someone's.

She loved belonging to one person. Always had, ever since she and her middle school friends sneaked their mothers' romance novels, reading them under the covers at sleepovers and giggling over the sexy bits. But Stevie had always loved the final declarations even more. When one person—usually a man, because heteronormativity—would confess that he couldn't live without the other person. He couldn't even breathe. That single-minded devotion always sent her heart racing. That union that felt both impossible and inevitable.

Six months single, Stevie still wasn't quite sure who she was on her own, which scared the shit out of her.

"Thank you," Adri said softly, squeezing her hand. "For doing this with me. I know the Empress isn't your first choice."

Stevie didn't know how to respond to that, so she said nothing. She simply squeezed Adri's hand back and let her go.

CHAPTER

NINE

THE EMPRESS WAS a tiny building between a laundromat and a cheap fortune-telling parlor. The brick facade sported a small marquee announcing the upcoming *Much Ado* production in rainbow ombre letters, though the *o* was crooked and fluttered a bit in the morning breeze. The glass ticket box, while a bit smudged and in need of cleaning, was encased in maple-colored wood and topped with vintage brass embellishments.

"It's charming," Iris said. She'd never been here before, but the more she thought about participating in an all-queer Shakespearean romp, the more she warmed to the idea.

"Isn't it?" Simon said, grinning and opening the door for her.

Inside, the lobby was small and modern, but with vintage touches here and there that Iris loved. The floor was poured cement, the walls exposed brick, the crown molding a deep purple. Swaths of rainbow silks layered the walls here and there, along with framed black-and-white photographs of previous plays. The lighting was soft and honeyed, adding a homey feel to the entire space. Despite this ambience, there was evidence of shabbiness everywhere, worn carpets and fraying curtains.

"Hi there!" A Latinx person in a lacy black blouse and black jeans sat behind a table near the closed theater doors. She was tapping away on a silver laptop, eyes shifting to Simon and Iris every other word. "Here for auditions?"

"Uh," Simon said, mouth practically hanging wide open as he stared at the woman.

Iris rolled her eyes. Queer as he may be, Simon was such a doofus sometimes when it came to talking to beautiful women. And there was no denying this woman was drop-dead gorgeous.

"Yes," Iris said, looping her arm through Simon's and giving him a yank. "Company."

"Great, great," the woman said, unearthing a clipboard from under a pile of books. "Our assistant director, Julian, is handling the company auditions in the back hall." She looked up at them and handed over the clipboard. "If you could just—"

The woman blinked, her eyes locked on Iris.

Iris blinked back. Glanced at Simon.

"You're her," the woman said.

"I am?" Iris asked.

The woman's smile grew so wide, Iris couldn't help but smile back. Jesus, her teeth were pristine.

"Yes!" the woman said. "You're Iris, right?"

"Um, wow, I . . ."

"I'm Vanessa." She reached out to shake Iris's hand. "I'm so excited to meet you. Does she know you're coming?"

"What?" Simon asked. "Does who—"

"Oh my god, it's a surprise," Vanessa said. "You're surprising her. That is so damn romantic."

"Um," Iris said again, brilliantly. "I'm sorry, who—"

"Hang on, hang on, let me get Adri," Vanessa said, then flung open the theater doors, holding one open with her butt.

"Babe!" she called down the aisle. "You'll never guess who's here!"

"Who?" a deeper voice called back, sultry and husky even with that one syllable.

"Iris!"

A beat of silence. Iris tightened her arm around Simon's, ready to make a run for it. He gave her a *What the fuck* look, which she readily returned.

Footsteps bounded up the aisle, and then a pretty woman appeared, deep green wavy hair cut to her chin and framing her heart-shaped face.

"Oh my god, it is you," she said, frowning. "She didn't tell us you were coming."

"I don't . . ." Iris shook her head. "What? We're here to audition for the company. That's it."

"Wonderful," Adri said, eyes flitting up and down Iris's body in a way that made Iris feel the need to check and make sure nothing was on her face or clothes. "You act?"

"Baby," Vanessa said before Iris could answer, grabbing onto Adri's arm. "Beatrice. You haven't found her yet, right?"

The two women looked at each other, Adri's mouth open in a thoughtful circle.

"Wouldn't that be perfect?" Vanessa asked.

"Oh, Van, I don't know," Adri said.

"Why not? We already know they have chemistry. And she'd be so happy," Vanessa said, her voice taking on a more tender tone.

"She'd be surprised," Adri said. "She doesn't always love surprises."

"She likes good surprises."

"Well, who the hell likes bad surprises?"

"No one, I guess," Vanessa said. "I'm just saying, I think she'd like this."

"Excuse me," Iris said, ready to get off this Willy Wonka roller coaster. "But what the hell is happening?"

Adri and Vanessa laughed.

"Sorry," Vanessa said. "We were just wondering if you'd like to read for Beatrice."

"Van," Adri said, folding her arms.

"What does it hurt to try?" Vanessa said.

"Beatrice?" Simon said. "As in . . . the lead?"

"Whoa, what?" Iris asked. She was vaguely familiar with *Much Ado About Nothing*. She'd read it in high school, seen the movie with Emma Thompson, but she couldn't really remember anyone's names.

"We have our Benedick," Adri said, eyes narrowing on Iris, "as I'm sure you know. We're still looking to fill the co-lead."

"You might be a great fit!" Vanessa said.

"Might," Adri said again.

"Me?" Iris asked, pointing to herself. "But I don't act."

"Yes, she does," Simon said.

"No, I don't." Iris elbowed him in the ribs. "Not officially."

"She's funny," Simon said, ticking off on his fingers. "She's dramatic. She's got flair, charisma, passion, you name it."

Adri smirked. "Sounds perfect for Beatrice, actually."

"Simon Everwood, you are dead to me," Iris said out of the side of her mouth.

Vanessa laughed, then reached out to tap Iris's arm. "What can one reading hurt, hmm? Let's just try it. If it doesn't work out, no harm done. Adri will send you back to the company audition with Julian and your friend here. Right, Adri?"

Adri sighed and rubbed her forehead. "Fine. I guess it doesn't hurt to do a reading."

Iris opened her mouth to protest—no way was she prepared to even think about playing a lead role—but Simon pushed her forward.

"She'll do it."

"Simon, goddammit."

"See?" he said. "Passion."

"I do see," Adri said, her eyes sliding up and down Iris yet again.

"All right, fine," Iris said, because she knew Simon would never let her turn around and come with him to the company audition. Best get this weird-as-hell experience over with.

Vanessa offered to take Simon to Julian, while Adri led Iris into the theater. It was small and brick-walled, with plush purple seats and an antiqued rainbow border framing the front of the modest stage. Lights and wires hung from the ceiling and Iris felt an unexplainable thrill swoop through her belly.

She'd never actually been in a play. Though her mother and siblings had told her more than once that she was dramatic enough to carry her own theater troupe, she'd dropped her high school class after a few weeks on account of Mr. Bristow's extreme creepiness. Now she had to admit that walking into an empty theater, the stage lit up and waiting, was kind of exciting.

"Okay," Adri said once they reached the stage, handing Iris a script already open to a scene. "Are you familiar with the story?"

"A bit," Iris said, suddenly nervous. "Some army arrives home, a dude falls in love with a girl."

Adri nods. "That's Claudio and Hero, though in our play, it's two men, one of them trans."

Iris smiled. "I love that."

Adri's whole face lit up. "I do too. But you're reading for Beatrice, Hero's cousin, a very sharp-witted woman who has zero time for foolishness."

"Sounds like a smart lady."

"She is," Adri said. "In this first scene, she insults Benedick, a soldier, as these two have a history of battling wits. He shows up—in our case, *she* shows up—and the two duke it out verbally. We'll have a revised script to account for pronouns and other adjustments once we get the cast set."

Iris nodded, eyes scanning over the lines. Shakespeare wasn't easy, by any means, but Iris had read enough in high school and college to understand most of it.

"I'll read the other parts," Adri said. "You just do Beatrice."

"Could I have a second to get my bearings?" she asked.

"Of course," Adri said. "I know you weren't prepared for Beatrice. Or were you?" She tilted her head, as though waiting for Iris to confess something.

Iris frowned. "No, I definitely wasn't."

Adri's eyes narrowed slightly, but she nodded and waved for Iris to take her second.

Iris turned away, chewing on her thumbnail as she read over the lines. *In our last conflict, four of his five wits went halting off, and now is the whole man governed with one . . .*

Iris couldn't help but laugh softly. Beatrice was funny. Smart. Undoubtedly sexy. Iris could do this. At least enough to get through the reading without making a total fool of herself. In the end, she'd join Simon in the company, and they'd have a laugh about the odd director who forced her into reading for the lead.

"I think I'm ready," Iris said, glancing up at Adri. Vanessa had come in while Iris studied, and the two were now staring at her with such interest, Iris actually did check her face for stray crumbs this time.

"Great," Adri said. "You can head up to the stage."

Iris did as she was told, lifting her long skirt so she didn't trip up the short flight of stairs on stage left. Or was it stage right? She could never keep it straight.

"Whenever you're comfortable," Adri said, following her up.

"Starting at line thirty." She stood a few feet away from Iris and was all Iris could really see. The stage lights were bright, making everything in the theater seem dreamlike, a gauzy black and white.

Iris rolled her shoulders back. She cleared her throat. Then she very nearly cracked up at what she was doing. Nervous energy propelled her forward, so her first line came out on a bubble of laughter.

"I pray you, is Signior Mountanto returned from the wars or no?"

It seemed to work, though, curling a bit of mirth through the words.

"I know none of that name, lady," Adri read as the messenger. Then, as Hero, *"My cousin means Signior Benedick of Padua."*

And so it went. Iris quickly warmed up to her character, this woman who was fed up with arrogant bullshit and at the same time clearly wanted to bang Benedick's brains out. It would be fascinating to see this played out between two queer women.

The idea spurred Iris on even more. Soon, she was moving around on stage, flourishing her hands, scoffing when the line called for it. Though when it came time for Benedick to arrive, she quieted down. Their verbal sparring was fast, vitriolic, but she infused it with . . . well, with lust, if she was being honest. It just felt right, and she remembered hearing this whole play—at least when it came to Beatrice and Benedick—was one giant exercise in foreplay.

"You always end with a jade's trick," she said, teeth slightly gritted as she read Beatrice's last line in scene 1. *"I know you of old."*

Silence.

A very long, charged, terrifying beat of silence.

Iris was breathing a bit heavily, and she realized she'd jutted her hand toward Adri, one coral-painted finger pointing at her face while she read Beatrice's lines.

Iris dropped her hand, cleared her throat. Waited.

Adri just stared, mouth slightly parted.

"So . . ." Iris said, "what now?"

"Wow," Vanessa said, clapping. "I mean, Adri, right?"

Adri started to say something, but before she could say anything, the theater doors banged open.

"Sorry, that took an eternity," a voice said. Iris looked out into the audience but could only see a shadowy form heading down the aisle. "Their lunch crowd is getting out of control."

Iris frowned, the voice somehow familiar. She squinted to see, but the figure was still a blur in the lights.

"No worries," Adri said, eyeing Iris. "Gave us some time to get to know your girl."

"My what?" the other person said.

"Their what?" Iris said at the same time. "I'm not—"

But then, the person—a woman with a curly shag haircut and amber-brown eyes—arrived at the edge of the stage, stopping next to Vanessa and staring up at Iris with her mouth hanging open.

"Stefania?" Iris said.

"Iris," Stefania said back, her voice breathy and shaky.

They stared at each other for a second. Iris's head swam. She never expected to see Stefania again—never wanted to, if she was being honest. Something flickered in the back of Iris's mind, puzzle pieces of this whole bat-shit experience coming together—the way Adri and Vanessa seemed to know who she was, her name, this *her* they kept talking about surprising.

What the hell was going on?

She opened her mouth to ask exactly that, but then, as though she was lit abruptly on fire, Stefania dropped a paper bag on the floor, hopped onto the stage, and pulled Iris into her arms.

CHAPTER

TEN

IRIS.

Iris was here.

At the Empress.

On stage.

Stevie felt dizzy, embarrassment clouding into her cheeks as she stared at the redhead she'd puked all over just seventy-two hours ago.

The redhead her entire friend group thought she was having sex with.

No, not just having sex with.

Dating.

Iris swam in her vision, and she knew she had to do something. Say something. Before she could really think through it, she dropped the sushi that took her nearly an hour to procure and ran up the stage steps.

Slid her arms around Iris's waist and pulled her close.

"Please," she whispered in Iris's ear.

It was all she could think to say.

Iris was stiff, shocked, as she damn well should be, but she also smelled amazing, all ginger and bergamot, the fabric of her light sweater like silk under Stevie's fingers.

"Please," Stevie said again when Iris didn't embrace her back. Which, Stevie knew, was a clear sign she should back off, but desperation to get out of this situation without her entire lie blowing up in front of Vanessa and Adri drove any other thought to the far corners of her mind.

Finally—thank Christ, finally—Iris softened and wrapped her arms around Stevie's shoulders, but not without a "What the hell" whispered back into Stevie's ear.

"I know. I'm sorry," Stevie said. "Just let me—"

"That is the cutest thing I've ever seen," Vanessa said, her voice floating up from the audience. "Right, babe?"

"Pretty cute," Adri said, though her tone was decidedly more thoughtful. It jolted Stevie back into reality and she pulled away from Iris.

Iris met her eyes, fire in all that green.

I'm sorry, Stevie mouthed again. She could fix this. Explain it. Iris had tucked her into bed, for god's sake. Surely she'd understand the need to save a little face in front of an ex.

Stevie cleared her throat and turned to face Adri and Vanessa, her fingers tangling with Iris's. Iris let her do it, and she felt buoyed by the permission.

"Um," she said. "So, this is Iris."

"Yes, we know," Vanessa said, grinning. "A romantic, if ever there was one."

Iris snorted, her fingers tightening on Stevie's to a painful degree. Stevie laughed nervously. "Yeah, I, um, I had no idea she was—"

"I wanted to surprise Stefania," Iris said, hand still squeezing Stevie's. "And I think I succeeded."

"Oh, you did," Stevie said, squeezing back. "You definitely did."

"Stefania?" Adri said, her thick brows lowering.

Stevie met her gaze. Swallowed. Adri knew all about how Stevie sometimes envisioned herself as a different person to get through a stressful situation. She also knew that Stevie didn't go by Stefania—the name given to her in honor of her Italian great-grandmother—with anyone.

"Yeah," Stevie said, lies unrolling onto her tongue. "When Iris and I met, I told her my full name. She liked it. Didn't you?" She nudged Iris's arm, and Iris glared at Stevie with enough fire to re-ignite a dwindling star.

"Right," Iris finally said, biting into the final *t* so loudly, the sound echoed through the theater. "Give us a second, will you?" she asked Adri and Vanessa, pulling Stevie by the hand toward the stage steps.

"Of course," Adri said.

"But don't leave, Iris," Vanessa said. "I'm sure Adri wants to talk to you about Beatrice."

"Van," Adri said sharply. "I'm the director here."

"I know, babe, but come on. Have you seen a better one?"

"Wait, really?" Iris asked, pausing on the steps.

"Beatrice?" Stevie asked, but Iris was staring at Adri.

Adri flattened her mouth. "I admit, Iris, you're perfect. I mean, we can do a reading with Stevie so you can get a feel for what it will be like with Benedick, but yes. You're the best Beatrice I've seen in . . . well, maybe ever. No question."

Iris blinked, a tiny smile on her beautiful mouth. But then it faded, and she looked at Stevie. "You're Benedick."

It wasn't a question, but Adri's resigned expression morphed into suspicion anyway. "You didn't know?"

Iris sniffed in response. Stevie had to get her out of here. Fix this.

"We'll be right back," Stevie said, changing direction and tug-ging Iris backstage.

It wasn't a huge space, a hallway mostly, full of pulleys and wires above, poured concrete below. Stevie didn't slow down until they were in the small dressing room the entire cast shared on performance nights. There were four lighted mirrors, two on each wall, mixmatched chairs set in front of the vanities. A green leather couch sat in one corner, a coffee table covered in books and scripts and a Nintendo Switch.

As soon as the door clicked shut, Iris rounded on Stevie.

"What the actual fuck?"

"I know," Stevie said. "I know, I'm sorry."

Iris folded her arms, long, tangled hair draping over her shoulders. She was gorgeous when she was mad, her green eyes a bit darker, red hair like fire—

Stevie shook her head. Focus. She needed to focus here.

"Who are you?" Iris asked. "Because you sure as hell aren't Stefania."

Stevie presented her palms. "I am. I just go by Stevie."

Iris's eyes softened, but only slightly. "Stevie."

Stevie nodded.

"So why did you tell me your name was Stefania?"

Stevie dropped her arms. "It's my name."

"You know what I mean."

Stevie nodded, rubbed her forehead. "Yeah. Sorry. I just . . ." She searched for a reason that would make her sound less pathetic, but there wasn't one. She *was* pathetic, and the sooner Iris knew it, the better.

Granted, she had already puked on the poor woman, so Iris was probably very aware already.

"I get nervous when I meet new people," Stevie said. "I'm not awesome with strangers, and you were so . . ."

Beautiful.

Hypnotic.

Perfect.

The words cascaded in Stevie's brain, but she couldn't say any of those things.

"Confident," she said. "So I acted like I was too. Thinking of myself as someone else helped. I mean, up to a point."

Iris watched her, mouth slightly pursed. "Okay. I guess I get that."

Stevie audibly exhaled, but Iris wasn't finished.

"What I don't get is why your friends seem to think I came here for you. That we know each other beyond a disastrous one-night stand."

Stevie winced. "Nice word choice."

Iris's brows lifted. "I think *disastrous* is pretty apt."

"No, yeah, it's perfect."

Silence spilled in between them. An awful, awkward silence.

And then, unexplainably, "I throw up when I'm really nervous" is how Stevie chose to fill it.

Iris's mouth dropped open. "Wow."

"Yeah. So that's fun."

"I'm sorry," Iris said softly. "You could've just said you didn't want to sleep with me. I'm a big girl, I can—"

"I did want to though," Stevie said.

Iris tilted her head. More awkward silence, but this time, Stevie kept her damn mouth shut. The blush in her cheeks probably said enough anyway.

"Okay," Iris said, pressing her fingers into her eyes. "Let's focus on the more pressing issue."

"My friends."

"Yeah."

"And Beatrice."

Iris dropped her hands, gaze on Stevie.

"You must be really good," Stevie said. "I've never seen Adri offer someone a part that fast."

That tiny smile again. "Really?"

Stevie nodded. "And I've known Adri for ten years."

Iris shook her head. "I didn't mean to audition for Beatrice. They pretty much made me. Well, them and my friend Simon, who's with the company somewhere."

"Yeah, Adri can be pushy."

"It was more the other one. Van?"

"Ah," Stevie said.

Iris folded her arms. "Now why would she do such a thing?"

Her tone dripped sarcasm. Stevie knew she needed to get this confession over with, and it all came out in a rush. "Probably because Ren—my friend I was with at the club that night—showed them a picture of you and me dancing at Lush and they were so excited that I'd hooked up with someone so very obviously out of my league that I let them believe we're kind of sort of maybe dating."

Iris squinted at her like she was trying to catch up.

"So," she said finally, "we're dating."

Stevie said nothing.

"Like, fake dating. In a rom-com," Iris said.

Stevie filled her cheeks with air, blew it out slowly. "It just sort of . . . happened. Adri and I used to date, and now she and Vanessa—"

"Oh my god, wait, what?" Iris said. "This is all about getting your ex back?"

"No," Stevie said, taking a step closer to Iris. "No, I don't want her back, I swear. But . . ." Fuck, it all sounded so ridiculous. When she spoke again, she closed her eyes and kept them squeezed shut. "I just wanted a minute to breathe. An hour, a day, where I wasn't the pathetic ex slash best friend everyone was worried about."

She opened her eyes. Iris was staring at her, mouth slightly parted.

"I figured, I'd let it play out for a couple of weeks, then tell them we broke up," Stevie said. "I didn't expect you—the real you—to come walking into my ex's theater."

Iris smiled a little at that. "Well, I am full of surprises."

"Yeah." Stevie smiled back. "You really, really are."

CHAPTER

ELEVEN

IRIS COULDN'T BELIEVE she'd somehow found herself in the middle of a romantic comedy.

Fake dating.

It was ridiculous.

It was absurd.

It was . . .

She looked at Stevie, whose shaggy curls fell into her eyes, making her look like some sort of adorable lesbian pop star. She wore a fitted gray T-shirt that said *I Put Reading on the Map!* and featured, inexplicably, a picture of a cartoon cat holding up a copy of *A Wrinkle in Time.* The shirt bordered on ridiculous, but paired with Stevie's low-hanging black jeans and boots, it worked.

Stevie was hot, there was no doubt about it.

And Iris got the distinct impression that she had no idea, which only made her hotter.

I just wanted a minute to breathe . . . where I wasn't the pathetic ex slash best friend everyone was worried about.

Stevie's words floated through Iris's skull, a collection of syllables and phonemes that found their way into the middle of her chest.

She couldn't say she didn't understand where Stevie was coming from here.

She did.

All too well.

And, sure, Stevie's tiny lie probably seemed harmless before Iris walked into the Empress. Empty words to take some pressure off. But now Iris was real.

Now Adri had offered Iris a lead part in the play.

And . . . Iris wanted it.

That was the real kick in the ass here. If she turned down the role, she could simply walk out the door—with a completely bonkers story to tell Simon on the drive home—and Stevie could carry on with her lie for a few weeks before relaying news of their breakup. Iris didn't have to do a thing. She could just go back to her life in Bright Falls. She'd help Claire and Delilah plan their wedding, and she'd endure more of her mother's random setups—hell, maybe Maeve's gynecologist *was* single—and everything would be just as it had always been. She'd continue to languish over her novel, freaking out on the daily that she was going to have to send back her advance and ruin her career before it even got started, all because she was burned out on romance and couldn't think of a decent idea, and—

She froze.

Fake dating.

It was one of Iris's least favorite tropes—she could never really imagine a situation in real life where fake dating would be necessary—and yet . . . here she was with Stevie-whatever-her-last-name-was standing before her, asking Iris to fake date her.

This might work. Iris had no interest writing the trope into her book—Tegan McKee didn't seem like the type, and Iris didn't know if she could pull it off believably, if she was being honest—but spending time with Stevie in a romantic setting could break through Iris's block. She could actually experience a little romance. A few dates. Hand holding. Get her head back in the true love game without a single messy string attached.

Because it was all fake.

Plus, she really wanted to do this play. Reading for Beatrice on stage, she'd felt excited. Passionate. It was *fun*, and if nothing else, Iris Kelly was all about fun.

"Okay," Iris said. "But if we do this, I'll need a few things from you."

"Wait . . ." Stevie said. "You actually want to fake date me?"

"I want to fake date *someone*. And I want to do this play, so I think we're at an impasse where *Much Ado* is concerned."

"I can just tell them the truth," Stevie said. "I'll go out there right now and—"

"No way in hell you can do that," Iris said. "Not if I'm playing Beatrice." If Stevie admitted to her friends—and her ex, who also happened to be the director—that she puked all over Iris and then lied that they were banging, that would make for some very awkward onstage dynamics. Not to mention the utter humiliation, and Stevie seemed like she'd already had enough of that. It was all a bit too much drama for any one person to take, even in this theatrical setting.

Stevie's shoulders visibly relaxed, but then her brows crinkled together. "Wait, did you say you *wanted* to fake date someone?"

Iris grinned. "Well, see, that's where you can help me—with research." But before she could explain any further, the door flew open to reveal Simon.

"Hey, there you are," he said. "That wondrously gorgeous woman out there told me they offered you Beatrice. Iris, that's amazing! Tell me you're going to accept. I refuse to let you pass—"

He froze, his gaze darting to Stevie.

"Oh. Sorry to interrupt," he said. "I was just . . . hang on." His pushed up his glasses, then pointed his finger at Stevie. "Aren't you the throw-up girl?"

"Simon, Jesus," Iris said.

"Sorry, just . . . well, aren't you?" Simon asked, his face an amalgam of confusion and amusement.

"Um, yeah . . . I guess that's me," Stevie said, swallowing over and over again like she just might do an encore of the vomit incident itself.

"She's also playing Benedick," Iris said, then grabbed Stevie's hand and laced their fingers together, "as well as my fake girlfriend."

A charged silence spilled in between them. Simon blinked at her, his mouth open, and Iris fought the urge to laugh.

"Isn't telling people we're fake dating sort of defeating the purpose?" Stevie asked quietly.

"With your crew, yes," Iris said. "My group? They'd never buy it."

"Why not?" Stevie asked.

"Because Iris doesn't do girlfriends," Simon said slowly, his expression still a model of *What the fuck?*

"Or partners of any kind," Iris said. "But it's fine. I don't need you to convince my friends that you love me. I just need you to hang out with me a little, *act* like my girlfriend, maybe go on a few romantic dates so I can get a feel for what it's like again."

"For what *what's* like?" Stevie asked.

"Love," Iris said, waving a hand. "Romance. You know, soul mates and stars and moons and all that shit."

Stevie blinked, but Simon face-palmed himself.

"Oh my god, this is for your book," he said.

"What book?" Stevie asked. "What the hell is happening?"

Iris released Stevie's sweaty palm and turned to face her. "I write romance novels and I'm a bit stuck. I just need a little inspiration, that's all. I'm hoping some good old-fashioned courting will get me back in the mood."

"And I can help you do that?" Stevie asked.

Iris nodded. "Totally. I'll be your fake girlfriend around your friends and when we're at the theater. You be my romance guinea pig."

Simon looked horrified.

"Okay, that didn't sound great," Iris said. "The guinea pig part, but it's not a big deal. I date you, you date me."

"Fakely," Stevie said.

"Hey, this was your idea," Iris said, folding her arms. "We can just tell Adri and her Aphrodite girlfriend that you lied and—"

"No," Stevie said, shaking her head. "I'm in. I can do it."

"I don't understand a fucking thing that's happening right now," Simon said, sending both hands through his hair. "They should make pills for this."

"I'm sure they do," Iris said, patting his cheek.

"Stevie?"

Footsteps sounded on the concrete, and Adri and Vanessa appeared in the hallway.

"Oh," Iris said quietly, "showtime. Simon, be cool."

"Be cool how?"

"Just shut up," Iris said to him and then yanked Stevie closer, arm curled around her waist. Stevie was a fucking brick wall next to her—that was going to need some work.

"Hey, there you are," Adri said, spotting them through the doorway. Her eyes flitted down to Iris's arm around Stevie, before lifting again. "Did you two want to do a reading? I'm happy to run that so you can get a feel for interacting with Stevie on the stage."

"No need," Iris said quickly. "I'll do the play."

Vanessa clapped her hands once, her mouth spreading into a lovely smile. "Wonderful! Amazing."

"That's great," Adri said. "We're excited."

Iris smiled. "Me too."

Adri glanced at Stevie, then cleared her throat. "Okay, so, some details. We usually hold the full company rehearsal in the evenings to accommodate our actors with day jobs, though I also conduct regular workshops for our principal actors if they can swing it."

"That works, I think," Iris said.

"Everything starts up next Friday with our principals' retreat at Vanessa's parents' house in Malibu. We have team building exercises, pair off to run lines, do some role reversal. I know it's last minute, but I'm afraid it's nonnegotiable."

"Malibu?" Simon said. "That's a bit far, isn't it?"

"Not for me," Iris said quickly, because *Malibu*. "I've never been and I've always wanted to go." And, Jesus, the idea of getting out of Bright Falls for a bit sounded nice.

Vanessa smiled. "My folks pay for everything, including airfare, so there are no worries there. They're big supporters of the arts, and this is part of their annual contribution to the Empress. They make themselves scarce while we're there, which is also appreciated." She laughed. "Things can get a little wild."

"I love wild," Iris said.

"She really does," Simon said, and Iris elbowed him in the ribs.

"So you're in?" Adri said, tucking her teal hair behind her heavily pierced ears.

Iris eyeballed Stevie, who was still staring straight ahead like she was facing down the barrel of a gun. Iris shook her a little, pressed their shoulders together and grinned at Stevie like the smitten kitten she was.

Well, *pretending* she was.

"I'm very much in," she crooned. God, she was already so good at this.

"Jesus Christ," Simon muttered under his breath, but Iris ignored him, nuzzling Stevie's neck a bit for good measure.

Iris wasn't positive, it happened so fast, but she could swear Adri's smile dimmed just a little.

"Wonderful," Vanessa said. "This is going to be so much fun. Right, Stevie?"

Iris heard Stevie inhale slowly, waiting a split second before she managed a whispered, "So much fun."

CHAPTER

TWELVE

FOUR DAYS LATER, Stevie was wearing a bathing suit that didn't fit.

She couldn't even remember the last time she'd been swimming, but now she stood on the warm deck of the Belmont Club's giant pool with Iris, trying to get the courage to take off her tank and shorts to reveal a one-piece she'd had since she was seventeen. It was orange and pink and white—which she was pretty sure she'd picked out as some sort of baby lesbian pride statement—and had a one-shoulder style. The strap was so tight, it felt like it was about to snap.

A few days ago, the day after their fraught reunion at the Empress, Iris had texted while Stevie was wiping down tables at Bitch's.

Iris: Hey sweetie

Stevie had stared at her phone. Of course, she and Iris had exchanged numbers before Iris left the Empress on Tuesday, but still, Iris's term of endearment threw Stevie off balance. Maybe Iris meant to text one of her friends. Stevie ignored the text and went on with her shift, only to have her phone buzz approximately seven minutes later.

Iris: Snookums

Iris: Oh that's horrible. Maybe just honey?

Iris: Baby. I like that one

Iris: Babe

Iris: Isn't it a requirement that all queer couples call each other babe? Judging from my friends, I think it is

Iris: Darling, if we want to get fancy

Iris: Nope never mind, that reminds me of my best friend's mom a little too much and *shudder*

Stevie just blinked at her screen as the texts piled in, unsure of what to say back. Finally, she settled for a very sophisticated Hey.

Iris: She lives!

Stevie: Sorry I'm at work

Iris: Where do you work?

Iris: I just realized we know nothing about each other. Might want to change that before rehearsals start.

She had a point there. All Stevie knew about Iris was that she was an author and lived in Bright Falls.

Stevie: Bitch's Brew. If you like a little bit of queer witch with your coffee, it's the place to be

Iris: I always prefer a little queer witch

Stevie: As do we all

Iris: I'll let you get back to work, but I wanted to ask you out on a date

Stevie: A date?

Iris: A "date" 😉

Stevie inhaled slowly. She'd agreed to this part of their deal, but figured Iris would simply . . . forget? Then again, Iris didn't seem like the kind of person who forgot anything. Nerves flared through Stevie's stomach, but she swallowed them down. She could do this. It wasn't like she actually had to impress Iris—she'd already humiliated herself in the worst way possible in front of the woman. Plus, Iris was sweet. A little hyper, but sweet.

And gorgeous.

God, Iris was so ridiculously beautiful, Stevie had a hard time breathing just thinking about her freckles, her red hair, her—

Iris: So?

Stevie shook her head to clear it and texted, What did you have in mind?

Which was exactly how Stevie found herself wearing her pubescent bathing suit on a Saturday morning at the Belmont Club's poolside Pride party in Portland. It was a fancy place that required membership, but every June for the last few years, they hosted a fundraiser for the Trevor Project and decked out their huge outdoor pool with all manner of rainbow paraphernalia. Apparently, Iris's friends were all going to celebrate an engagement, and Iris wanted Stevie to go with her.

Be my date, she'd texted. We can get to know each other more and maybe it'll be less awkward for you if we start in a group setting.

It was actually kind of sweet of Iris to think of Stevie's comfort level like that, and the woman was already doing Stevie a huge favor by acting like her girlfriend during the play. The least Stevie could do was go to a queer pool party for a good cause. She'd certainly had her share of friends back in high school who'd needed some of the Trevor Project's resources, and she knew the organization had saved more than a few lives.

But now, ten minutes after meeting Iris in the Belmont's lobby, Stevie stood frozen by the pool as partygoers continued to arrive. And it didn't help the situation that Iris looked . . .

Well, she looked fucking radiant. She wore a white tank top that was thin enough to reveal a bikini underneath—red, yellow, pink, and orange flowers, tied around her neck with a very thin string— and a pair of tiny denim shorts with the pockets hanging below the hem line. Her hair was up in a messy bun, and when she whipped off her tank top, Stevie nearly stopped breathing.

"You okay?" Iris asked as she started slathering on SPF 50.

Stevie nodded but still didn't make a move to take off her own green tank. She glanced around, taking in the scene instead. It was pretty impressive, she had to admit. The pool was large and sparkling, and there were rainbow flags and banners everywhere, along with specific identity flags blowing in Mason jars on the patio tables lining the area. The deck sported teak sun chairs and large umbrellas in an array of colors, and a bar offered a variety of drinks featuring tiny rainbow umbrellas. It seemed to be a family affair as well, with a lot of couples of all genders sitting on the side of the pool while their kids splashed in the water.

"This is pretty amazing," Stevie said.

"I told you," Iris said, then held out the tube of sunscreen to Stevie. "Will you put this on my back?"

Stevie's eyes went wide, but she took the cream, smearing a blob onto her hand as Iris turned around. Her back was smooth and freckled, and the only thing interrupting the swath of skin were two itty-bitty strings tied around her neck and ribs. Stevie started between her shoulders—a safe place—but as soon as she touched Iris, her knees wobbled a little. Iris seemed steady as a rock, but then she grinned coyly over her shoulder.

"Such a romantic gesture, sweetie pie, thank you."

Stevie couldn't help but smile at this new term of endearment. Iris's joking tone helped calm her stomach, distract her from all the skin under her fingertips. "Sure thing, baby cakes."

Iris laughed, then tilted her head forward to give Stevie access to her neck. Stevie finished the job quickly and was wiping her hands off on her towel when her phone buzzed in her bag. Digging into its depths, she saw Adri's name flash across the phone's screen. She grabbed the device and squinted at the text.

Adri: Hey how's it going?

Stevie: Good. You?

Adri: Fine. How's Iris? Things going okay?

Stevie glanced at Iris, who was currently slathering her curvy thigh with sunscreen. Their gazes caught, and Iris winked.

"Muffin," she said, then made a kissy face.

Stevie snorted back a laugh.

Great, she texted Adri. Really great.

Adri: Good

Adri: So I was hoping we could get together to talk about the script

Stevie: Oh?

Adri: This project did start with you and me in a shitty apartment, after all

Stevie: And really bad pizza

Adri: God, so bad. It smelled like feet. Am I remembering that right? Didn't it smell like feet?

Stevie: It totally did. But it was five bucks a pop and we were broke

Adri: Facts. So what do you say? Could you meet me at our place this afternoon?

Stevie: Our place?

Adri: Sorry. You know what I mean

Stevie did, but she hadn't been to the apartment she'd once shared with Adri since she moved out, and she honestly wasn't too keen to change that, particularly now that Vanessa lived there. Stevie winced, thumbs hovering over the keys. She looked up at Iris again, who was now waving to a group of people heading toward them.

Stevie: I can't today. I'm actually at the Belmont with Iris

Three dots bounced onto the screen, then disappeared before appearing again. Stevie felt her throat go a little tight. But she and Adri were over. Friends only. Dating other people. Adri would understand.

Adri: Got it. No worries then

Stevie pressed a hand to her stomach. Dammit, she hated texting for this very reason. She knew Adri and there was definitely a *tone* to her response, but Stevie also knew if she asked about the tone, Adri—and most people, it was a fucking text for Christ's sake—wouldn't have a clue what she was talking about and then Stevie would feel like an idiot.

So she swallowed several hundred times, took five thousand deep breaths, and dropped her phone back into her bag.

"Hey!" Iris called to the incoming group, then turned to grab Stevie's hand, whipping her to her side before Stevie had even finished zipping up her tote.

"Oh, okay," Stevie said, stumbling against her.

"Pucker up, buttercup," Iris whispered, and Stevie laughed again, feeling herself instantly relax.

"This place is gorgeous," a pretty brunette with glasses said. She had on a vintage-style polka-dotted one-piece, a wrap skirt around her waist. She held hands with a curly-haired woman in a black tank top and shorts, an array of arm tattoos gleaming under the sun.

"Isn't it?" Iris said.

"Of course it is, it's the Belmont." This from a refined-looking blonde with shaggy bangs, her hand tucked in the palm of a woman with reddish-brown hair cut short and shaved on one side.

"You can take the girl out of the cotillion, but you can't take the cotillion out of the girl," the tattooed woman said.

"Flip her off, Astrid," Iris said to the blonde. "I beg you."

Astrid just pursed her mouth and shook her head.

"Point," the tattooed woman said.

"Fuck, it's hot," the guy Stevie remembered as Simon from the Empress said. "Is it supposed to be this hot in June?"

"Global warming, baby," a Black person with a halo of dark curls said.

Iris just beamed at all of them, then slid her arm around Stevie's waist. "Everyone, this is Stevie."

At that point, the entire six-person group seemed to freeze, as though they just realized Stevie was there.

"Holy shit," Tattoos said.

"Sweetie," the brunette in glasses said to Iris, her brown eyes wide and her mouth slightly open. "Did you . . . did you bring a date?"

"Oh god," Simon said, shaking his head.

"What?" his partner asked.

Iris laughed. "It's nothing as dramatic as that. Stevie's my fake girlfriend."

All the friends blinked as one, like some sort of weird group-think.

"She's what?" Astrid asked.

"I told you this was a bad idea," Simon said.

"Iris, what are you talking about?" the brunette asked.

Iris sighed and Stevie truly wanted the earth to swallow her whole right now. This was beyond awkward. She wasn't sure why she thought this would go well, or that she could do it without feeling like a complete idiot.

"Okay, just listen," Iris said, then she proceeded to explain about meeting Stevie at Lush and running into her again at the Empress. She didn't mention Stevie's lies, nor did she mention the fact that they were fake dating for real—or fakely? God, this was confusing—for Stevie's friends. She simply said Stevie agreed to go on some dates with her for the sake of research.

"Research," Astrid said. It wasn't a question. More like an accusation.

"Yes," Iris said. "And I'd really appreciate it if you'd all just get over it, because Stevie here is lovely and being a very good sport."

They all exchanged glances and Stevie felt herself shrinking even more. Iris's grip on her tightened, and then the woman in glasses stepped forward and held out her hand.

"I'm sorry, Stevie, we're being so rude. It's really nice to meet you. I'm Claire."

"Hi, Claire," Stevie said, shaking her hand. "I know this is weird."

"It's *Iris*," the tattooed woman said. "Think nothing of it. I'm Delilah."

Stevie smiled and waved, then the others introduced themselves as Astrid, Jordan, and Emery.

"Great," Iris said lightly, but her voice was a bit tight. "Now that that's over with, my girl and I are going to take a dip." She turned toward Stevie. "Shall we?"

"Um, sure," Stevie said, letting Iris lead her away. As they went, she heard a whispered "What the fuck" from someone in the group, but Iris just kept moving. They stopped at another set of chairs and Iris shucked off her shorts and . . .

Stevie nearly passed out.

See, part of the problem with fake dating a ridiculously hot woman was that Stevie still hadn't scratched that itch for some physical activity that had reared its ugly head in Bitch's last week when she'd tried to nuzzle Adri. And now, standing here under the sun while a very beautiful and curvy Iris stripped down to her tiny bikini . . . well, Stevie was having feelings.

"Well?" Iris asked. "Are you coming in with me, my little rosebud?"

Stevie cracked up at the name, which again helped her relax. "I guess I am, mon petit chou."

Iris laughed. "French, already? I'm flattered."

"It means my little cabbage. I'm not sure how flattered you should really be."

"Vegetable talk. That's hot."

Stevie shook her head, the blush creeping over her cheeks irrepressible.

Iris tilted her head, gaze narrowing. "It's not an act, is it?"

"What?"

"The shy thing."

Stevie choked on a laugh. "Um . . . no, not at all. You *were* there the night we met, right?"

Iris shrugged. "I remember a really sexy woman kissing me first."

"Followed by evidence that I am the worst seductress in the Pacific Northwest," Stevie said.

Iris's expression remained thoughtful as she stepped forward, fingers sliding under the hem of Stevie's tank. "Then allow me to take the lead. May I?"

Stevie swallowed, acutely aware at how close Iris was. She knew it was fake—this wild woman playing at romance to get into a character's head or something—but with Iris a mere breath away, Stevie could count every single freckle on her face, and her lungs were having a hard time remembering how to function.

She managed to nod though, and Iris lifted her shirt up, prompting Stevie to raise her arms. The fabric slid slowly—way more slowly than it really needed to, in Stevie's opinion—and when the tank slipped free, Iris was smirking.

"What?" Stevie asked, rolling her shoulders back. The single strap of her bathing suit pulled at her neck.

"Nothing," Iris said. "You're just cute, that's all."

Stevie snorted. "Is that a line for your research?"

Iris's smile slipped, but only for a second. "Of course it is, my adorable button."

Stevie took care of her shorts—no way she could handle a woman who could most certainly be featured on some Sexiest People of the Year list taking off her pants—and she and Iris approached the edge of the pool, the water already undulating with swimmers. Stevie spotted Iris's friends wading by the stairs, half of them with umbrellaed drinks in their hands already.

"Ready?" Iris asked, slotting her fingers between Stevie's.

Stevie pulled on her suit's strap, which felt about as thin as a spaghetti noodle. It barely gave, digging into Stevie's shoulder like a wire. Still, she nodded and tightened her grip on Iris's hand.

"One . . ." Iris said, "two . . . three!"

Stevie leaped, throwing her free arm back and jumping. The water hit her like a slap—sudden and freezing cold. Still, she felt liberated and wild. She lost Iris's hand on impact, and she let her knees bend all the way, her feet scraping the bottom before she rocketed herself back to the surface. She broke into the sun, swiping her hair back from her face and laughing.

"That was amazing," she said, blinking into the light and trying to find Iris. "I should do that more—"

"Oh shit," Iris said, her eyes wide on Stevie's chest.

Then Stevie realized exactly why she felt so wild and free upon hitting the water—her bathing suit strap had snapped and was currently drifting in front of her while the pool's waves lapped at her . . .

"Fucking hell," she said, crossing her arms to cover herself, because despite the vigorous dive, she and Iris had jumped into the shallow end and her boobs were on full display at this family affair.

"Okay, okay, it's okay," Iris said, swimming toward her. She grabbed the floating strap and pulled up, nudging Stevie's arms out of the way so she could hook it around her neck. Iris moved behind her and Stevie felt tugging.

"Everyone okay?" Claire asked, moving through the water toward them.

"I'd say that's a no," Delilah said, but not unkindly. She winced at Stevie, her expression pure sympathy.

"Can you tie it to something?" Astrid asked, now behind Stevie too as she and Iris tried to troubleshoot her ancient swimsuit into functionality. Soon the entire crew had swarmed Stevie, all of them closing ranks to cover her from public view.

Still, Stevie felt like she was five seconds from flashing all of them, and that was not her idea of a great first impression.

"Well, baby doll," Iris said, "there just doesn't seem to be any way to salvage this." She tugged a bit more.

"I can just go," Stevie said. "I don't want to ruin your party."

"Hell no," Iris said. "My woman is in trouble, and I'm going to fix it." She released the strap slowly so Stevie could hold the swimsuit to her chest herself. "They sell suits in the club."

Stevie nodded and let Iris help her out of the pool via the stairs. A few middle school–aged boys pointed and laughed, and Stevie felt like she was eleven years old again as she climbed out of the water and Iris wrapped a towel around her.

"Some romantic first date," Stevie said.

Iris laughed. "You always make it interesting, I'll give you that."

"So . . . how much did you see? Before I covered myself up?"

Iris's mouth twitched as she tugged the towel tighter. "Let's just say the curiosity that never got satisfied the night we met has been fully quenched."

"Oh god," Stevie said, covering her eyes.

"Hey, you've got no need to be embarrassed."

Stevie peeked out from between her fingers. "No?"

"Not even a little tit. I mean bit."

Stevie froze for a second—she couldn't believe Iris said that—but then a laugh bubbled into her chest and flew from her mouth. Soon they were cracking up, literally hanging on to each other's shoulders for support. Stevie couldn't remember the last time she'd laughed so hard her stomach muscles hurt.

"Oh god, I needed that," she said wiping her eyes.

"Everyone in the club needed that," Iris said, and Stevie devolved into giggles again as Iris took her hand and led her toward the club.

"Now," Iris said as she opened the glass door and the cool air rushed out to meet them, "for your next selection, I'm thinking something at least three sizes too small with nothing but a string to cover your ass."

"Maybe I'll just leave off the bottoms altogether," Stevie said. "Just really lean into this public indecency vibe I've got going on."

Iris laughed harder as they walked through the lobby, which was all glass and rich wood. Stevie felt a swell of pride—it felt like a huge accomplishment, making a woman like Iris laugh like that. They were nearly to the club's shop when Iris jolted to a stop so quickly, Stevie bumped into her.

Iris hardly seemed to notice though. She was frozen, her already pale skin now a shade that could only be described as puce.

"Hey," Stevie said gently. "You okay?"

Iris just blinked, her eyes wide on a woman about twenty feet in front of them at the front desk. She was tall, with ice-blond hair cut short on the sides and long on top, dressed in a white tank, navy board shorts, and white sneakers. She looked to be paying for tickets to the party and was soon joined by another woman with long dark hair in a tie-dyed cover-up, a bag filled with beach towels on her shoulder, along with a kid with light brown hair who looked like he was about nine or ten.

"Ready, baby?" the blonde said, then linked hands with the brunette and started toward Iris and Stevie.

As she got closer, the blond woman locked eyes with Iris, her mouth parting. Then she shook her head ever so slightly and sped up, but the brunette had also seen Iris.

"Oh my god," she said, rearing back as though Iris had spit venom. "You."

"Lucy, come on," the blonde said. "Let's just go."

But Lucy wasn't having it. She wrenched her hand free and whirled on her partner. "Did you know she was going to be here? Are you still fucking her? Goddammit, Jillian, I thought we'd moved through this!"

"Mama, what's wrong?" the kid asked.

The blonde—Jillian—just shook her head, while Iris seemed locked into place. Stevie squeezed her hand, trying to jolt her back into herself, but all that did was cause Iris's lower lip to tremble.

"Nothing, sweetie," Jillian said to the kid, then glared at Iris. "Why are you still standing here? Can you please leave?"

Iris blinked, her mouth opening and closing like a fish.

"Oh no," Lucy said, folding her arms. "No one is moving until I get some answers. I think we need to call our therapist. Right now."

"Hey," Stevie said as firmly as she could. She wasn't sure who the hell these people were, but they were pissing her off. Suddenly, the bold and brash Stefania seemed to take over, and Stefania couldn't stand to see Iris cowering beside her any longer.

"I don't know who you two are," she said, "but my girlfriend hasn't done anything to you."

"Girlfriend," Lucy said, snorting. "Better be careful, she likes to sleep with married women."

"Lucy," Jillian said.

"Am I wrong?" Lucy asked, her voice shrill. Tears shined in her eyes, but Stevie had had enough.

Holding up her broken bathing suit with one hand, she pulled a still-pale Iris away until they reached the gender-neutral locker room, intent on getting Iris as far away from those two assholes as possible.

CHAPTER

THIRTEEN

JILLIAN.

Of all the fucking people.

Iris knew Jillian lived in Portland, but Iris still hadn't seen her former lover since the morning of Claire and Delilah's housewarming party last year.

On that night, Lucy had called Iris—on the phone Jillian had accidentally left behind—and the whole affair had broken wide open. Lucy had even cried to Iris as they'd sort of lamented the injustice together. Now, clearly, anger had replaced any commiseration.

"Hey," Stevie said.

Iris blinked at the locker room around her, all smooth teak lockers and marble tile. Plush white towels were stacked on shelves, and wooden beams stretched across the ceiling. Gleaming bowl-style sinks lined the shiny counters, and the air smelled of herbs—lavender and basil and mint.

"Jesus, this place is fancy," Iris said. Her voice sounded off, barely there.

Stevie laughed. "Yeah, I don't think I'll be acquiring a membership anytime soon."

Iris nodded, still gazing around at all the glamor. The room was empty, but when she spotted a sauna in the back corner of the room, she headed straight for it.

The space was warm, though not sweltering, but Iris still plopped onto the teak bench and flung off her towel. Leaned her head back and closed her eyes.

She heard Stevie come in and settle across from her, towel brushing Iris's ankles.

"That was quite the heroic scene out there," Iris said without opening her eyes. "Stefania in action?"

Stevie didn't say anything.

Iris squeezed her eyes even tighter. She didn't want to look at Stevie. Didn't want to see the questions there, the judgment. Shame clouded into Iris's chest, her fingers curling into fists. She didn't think of Jillian often. After it all went down over a year ago, it had taken Iris a few weeks to really process the whole affair, and she liked to think she'd reconciled that it wasn't her fault, that she hadn't known anything about Jillian's marriage or her lies. But there were moments, brief flashes where Iris's brain would go back through the entire thing, from the moment Jillian walked into her shop to the night Lucy called, and then it was hard to breathe.

Hard to look at herself in the mirror.

Iris hadn't loved Jillian. She knew that—it wasn't about love. The sex had been unreal, true, and they had done things together that didn't involve orgasms, nights out at chic bars and a few art shows at fancy Portland galleries. But more than any of that, it was the fact that Jillian had *picked* Iris.

She'd singled her out.

She'd found her on Instagram, hired her to design a custom planner, then promptly fucked her behind her wife's back when the job was done.

And Iris had just . . . let her do it.

"Fuck," Iris said now, pressing her knuckles into her eyes. "I'm sure you're wondering what the hell that was all about."

"You don't have to tell me," Stevie said. "But are you okay?"

Iris finally opened her eyes. Stevie's gaze was soft, so brown and deep and intense, Iris didn't even bother to lie.

"I don't know," she said, and something about the admission caused tears to swell into her eyes. She swiped at them uselessly. "Dammit. Sorry."

"Hey, it's okay," Stevie said. "One time, I threw up on this woman I was trying to get into bed, so, you know, could be worse."

Iris's eyes went wide for a second before she bust up laughing. "Holy shit."

"I know, worst date story you've ever heard, right?"

Iris kept laughing, her shoulders shaking. Thankfully, Stevie started laughing too because, Christ, it *was* funny.

In retrospect, at least.

The two of them laughed for a good two minutes, so much so that Iris's stomach muscles started hurting. Stevie had a great laugh, soft, but strong and passionate.

"Wow, I needed that," Iris said, sitting back against the warm wood, her legs splayed. "You'll have to thank the girl you puked on for the comic relief. From me to her."

Stevie grinned. "I'll do that."

Iris gazed up at the ceiling, reality settling back in again. "I dated her. The blond one. Her name is Jillian."

Then, the whole story spilled out. She didn't want to talk about it, but at the same time, she *did*. She wanted to explain to Stevie, but she also just felt heavy, like the words and feelings of the entire ordeal were stuck to her ribs, slowing down her movements and thoughts.

When she was finished, she leaned her head against the wall, suddenly exhausted.

"So that's my sad little story," Iris said. "Want to hear about my boyfriend of three years who dumped me because I didn't want to have his babies? That's a good one too." Iris rolled her head to look at Stevie, because at some point, she'd moved next to Iris, still holding her bathing suit to her chest, wet hair frizzing around her face.

"None of that was your fault," Stevie said.

"What? The babies or the cheating wife?"

"Both," Stevie said.

"Yeah, my friends all say the same thing."

"Of course they do. But maybe you need to hear it from someone who barely knows you and has no stake in the game. Because it doesn't seem like you quite believe it."

Iris shook her head, looked away. "I believe it." But even to her own ears, her voice sounded hollow. "It's just . . . do you ever feel like the *you* you want to be isn't the person anyone else wants?"

Stevie laughed, but it wasn't a happy sound. "Yeah. All the fucking time."

Iris tilted her head. "Why?"

Stevie sighed and pulled one leg up on the bench, wrapped an arm around her knee. "I have Generalized Anxiety Disorder. Have since I was a kid. And it makes things . . . tricky. I don't always know what's going to trigger my anxiety, and it's like, the whole fucking world won't slow down, you know? To keep up, I have to *do* and *be* and *act* and move to that city and say no to that person and be fine when my ex says we should break up even though I'm terrified to do life by myself."

"And be fine when that ex starts dating your best friend?" Iris asked. She hadn't exactly been told that Vanessa was Stevie's close friend, but she got that vibe—that queer coven energy she knew and loved well.

Stevie sighed, shrugging. "Yeah. And I *am* fine."

Iris smiled. "Just like I believe it's not my fault." She and Stevie watched each other for a few seconds, seconds that suddenly made Iris want to pull Stevie to her, bury her face into her neck and breathe in deep.

"This isn't very romantic," Iris finally said. She needed to break this spell.

"No, it's not. And it's hot as ever-loving fuck." Stevie wiped at her forehead, slicking her hair back, then grew serious again. "Do you want to go back to the pool?"

"Not even a little."

"Oh thank god," Stevie said. "I mean, I *could* pay two hundred bucks for a club bathing suit, but then I wouldn't be able to buy groceries for like a month, so."

"Understood."

Still, neither woman moved. It was true Iris didn't want to risk seeing Jillian again or explain to her friends what had happened, but she also didn't want to go home.

She didn't want Stevie to go home.

For the first time in a long time, despite her encounter with Jillian, she felt . . . relaxed. She wasn't thinking about her disaster of a book. She wasn't thinking about how things were changing in her friend group. She wasn't thinking about how everyone seemed to be moving on, growing, changing without her.

She simply *was*, with another disaster by her side—because Stevie was one hundred percent an adorable disaster—and it felt like that first gulp of cold water after a long hike.

"You know, pumpkin," she said, sitting up and wrapping her towel back around her waist, "I think I could go for a super queer and witchy flat white."

Stevie lifted a brow. "Really."

"You know a place?"

"I might. Get a hell of a discount there too."

Iris grinned. "Great. But, honeybee, you have to go collect our shit out by the pool, because there's no way I'm going out there again."

CHAPTER

FOURTEEN

IT WASN'T A long drive to Bitch's, but Stevie hadn't been in Iris's car since *that night*, and she was having visceral flashbacks that left her both horrified and a little . . . charged.

Unhelped by the fact that she had no underwear on.

After she'd grabbed their stuff from the pool deck and explained to Iris's crew that Iris had a headache, she'd taken off her bathing suit in the locker room and adorned her tank and shorts. As she'd met Iris at the Belmont already wearing her ill-fitting suit, she hadn't even thought to bring undergarments to change into. Granted, her chest wasn't exactly crying out for constant support, and she didn't wear a bra half the time anyway.

"God, I love the city," Iris said, stepping out of her car about two blocks from Bitch's. She spread her arms on the sidewalk and lifted her face to the sun, a cloud just passing over the light and sending her face into shadow. Passersby looked at her sideways as they edged around her, and it was clear Iris did not give two shits.

Stevie couldn't help but smile at her. "Have you always lived in Bright Falls?"

Iris dropped her arms and twirled around once, then linked elbows with Stevie as they started walking. "Yep. Well, since I was ten when we moved there from San Francisco. And I went to college at Berkeley."

"So you've got plenty of city blood in you," Stevie said.

Iris nodded. "I guess so. I love small towns, but this . . ." She waved her hands at the street. "The buzz, the lights, the people. The rainbow flags. It's not Bright Falls."

"Have you ever thought about moving?"

A frown creased Iris's forehead, her mouth dropping open for a second before snapping shut. She shook her head. "Everyone I love is in Bright Falls."

Stevie nodded. "Everyone I love is here."

Iris smiled at her, then nudged her with her shoulder. "What about you? Born and bred in the city?"

"Oh, god no. I was born in Petaluma."

"Is that in California?"

"Yeah, super small town. My mom's still there. She's a veterinarian. It was just her and me growing up, and it was great, but when I turned eighteen . . . I don't know. It wasn't easy being queer there."

Iris squeezed her arm. "I can imagine. It was only bearable for me in Bright Falls because of Claire. Plus, I didn't really understand I was bi until college. You were young when you realized?"

"Yeah. Thirteen. Add my anxiety into the mix and it was interesting. My mom was always really supportive though."

"At least there's that."

"Way more than a lot of kids in my town got." They stopped at the crosswalk between blocks. "What about your family?"

Iris took a deep breath. "Mostly supportive. Catholic. Middle child fuck-up to a perfect older brother and younger sister."

"Fuck-up?" Stevie asked, frowning. "How?"

Iris shrugged and they started walking again. "No spouse and no kids and no plans to change my status in the future? Plus, I like sex a little too much, so there's that."

"Oh."

"Yeah." Iris shot her a smile that didn't reach her eyes. "They love me, but . . . well . . . my mother *worries*." She hooked finger quotes around the last word.

Stevie opened her mouth to ask more, but Bitch's came up on the left and Iris's smile turned real.

"This place looks amazing." She motioned to the various Pride flags blowing in the wind by the dark oak door, coupled with the witchy font declaring the shop name on the window. "In Bright Falls, there are only a couple places that go all in for Pride."

Stevie laughed. "Here, it's like a parade every day."

"I love it."

Stevie's smile broadened as she watched Iris take in the decor and was just about to open the door when she saw her.

Adri.

Through the window.

Staring right at them with wide eyes and a copy of *Much Ado* in her hands.

"Oh shit," Stevie said on an exhale.

"What?" Iris asked, looking around. Stevie knew the second Iris spotted Adri too, because her whole body stiffened. "Oh. Okay. Showtime, then."

"Fuck," Stevie said, her oxygen level immediately depleting. She wasn't prepared for this. Hadn't even considered that one of her friends might be at Bitch's, much less Adri herself, but she should've. She should've known or foreseen or—

"Hey," Iris said softly. She waved at Adri, then moved them both closer to the door so they were out of her line of sight. "It's okay."

"Fuck, fuck." It was all Stevie could think to say.

"You're really freaked out."

"I just . . . I'm not great with surprises."

"I've noticed."

"Sorry," Stevie said. Fuck, she was such a mess.

"It's okay," Iris said. "This is the first time we really have to do this. You just need to get into the mood a little. Let's practice. Just us." Her fingers brushed Stevie's, lightly at first, then she linked their hands together. Stevie's stomach swooped at the contact, but she knew this was just part of the game.

"All right?" Iris asked.

Stevie nodded, breathed.

"We'll be fine," Iris said. "A little hand holding, a little leaning. That's it. It's not like we have to have sex on a table in there to prove we're together."

"Jesus, I hope not," Stevie said, but she was laughing, her breathing already slower. Iris's thumbs swiped over the backs of her hands, a soothing rhythm.

"And you're a great actor," Iris said.

"You've never even seen me act."

Iris tilted her head. "Well, my precious little beetle, you said Adri only casts the best, so. You've got this."

Stevie smiled. "Precious little beetle?"

Iris shrugged. "I'm improvising. See? We're so good at this already."

Stevie laughed, then rolled her shoulders back. She was tempted to bring Stefania into the mix, but somehow, that just didn't feel right. Not this time.

"Okay," she said. "I'm ready."

Iris opened the door and ushered Stevie inside, her hand pressed to the small of her back. Such a small touch, but somehow, it worked to ground Stevie into her body. Feet on the floor. Fingertips brushing Iris's as they moved to the line.

She waved at Adri, who waved back, her eyes following them toward the register.

"Doing great," Iris said, pressing herself a little closer to Stevie's side to whisper in her ear. Stevie shivered and Iris laughed. God, the woman practically emanated sex.

Stevie was pretty sure the only thing she ever emanated were stress hormones.

At the register, Stevie greeted Ravi, a part-timer who just started a few weeks ago, and ordered Iris a flat white, along with a cold brew for herself.

"God, we're such fucking hipsters," Iris said as they collected their drinks and headed toward Adri.

Stevie laughed. "I've got some glasses in my bag."

"Do you?"

"No, but is a hipster really a hipster without glasses?"

"Okay, so we're very bad hipsters."

Stevie laughed again, the conversation flowing so naturally she hadn't even realized they'd reached Adri's table.

"Hey," Adri said, standing. "Iris, nice to see you again."

"You too," Iris said brightly. "I can't wait for the Malibu trip."

Adri just lifted a single brow. "I'm sure you can't."

Iris's energy dimmed a bit at Adri's tone, but she simply sat down and crossed her legs. Adri sat too, followed by Stevie, who sank into the chair next to Iris like slipping into quicksand.

Iris draped an arm over the back of Stevie's chair, fingers playing with the ends of her hair. Adri's gaze followed the movement, and Stevie cleared her throat.

"Revising the script?" she asked.

Adri blinked, then looked down at her book and open laptop. "Yeah. It's coming along nicely, I think."

"What specifically are you working on?" Iris asked, sipping her drink. "Are you rewriting it?"

Adri's smile was more akin to a flash of teeth. "You don't rewrite

Shakespeare. I'm just making subtle changes to adjust for our queer cast."

Iris nodded. "I love that. Such a great idea."

This time, Adri's smile was genuine, and Stevie felt her shoulders release their hold on her neck.

"We think so," Adri said, glancing at Stevie. "We first started working on this interpretation back in college."

"Oh? You went to college together?" Iris asked.

Adri's eyes narrowed. "You didn't know?"

Iris sniffed. "I'm sure we would've gotten around to it. We're not exactly spending all of our time talking about our exes." She leaned over and kissed Stevie's cheek. And not a sweet peck either, a slow, sort of open-mouthed press-and-seal just next to Stevie's ear. Goose bumps erupted up and down her arms and she met Iris's gaze as Iris leaned back into her own space.

Iris winked.

Fuck, she was good at this.

Stevie smiled at her—a real smile—but it dimmed quickly as she looked back at Adri, who was staring at them with her thick brows pressed together. Clearly, Stevie was actually a horrible actress.

"You know," Adri said, leaning back in her chair. "Beatrice is a really difficult part."

Iris tilted her head. "I would imagine. It's Shakespeare."

"She's complex," Adri went on. "Takes a certain amount of subtlety I'm not sure you possess."

"Adri," Stevie said.

"I'm just being honest," Adri said. "I cast Iris and I stand by my choice, but I want her to be prepared to work."

Iris pursed her mouth. "I can be subtle. I can be anything you need me to be."

"So you're saying you have no theatrical identity?"

"Adri, what the hell?" Stevie asked.

"It's okay," Iris said. "Adri's just doing her job."

"I am," Adri said.

This time, *Iris's* smile was a quick flash of teeth, and Stevie could feel her panic flaring again. Adri was a tough director, she knew. She'd been on the receiving end of her criticism more than once, which was fine, and Stevie was prepared for feedback. That was theater. And she'd certainly seen Adri dress down other actors—even caused more than one to cry and run off stage—but they weren't in the theater right now. In this coffee shop, an accidental social interaction, Iris was Stevie's girlfriend, not Adri's lead actor.

"I think we should get going," Stevie said, standing up. They'd barely touched their drinks but fuck it. There were a hundred other places Stevie could get Iris a flat white if she really wanted one.

"Right," Iris said, not missing a beat. "Movie at my place tonight." She laced her fingers with Stevie's and pressed a kiss to the back of her hand, their fake plans rolling off her tongue like silk.

"See you next week?" Stevie asked Adri.

Adri nodded and smiled. "In Malibu. Don't forget your meds, okay?"

Stevie frowned. "You know I won't."

"Just making sure," Adri said, leaning back. "Remember that time we went to Austin? We had to call your doctor to send a prescription to a pharmacy there. It was a pretty big hassle and I need you on point for the retreat."

Stevie just nodded but felt Iris's gaze on hers. Iris didn't know about her meds. Stevie wasn't ashamed, not at all, and she figured she'd tell Iris eventually, but it wasn't the sort of information she offered to anyone on the street.

Then again, Iris wasn't exactly anyone.

Still, Iris didn't ask for more details, and Stevie knew she wouldn't. Not in front of Adri.

"Bye," Stevie said, then she didn't even wait for Adri to reciprocate. She simply turned and led Iris out of the shop and back into the warm summer air. She didn't stop there, either, but kept walking, gripping Iris's hand until they reached Iris's car.

"Well," Iris said, pulling away so she could dig into her bag for her keys, "that was interesting."

"I'm sorry," Stevie said, scrubbing her hand over her face. "I don't think Adri's buying this whole dating thing between us."

Iris froze, then lifted her keys out, jangling them into her palm. "You think that was Adri not buying it?"

"Yeah. I mean, she was acting like a total bitch, like she was trying to catch us in a lie or something."

Iris pursed her mouth, like she was fighting a grin. "Okay."

"You don't think so?"

Iris pressed a button to unlock the car, then slid into the driver's seat. Stevie followed, closing herself in the sun-heated seat on the passenger side.

"I'll just say this," Iris said. "I think Adri believes us. I think she believes the hell out of this relationship."

"Really?"

Iris nodded, then started the engine. "Where to?"

"I don't know. You can drop me at my place, I guess."

Iris's shoulders went a little soft, and she stared out the front window for a few seconds.

"You know," she said finally, "so far, we're really fucking bad at crafting a romantic date."

Stevie winced. "What, my bathing suit literally breaking, followed by an encounter with a power femme and topped off with my cranky ex isn't romantic?"

Iris laughed. "Shocker, I know."

"What can we do to fix that?" Stevie asked, because she wanted to fix it. She wanted to help Iris, hold up her end of the bargain.

And maybe, a little part of her didn't want to go home to her empty apartment and listen to the pipes squeak while her neighbor next door took their fifth shower of the day.

"Well," Iris said, "I've heard that watching a movie with some popcorn and an obscene amount of wine in a small town can be pretty romantic."

Stevie tapped her chin, pretending to think. "That'd be a pretty good research opportunity for you, I think. I'm in."

Iris grinned and threw the car into reverse.

IRIS'S APARTMENT WAS open and eclectic, with turquoise appliances in the kitchen, a vibrant red L-shaped couch, colorful pillows strewn around haphazardly. There were potted plants everywhere, herbs on tables and windowsills, various art on the walls, and twinkle lights twisted around the large main window's curtain rod. In the adjacent room, there was a huge bookshelf, books organized in a rainbow of color.

It was all very . . . Iris. Even though Stevie didn't know Iris that well, the apartment's vibe fit her somehow.

"You have a lot of books," Stevie said, then winced at the banality of her conversation. Clearly Iris had a lot of books.

"I do," Iris said, heading down the hall. "Just let me change really quickly."

Stevie nodded and perused Iris's bookshelves, finding many of her favorites among the rainbow.

"Want a drink?" Iris said, coming back into the living and kitchen area wearing tight yoga pants and a fitted green tee, the color making her eyes look like emeralds. Her hair was still damp, drying in varying curly and wavy patterns.

"Um, water, if that's cool," Stevie said.

Iris's hand froze on a wine bottle.

"You can drink," Stevie said quickly. "I just shouldn't on my meds."

Iris nodded and put back the bottle. "No problem, sweetums. I've got seltzer."

Stevie laughed and shook her head as Iris dug into the fridge and came out with two cans of LaCroix, handing one to Stevie as she headed for the pantry. She grabbed a giant bag of white cheddar popcorn and nodded toward her red sofa.

"Okay, so," she said, plopping onto the couch and turning on her TV. "We've got all the basic streaming choices available. The question is, which romantic comedy is *the* most romantic?"

Stevie settled in the opposite corner and popped open her drink. "Hands down, *Serendipity*."

Iris laughed. "Oh my god, a John Cusack fan?"

Stevie shrugged and hid her blushing cheeks behind the cool can. "I mean, he's not my type at all, but I love the fate aspect of it."

"Ah. Kate Beckinsale, then."

Stevie grinned. "Like any self-respecting sapphic our age, Kate was part of my formative experience. I saw that movie for the first time when I was, like, eleven, and . . . yeah. I found her pretty."

Iris smiled. "For me, it was *Blue Crush*."

"Which girl?"

"All of them?"

Stevie laughed. "You're bi, right?"

Iris nodded. "I guess that's important information for my fake girlfriend to know."

"It is."

They smiled at each other for a few seconds, and then Iris found *Serendipity* and started the stream. She ripped open the bag of popcorn as John and Kate grabbed for the same glove during Christmastime in Bloomingdale's, and Stevie had to scoot closer to get a handful.

"I love New York," Iris said as the actors ice-skated through Central Park.

"Have you gone there a lot?" Stevie asked.

Iris shrugged. "A few times, with my friend Claire and her . . ." She took a deep breath. "Her fiancée. Wow. First time I've said that out loud."

Stevie tilted her head. "Yeah?"

Iris nodded but her eyes went a little shiny and she waved a hand through the air. "Anyway, New York is . . . I don't know. It's the only place I've ever been that felt exactly like I expected it to, exactly like every story and movie and poem about it. Like magic and realism all twisted up together."

"Wow," Stevie said, smiling softly at Iris. "You are a writer."

"Oh my god, shut up," Iris said, but she smiled back. Still, a certain longing rose up in Stevie's chest as New York unfolded on the screen before her. The city had always been mythical to her, a theatrical utopia, but unattainable, an ethereal monster capable of swallowing Stevie whole, no matter how much Ren believed that's where Stevie was meant to be. Despite all that, Iris's poetic—if brief— endorsement was enough to spark something in the center of Stevie's chest.

But she'd gotten really good at ignoring those kinds of sparks over the years, so that's exactly what she did now, taking in the movie, that spark itself, like she would a fantasy novel or film. It was breathtaking, beautiful, but at the end of the day, an impossibility.

"My best friend Astrid?" Iris said after a while, John running rampant through New York with Jeremy Piven, searching for clues and signs. "She and her girlfriend, Jordan, are pretty big on fate." Then Iris told Stevie all about how Jordan drew a Two of Cups tarot card for months, and Astrid drew the same one after they'd sort of broken up.

"Astrid wooed her back with, like, twenty Two of Cups cards strewn all over the Everwood Inn."

"God, that's romantic," Stevie said.

"True," Iris said. "But not as romantic as getting puked on by a one-night stand and then fake dating them."

Stevie laughed. "Jesus, what a story." She wasn't sure she'd ever think of that night without cringing, but at least it was becoming a sort of joke between them.

Iris tilted her head, eyes on Stevie. "Can I ask you a question?"

"Sure," Stevie said slowly. That question hardly ever preceded an easy answer.

"Why were you so nervous to sleep with me? Was it your anxiety, or . . ."

Yep, yep, Stevie was right. Definitely not an easy answer. "Oh. Um . . . well . . ."

"You don't have to tell me," Iris said.

"No, it's okay," Stevie said. If they were going to do this fake dating thing, it was probably best if Iris knew exactly what she was getting herself into.

"I don't do that a lot," Stevie said. "Sleep with strangers. And by a lot, I mean ever."

Iris's brows lifted. "Like . . . never?"

Stevie shook her head. "Anxiety definitely has a lot to do with it, but it's hard to tell if it's from my disorder or if it's just me, or what. It's not always easy to separate myself from my illness, or to even understand if I should separate myself at all? Like, what is my personality and what is my anxiety? Or are they the same thing? It's confusing sometimes."

"It sounds like it," Iris said softly.

"I'm on meds and they help, but I think I got a little too in my head the night we met."

"Stefania didn't see you through, huh?"

Stevie laughed, swiped a hand through her hair. "No. She only helps to a point. It's probably good that you know all of this now though. I might be really horrible at even *pretending* to be having sex with someone."

Iris frowned. "You're an actress. Pretending is part of your job."

"Yeah, but with acting, I have a script. That's why I love it so much. No surprises. Even if I have to kiss someone on stage, I know when it's coming. I know what I say and what my partner says right before it happens. I know exactly what to do and say afterward. It's different than actual life."

"You managed to kiss me on the night we met," Iris said.

Stevie laughed bitterly. "Yeah, and promptly threw up all over you."

Iris winced. "Okay, I see your point."

"I get that what we're doing is fake or for research or whatever, but . . ." She shook her head, cheeks flaming.

"But what?" Iris asked, nudging her knee. "Come on, tell me."

Stevie pressed her hands to her face. "It's so embarrassing."

"More embarrassing than vomiting on your date?"

"No, exactly that embarrassing." She leaned her head back on the sofa as John's fiancée gave him a wedding present on the screen. Maybe she could say it more clearly if she wasn't looking at Iris, Sex Goddess of Bright Falls. "I've only ever slept with Adri. And that took me four years of flirting and freaking out in private. It took four years of getting to know her and really understanding that she loved me and wouldn't judge me or leave me. Well . . . at least not right away."

"Oh."

"Yeah." Stevie felt Iris shift, but she didn't glance her way. She focused on patterns in the plastered ceiling. "But I don't *have* four years now—I mean, after you and I fake break up or whatever. I don't want to take that long. I actually do want a real girlfriend eventually. And until that happens, I *want* to hook up and have sex. It's been . . . well, never mind how long it's been, but you saw firsthand the results when I try to sleep with someone I don't know very well."

"Not everyone's into casual sex, Stevie. My best friend, Claire, is now engaged to the only person she's ever tried to have a purely sexual relationship with."

Stevie smiled. "That's sweet."

"Nauseatingly so," Iris said, rolling her eyes, but then she grew serious again. "Plus, have you, I don't know, considered another alternative? Like, do you think you're demisexual? Or on the ace spectrum somewhere?"

Stevie tucked her legs to her chest, mirroring Iris's position. Iris was looking at her so patiently, so . . . tenderly, Stevie felt herself relax more and more by the second.

"I've considered that, yeah," she said. "But I do feel sexual attraction to people I don't have an emotional connection with. Like I told you back at the Empress, I really did want to sleep with you."

"Well," Iris said, grinning and flipping her hair. "Who wouldn't?"

Stevie laughed, but noticed Iris's smile didn't quite reach her eyes.

"Anyway," Stevie said, "It's less about attraction and more about my brain. When I was with you the other night, I couldn't slow it down. I kept worrying I'd do something wrong, or I'd be bad at something, or how my boobs are a lot smaller than yours, or how the idea of being naked with you made me feel like I needed to—"

"Puke?" Iris deadpanned.

Stevie groaned and covered her eyes. "Not very flattering, I know, but it's not you, I promise. If anything, I wish I could be more like you."

"Me?"

"You were so fucking suave the night we met. A pro."

"A pro at sex."

Stevie laughed. "I mean . . . yeah? Like you knew exactly what you wanted. You were relaxed. Cool. Sexy. I wish I had half that confidence."

Iris didn't say anything for a few beats, long enough for Stevie to turn her head to look at her. Iris chewed on her bottom lip, eyes a little distant.

Stevie nudged her knee. "Hey. I mean all that in a good way."

Iris's expression cleared. "No, no, I know. But Stevie . . ." She sighed, pursed her mouth a little. "All that confidence bullshit is *learned.* I'm confident and loud and funny because I had to be growing up. I like sex, yeah, but it's not like every single encounter I have is amazing. At least half are mediocre at best. Some are truly abysmal. And I will tell you right now, the first few people I slept with? I was *not* this radiant goddess you see before you." She waved her hand down her body, a smile turning up one corner of her mouth. "Sex is just like anything else. Practice makes perfect. Or at least, it makes better."

"Makes non-puking."

Iris laughed. "Exactly."

"But that's the problem, I have no way to practice. How do you practice relaxing while taking off your shirt in front of a stranger, when that's the exact thing making me anxious?"

"I don't know," Iris said, laughing. "Maybe there's a gal out there in a bar somewhere with a sex lessons kink."

Stevie laughed too but then froze, her mouth hanging wide open as an idea bloomed into her brain.

"What?" Iris asked.

Stevie snapped her mouth shut. "Nothing."

"That was not a look that meant nothing."

Stevie shook her head, her face as warm as an Alabama summer. "I just . . . well . . . um . . ." God, she couldn't say it. Couldn't ask it in a million years.

"Out with it," Iris said. "I can tell you want to say it, so take a deep breath and do it."

Stevie couldn't help but smile at the firm yet gentle way Iris commanded her. Very . . . teacher-like.

"You're sort of making my point here," she said.

"The point you haven't said out loud yet?" Iris asked, folding her arms.

"Yeah, that one." Stevie tucked her frizzing hair behind her ear. "Okay, what if . . . you helped me?"

Iris canted her head. "Helped you with what?"

Stevie's mouth worked, trying to get the words out. How do you say *sexy stuff* without saying, well, *sexy stuff*? Still, if she was really asking for this—if by some chance Iris said *yes*—she'd be doing a lot more than just saying the words.

Oh god.

This was a preposterous idea.

Her stomach lurched into her throat, and she swallowed hard. She *wanted* to be more confident. She *wanted* to hook up with someone, even just kiss someone, without throwing up. Her anxiety was what it was. It would always factor into everything she did. But behavioral therapy was a big part of her treatment. Her therapist, Keisha, was always giving her little challenges to help her feel more comfortable—go to a movie by herself, take a class to learn something she felt incompetent at, take a trusted friend to a bar and ask someone out.

And she'd done it. She'd met Iris, even kissed Iris, but clearly, she needed more practice beyond that first interaction. She needed to take it to the next level.

"Hey," Iris said, nudging her knee. "Help with—"

"Sexy stuff," Stevie blurted out before she could talk herself out of it.

Iris's eyes rounded. "Stevie, *I* do not have a sex lessons kink."

"No, yeah, I know, but hear me out." Stevie shifted so she was sitting on her knees, then grabbed the remote and paused John and Kate's snowy Central Park reunion. She started ticking off on her fingers, adrenaline pushing her forward. "We've already kissed."

"True. Best kiss of your life."

Stevie fought a laugh and kept going. "You've already seen my . . . my . . . you know." She waved her hand around her chest.

"God, Stevie, you can't even say boobs."

"I can so."

"Then say it." Iris pursed her mouth in challenge.

"What are we, middle schoolers?"

"Boobs, boobs, boobs," Iris chanted.

Stevie laughed. "Okay, fine, boobs, there, I said it."

"Now say tits."

Stevie groaned. "Why?"

"Lesson number one."

"Really?" Stevie's stomach fluttered. "So you'll do it?"

Iris just lifted a brow and folded her arms.

Stevie blew out a breath, ruffling her bangs. "T-tits."

"Okay," Iris said slowly. "Now with gusto."

"Tits!" Stevie yelled.

Iris laughed. "Now we're talking. Next word: pus—"

"Oh, Jesus, baby steps, okay?" Stevie said, covering her face with her hands. Iris went silent and Stevie peeked at her from between her fingers. "So?"

Iris sighed and turned so she was facing Stevie, crisscrossing her legs. "Tell me more. What do you actually want me to do?"

Stevie dropped her hands. "I don't know."

"Then I can't do it. You have to know, Stevie. Especially with this sort of thing."

Stevie felt herself relax a little at Iris's soft tone. Not only that, but her words too—the gentle way she was taking Stevie seriously, despite her jokes. How it was very clear that Iris, for all her bravado, took sex pretty seriously too.

Which was exactly why she was the perfect person to help Stevie.

"Okay," Stevie said. "I want to be able to talk to potential romantic partners—"

"Romantic, or sexual?" Iris asked. "Not always the same thing."

"Both," Stevie said. "Yeah, both. I want to talk to them without feeling like I need a shot of tequila, which I can't have anyway. I want to . . . kiss them as *me*. Not Stefania. I want to get naked with them without throwing up."

"That would be preferable for them, yeah."

Stevie smiled. "And I want to actually sleep with someone I haven't spent four years pining over. I . . . well, I want to be more like you, I guess."

Iris frowned but said nothing. She stared at Kate's frozen face for a few seconds then turned back to Stevie. "If we do this, you're in charge. By which I mean, you have to set the boundaries, the rules. I don't want to accidentally do anything you're uncomfortable with."

Stevie nodded. "I mean, you too. I don't want you to be uncomfortable either."

Iris smirked. "There's not a lot about sex that makes me uncomfortable."

"What about romance?" Stevie asked, another idea popping into her mind. If they really were going to do this, she wanted Iris to get something from it too. The woman was risking getting vomited on again, coaching a hopeless twenty-eight-year-old in the ways of hookups. The least Stevie could do was give her a reason to persevere.

"What about it?" Iris asked.

"Romance makes you uncomfortable, doesn't it?"

Iris sighed. "Not uncomfortable so much as . . . currently uninterested."

"But you *need* to be interested, right? For your book?"

"What's your point?"

"Well, I mean, one day, when I do finally hook up with someone, I still want it to feel . . . nice."

"Nice."

"Romantic. Even if it's just a one-night stand, I like music and soft lights and, shit, I don't know. Romance."

Iris looked at her like she'd lost her mind. "Still waiting for your point, Stevie."

"You help me with . . ."

"Showing your tits."

"Yes. That. And I'll make it romantic. For you. So you can, you know, have more research for your book. That's half the point of our partnership, isn't it?"

Iris narrowed her eyes, but then her brows lifted. "Okay, your point is valid. But let me make sure I've got this straight. We're fake dating in front of your friends."

"Yes."

"And I now have a sex lessons kink."

Stevie grinned. "I mean, call it what you want."

"And you have a romance lessons kink."

"Look how symbiotic we are."

"It's a beautiful thing," Iris said dryly, then her tone softened. "Are you sure?"

"I am," Stevie said, then stood up. Her blood sped through her body, making her fingertips tingle, her heart drum against her ribs. "And I think we should start right now."

"Right now?"

"Right now."

She knew herself—if she went home, slept on it, she'd talk herself out of this, and then she'd still be the horny yet terrified wannabe thespian who nuzzled her ex's neck.

Iris got up too, but then they both simply stood there, unsure of how to move on. Somehow, even though Iris was the expert here, her uncertainty made Stevie's shoulders relax.

"Okay," Iris said finally, "if we're really doing this, I think we should start where things went wrong with us."

"Yeah," Stevie said, "makes sense."

"It was dark," Iris said. "We had music on."

Stevie nodded, but as she looked around at Iris's apartment, the dusky evening light filtering purple into her living room, *Serendipity* still frozen on the screen, bits of popcorn dotting the sofa and floor, she felt anything but romantic.

And if this was going to be useful for Iris too, she needed to set the mood.

"We need candles," Stevie said, looking around.

"What? We did not have candles the other week."

"No, I know, but we need a little ambience, don't you think?"

"Ambience?"

"Jesus, you really are bad at this romance stuff," Stevie said.

Iris groaned and rubbed her forehead. "God, I know. My brain is a fucking blank when it comes to that shit. The last hookup I had—before you, I mean—was in a . . ."

She trailed off, pursing her mouth and shaking her head.

"Was in a what?" Stevie asked.

"Never mind."

"You made me tell you my bonkers idea." She popped her hands on her hips. "Iris."

"Fine," Iris said on a sigh. "The last person I slept with, we fucked in a bathroom stall."

"Really?"

"Really."

"I'm sure a lot of people do that."

"At Topgolf?"

Stevie nearly choked on a laugh. "Topgolf."

"I was there with my friends and the bartender was hot, okay?"

Stevie laughed. "I'm sure they were."

"So, yeah, romance? Not really part of my repertoire lately."

"Well, luckily, I can barely think of kissing someone without a bubble bath and some moody music. Do you have candles?"

Iris nodded, waving to a few sprinkled around the room. "There are more in my bedroom."

"Okay, you go get us some dinner," Stevie said, glancing at the time on her phone. "I'll set up here."

"Dinner," Iris said. "Yeah, I am hungry, actually."

"Same. I'll eat whatever."

"That's what she said."

Stevie shook her head, a laugh bubbling into her mouth. "Go."

"I'm going, I'm going," Iris said, picking up her keys and phone. "Just don't burn the place down."

"Romance would never."

Iris smiled, eyes roaming Stevie's face for a split second before she opened the door and left.

Stevie turned back to the empty apartment, shut off the TV, and got to work before she came to her senses.

CHAPTER

FIFTEEN

IRIS WAS NERVOUS.

As she walked back from Moonpies—ironically, the café that had taken over the space where her paper shop used to reside—with her hand in a bag full of the best fries she'd ever eaten, she could barely swallow the greasy things down.

Sexy stuff, as Stevie called it, she could handle. Granted, she'd never exactly been in this situation before, where she was pretty much coaching someone through foreplay, but it was sex. Or pre-sex. All of those things had always come easily to her. She liked her body, knew she was pretty hot, and had no problem getting naked in front of other people as long as everyone consented.

But romance . . . well, she hadn't engaged in that in a long-ass time. Since Grant, and usually he was the one who set all that shit up. He booked the romantic dinners. He suggested a riverside walk at twilight. He whispered sweet nothings in her ear while they fucked.

Or *made love,* as he would say.

And she liked it. She adored romance novels. Always had. She loved the grand gestures, the quirky towns, the haphazard heroines looking for true love. She craved the idea of herself caught up in romance, an Iris Kelly completely thrown over by love.

Softened.

Changed.

As she stopped in front of her building and paused on the front step, she flashed back to all those purportedly romantic times with Grant, the times he wanted to look her right in the eyes when she came, and she could never go through with it. She tried, but right as the orgasm rushed through her, she'd always snap her eyes shut.

She'd crack jokes during the twilight river walk.

She'd make a game out of what other couples were talking about during the fancy romantic dinner.

She simply wasn't built for that kind of romance, no matter how badly she might've wanted it in the past, so she wasn't exactly sure how these lessons were going to go.

Climbing the steps to her unit, she focused on Stevie and how she could help her, running through what sort of things they could do that Stevie would be comfortable with. She'd only made it to kissing—which they'd already done—when she swung open her door and gasped.

The place was aglow.

Tiny flames flickered everywhere. Iris had always loved candles. Bought them every time she took a trip to the flea market in Sotheby, but she usually only lit one or two at a time. Now, every single candle she owned was aflame and spread out through the living room. The twinkle lights snaking around her curtain rod were on as well, turning the whole room amber and gold.

"Wow," she said. Soft music—something modern, yet instrumental—filtered out of Iris's Bluetooth speaker.

"Yeah?" Stevie asked. She stood up from the couch where she'd been looking at something on her phone. "What do you think?"

"I think . . ." Iris set the food on the counter. "Wow."

Stevie smiled. "You already said that."

Iris just nodded, her stomach fluttering.

Actual *fluttering*.

She couldn't remember the last time that had happened. When she made this whole arrangement with Stevie back at the Empress, she hadn't fully envisioned what romance might entail. She pictured outings. Dates. That was it. Walking hand in hand through the park.

Not . . . this.

"You okay?" Stevie asked.

Iris nodded. She could do this. She *had* to do this. She'd become pretty fucking jaded if a few candles freaked her out this much, and her novel's deadline loomed like a gathering storm.

"How do we start?" Iris asked, because hell if she knew. She thought about tacking some new cheesy term of endearment onto her question—*lovebug* or *my little cinnamon stick*—but suddenly, her romance jokes didn't feel very . . . well, jokey.

Stevie, however, just nodded and set her phone down. "You don't want to eat first?"

"And kiss you with veggie burger breath? I'll pass."

Stevie laughed, but she clutched at her stomach a little, which Iris recognized now as something she did when she was nervous. Well, good. At least Iris wasn't alone in that.

"In that case, I think we should dance first," Stevie said.

"Dance."

Stevie nodded. Iris didn't move. The current song was slow and languid, nothing like the fast beat they'd first essentially dry humped to at Lush.

Dry humping, Iris could do.

This?

Not so sure.

She inhaled slowly then stood stock-still until Stevie came over and took her hand, leading her over to the more open space between the coffee table and the TV.

"Okay, imagine we've just been out on the town," Stevie said, wrapping one arm around Iris's waist. "We met at . . . I don't know. What's a rom-com type meet-cute?"

"A wine tasting," Iris said as Stevie set one of Iris's hands on her shoulder. "I'm a vintner. You're a wine critic."

Stevie smiled. "I like that. Am I terribly mean?"

"You are. Gave my winery a horrible review and now I hate you."

"But you also find me ridiculously attractive, and we ran into each other at another winery's opening. Your best friend's."

"And my friend thinks we really need to hate fuck each other and get it out of our systems," Iris said.

"Except I don't hate you. Secretly, I want to wine and dine you," Stevie said, lacing their free hands together and holding them right above her heart. She spun Iris around and pressed closer.

"Shit," Iris said, her voice a little shaky. She cleared her throat. "How are you so good at this?"

Stevie shrugged. "Am I?"

"Yes, extremely."

"I don't know." Stevie sighed, bit her lower lip. "I've never had a day without anxiety, which meant making friends when I was a kid was hard. I think that sort of made me want the emotional parts of a relationship even more. Don't get me wrong, feelings are still scary, but it's like a language that I understand. Fear. Happiness. Hope. Despair. Anger. I get what those things are, what they mean. But the physical stuff, using my body to talk when my body feels constantly at war with my brain . . . I might as well try to communicate with people on another planet."

Iris shook her head. "God, it's the total opposite for me."

"That's actually what I love most about romances," Stevie went on. "The sex scenes are hot, sure, but it's that HEA that makes me keep reading, you know? The feeling of finding someone who loves you for exactly who you are. No more, no less."

Iris snorted. "Have you ever found that person in real life? Because I sure as hell haven't."

Stevie frowned and was silent for a few seconds. "No," she said finally. "I guess I haven't."

They continued to sway to the music, and Stevie pressed their foreheads together. Iris knew it was a move, a romantic gesture, but in the moment, Stevie's lashes literally fluttering against her cheeks, Iris's whole body went soft and warm. She opened her eyes to find Stevie watching her, the brown so dark in the dim light, Iris found herself writing a line in her head.

. . . *the kind of eyes you could get lost in, drown in, and never even try to take a breath.*

Jesus, that was some romantic bullshit right there. Which meant this was working—Iris's romance writer gears were starting to turn in a rusty circle.

But as she and Stevie kept moving, their eyes locked on each other, Stevie's hand drifting up and down Iris's back, the less . . . fake it all felt.

Iris shook herself, forcing her mind to focus on their task and put some space between them. "Okay, romantic achievement unlocked."

Stevie smiled. "Good."

Her voice was way too fucking soft.

"Your turn," Iris said firmly and shifted both of her hands to Stevie's waist.

Stevie went a little rigid. "Oh. Shit. Now?"

"Now," Iris said. She wasn't sure she could take much more languid swaying and lowered lashes before something inside her shut down. She felt a bit woozy, like she'd eaten a weed gummy on an empty stomach. Plus, she'd gotten a line, a flash of that elusive romantic spark. She didn't want to press her luck.

"Last time we did this, where did you shut down?" she asked Stevie.

"Um . . ." Stevie rubbed her forehead, blew out a long breath.

Iris squeezed her hips in reassurance. "You can do this. Think with your body, not your mind."

"Is that what you do? When you hook up with someone?"

Iris nodded. "Just cut the two off from each other."

"And that really works?"

Iris hesitated, something in her chest tugging slightly, but she shook it off. "Totally."

"Um, yeah, okay." Stevie took a deep breath. "Last time, it was after you took off your shirt. I just . . . freaked out at the idea of taking mine off too."

"Okay, we can work with that. Do you want me to take off my shirt?"

Stevie's laugh was shaky. "I mean, are you okay doing that?"

"I'm fully okay with that, but I also don't want to come across as some weird creeper talking you into stuff. It's your call."

"You're not a creeper. This was my idea."

Iris nodded, then dropped her hands from Stevie's waist and took a step back, tapping her chin. "I actually think it might help if you took control over this whole thing."

"What do you mean?"

"I mean *you* take off my shirt. At your pace."

At first, Iris could tell Stevie inwardly recoiled, her entire body tightening, but then she released a long breath.

"That actually makes sense," she said. "If I'm in control, then . . . well, I'm in control."

"Exactly."

"And I have your consent?"

Iris smiled. "Enthusiastic consent."

Stevie nodded, then just stood there for a few seconds, hands on her hips.

"Maybe start with an easier touch," Iris said. "My arms or shoulders or something."

"Yeah. Yeah, good idea." Stevie took a step closer to Iris, closed her fingers around Iris's wrists. She slowly trailed her hands up . . . up . . . all the way to Iris's neck. Her touch was soft and . . . shit, really nice. Goose bumps erupted over Iris's skin, but she didn't call attention to them. She didn't close her eyes or sigh like she wanted to— she didn't want to freak Stevie out too much here—instead, she kept her face impassive, yet inviting. Open, but mostly expressionless.

Stevie's eyes followed her own fingers, drifting down Iris's neck, thumbs swiping over her collarbone, mouth open just a little. Iris could hear Stevie's breathing go ragged. She had to clench her legs together because . . . fuck, she was getting turned on, that telltale thrum blooming between her thighs.

"Maybe you should kiss me," she said, her own breathing a little jagged too. "Or not. Whatever you want."

Stevie nodded, her eyes drifting to Iris's mouth. She only hesitated a moment before she leaned in, taking Iris's lower lip between hers in a way that made Iris want to groan.

She didn't.

But it was a goddamn feat to hold it in, because lack of confidence or not, Stevie was a fucking amazing kisser.

Stevie turned her head, her tongue dipping into Iris's mouth like a tease before retreating again, before her teeth tugged on Iris's lip and then swept over Iris's own tongue again.

Fucking hell.

"Can I touch you too?" Iris asked, because Jesus, she had to do something.

"Yeah," Stevie said against her mouth, then kissed her again, a wild but slow dance of tongue and teeth Iris was pretty sure she'd never experienced before.

Iris fisted her hands at Stevie's hips, desperate to pull them closer. She didn't though. She forced herself still as Stevie's fingers drifted down her arms again, then played at the hem of her T-shirt.

"Whenever you're ready," Iris said, her voice raspy as Stevie's mouth slid to her ear. "I'm good to go."

A little *too* good, but whatever. Iris's thoughts clouded, her hips undulating ever so slightly against Stevie's. She needed to get a goddamn grip, but before she could, Stevie tugged on Iris's shirt, lifting it so Iris had to let go of Stevie and raise her arms. The fabric slid over her skin, making her shiver as the cool air hit her stomach and chest.

Stevie dropped the shirt on the floor and stepped back a little. "I remember this," she whispered.

"What?"

"How fucking gorgeous you are."

Her eyes roamed over Iris's body, pausing not only at her breasts in her pink cotton bra, but her neck and stomach and hips as well. It made Iris feel incredibly seen and vulnerable and . . . she wasn't sure she liked it.

"Okay," she said, forcing her head back in this game. "What's next?"

Stevie looked down at her own tank top, her mouth pink and a little swollen from kissing. "I . . . I remember this too. That night, I wasn't wearing a bra and I think that's part of what made me spiral. Like, just automatic exposure."

"Well, I've already seen your tits, as you pointed out earlier."

"Yeah, but that was an accident. This is . . ."

"Not an accident."

"Yeah."

"So what would help you here? Or we can stop."

Stevie shook her head. "I don't think I want to stop."

"Okay," Iris said softly. "Take your time. You're in control. You call the shots."

Stevie looked down for a few seconds, but then stepped closer to Iris again, hand circling her waist. Iris suppressed a shiver, but her own hands went to Stevie's forearms, pulling their bodies together even tighter. Stevie kissed her again, once . . . twice . . . before her fingers drifted to Iris's bra's clasp.

"Is this okay?" Stevie asked.

And goddammit, it was more than okay. Iris nodded, then said "Yes" out loud. Stevie unhooked the bra and this time, Iris couldn't hold back a sigh as the straps slid down her arms. She dropped her hands and the garment fell to the floor, her breasts swaying freely.

"Shit," Stevie said. She held Iris by the waist, her thumbs swiping at her hips.

"Is that a good expletive or . . ."

"It's good," Stevie said, lifting her eyes to Iris's. "You're a fucking goddess."

Iris laughed, feeling suddenly shy. "No. I'm just me. Remember that, okay? Whoever you do this with for real is just a person, exactly like you."

Stevie nodded then kissed her again. It was a sweet kiss this time, tender, and Iris had to resist the urge to turn it hard. Soon, though, Stevie did that for herself, her mouth going hungry, tiny moans slipping from her throat. She reached down to her tank's hem and lifted, all in one motion, whipping it over her head as though tearing off a Band-Aid.

She stood there for a second, her eyes closed, breathing heavily. Iris reached out and touched her waist gently but went no further.

"You're beautiful, Stevie," she said, and she was. There was a tiny black heart tattoo at the base of her throat Iris hadn't noticed before, delicate and understated. Her breasts were smaller than Iris's, it was true, but they were lovely—creamy and pert, with perfect pink nipples Iris couldn't help but visualize sucking into her mouth.

Stevie's eyes popped open, and she pulled Iris closer . . . closer. When their breasts touched, both women let out a low moan, Iris's breathing instantly harsh and ragged again. She was fucking soaked, and her head was getting increasingly fuzzy again. Stevie touched their foreheads together, both of their hips pressing, seeking.

Stevie slotted her leg between Iris's and Iris moaned again. Loudly, with an *oh god* flowing from her mouth, because fuck, it felt good, so goddamn good, and moaning was what she would do if this were all real.

But it wasn't.

And she felt the second Stevie remembered it. Stevie froze, then stepped back so far, the inches between them turned into feet before Iris could blink.

"Shit," Iris said. "Stevie, I'm sorry."

"No, no, it's fine," Stevie said, shaking her head. "I'm the one who took it to the next level. I should've asked."

"You're freaking out."

Stevie closed her eyes, suddenly breathing like a struggling air-conditioning unit. "A bit. It's not your fault, I promise. I just need a second."

"What can I do?"

Stevie shook her head, arms crossing over her chest. "Hand me my shirt?"

Iris scooped up the tank, then looped it over Stevie's head in the least sexy way possible. Stevie pulled it down around her hips, her breathing a little slower, but not quite back to normal. Iris grabbed her own shirt and slipped it on while Stevie's chest continued to heave.

"Should I get a bucket?" Iris asked.

And that did it.

Stevie's eyes went wide, then her harsh breathing stopped abruptly before it shifted into laughter. It was a deep laugh, full-mouthed and beautiful, and Iris cracked up too. Soon, the two of them were laughing so hard, Iris's stomach hurt, and they collapsed onto the sofa, the candles still flickering all around them.

"Well," Stevie said when they'd stopped. "I made it further than last time, at least."

"You did." Iris sat up and wiped her eyes. "And it didn't end in vomit, which is always a plus."

"Growth." Stevie sat up too, leaning her elbows on her knees. "Thank you."

Iris met her gaze, and they both held it for what felt like a second too long. She cleared her throat. "I'm not sure how much I actually helped."

"You helped," Stevie said. "A lot. Just talking me through it. Reminding me of control, reminding me of, well, *me*."

Iris nodded, but for some reason, she couldn't look at Stevie anymore. "Well, thanks for the romance help."

"You're welcome."

They sat there, the languid music still curling around them, and Iris suddenly needed to be alone like she needed a cold shower. This wasn't new—every now and then, despite her raging extroverted nature, she needed silence, quiet, time to process, and hell if she didn't need to process a bit now. Her limbs felt shaky, her heart beating a little too fast, and it didn't help that her clit still thrummed between her legs after her and Stevie's . . .

Lesson.

That's all it was.

She got up and started blowing out the candles. "I think we better call it a night," she said in between puffs.

"Yeah," Stevie said, rising as well and helping Iris darken the room. Soon, only the twinkle lights lit the room, which still felt far too fucking romantic for Iris's taste. She yanked the plug from the wall by the window, plunging them into momentary darkness.

HOURS AFTER STEVIE left, after they'd agreed that Iris would meet Stevie at her apartment in Portland next Friday to go to the airport for the LA trip together, Iris still couldn't sleep.

She laid in her bed, eyes wide open on her ceiling fan, playing the night—the whole day, actually—over and over in her head. She couldn't shake this restless feeling. She'd already gotten herself off—no way she could function properly after what she and Stevie did without some relief—and she'd reheated and eaten her Moonpies burger. She'd showered, cleaned up the popcorn, put all the candles back in their rightful spots.

And yet.

She groaned and rolled over, squeezing her eyes shut to force them into slumber. Still, when her phone buzzed on her nightstand, she leaped into action, glad for another distraction. She saw a message from Claire in the group chat, whose name had now changed to *So Many Queerstions*.

> **Claire:** Are we just going to ignore the fact that Iris brought a fake girlfriend to the pool today?

> **Iris:** Ideally, yes

> **Astrid:** Oh thank god. I've got so many questions

> **Iris:** Ah, so you're the name-changing culprit

> **Delilah:** No that was me. Queerly

Jordan: She's cute, Iris

Claire: So cute. SO WHY IS SHE FAKE?

Iris: Easy killer

Claire: The question stands

Iris: I think you mean queerstion

Jordan: Doesn't exactly roll off the tongue

Delilah: Speaking of tongues, are you fake fucking too?

Claire: Babe

Astrid: Delilah

Delilah: It's a valid queerstion!

Iris sighed, then tapped out a quick explanation about the play and Stevie's ex. The group erupted in congratulations at her playing Beatrice, which Iris had to admit, felt pretty nice, but then they got back down to the real business at hand, because of course they did.

Delilah: So you're Stevie's hero

Iris: It's mutually beneficial

Astrid: Are you really that desperate for romantic content?

Delilah: Nice choice of words

Astrid: Did I accidentally go all Isabel again?

Jordan: A bit, babe

Astrid: Sorry

Iris pressed her fingers into her eyes.

Iris: Look it's fine. Stevie's nice and we're helping each
other out, that's all this is

A flash of Stevie's mouth, her fingers like silk on Iris's bare
back . . .

"Fuck," Iris said, squeezing her thighs together and sitting up in
bed. She tapped out a quick good night to the group, then turned her
phone off. She sat there, breathing heavily for a second, before she
grabbed her laptop from her nightstand and opened it up to her
Tegan McKee draft.

Which consisted of all of two words.

Tegan McKee . . .

She stared at the screen, but the only thing in her head was slow-
dancing and the slow slide of cotton over skin . . . a mouth that tasted
like summer and mint.

She tossed her computer aside and got out her iPad instead, opening her drawing program and starting a new file. She slipped her
stylus from its holder and started drawing. Quick strokes, very little
planning. Just lines, arches, shading to process her thoughts. She'd
always used drawing and illustrations to do this—reorder the world
in her head, expel her worries, her fears, her hopes. When she was a
kid, she'd spend hours drawing everything in her life—her family,

Claire and Astrid, her first kiss. In college, when her art turned into something a bit more practical—a planner she created for Astrid to help with her stress level—Paper Wishes was soon born. Still, she always came back to the blank page when the shit went down. She had file after file chronicling her friendships, Claire's daughter, Ruby, at her first birthday, Iris's breakup with Grant, Astrid's doomed engagement with that shit boot Spencer, Claire and Delilah when they first got together.

Jillian.

Now, as she drew, she could feel the restlessness settling, her mind quieting as a figure formed on the page—shaggy curls, a striped crop top, and plaid pants. Iris added more details. Lush as a sultry background. The lacquered bar Stevie was leaning against when Iris first saw her, that slightly terrified yet hungry look in Stevie's eyes.

It took a bit of time, the night creeping into early morning, but when Iris finished the last stroke, she had a complete drawing.

A scene.

She blinked at the black-and-white illustration, already thinking of the colors she'd use, even words she'd pair with it. She never reached the color phase of her drawings, using them mostly as an emotional outlet, but this one . . .

She stared down at Stevie's face, that lovely mouth slightly parted. Excitement zinged through her like electricity, that familiar, creative-spark feeling, so Iris saved the file as "Meet-Cute" and exited out of the program. Then she grabbed her computer again, opened up her novel drafting program, and finally started to write.

CHAPTER SIXTEEN

"HOLY SHIT, IS this real?" Iris asked.

Stevie watched as Iris gazed up at the modern-style white house, all glass and reclaimed wood and ninety-degree angles, her mouth hanging open adorably. The breeze blowing through the palm trees was sultry and warm, and Stevie could just make out the sound of the Pacific rolling behind the house.

"It's real," Stevie said, smiling at her over their rideshare's roof. Their driver popped the trunk and lifted out their luggage, then promptly took off down Yerba Buena Road. Stevie rolled both suitcases toward where Iris stood on the cobbled driveway. "Welcome to the Riveros' ridiculously opulent seaside mansion."

"I'll take ridiculous," Iris said. "I'll take this kind of ridiculous every day."

Stevie laughed then took advantage of that fact that Iris was still staring up at the house to . . . well, stare at Iris. Not that she hadn't been doing the same thing all morning whenever she could, since the moment Iris picked her up to head to the airport, and then again throughout their entire two-and-a-half-hour flight.

She just couldn't seem to stop.

Stevie wasn't sure if she was staring because Iris was beautiful—she was, completely radiant with her bright hair in a fishtail braid, a grass-green sundress flowing over her freckled skin—or because she was still trying to process the last time they were together.

Their . . . lessons.

She and Iris had only texted a few times since, discussing trip details, packing lists. Once, Iris had asked about a certain line in *Much Ado*, and she and Stevie had then watched the Emma Thompson movie while texting constant comments and ideas. But neither woman had said anything about the kissing, the shirtless pressing.

The moaning.

God, the moaning—Stevie didn't think she'd ever forget the sound Iris made when she'd slid her leg between Iris's thighs. It was gorgeous. Raspy and hot and had promptly sent Stevie in a tailspin of too many thoughts and not enough time to slow them down.

In the last week, Stevie had relived that sound over and over again, and she wasn't sure she could ever admit to anyone how many times she'd gotten herself all worked up, underwear completely drenched in seconds, just thinking about it. On the one hand, the lesson Iris guided her through seemed to have worked—she'd felt more relaxed as they'd kissed, she was able to undress them both without needing to dry heave. On top of that, the moan Iris emitted was real, and Stevie felt a surge of pride and hope that one day she might actually be able to do that to someone in an organic situation that would end in actual sex.

On the other hand . . .

Yeah, Stevie couldn't stop staring at Iris.

Maybe she just needed to work on this a little more—if Iris making sounds of pleasure threw her off, maybe she simply needed Iris to help her through a lesson where there were . . . more moans of pleasure?

Jesus, she sounded absurd. She yanked her gaze from Iris and scrubbed her face with one hand. She one hundred percent had to stop thinking about moaning. For many reasons.

Not the least of which was the fact that Adri, Vanessa, and Ren were already at the Riveros'—they'd flown down yesterday to get things set up—and Iris and Stevie had to put on their fake dating game faces. The rest of the principal cast was arriving tomorrow, which gave Stevie a bit of time with her friends to settle into . . . whatever the hell she and Iris were.

"You ready for this?" Iris asked.

"Honestly?" Stevie said. "Not really, no."

"It'll be fine. You did great at Bitch's the other day."

"Did I? Adri wasn't very pleasant."

Iris smirked. "Again, unrelated to our lie."

"You still think that?"

"We're very convincing, trust me. And, you know, the other night . . . I really believed you."

Stevie frowned. "Believed me about what?"

"That you really wanted to get me naked and have your wicked way with me." Iris winked, but her cheeks went a little pink.

Stevie's, of course, flamed supernova. "Iris, that . . ."

But . . . what? It wasn't real. She didn't actually want to get Iris naked and have her wicked way with her. They'd tried that—disaster. So this really was acting, a part they were both playing, as was pretty much every single thing they were going to do for the next two days, *Much Ado*–related or not.

Stevie shook her head. Got back into her character.

Except she wasn't exactly sure who the hell that character was.

"Hey, you two!"

Vanessa's voice sounded from the front door, which Stevie hadn't even heard open. Adri appeared next to Van, what looked like a mimosa in her hand. She looked beautiful, as always, her hair a deep teal, her natural dark strands mixing throughout, and she wore a black tank top with tiny swim shorts dotted with coral-colored Hawaiian flowers.

"Hey," Stevie said as Iris slipped her fingers between Stevie's.

"You made it," Adri said, her eyes flitting to their hands and back up. "Iris, nice to see you again."

"You too," Iris said. "Thank you so much for having me here. I'm so excited."

"Of course," Vanessa said. She wore a hot pink triangle top bikini, a sheer floral wrap around her waist. "This is my favorite weekend of the year."

"Yeah, because you get to sit around in your bathing suit and drink while the rest of us work," Adri said.

Her tone was light, teasing, but Van's expression still dimmed.

Iris squeezed Stevie's fingers and laughed. "Sounds like a dream to me."

Vanessa smiled. "I mean, right?"

Adri slid her arm around Van's waist, then pressed a kiss to her temple and whispered something in her ear. Vanessa relaxed, and Stevie felt the sudden need to touch Iris too, push close to her side.

No. Hell, no, she was not going to get into a PDA battle with her ex. Plus, Adri's the one who had instigated their breakup in the first place—it wasn't like Stevie could succeed in making her jealous, even if she wanted to.

"Interesting," Iris said quietly.

"What is?" Stevie asked.

But Iris just looked at her for a second, then shook her head. Before Stevie could question her any further, Van called out to them.

"Come in, come in," she said, waving them forward.

Stepping inside the Riveros' house was always a stark reminder that no, rich people were not just like everyone else. Not by a long shot. The downstairs area was one wide-open space, with marble floors in the kitchen transitioning into a gorgeous driftwood in the living spaces. The living room was huge—there was enough seating for twenty people, at least—sporting a giant white sectional as the centerpiece with light blue and gray armchairs sprinkled throughout, and pillows in ocean colors of seafoam, navy, and turquoise to complete the beach-retreat look. The back wall wasn't a wall at all, but floor-to-ceiling windows with a sliding door that opened up onto the back deck. The infinity pool glowed aquamarine under the sun, and the Pacific rolled just beyond that.

"Holy shit," Iris said.

"You already said that," Stevie said.

"I'll say it again—holy shit. What do Vanessa's parents do again?"

"Family money," Stevie whispered. "Van's great-great-grandparents immigrated from Columbia and started a tiny vineyard up in Northern California that became super successful. But Van's mom and dad are also pretty big agents with William Morris Endeavor."

"Ah. Hollywood types."

"Yep."

Stevie took a breath, inhaling the familiar smell of sunscreen and expensive natural cleaners. The last time Stevie had been on this retreat, she and Adri were still a year away from breaking up, but the fissures were already there, tiny cracks of evidence that they were out of love and nearly out of time. But on the retreat, it was like all that disappeared. She and Adri even had sex while on the last trip—probably the last time before the breakup—a wild tangle of limbs in the shower fueled by too much sun and rich food, the heady drug of working on a play together, which had always been like a virtual Viagra for their sex life.

Stevie shoved the memories away. In front of them, Vanessa turned and smiled. "I have the best room for you two."

"Oh," Stevie said. "You didn't have—"

"Actually, babe," Adri said, "I had to move them to the Jasmine Room."

Vanessa frowned. "Why?"

Adri took a sip of her drink. "Satchi and Nina really wanted the Hyacinth. And they've been together longer."

"When did they tell you that?" Van asked.

"They texted me when I asked them about room assignments. You know they've always loved that room, and I—"

"It's fine," Iris said, waving her free hand. "We're fine wherever you put us. I'd sleep on the back deck, honestly."

"Yeah," Stevie said, her palm growing sweaty in Iris's hand. She'd never seen Van and Adri bicker like this before. But she honestly didn't care what room they stayed in. She could never keep all the names the Riveros had for their ten bedrooms straight in her head, but there was no such thing as a bad room in this house. "We're fine."

"Good," Adri said. "I can take you up."

Vanessa blinked. "I'll just get some drinks started." Then she turned and speed-walked into the expansive kitchen before Stevie could call out her thanks.

Stevie and Iris followed Adri up the floating staircase, carrying their suitcases with them, and down an open hallway to a room at the very end. Adri swung the door open and bright light spilled inside.

"Here we are," she said, waving them ahead of her.

Stevie stepped into a lovely space—every bedroom was at the back of the house, so they all had balcony access and ocean views. The bed linens were white and bedecked with colorful pillows that matched those downstairs, and the en suite bathroom boasted mosaic tiles and a huge glass shower.

"Ah," Iris said, nodding as she looked around.

"What?" Stevie asked.

Iris's brow lifted, but she just turned to Adri. "Thank you, this is lovely."

Adri smiled. "I'll leave you to get settled in." Then she turned, squeezing Stevie's shoulder as she left.

"Wow," Iris said once they heard Adri's footfalls on the stairs.

"What?" Stevie asked. "What's so *wow*?"

"Who are Nina and Satchi?" Iris asked.

"Regulars with the Empress. They're playing Don Pedro and Don John. Been together for, like, five years, I think."

Iris laughed and pushed her suitcase toward the driftwood dresser. "Right."

"What?"

"Really? You don't see it?"

"See what?"

Iris waved her hand at the room.

Stevie just stared at her.

"Adri changing our room last minute?" Iris said. "To this room?"

"I mean, I figured they'd put us in the same room. If what you say is true and Adri does believe we're dating, then of course—"

"Yeah," Iris said. "But *this* room is for roomies. Not lovers."

"What are you talking—"

But then she saw it.

Beds.

As in two.

Two twin beds. Opulently appointed, of course, but yeah, this was definitely a room to be shared by people who were not sleeping together. Panic surged into Stevie's throat.

"Shit," she said, already breathing more heavily. "She knows, doesn't she? She knows we're faking, and fuck, that is so humiliating, and I—"

Hands on her face. Soft and sweet, scents of ginger and bergamot washing over her. She immediately calmed down, more from the shock of Iris's closeness than anything else.

"No," Iris said. "Stevie, I don't think she knows."

"Still?"

"Still." Iris tilted her head, swiped her thumbs over Stevie's cheeks. "You're sort of adorable, you know that?"

Stevie just stared at her. Iris stared back. It felt like a lifetime of just . . . *looking*.

And nothing about it felt fake at all.

"Then why do we have the twin bed room?" Stevie asked.

Iris smiled softly. "Why indeed."

"I'm confused."

Iris laughed and pulled away, heading to her suitcase and heaving it up on one of the beds. "You'll figure it out. As for me, I'm going to put on my sexiest bikini and get in that pool as soon as possible."

She glanced at Stevie, brows lifted in a question. Stevie, however, didn't know the answer. She only knew that she wasn't sure she could take a bikini much sexier than the one she'd already seen Iris wear at the Belmont.

"Join me?" Iris asked.

"Um . . ."

"That wasn't actually a question."

"Right. Yeah. Okay."

"You did get a new bathing suit, right?" Iris asked.

"I did, yeah."

"Is it sexy? It really needs to be sexy, Stevie."

Stevie laughed. She couldn't help it. Iris's tone was both teasing and firm, and smiling just seemed to come naturally around this woman.

"I think it'll do," she said, and hoped to hell Iris agreed.

CHAPTER

SEVENTEEN

"WILL THIS DO?" Stevie asked, smoothing her hands down her bare stomach as she came out of the bathroom.

Iris smiled, forcing her jaw to keep from dropping. Stevie's swim top was halter-style and black, but it had a bit of lace bordering the edges. She had on a colorful blue-and-orange-patterned jacket-style cover-up, that mysterious heart tattoo on display. The look was somehow feminine and neutral at the same time, and it worked. It really, really worked.

"Yeah, that's . . . that's perfect," Iris said. "What about me?" She spread her arms, revealing what she knew was a killer green bikini. Triangle cups, strings everywhere. It barely covered her ass, which was half the draw, especially since it was clear Iris's purpose here was a little more convoluted than a simple fake dating scheme.

Granted, fake dating wasn't exactly *simple* in nature, but this was no longer just about Stevie saving face with her friends and ensuring a smooth Shakespeare production.

This was about jealousy.

Iris couldn't believe Stevie didn't see it—the glances, the sniping at Van, the room change.

Adri was jealous as fuck.

Iris had suspected as much when she and Stevie had run into Adri at Bitch's last week, but now she was positive. And she wasn't sure how she felt about it, or how Stevie would feel once she figured out what Adri was doing. Iris didn't want to point it out, more because it was possible she'd read the entire situation wrong and didn't want to cause Stevie any more anxiety than necessary. Iris didn't know Adri. She barely knew Stevie. Hell, maybe this was all some big cosmic plot to get the two of them back together.

They'd been together for six years.

Iris hadn't had anything for six years. A plant, maybe. She was good with succulents. Even her business, successful as it was, had only lasted around five years by the time she'd really gotten it up and running and pulling a profit. So, maybe Iris was just paving the way for a reconciliation.

Which was fine.

Iris looked at Stevie, whose mouth was parted slightly as her gaze trailed down Iris's form and back up to her face. Stevie swallowed hard, and goose bumps broke out all over Iris's body, just from Stevie's simple observation.

Iris pressed her thighs together.

Practice, she told herself. *Fake.* They didn't want to muddy with the waters with earnest fucking, even if that earnestness meant nothing but an active libido.

"Yeah," Stevie said, looking away. "That'll do."

Iris smiled. "Let's get this show on the road, then."

IRIS WAS PRETTY sure she'd never been anywhere she would describe as *paradise*.

Until now.

They spent the afternoon swimming in the infinity pool, which sparkled like a fountain of youth, all with the Pacific crashing onto the beach below. Iris was never without a beverage in her hand, first mimosas with a poolside lunch of fruit and cheese and fancy crackers, then Aperol spritzes in the afternoon. She drank a ton of water too—no need to get sloppy drunk and let something slip.

Iris used the time to study Adri, who, Iris discovered, had a tiny heart tattoo at the base of her throat that matched Stevie's. So there was that. She was also beautiful, smart, and always had a hand on Vanessa. A kiss here, a waist-squeeze there. But her eyes followed Stevie, and Iris didn't think she was the only one who noticed.

More than once, Iris caught Ren—Stevie's chic friend from Lush who helped with the Empress's costumes—watching Adri too. Vanessa didn't seem to notice, or if she did, she didn't show it. Stevie was also clueless, or so it seemed. Iris made sure to stay close to her. She didn't want to paw at her—that felt a bit creepy, to be honest—so she let Stevie lead the way in terms of physical affection.

Which wasn't very much at all. Stevie sipped her club soda with lime, laughed with her friends and Iris, got into an in-depth discussion with Adri while they were in the hot tub about ways to shift Benedick into more of an arrogant ass as opposed to an arrogant misogynistic ass. They talked about the other roles, how the Dons were both played by women, how two gay men—one of them trans—played Hero and Claudio, and the adjustments Adri had made to the script to accommodate all the glorious queerness, which included they/them pronouns for an agender actor playing Leonato. Meanwhile, Iris sat next to Stevie, waiting for Stevie to put her arm around her shoulder, to rub her knee or kiss her cheek, *something* to show their togetherness in front of Adri.

But Stevie never did any of that.

Which was fine. This was Stevie's show; Iris was just here for support.

Still, by the time they'd all showered and dressed for dinner, Iris was grumpy. Too much sun and alcohol, most likely, and she was ravenous. That cheese hadn't lasted long, and she was definitely the kind of person her friends tended to avoid when she was hungry—or feed immediately.

She sat down at the expansive driftwood table and thanked all the gods that there was a bread basket already present. Candles were set out along the sideboard, and a modern, branch-shaped chandelier glowed above them. She tore a hunk out of the warm brown bread as Vanessa emerged from the kitchen with a giant dish of lasagna, followed by Adri and a bowl filled with leafy green salad.

"We went simple tonight," Vanessa said. "Hope that's okay."

"It's perfect," Iris said, accepting a glass of red wine from Ren.

"So, Iris," Adri said once they all had full plates and were cutting into their food. "What do you do when you're not taking the community theater world by storm?"

Iris smiled. "I'm a romance author. And I have a line of digital planners I sell through an Etsy shop called Paper Wishes."

"A renaissance woman," Vanessa said. "Would we know any of your books?"

"Stevie loves romance," Adri said, her eyes on Stevie.

"I know," Iris said, and shit, she just could not resist taking Stevie's free hand, then leaning over to kiss her cheek. Stevie laughed softly, meeting Iris's eyes briefly before taking her hand back.

"And no, Vanessa, you probably wouldn't know my books yet," Iris said, ripping another piece of bread in half.

"Not very popular?" Adri asked.

"Babe," Vanessa said.

"What?"

"Subtle as always, A," Ren said.

Stevie cleared her throat but said nothing.

"I haven't published yet," Iris said, keeping her eyes on Adri. "My first book comes out in October."

"Oh, that's exciting," Van said. "Congrats."

Iris tipped her glass at her. "I hope you'll all come to the launch party in Bright Falls."

Adri's gaze flicked to Stevie then back to Iris. "If you still want us to by then, I'm sure we will."

Silence spilled over the table, her insinuation like a finger snuffing out a flame. Iris was trying to figure out how to play this—Adri was her director after all, and this passive aggression seemed to be the way she was planning to interact with Iris. She'd just decided that a change of subject was the best course of action when Adri went on.

"Stevie's special, you know," Adri said.

"Adri," Stevie said.

"What? You are. You're a gifted actor, Stevie, but you're sensitive. I just want to make sure Iris here knows that."

"I can tell her just how sensitive I am myself."

"Can you?"

"Adri, what are you doing?" Vanessa asked. Her brows were furrowed, eyes glistening in the dim light.

Adri sighed and let her fork clatter to her plate. "I'm looking out for our friend. Is that a crime?"

"Stevie can look after herself," Ren said.

"Except Stevie struggles with that, Ren," Adri said. "Always has. You know she does. And I'm sorry, I'm happy Stevie has found someone, and Iris, you seem amazing, truly, but you're not exactly a gentle person. At least from what I've seen. I'm just looking out for her. Stevie is—"

"*Stevie* is right fucking here."

Stevie's voice cut through Adri's soliloquy. She stared at Adri, but not with vitriol like Iris expected—like Iris sort of wanted, if she was being honest—but with wonder.

"Excuse me," Stevie said, then got up from the table and disappeared out the back door toward the beach.

Iris picked up her wine and took a sip, glaring at Adri as she did so. Fuck the fact that Adri was essentially her boss for the play. It was too late to replace her as Beatrice anyway.

"Well," Ren said. "Dessert anyone?"

Vanessa tossed her napkin on her plate and rose, then walked off down the hall without another word to anyone.

"Jesus, Adri," Ren said.

"Oh, fuck off, Ren," Adri said. "You have no idea what it's like to be with someone for six years. All that care and concern doesn't just go away, okay?"

"Sure as hell seemed like it all went away when you started fucking Van two months after the breakup."

Adri pursed her mouth, a muscle jumping in her jaw. Finally, she stood up too, and left out the back door just like Stevie.

Iris sat there, her pulse galloping against her ribs more than she'd like to admit. She wasn't one to back away from conflict, but this . . . she wasn't sure what role she played here among this group of people who had known one another for a decade. She didn't know if she should go after Stevie or give her time to cool off. Because the truth was, she didn't really know Stevie at all.

Ren scrubbed a hand over their face, then lifted their glass in a toast. "Welcome to the fam, Iris."

CHAPTER

EIGHTEEN

WHILE IN PORTLAND, Stevie always forgot how much she loved the ocean. The vastness of it. She spent her days fighting huge emotions and thoughts, constantly working to keep herself from spilling over. But here, in front of the Pacific at twilight, with nothing around except water and rocks and sky, she remembered just how small she was, how insignificant in the scheme of the universe.

It was a good reminder, healthy perspective and all that, particularly as she sat in the sand, tears on a free-for-all down her cheeks. She'd barely set them loose, her chest opening up in relief, when she caught a shadow to her right. Wiping at her face, she glanced over, expecting to see a redhead walking toward her, but instead saw her ex.

Her heart did something funny in her chest—a leap, a flutter, she wasn't sure—and she had no idea what it meant. She turned back to the ocean, focused on all that power, that mystery.

Adri, of course, was undeterred by Stevie's silence. She settled next to her, and Stevie was momentarily overwhelmed by familiarity—Adri's rosewater scent, the familiar way a sigh slipped from her throat.

The way she pressed her shoulder into Stevie's. That touch was like a fingerprint—she'd know Adri blindfolded.

"I'm sorry," Adri said.

"Are you?" Stevie asked, still not looking at her. Ocean. Water. Waves.

"Yeah. I am."

"For what exactly?"

Adri didn't answer for a while, but it was a fair question. She wrapped her arms around her knees, leaned forward a little, and the wind whipped her hair into the sky, the fading light turning the color a dark green.

"For being an ass to Iris?" Adri finally said.

"Is that a question? Because you were definitely an ass to Iris. Have been, actually, since the audition."

Adri nodded. "Yeah. I'm sorry for being an ass to Iris."

"Okay. That's a start."

Adri sighed and shook her head. "Look, I guess I wasn't exactly prepared for this."

"You offered her the role. You knew she would be here."

"Not Iris *here*. Iris and you."

Stevie felt the words like a shove to the chest. She must've heard wrong. Adri was with Vanessa. Vanessa, who was sweet and smart and beautiful and not a fucking mess all the time. Adri was the one who started the entire conversation that led to her and Stevie's breakup, brought it up in bed one night back in January, after they'd already brushed their teeth and turned out the lights and said good night.

I think we should talk about breaking up.

That's what Adri said, her exact words, and Stevie had felt them like a bomb finally detonating, a bomb she'd been watching falling from the sky for months. Of course Stevie had agreed—she always agreed with Adri, with everyone—and once your partner says some-

thing like that, something so final and shattering, there was no going back anyway.

So they'd broken up.

And Stevie had been lost for months, wondering if she'd ever have
had the courage to end things if Adri hadn't spoken up first, which
had brought on a spiral of self-pity and hatred that pretty much
locked Stevie into place until very recently.

She knew she and Adri didn't have what she wanted, didn't have
what Adri wanted either, but she also craved familiarity.

Safety.

And she and Adri had been so, so safe. Even now, that safety was
like a clear eye in a hurricane—wide open and calm. No one-night
stands, no nervous puking, no lessons.

No wild redhead who made Stevie—

She squeezed her eyes shut, stopping the thought. This wasn't
about Iris. Not at its core. Couldn't be. She and Iris weren't even real.

"You wanted this," Stevie finally said. "You're the one who put this
whole thing into motion. You're with Van. You're *living* with Van."

"I know," Adri said. "And I . . . I'm not saying that I . . . fuck." She
rubbed her forehead, sent her fingers through her wavy hair.

"What? You're not saying what?"

Adri dropped her hands. "I'm not saying I want to get back together, okay?"

Stevie shook her head. "This conversation is making me feel like
shit, Adri."

"I'm sorry. Dammit." Adri turned so she was facing Stevie, took
one of her hands in hers. "I don't mean to do that. Really. I just . . .
look, we were together a long time. That doesn't just go away,
does it?"

Stevie's throat went tight. Too tight, but she managed a raspy, "No."

"And I miss you. I do."

Tears welled into Stevie's eyes. "Fuck, Adri."

"I know."

"You're with Van," Stevie said again.

"And you're with Iris."

Stevie swallowed. "I am."

Adri leaned closer, rested her chin on Stevie's shoulder. She was so close. So . . . familiar.

"See?" Adri said softly. "A lot of different things can be true at once."

Stevie leaned her head against Adri's—so easy, so *normal*, even as her mind whirled like the ocean wind.

"I worry about you," Adri said after a while. "I don't want you to get hurt. And Iris seems like a lot."

"So . . . what? You want me to break up with her?" Stevie asked. "Are *you* breaking up with Van?"

Adri said nothing. Stevie wasn't even sure what she wanted that answer to be—she loved Vanessa. And Stevie didn't want to get back with Adri, but god, she had to admit the thought was intoxicating. Sinking back into something she knew, something she understood, even if it was somewhat lackluster as far as great love stories went.

But maybe Iris was right.

Maybe those kinds of stories were simply that—stories. Myths humanity wove to thread hope through the meaningless chaos of life.

Still, that hope of a great love was there, fanned into an even stronger flame since she and Adri separated, and Stevie didn't think she could ignore it now.

And she didn't think Adri wanted to ignore it either.

Stevie pulled back to look at her ex. "You're not breaking up with her."

It wasn't a question.

Adri's teeth closed over her lower lip, and she shook her head. "I love Van. I do. But I love you too."

Clarity glimmered on the edge of Stevie's thoughts, a glimmer of light in the middle of a storm. Adri's attitude with Iris. The way she was all over Vanessa at the pool. This conversation right here, which felt like tentacles reaching out to lock Stevie back into place, back into Adri.

Tears spilled over and raced down Stevie's cheeks, but she forced herself to stand up. She knew she needed to say more. Needed to tell Adri to stop, to let her go, but she couldn't get the words together in her head. They jumbled together, a mishmash of things she knew were true and things that terrified her, that illusive clarity still hovering out of reach. But she knew she couldn't stay here, and those words were, at least, easier to say.

"I need to go."

"Stevie—"

But Stevie kept walking, and the wind and waves swallowed up whatever Adri was going to say to stop her.

CHAPTER

NINETEEN

IRIS WATCHED STEVIE lean her head against Adri's.

She hadn't meant to see. She'd come up to the room to grab a hair tie so she could go out on the beach to find Stevie. As she secured her still-damp hair into a low ponytail, she'd stepped out onto the balcony to look for her fake girlfriend, glancing left and right so she knew which way to head.

And there she was, sitting in the sand and staring at the waves, a tiny shape a few hundred yards down the beach. But just as Iris was about to turn away to head downstairs and outside, she'd seen Adri.

She'd seen Adri sit down next to Stevie.

She'd seen her press in close.

She'd seen her rest her chin on Stevie's shoulder.

Which was all fine.

Whatever was going on between Stevie and Adri, it was complicated. Iris knew it wasn't really about her—it was about six years of emotions and togetherness, and there was no way Iris could really relate to that.

There was no way Iris could compete with that.

Not that she was even trying. She was here to help Stevie. She was here for a play, a play Iris herself wanted to do.

After she came back inside the room and closed the sliding balcony door, she decided to focus on Beatrice. She washed up and then settled in her tiny twin bed and tried to read through the revised script Adri had given her before dinner. But she couldn't concentrate. She kept seeing Stevie, wondering about Stevie, worrying about Stevie. Finally, she tossed her script aside and took out her iPad, opening up a folder now labeled "S & I."

In the last week, she'd been drawing a lot. She'd written a lot too, her novel finally taking on somewhat of a shape, enough that she could breathe a little bit when thinking about her deadline. But she had a lot of illustrations too—a scene of Iris tucking Stevie into her bed the night they met, the shock of seeing each other at the Empress, their conversation backstage. The Belmont. Her friends' incredulous expressions as she introduced them to Stevie.

Their lessons that night.

She nearly opened up that file, her finger hovering, her mind already re-creating their mouths on each other, Stevie's fingertips as she dragged Iris's bra straps down her arms.

But she didn't.

In fact, she hadn't gone back to review any of the scenes she'd drawn, and she couldn't really explain why. She started a new file and started sketching Stevie sitting on the beach, alone, a closer view than Iris could actually see. She drew the details of her hair, curls in the wind, the uncertain roll in her shoulders. She was deep into adding details to the twilit ocean when the door opened, revealing Stevie in the doorway.

Iris honestly hadn't expected Stevie to come back to their room tonight, but seeing her here now, she couldn't stop the flare of . . . something in her chest.

Relief?

Confusion?

Maybe both.

Iris let herself exhale, told herself she was just glad to know Stevie was safe.

"Hey," she said, clicking her iPad to dark and sitting up in bed as Stevie closed the door. "You okay?"

Stevie looked at her. *Really* looked at her. Her hair was a mess— wind-tossed and frizzy from the humidity, and her cheeks were a little red. Stevie didn't wear makeup, so there were no telltale mascara streaks, but Iris could tell she'd been crying.

"What happened?" Iris asked.

Stevie shook her head and came to sit on the end of Iris's bed. Iris pulled her feet up to make room.

"Nothing," Stevie said. She was breathing heavily, her fingers shaking.

"Hey." Iris reached out and tangled their fingers together, an instinct. "It's okay. Just take a breath."

"I'm fine," she said, pulling her hand back. "I'm fine. Really. Do you think we could have a lesson?"

Her words were coming fast, so fast it took Iris a second to register them.

"A lesson," she said.

Stevie nodded. Tears glimmered in her eyes. "I need one."

"Now?"

"Yes, fucking now."

Iris reared back. "Okay, what's going on?"

Stevie swiped at her eyes. "Nothing. Everything. I don't know. I just know that I have to move on. I have to move on now, and if I don't figure out how to be with someone else, I'm going to . . . Adri and I will . . ."

The tears spilled over, and Iris scooted closer to her. "Hey. Just stop for a second."

"No," Stevie said, standing up. She crossed her arms, her whole body vibrating with . . . what? Iris couldn't really tell. Energy, sure, but there was something else there. Something that looked like panic.

Iris shoved her covers back and stood up too. "Stevie. Let's just slow down."

"I don't need to slow down, Iris. If I slow down, I'll *think*, and if I think, I'll never go through with it. I'll talk myself out of it, like I talk myself out of everything that scares the shit out of me, and then I'll be stuck. Or worse, I'll go back to someone who doesn't even want to actually be with me because . . . I don't even know why. Because it's easy, because it's safe."

She stepped closer to Iris, slid her hands up Iris's arms. "What's my next lesson? We can do something super romantic tomorrow, okay? But can we . . . for tonight . . ."

She trailed off and Iris shifted to take her hands, lacing their fingers together. She stared at Stevie and Stevie stared back, and goddammit, Iris wished she could give Stevie what she thought she wanted.

But she couldn't.

Call it lessons, call it preparation or exposure therapy or whatever the hell they wanted, but it was still *physical*, bodies pressing together, impossible to separate completely from the mind, and Iris couldn't do that with Stevie shaking like this. She couldn't do it with tear tracks on Stevie's cheeks.

"Stevie," she said gently, tugging on her hands. "Come sit with me."

Stevie shook her head, didn't move. "Iris, please."

Iris sighed. "We're not doing that tonight. I'm sorry, but not like this."

Stevie's expression fell and she pulled her hands free. "Not like what?"

"Not with you this upset. Let's just talk, okay? Or go to sleep. It's been a long day, and I think you just need to—"

"Fuck, you too?" Stevie's tone was sharp.

"Me too what?" Iris asked.

"Someone else telling me what to do, telling me what's right for me. Because Stevie's just a useless sack of skin on her own, right?"

"What?" She reached for Stevie's hand, but Stevie stepped back. "No, that's not—"

"Forget it," Stevie said. She hauled her suitcase onto the other bed and unzipped it.

"Stevie, hang on. Talk to me."

But Stevie didn't answer. She simply grabbed her toiletry bag and disappeared into the bathroom. A few minutes later, the shower turned on, and Iris was left standing in the middle of a room in Malibu, wondering if she and her fake girlfriend had just broken up.

IRIS COULDN'T SLEEP.

Normally, she slept like a baby, nothing to keep her up, nothing to keep her heart and mind churning deep into the night. But now she felt too hot, then five minutes after kicking off her covers, the ceiling fan set her skin to shivering.

She didn't seem to be the only one having a hard time, as Stevie kept shifting around on her bed too, flopping onto her back to stare into space, then onto her side, facing away from Iris.

Well past midnight, Iris was still awake to see Stevie sit up and take a deep, shaky breath. Iris didn't move, lying on her side and watching as Stevie fiddled with a loose string on her sheet in the moonlit dark, the ocean a quiet lullaby outside their open balcony door.

Finally, Stevie turned to look at Iris.

Their eyes locked and Iris felt her breath catch. Stevie looked wrecked. Small and scared and exhausted, so Iris didn't even stop to think through what she was doing when she propped herself up on one elbow and peeled her covers back. She shifted to the left, placing her hand on the now open space in her tiny bed.

Stevie followed her movements, only hesitated for a moment. She got out of her own bed, wearing a thin tank top and black boxers with a rainbow waistband, and slid in beside Iris.

She laid down immediately on her side, tucking both hands under her head, her back to Iris. Iris waited for a beat, just to make sure Stevie really wanted to be there, before she covered them both with the sheet.

Iris settled on the mattress slowly, her front pressing inevitably to Stevie's back in the small space. Stevie was warm, her breathing calm and even, and she smelled like the sea, like sun and salt and something else uniquely Stevie.

"Is this okay?" Iris said quietly as she wrapped her arms around Stevie. There was simply no other place for her arms to go.

"Yeah," Stevie said.

Iris rested her head on the pillow, but then Stevie scooted back, fitting herself tighter against Iris. It wasn't even sexual, just . . . close.

Intimate.

Iris held her breath for a second, trying to figure out what to do with her torso, her legs. She hadn't done this in years—cuddling. Not since Grant. She and Jillian, despite the many actual dates they went on, never had this kind of relationship. Theirs was all fine dining and fucking, followed by Jillian declaring she had an early meeting in Portland while she slipped on her five-hundred-dollar shoes. And Iris's dalliances of late . . . well, she never let it get this far, always leaving ten minutes post-orgasm.

She wasn't sure she even remembered how to cuddle, but as Stevie seemed to sink against her, she found herself doing the same, her body acting and reacting on its own. She pressed her face to Stevie's hair, slotted her knees behind Stevie's legs in a perfect spoon. Stevie's hands tangled with hers, and they both exhaled together, like a song or dance—Iris wasn't sure which.

Iris wasn't sure about a lot of things right now.

But soon it didn't matter, because Stevie's breathing went deep and even. Iris's own eyes grew heavy, Stevie's rhythm and warmth pulling her into an easy sleep.

CHAPTER

TWENTY

STEVIE WOKE BEFORE Iris. It took her a few seconds to remember where she was, why she was there. She kept still, not daring to move or let herself roll over and do something pathetic, like gaze at Iris while she slept.

Stevie had simply needed some comfort last night. That was all that was. Desperation brought on by confusion, anger, exhaustion.

Some of that still lingered, but it was clearer now.

Adri was clearer.

Her best friend, first and only lover, partner for six years. Adri did love her. Stevie believed that. Adri was used to taking care of Stevie, used to helping her navigate the world, their relationship, their sex life, even theater.

Stevie was used to that too.

She supposed they were both having a hard time letting go, but Stevie knew she needed to. Beyond the stage, Adri had zero faith in her, that much was clear now. And maybe part of that was Stevie's fault—she didn't have much faith in herself—but she knew Ren was right.

Stevie was stuck.

And if she didn't figure out how to take care of herself, do what *she* wanted when she wanted it, she'd always be right where she was.

Next to her, Iris stirred, and Stevie's body instinctively turned over.

Big mistake.

Because Iris Kelly was fucking gorgeous in the morning.

Stevie imagined her own hair was a rat's nest from the tear-soaked wash she managed in the shower last night, followed by sleeping on her curls half wet. But Iris? Iris was glowing in the morning sun that streamed through the windows, her hair a bright ruby, her eyes a seafoam green from the light. Long lashes blinked heavily, then opened fully when her eyes landed on Stevie.

"Hi," Iris said, her voice adorably muzzy. "Did you sleep?"

"I did," Stevie said. She tucked her hands together under her head, shifted her legs so they barely brushed Iris's knees. "You?"

Iris nodded and yawned, but then her expression went serious, eyes searching Stevie's. "I'm sorry about last night."

Stevie shook her head. "It's fine. I'm sorry I acted like a brat."

"You didn't."

"I kind of did. And you were right. I was way too amped up to . . . learn anything."

Iris smiled. "Yeah, I mean, what's the point if all my extensive knowledge doesn't really sink in, right?"

"Exactly."

Stevie tracked Iris's freckles across her face. She had one blue one, right under her eye.

"Tell me about this," Iris said. Her fingertips brushed the tiny heart tattoo at Stevie's throat, then retreated.

"Oh." Stevie touched the spot too, though she couldn't feel anything there after so many years. "Adri and I got it together."

"I figured," Iris said. "I noticed hers too."

"We'd been dating for about a year. I'd always wanted one—a tattoo, I mean—but I was scared to get it on my own, because of course I was."

Iris's brows dipped a little, but she said nothing.

"Anyway, it was sort of spontaneous. We were out on the night of our anniversary and passed a tattoo shop. Adri suggested doing something together. I agreed. That's it. Nothing too fancy or romantic, actually."

Iris's eyes slipped to the tattoo, then back to Stevie's face again. "I think you're a lot braver than you give yourself credit for."

Stevie closed her eyes for a split second. "I'm not. But thank you for saying that."

"Stevie. I'm not just blowing smoke up your ass here."

Stevie gazed at her, that blue freckle like a little spark among all the brown. "I want that to be true. I'm trying."

"You're doing amazing, okay?"

Stevie nodded, her chest opening up at Iris's words. She hadn't realized how much she needed to hear that from someone until this moment. Still, it wasn't enough to be trying. She had to *do*. If she didn't, she'd stay stuck. She'd fall right back into Adri—all her ex had to do was ask. Stevie couldn't believe how close she came last night to giving in to the feeling of it, of *Adri and Stevie*, the solid fact of being a part of a real couple. If it hadn't been for Vanessa hovering at the edge of her mind, and Adri's declaration that she loved Van, Stevie knew she wouldn't be in this bed with Iris right now.

"I still want to keep practicing," she said. "If that's okay with you."

Iris shifted, propping herself up on her elbow. "Are you sure? You did pretty great last time."

Stevie's cheeks grew warm, blood rushing to the surface, and she pointed at them. "Look at this. I can't even think of being with someone like that without blushing."

"Blushing isn't a crime, Stevie. It's actually pretty adorable."

"To you, maybe. But you . . . we . . . this isn't really happening. You and me. There's no risk here, right?"

Iris swallowed. "Right."

"When it's really happening, I don't want to fumble and shake and fight for breath. I don't want to have to *tell* someone why I'm shaking and fighting for breath. God. I want to feel sexy. I want to *be* sexy. There's nothing sexy about a panic attack."

"Okay," Iris said. "What do you want to do?"

Stevie laughed and turned onto her back, staring up at the ceiling. "Aren't you the teacher?"

"Yeah. And I'm telling you, like I told you last time, to take control. That's how you're going to feel sexy. By owning it and *doing* it. So do it."

Stevie glanced at her. "Now?"

"Now."

They looked at each other for a second, Iris's mouth parted just a little.

"You're sure?" Stevie asked.

Iris smiled. "Once again, you have my enthusiastic consent."

Stevie nodded, then worked herself out from under the covers and sat up on her knees. Took a few deep breaths. She gazed down at Iris, who was still propped up on her elbow, the sheet covering her body to her ribs.

"Lie back," Stevie said.

Iris did as she was told, sinking against the pillows. Stevie let her settle for a moment—let herself settle, because her hands were already starting to shake. But then she closed her eyes and pictured it—taking control, just like Iris said. She formed the scene in her mind, exactly what she wanted to do to Iris, how she wanted to make her feel, and she didn't slip into some other person.

She slipped into herself, Stevie Scott, but a Stevie Scott who did what she wanted. A Stevie who knew she could.

One more slightly shaky breath, and then she reached up and pulled the sheet down slowly, revealing Iris's body inch by beautiful inch, her tank top, a sliver of creamy skin at her belly button, and then . . .

Her underwear.

She wasn't wearing shorts or pants. Just a pair of bright purple bikinis.

"Shit, sorry," Iris said, wincing. "I should've warned you."

Stevie shook her head, forcing her eyes back to Iris's. "It's fine."

"Very sexy move though," Iris said. "That slow tug of the covers."

"Yeah?"

"Yeah."

Stevie's mouth curved into a tiny smile. Her pulse sped up as she thought about what she should do next, honestly shocked when the answer was so clear. She barely even second-guessed herself as she pressed a hand to Iris's stomach, gently, then straddled her, sliding her thigh over Iris's hips until she sat above her. Iris sucked in a breath but didn't move. Didn't say a word.

"Okay?" Stevie asked.

Iris just nodded, her eyes tracking Stevie's.

Stevie ran her hands up Iris's torso to her ribs, thumbs meeting at her sternum. Iris didn't have on a bra, and her nipples were already peaked, pressing into the thin cotton. Stevie grabbed the hem of her tank, lifting until Iris raised her arms, and soon Iris was shirtless, bared to Stevie in a way that made Stevie feel the need to moan.

She didn't. But Christ. Iris was goddamn gorgeous, her breasts full, her nipples pink, the tips hard and begging for Stevie's mouth. Stevie wasn't sure if that would be over the line or not, so she settled for trailing her fingers just under that lovely swell. Iris's body arched into her touch, her eyes fluttering closed.

"Fuck," Iris said.

"Okay?" Stevie asked, pausing.

"Yeah," Iris said, laughing. "Very okay. You're . . . you're doing great."

"Good," Stevie said, then she lifted her own shirt and Iris's eyes snapped open. Stevie watched her throat move in a hard swallow, Iris's hands resting on Stevie's thighs.

Still, Iris didn't touch her anywhere else, even though Stevie knew her nipples were just as hard and taut as Iris's. Stevie wasn't sure if it was inappropriate to ask to be touched, seeing as how this was Stevie's lesson.

So she concentrated on Iris, lowering herself until their breasts met, their labored breathing tangling together in the space between them. She kissed Iris . . . once . . . twice . . . before settling onto her lips in earnest, sweeping her tongue into Iris's mouth. Iris met her, press for press, little moans rolling up from Iris's throat. Stevie smiled against her. This time, the sounds Iris was making didn't freak her out at all. They were like music, soft and light and gorgeous.

Stevie took Iris's hands off her thighs, then stretched them above Iris's head, sitting up a little to look at her. She was beautiful like this, writhing underneath Stevie. Stevie kept waiting for the panic to start its inevitable rise. Her stomach did flutter a bit, her fingers betraying the slightest shake, but she kept it together, the panic barely swelling.

Because she liked this.

No, she *loved* it.

The control. The way she was making Iris gasp and squirm. *She* was the reason Iris's pupils were blown wide. *She* was the reason Iris's hips lifted, circled, seeking pressure.

And Stevie wanted to let her find it. She wanted to make Iris feel good, so she would know that she *could*, so she could make someone else feel good when it was real.

Still, nothing about this felt fake as Stevie slid off of Iris and onto her side.

"Stay still," she told Iris. "Keep your arms above your head."

Iris obeyed, turning her head slightly to meet Stevie's gaze. Stevie leaned in to kiss her, a hard and fast tug of lips, the glide of their tongues like nothing Stevie had ever felt before. She slid her hand down her own thigh, then drifted back up between Iris's legs, just the barest touch before she placed her hand between Iris's breasts, drifting over to one nipple before visiting the other.

Iris gasped when Stevie took one between her thumb and forefinger, eyes slamming closed. Stevie smiled, trailing her fingertips down Iris's stomach, following the freckles to her belly button and lower. She dragged a finger over the band of her underwear, pausing.

God, she wanted to touch her.

Wanted to make her moan, make her come.

"Can I?" Stevie asked quietly, her own breathing just as ragged as Iris's.

Iris hesitated, watching Stevie for what she assumed were signs of her own doubt, but Stevie was sure.

She'd never been more sure of anything.

Finally, Iris nodded, added a whispered *"Yes"* to her consent. Stevie pressed her mouth to Iris's shoulder, moving her fingers over Iris's pelvic bone. She stayed above her underwear, unsure if touching Iris's skin would be too much for either of them, but she could already tell Iris was soaked. She felt her wetness as she slid her fingers down to Iris's sex, pressing slow circles into the cotton.

"Oh my god," Iris said, back arching, hips reaching up for more contact.

Stevie opened her mouth on Iris's arm, tongue swiping at her skin, teeth grazing as her fingers explored, spreading Iris's pussy under her underwear, dragging more wetness up toward her clit.

"Fuck," Iris said. "Stevie." Her breathing grew even more raspy, desperate, and Stevie applied more pressure, circling until Iris couldn't even manage expletives anymore. She was just moans and breaths and Stevie had never felt more powerful.

More like herself.

She hooked her leg around Iris's, dragging Iris's thighs open even more, giving her more access to Iris's clit. Iris grabbed Stevie's wrist, her moans becoming whimpers.

Stevie had just started circling faster when Iris tugged Stevie's hand away.

"Hang on a sec," Iris said, her chest heaving. She kept her fingers on Stevie's wrist, both their hands resting on Iris's stomach.

Stevie leaned up on her elbow. "Are you okay?"

Iris laughed, blew out a long breath. "Yeah. Yeah, more than okay. I just . . ." She met Stevie's gaze, curled Stevie's hand to her chest. She searched Stevie's eyes, her own a little watery-looking. Her lower lip trembled, just barely, but Stevie saw it.

"Iris."

"I'm okay, I swear." Iris laughed again. "You were great. Incredible, okay? I just . . . I think that's probably enough, don't you?"

Stevie frowned. "You didn't want—"

"I did," Iris said. "And I was about to, I promise. But this . . . this is for you. And you did it. You seduced me." Iris winked at her then, even though her cheeks were flushed, her breathing a little uneven. "A-plus."

Stevie managed a smile as she took her hand back and waited to feel relieved. Triumphant, or confident and sexy. And yeah, some of all that was there, but mostly, she just felt . . .

She wasn't sure. Or maybe she was, and she just didn't want to name the sinking feeling in her chest, that letdown in the pit of her stomach.

"Okay," she said, nodding. "Yeah."

"You're a fabulous student," Iris said.

Stevie smiled at her. "I have a great teacher."

Iris nodded and sat up. She swung her legs off the other side of the bed, then rounded the end and grabbed her tank top from where it had landed on the floor. She slipped it on and then headed toward the bathroom. "I'm just going to wash up."

"Okay," Stevie said, but as Iris closed the door, she didn't feel like she'd made progress, taken another step toward her goal.

She didn't feel like that at all.

CHAPTER

TWENTY-ONE

IRIS PRESSED HER palms to the cool tile in the bathroom. It still wasn't enough to calm her down, so she flipped on the faucet, splashing cold water on her face over and over until she felt sufficiently quelled.

Drying her face, she stared at herself in the mirror, eyes still a little glassy from her and Stevie's . . . what?

Lesson?

That sure as shit didn't feel like a lesson.

It felt fucking amazing.

Fun and sexy and wild. Stevie teased her, controlled her, and Iris loved it. Then . . . god, Stevie's touch. Even above her underwear, it had been intense, perfect, pressing and circling in random patterns in a way that got Iris there so fast, the impending orgasm had taken her a bit by surprise.

She hadn't expected to come during these lessons.

She hadn't expected to be so *desperate* to come.

And she sure as hell didn't expect herself to stop the whole thing.

Iris wasn't sure what made her do it. But suddenly, the idea of crying out under Stevie's fingers, of Stevie seeing her that exposed and vulnerable . . . Iris couldn't do it. Which made absolutely zero sense because Iris always came. Every encounter she had—she made sure of it. Even when she barely remembered her partner's name, even when she was bored or tired or a little too buzzed from a couple of drinks. And she never felt like she was exposing some part of herself to her partner. Orgasms were simple science, a bundle of nerves reacting to stimuli.

Stevie shouldn't be any different.

But somehow, she was.

Iris told herself the instructive aspect simply threw her off. She'd certainly never given anyone actual sex lessons before, and she didn't want to come across as creepy, racking up orgasms while Stevie asked her if she was doing it right. What happened on that bed was for *Stevie*, and Iris had helped Stevie take control, which was clearly what Stevie needed to feel confident in bed.

Maybe Adri had never given her that before. Adri certainly radiated some big top energy, so it was fully possibly that when it came to sex, Adri and Stevie—

Iris closed her eyes. She didn't want to bring Adri into her thought process. The way Adri spoke to Stevie last night still made Iris want to light something on fire, but she also knew their sex life—and whatever messy and complicated thing was still going on with them—was none of her business.

All of which was why Iris stopped Stevie. She even wondered if Stevie could manage on her own from this point forward, meet someone for real, and Iris needed to concentrate on her book.

On the play.

On anything but the sound Stevie made when she'd touched Iris, that barely-there hitch in her breath that had made Iris so wet, she—

Iris squeezed her eyes shut again. This was just unfulfilled lust.

That's all it was. Once they got back to Oregon, Iris would return to Lush. Find someone to be with who was uncomplicated and nameless.

Someone Iris could easily forget.

She quickly plaited her hair into a braid and brushed her teeth, trying to think through the next scene in her book, maybe something with a moonlit beach walk or drive along Pacific Coast Highway.

Problem was, she couldn't get Tegan McKee's face clear in her mind, nor her adorably clumsy love interest, Briony. In the scenes that drifted through Iris's brain right now, there was only a honey-eyed woman, messy curls spiraling over her forehead, filling every single page.

———

BY THE TIME Iris got herself together and emerged from the bathroom, Stevie was gone. She ignored the way her stomach knotted at the empty room—they had a lot of work to do today, after all, and honestly, Iris couldn't wait to see Stevie as Benedick.

When Iris got downstairs, dressed in a rainbow-striped jumpsuit, the rest of the principal crew had arrived. Stevie was at the breakfast table, a cup of coffee in her hands, Adri sitting across from her, wearing a pair of clear-framed glasses and focused on her iPad.

Iris watched them for a few seconds, unsure of what she was looking for.

Camaraderie?

Love?

Lust?

Hell, Iris didn't know why she was even looking for anything. She cleared her throat, and several other people's eyes snapped to hers.

"Hey, you must be Iris!" a Black man with a septum piercing said. "I'm Peter. I'm playing Claudio."

"Oh, hey," Iris said, accepting his kiss on her cheek. "It's wonderful to meet you."

"And I'm Jasper," a white man said from near the coffeemaker. "Hero. And that's Satchi and Nina." He pointed to a Japanese American woman with a middle part and dyed purple tips, and a white woman with strawberry blond pigtails. "They're Don Pedro and Don John."

"Hi," Iris said, and they waved in greeting.

"How's the Jasmine Room, Satch?" Ren piped up from where they were cooking up a giant pan of scrambled eggs.

"Is that what it's called?" Satchi said, pouring herself some grapefruit juice. "I can never keep all the room names straight in this place."

"Yeah," Ren said, glancing at Adri, who was very pointedly not glancing at anyone. "Me neither."

"Ren," Stevie said softly.

"What?" Ren asked, turning off the burner.

Stevie sighed and sipped her coffee, her eyes connecting with Iris's for a split second before she looked away again.

"All right, what'd we miss?" Peter said, eyebrows lifted at Ren. "Drama already? We haven't even done a read-through."

"Speaking of," Adri said, standing and pushing her glasses up her nose. "Let's get started. Where the hell is—"

"I'm here, I'm here, thank god almighty, I'm here." A person with deep brown skin and a mop of dark curls blew into the kitchen. They wore a bright red crop top and cutoff jean shorts. "Sorry, my rideshare driver was too cute and I lost track of time."

Adri pursed her mouth. "Iris, this is Zayn. They're playing Leonato."

"Oh, fresh blood," Zayn said, winking a heavily lined eye at Iris. Iris couldn't help but laugh, and she liked Zayn immediately.

"Go easy on me," she said.

"Never," they said, but they were smiling.

"All right, let's all meet out by the pool for the read-through as soon as possible," Adri said, decidedly not smiling as she swept from the room. Iris wasn't sure if she was in full-throttle director mode or if she was simply in a bitchy mood.

Everyone gobbled up their food and started toward the back deck. Iris hesitated over her own eggs, waiting for Stevie.

"Hey," she said when it was just the two of them left. "You okay?"

Stevie nodded. Didn't look at her. "I'm fine."

"Okay," Iris said, feeling suddenly and strangely shy. "I just wanted to check, because—"

"I'm fine," Stevie said, her tone snappish. She sighed and pressed her fingers into her eyes. "Sorry. I'm just . . . Adri has me on edge."

"Are you sure that's all it is?" Iris asked, then immediately wished she could swallow the question down. She wasn't sure what she would do if the source of Stevie's worry was something else.

If it was *Iris*.

"I'm sure," Stevie said, but her smile didn't quite reach her eyes. She played with the hem of her shirt, a white fitted tee with a picture of Ruth Bader Ginsburg printed on the front.

"What can I do to help?" Iris asked.

Stevie shook her head, but then froze. She met Iris's gaze and inhaled slowly. "Take me out when we get back to Oregon?"

Iris frowned. "Take you out? Like on a date, or—"

"No. I mean, yeah, we can do that too for you. For your book. But I mean, I need to go *out*. Somewhere safe. A place where I can meet someone and try to . . . I don't know." Stevie's lower lip trembled just a little. She bit down on it and shrugged. "*Try*."

"Hey," Iris said, taking a step closer to her. "You don't have to rush this, you know."

"No, I know, but I do." Stevie shook her head. "I have to prove it to myself. Because no one else is going to see me as anything other than my anxiety until I do. Until *I* see myself that way."

Her voice was rising again, just like it had last night when she'd come into their room shaking.

"Okay," Iris took both of her hands in hers. "We can do that. We'll go to Stella's in Bright Falls next week. I know every queer person in town, and they all come out for line dancing night. Totally safe space."

"Line dancing?" Stevie asked.

"What, it's fun," Iris said. "I'll be with you the whole time. Plus, you don't have to dance that much if you don't want."

Stevie nodded, laughing, even as a tear slipped down her cheek. Iris couldn't resist swiping it way with her thumb, then pressing her forehead to Stevie's. It was an intimate gesture, but it felt so natural, so . . . easy. Stevie gripped Iris's waist, rubbing the jumpsuit's material between her fingers, and Iris felt herself relax. She breathed Stevie in, all clean cotton and sea salt, and her eyes had just drifted closed when Stevie lifted her head away.

"You're really good at this," Stevie said.

Iris frowned. "At what?"

"At being a fake girlfriend."

Stevie's voice was soft, almost like a question. Her eyes searched Iris's, and Iris searched right back because for a split second there, she'd forgotten.

Maybe she'd been forgetting for a while now.

Her throat went a little tight, her breath suddenly elusive. All the reasons she stopped Stevie this morning in bed came rushing back at her, clearer than ever, and every single one was terrifying.

Every single one represented everything that Iris Kelly was not.

She shook her head and laughed, dropped Stevie's hands and did a little twirl, followed by a dramatic bow. This was the Iris she knew. This was the Iris she understood.

The Iris everyone understood.

"Well, I am a fucking great actress," she said, "as you're about to find out in full."

Stevie didn't laugh. She just offered a half smile and nodded, then took Iris's hand and led her outside to join the rest of the cast.

AS IT TURNED out, Iris loved acting.

The cast sat around the pool under the morning clouds, bare legs dipping into the water, Adri tucked into a chair with her iPad, and they made a wild and unlikely love story come alive. Iris felt drunk with the feeling of slipping into someone else's psyche, thinking through their motivations and emotions. It was like writing, but in full color, swelling with all the flavors and sounds and feelings of real life.

The rest of the cast was talented as hell—Iris could see why Adri had cast each one of them as she did—and she especially enjoyed watching Peter and Jasper act out the young Hero and Claudio, with their innocent love and trusting personas. Shakespeare was brilliant, sure, but seeing his characters played out as queer, as identities the world had so often tried to stifle and beat down . . . well, it was powerful.

It was beautiful.

And then there was Stevie.

Iris had known she was good—like Stevie had said, Adri didn't cast anyone who wasn't—but she'd been unprepared for Stevie in full throttle. She approached Benedick in a way Iris never would've imagined—arrogant, for sure, but tender. Even shy. A woman—in their version, at least—who wore a mask for the world to hide a deeper fear of being seen.

Of being loved . . . and left.

Of course, the lines Stevie read didn't say any of that, but Iris felt it. She knew everyone else felt it too, a distinct hush falling over them all whenever Benedick had a longer speech.

As for Iris, she read Beatrice on instinct, a feeling that had started with that strange audition with Adri. Iris's Beatrice was angry, yes. Annoyed and a little bitter, but more than anything, exhaustion encapsulated her Beatrice, a bone-deep weariness from living in a world that constantly asked her to be someone she simply wasn't.

But love changed her.

"And Benedick," Iris read from act 3, scene 1. *"Love on; I will requite thee, taming my wild heart to thy loving hand."*

She glanced at Stevie then, who was sitting across from her near the shallow end, watching her with her mouth slightly open. Iris felt triumphant at first—she'd read the line softly, but a little angrily, a bullet wrapped in a feather. It felt right, perfect even, but then Adri interrupted the moment.

"Let's add a little more wistfulness there, Iris," she said, scribbling something on her iPad with her stylus. "Okay, on to scene 2. I think—"

"I disagree," Iris said.

Adri lifted a brow. "Oh?"

Iris cleared her throat. "I just think Beatrice isn't really sure about loving Benedick. Not yet. She says she'll give him her heart, but that scares her, even pisses her off that she's caught feelings, so she says it with a little . . . I don't know."

"Oomph," Zayn said.

"Yeah," Iris said, smiling at them. "Oomph."

Adri pursed her mouth. "This is Beatrice's first realization of love, Iris. It's important that it's infused with care. With a little bit of awe."

"I get that," Iris said. "But I don't think Beatrice is in awe here. I think she's fucking terrified."

"She says *I will requite thee*," Adri said.

"Because deep down she does crave love," Iris said, "not because she's not scared. She's talking to herself here. She knows what her heart wants, but she also knows her heart is wild, and she—"

"She wants to love Benedick, so she will," Adri said.

"It's really that simple for you?" Iris said. "I would think as a director, you'd press for a little more nuance in these characters, particularly as the play is queer and we're all—"

"What I want as a director," Adri said, her voice bordering on deadly, "is for my actors to take my notes and shut the fuck up about it."

Silence fell on the group. Iris stared Adri down, her chest swelling with a strange sense of accomplishment. She was right about Beatrice—she knew she was—but suddenly, she was very aware that Beatrice's emotional state in this scene had very little to do with why Iris had decided to go toe-to-toe with Adri.

"Well, here's what I want," Iris said, but before she could go any further, Stevie stood up so quickly, waves undulated through the pool as she whipped her legs free.

"I think we could all use a break, yeah?" she said, her eyes widening on Iris.

"Good idea," Ren said. They were sitting under the umbrella at the patio table, working on a laptop. They barely even broke their stride tapping at the keys as they spoke. "I'll make sure Adri gets a drink."

"I don't drink while I work," Adri said. She hadn't moved from her chair, her eyes still locked on Iris.

"Maybe you should," Iris said, fully aware that she was pushing her luck here. Next thing she knew, she'd be out on her ass with this play, but she couldn't seem to keep her mouth shut.

"Iris," Stevie said, appearing next to her. She slotted their fingers together. "Let's go for a walk."

"Drama, drama, drama," Peter said as Iris let Stevie lead her away.

"We knew it would be with those two," Nina said, chin-nodding toward Adri.

"I fucking love it," Zayn said.

"Will you all shut up?" Stevie said, pulling Iris toward the stairs that led to the beach. Her tone held no vitriol though—more like a sister fussing at her siblings.

She kept moving too, walking fast until she and Iris hit the rocky beach. Iris's bare feet sank into the sand, and she let Stevie yank her toward the water at nearly a running pace.

"Okay, slow down," Iris said once they'd reached the waves.

"Sorry," Stevie said, doing as Iris asked. They started walking north, their fingers still tangled together.

Iris sighed, looking back over her shoulder at the house. Adri stood at the stairs now, watching them, her green hair blowing in the wind.

"Does she want to get back together with you?" Iris asked. "Is that what this is all about?"

Stevie sighed. "What do you mean *this*? You started that argument."

"I simply voiced my artistic opinion."

Stevie snorted.

"Okay," Iris said. "Fine. I wanted to get under her skin. Doesn't mean I'm not right about Beatrice."

Stevie glanced at her. "No, I think you're right. But that's not the point. Why?"

"Why what?"

"Why get under her skin?"

Iris sniffed and looked out at the water. It was a dull gray today, the clouds overhead growing thicker and darker by the minute. The wind picked up, ruffling her clothes and pulling strands of hair from her braid.

"I don't know," Iris said, even though she did. The more she thought about that whole scene last night, the more it bothered her. Adri's bullying, the room switch, how upset Stevie had been when she'd come back from the beach. She didn't like the way Adri treated Stevie, plain and simple, but neither did she want Stevie to feel like she needed Iris to do anything about it.

"Really?" Stevie stopped, turned to face her. "Because you're acting like a jealous girlfriend."

Iris smirked. "Isn't that what I'm supposed to be?"

Stevie just stared at her for a moment, arms folded, her eyes like shovels trying to dig underneath Iris's cool expression.

"What?" Iris asked, starting to squirm. She'd lose in a staring contest against Stevie, every single time.

"Why don't you actually date, Iris?" Stevie asked softly.

"What? That was out of left field."

Stevie's gaze stayed with her. "I'm just curious. I know you write romance and you're a middle child and your friends love you a lot, but I don't know anything else about you. Not really. I'm just trying to understand."

Iris's heart sped up, a too-tender nudging under her ribs. "Why? It's not like we're—"

"Real, god, I know." Stevie lifted her arms, then let them slap against her side. "But a lot about this *is* real. My life. This play. Your book. Adri and me. You and me affect real shit, Iris, whether you want to admit it or not. And I just . . . I want to understand why you're picking fights with my ex and why you're even here with me at all. Why aren't you with someone else?"

Iris's clenched her jaw, looked away. It wasn't like her friends hadn't asked her this very question multiple times in the past year. *Why don't you try dating, Iris? You're so amazing, Iris. Anyone would be lucky to have you, Iris. It's their loss, Iris.*

But was it? When every romantic step Iris had ever taken left her alone and wondering what the hell she did wrong? Why she couldn't be different?

"Are you aromantic?" Stevie asked. "It's great if you are, I just want to—"

"No," Iris said. That would be so easy, wouldn't it? Especially with Stevie, who barely knew her, but no way in hell was she going to co-opt someone's actual identity. And she knew that wasn't it. "I like romance, okay? I'm interested in it. I just . . ."

Stevie waited, her eyes all soft and patient.

"I really wish you wouldn't look at me like that," Iris said.

"Like what?"

"Like I'm some sad sack because I've made a logical decision."

"Logical . . . decision," Stevie said slowly.

Iris nodded. "Look, I'm not going to get into my sad romantic history again. You already know about Jillian and Grant."

Stevie frowned. "So one asshole and a guy who really loved you but wanted different things means . . . what?"

"It's not just them, okay?" Iris said.

Her throat went a little thick, but she swallowed hard, kept talking. If she said just enough, Stevie would get it. She'd understand, agree with Iris even, and they could move the fuck on.

"It's my whole goddamn life," she said. "It's my blissfully-in-love parents constantly telling me to get serious, my mother's setups because she knows I can't be trusted to find someone decent on my own. It's every guy in high school making me feel like a toy to be passed around the soccer team. And I let them do it, because yeah, even back then, I liked sex, okay? Sue me."

"Iris, I—"

"And then, once I came out as bi in college?" Iris plowed ahead, eyes stinging. "Suddenly the fact that I liked sex became a huge moral failing. I was *greedy*. And, Jesus, the threesome requests. Not jokes, mind you, actual *requests* from guys who approached me in the student center, in the gym, in the middle of a fucking lecture hall, like I was nothing more than a business opportunity. And don't you dare tell me everyone who's bisexual deals with that—my best friend, Claire, came out in high school and never once got propositioned. Not once. And why? Because she's sweet. She's *relationship* material. I'm not serious, Stevie. I'm just the girl you fuck."

Iris's lungs ached and she looked away—she didn't want to see Stevie's expression, whatever it was. She swiped at the moisture leaking from her eyes. Fucking wind.

"And Jillian?" she said, folding her arms and gazing at the waves. "Jillian was just the icing on a really big-ass cake."

For a good while—felt like forever—Stevie didn't say anything. She was quiet for so long, Iris glanced at her to make sure she was still there, but she was, gazing out at the waves too.

"Was that enough information about me?" Iris asked. "Did I shock you good and proper?"

Stevie looked at her, smiled softly. "I think I owe you a romantic outing."

Iris frowned. "What?"

"You heard me. So far, we've only had one romance lesson."

Iris's cheeks warmed, the memory of slow-dancing with Stevie in her living room rushing back like a gust of wind. "You don't have to do that."

"It's part of our deal," Stevie said.

Iris had a sudden, inexplicable desire to say *fuck the deal*, but pressed her mouth closed.

Stevie gestured around them. "Plus, we *are* on a beach."

It was cloudy, and the ocean's waves were wild, roiling and peaking with foam.

"Like . . . a *Wuthering Heights* kind of beach, maybe," Iris said.

Stevie laughed. "Fair. But, okay, if you were Heathcliff and I was Catherine, what would you do right now?"

"Um, leave you the hell alone? Heathcliff was a horrible person. Have you even read *Wuthering Heights*?"

"You brought it up!"

"Yeah, as an antithesis to romance."

Stevie swiped a hand through her hair. "Okay, well, narcissistic heroes notwithstanding, we should walk."

"Walk."

"Hand in hand."

"Lazily, while we search for shells to leave on each other's pillows?"

Stevie held out her hand. "Now you're getting it."

Iris eyed Stevie's hand, hesitating only a second before slipping her fingers into Stevie's palm. The contact zinged up her arm, causing an eruption of goose bumps, which was ridiculous.

Romance was nothing but brain chemicals and some pretty words, a nice setting. That's all it was. A fiction brains told to hearts.

Still, Iris gave in to it, if just for Stevie's sake. They walked along the shore for a while, swinging their hands between them. They searched for shells, scooping up the unbroken pink-and-white treasures in the sand and slipping them into their pockets. They talked about nothing, about everything. Iris learned that Stevie was allergic to strawberries, a tragedy in her mind, and she told Stevie about Paper Wishes and how she had to close it down last year.

"Tell me about your book," Stevie asked. "The one you're writing. I already read up on *Until We Meet Again*."

Iris smiled. "You did?"

Stevie gave her a look. "Of course I did."

"Well," Iris said, her cheeks warming, "this new one is about . . ."

She hesitated, feeling suddenly shy about the turn her book had taken.

"What?" Stevie asked. "What's it about?"

Iris squeezed Stevie's fingers. "It's about a vintner and a wine critic."

Stevie's eyes went wide, and she stopped, twirling Iris around to face her, a grin on her mouth. "Like, your idea from the other night in your apartment?"

Iris nodded. "It was a good idea. And you really did help make it feel . . . real."

Stevie beamed, her amber eyes bright even under the darkening clouds. "I'm so glad. It *was* a good idea. I can't wait to read it."

Iris grinned back, but it fell away as the first drops fell from the sky. The shower quickly turned into a steady rain, soaking both of them within seconds.

"Oh my god," Stevie said, wiping her hair from her face. "I guess we should head back."

Iris nodded and started to turn back toward the house, then froze.

"Hang on," she said, taking Stevie's hand.

"You okay?" Stevie asked.

Iris nodded, rain sluicing down her face. She watched beads of water gather on Stevie's mouth, had the sudden urge to lick them away.

Instead, she pulled Stevie close.

"This feels like something we should do," she said. "Dance in the rain on the beach."

Stevie's mouth opened a little, but then she smiled. "Look at you."

"I'm a fast learner."

"I see that," Stevie said softly. "Is that going to be our thing—or your characters' thing? They dance all over the city, finding super weird and unique situations to dance?"

"Maybe it is," Iris said. "I'll have to give you some author credit here pretty soon."

Stevie waved a hand. "I'd settle for a mention in the acknowledgments."

"Done," Iris said, then wrapped her arm around Stevie's waist. She had no clue what had gotten into her, but this felt right. It felt like the next step, for Iris—or, really, Tegan—to initiate a little romance.

And Stevie came into her arms so willingly, so perfectly. Stevie was just an inch or two taller than Iris, just enough for Iris to press her mouth to Stevie's shoulder. One of Stevie's hands went into Iris's hair, and fuck if Iris didn't exhale at the touch.

Didn't swoon. Just a little.

And for now, she let herself feel it, the warm rain on her skin, the gentle press of Stevie's hips. She let herself soak it in, believe it, if not for her own love story, then for Tegan and Briony's.

⁓

THAT NIGHT, AFTER a grueling afternoon featuring a second read-through full of Adri's copious notes—and Iris playing as nice as she could for Stevie's sake—Iris came out of the bathroom to find Stevie already in her own bed, completely passed out.

Iris watched her for a second, something like disappointment clouding into her chest that they were clearly sleeping separately tonight.

She shook it off—of course they were sleeping separately—and braided her shower-wet hair into a side plait while walking toward her own bed. She pulled the covers back, ready to crash, then froze.

There, set right in the middle of her pillow, was a perfectly pink sea scallop shell.

CHAPTER

TWENTY-TWO

THE NEXT WEEK flew by in a whirl of shifts at Bitch's, Effie constantly grumping about how corporations had taken over Pride, and rehearsals.

Stevie only saw Iris at the Empress, which was probably a good thing. Malibu had been intense, and Stevie definitely needed some space to get her emotions in check.

She and Iris put on a good show at the theater—holding hands here and there, a kiss on the cheek between scenes, sitting together in the audience when Adri ran a scene that didn't feature them—but honestly, the line between what was real and what wasn't was growing increasingly fuzzy in Stevie's mind, and she wasn't sure how to clear it all up.

Iris, for her part, was radiant. A star. Not only as Beatrice on the stage, but with Stevie too, winking at her when they caught each other's eye across the theater, sliding her hand over Stevie's hair as she passed by, resting her head on Stevie's shoulder when they were on break or sat watching another scene.

Stevie hadn't really been prepared for all of that—the physical intimacy that came with making up a relationship. An intimacy that felt . . . emotional. But she knew emotions were tricky, easily misunderstood, easily mistaken for something else. So she forged on, playing the adoring girlfriend, meeting each touch from Iris with one of her own.

Still, by Friday's rehearsal, she was exhausted, the effort it took to play not one character, but two, sapping most of her energy. True, she slept like a rock at night, but now, the day she and Iris were supposed to go to Stella's in Bright Falls for line dancing, she felt like a wire pulled taut and fraying at the ends.

And the *Much Ado* scene they were working on didn't help matters.

"Again," Adri said, pacing the front of the stage, glasses on and her red lipstick perfectly in place even after three hours of rehearsal. "This scene is critical."

"We know," Stevie said. They were working on act 4, scene 1, where Benedick and Beatrice profess their love, followed by Beatrice's insistence that Benedick slay Claudio to uphold Hero's good name.

"Then do it right," Adri said. "This interaction is painful. The cruel world coming into focus. But it's also tender. *Feel* that."

Iris lifted a brow at Stevie and mouthed *feel that*, causing Stevie to cover her laugh with her hand. Still, Iris said nothing to Adri directly. She'd been shockingly docile with their director this week, and Stevie, to be honest, was grateful. She wasn't sure she could handle her own swirling emotions *and* Iris Kelly going full throttle at her ex.

"By my sword, Beatrice, thou lovest me!" Stevie said as Benedick, pouring as much longing as she could into her words.

"Do not swear and eat it," Iris bit back as Beatrice.

Their eyes locked, a pause neither of them planned clouding between them.

"Yes," Adri said as the tension thickened. "Good."

"I will swear by it that you love me, and I will make him eat it that says I love not you," Stevie went on.

"Will you not eat your word?" Iris asked, her question a mere whisper.

"With no sauce can that be devised to it," Stevie said. *"I protest I love thee."*

"Why then, God forgive me."

Iris's eyes shined with actual tears, but not overtly so. Her words were whispered, a rhythmic wave on her mouth. Stevie heard the hush in the audience, the rest of the principals watching.

"What offense, sweet Beatrice?"

Iris laughed, a beautiful, vulnerable sound. *"You have stayed me in a happy hour. I was about to protest I love you."*

They circled each other, their steps bringing them closer . . . closer, until Stevie looped an arm around Iris's waist and yanked her into an embrace. Iris gasped, hand flying to Stevie's shoulders and her pupils blown wide as Stevie tilted her head, ran a finger along Iris's jaw.

"And do it with all thy heart," Stevie whispered, her mouth an inch from Iris's. They watched each other, eyes glimmering under the lights, Iris's lips gently parted, so gorgeous and full and—

"Good, let's stop there," Adri said softly, breaking the spell. Stevie stepped back, releasing Iris slowly.

"Well, shit," Jasper said from the audience.

"Say that again," Zayn said, fanning himself. "I think I need a cold shower."

The principals laughed and Iris joined in, performing a cute little bow. Stevie waved them off, a blush creeping into her cheeks. Her heart was flying under her ribs, wings and feathers and all. Adrenaline wasn't unusual when she was on stage—she needed it to get through especially tricky scenes, but this . . . yeah, this wasn't just adrenaline. Her heart raced, sure, but there was also a distinct thrum between her legs she was trying to ignore, a shortness to her breath that had nothing to do with acting.

"Can we take five?" she asked, swiping her hair back from her face.

"Sure," Adri said, head tilted at Stevie. "You okay?"

"Fine," she said, and she was. She just needed a second to herself, a bit of fresh air. She jogged down the steps and grabbed her water bottle from her seat, then headed up the aisle toward the back of the theater.

She was nearly to the double doors, eyes scanning her phone for a distraction, when she heard her name.

"Stevie Scott."

The voice was low and firm. Familiar. Her head shot up, looking around for the source. There, sitting in a purple velvet seat against the back brick wall, was a Black woman with long box braids, one ankle propped on her knee.

She grinned at Stevie.

"Dr. Calloway," Stevie said. "Oh my god, what are you doing here?"

Dr. Thayer Calloway was Stevie's favorite theater professor at Reed. She was queer, brilliant, and had been the first person to make Stevie truly believe she *could*. Dr. Calloway was tough and demanding and made Stevie cry more than once, but she also made Stevie into the actor she was today.

Whatever kind of actor that might be.

"I'm in town for my sister's birthday," Dr. Calloway said. "Horrific affair at a karaoke bar downtown. I can't seem to get 'My Heart Will Go On' out of my head."

Stevie laughed. "It's so good to see you."

Dr. Calloway stood up, dapper in her butch style of dark jeans and a white T-shirt under a navy blazer, flat brown loafers on her feet.

"I'm actually on my way to the airport," she said, motioning toward her rolling suitcase, "but I couldn't resist stopping by to check on my favorite students and the Empress."

Stevie smiled. "We're still here."

"So I see." Dr. Calloway smiled. "And thriving."

"It's all Adri. She's very determined."

"It's not only Adri." Dr. Calloway's eyes narrowed on Stevie, a familiar gaze that always made Stevie simultaneously squirm and straighten her shoulders. Dr. Calloway had once stared at her for a full fifteen minutes in front of their entire class, asking her the same question about the character she was playing at the time over and over again—*What does Angelica want, Stevie?*—until Stevie gave an acceptable answer.

"That was quite impressive," Dr. Calloway said, motioning toward the stage. "A Benedick unlike one I've ever seen."

Stevie waved a hand. "It's noth—"

"It's not nothing, Stevie." She lifted a brow, and Stevie nodded.

"Right. Sorry. I mean, thank you, Dr. Calloway."

"Call me Thayer, please. We're not in school anymore."

"Thayer," Stevie said, then immediately blushed. Half the theater department had been in love with Thayer Calloway, lesbians and bi and pan girls flocking to her queer energy like hens to their feed, along with a few women who had always assumed they were straight. And Stevie had been no different.

"Anyway, I do want to say hello to Adri and Ren, but I'm glad I caught you alone first," Thayer said.

"Oh?"

Thayer smiled. "I'm in New York now, as you probably know."

"I do. How's it going?"

"Very well, actually. I've just been asked to direct *As You Like It* for Shakespeare in the Park this summer. At the Delacorte."

Stevie's eyes widened. Half of Stevie's dramatic education at Reed had been studying actors on the famous Central Park Delacorte stage, everyone from Anne Hathaway to Meryl Streep to Rosario Dawson.

"Oh my god," she said. "That's wonderful. Congratulations, Dr.—Thayer. That's a dream come true."

Thayer smiled, showing all of her teeth, dimples pressing into her cheeks. "It is. And I want to offer you a role."

Stevie froze, her mouth dropping open without her permission. It was as though the letters were particles in the air, slowly coming together to form words, sentences.

"Wait, what?" Stevie finally asked.

"You heard me, Stevie."

"I . . . I'm not sure—"

"Before you say you can't," Thayer said, holding up her hand. "Think about it. I want you to play Rosalind."

"Rosalind. As in—"

"The lead."

Stevie's head spun. "I don't understand. There must be a hundred other people you could cast as Rosalind. Famous people. Freaking Natalie Portman."

Thayer nodded. "True. But I don't want Natalie Portman. I want what I just saw on that stage. I want what I saw hints of even back when you were eighteen years old and could barely look me in the eyes. I want Stevie Scott."

This wasn't real. This had to be a dream. "I just . . . I'm overwhelmed."

"I understand that," Thayer said. "I'm a bit overwhelmed myself. I honestly walked in here hoping to say hello to Adri. And only Adri. I'm surprised to find you still in Portland."

Stevie's mouth opened, but nothing came out.

"Anyway, as soon as I saw you up there, I knew I was looking at my Rosalind," Thayer said. She took a manila folder out of her messenger bag and started flipping through the papers inside. "Somewhere in here is a rehearsal schedule, dates the show will run, all those details. I'll email it to you as well, but I want you to have this now. Oh, hell, just take the whole thing."

She held out the folder and Stevie took it, her hand already trembling. She could barely process what Thayer was saying, much less what it meant.

"I'll need an answer by September first," Thayer said, "before our auditions officially start. I can help with housing, board, all those details, so don't let that hold you back. Please promise me you'll think about it."

"I . . ."

"Is that Thayer Calloway?" Ren's voice echoed from the stage, where they'd just emerged from backstage draped in various fabrics and materials. They held their hand up to their eyes, shading the lights to see to the back of the theater. "Holy shit, it is!"

"What?" Adri said, leaping up from where she was sitting in the front row. "Where?"

"Hi, you two," Thayer said, waving.

Ren jumped off the stage, all but hurling themself up the aisle, followed closely by Adri.

"Think about it," Thayer said one more time, squeezing Stevie's arm before Ren and Adri reached them.

The three of them immediately fell into catching up, Adri telling Thayer about the fundraiser dinner that will go along with the play, both Ren and Adri losing their minds when Thayer mentioned Shakespeare in the Park.

"I've just asked Stevie here to come work for me in New York," Thayer said.

Stevie closed her eyes for a split second while the news landed.

"Holy. Shit," Ren said, turning to her. "Yes. She'll do it."

"Ren," Stevie said.

"You're seriously considering *not*? Stevie."

"I don't know," Stevie said, panic rising in her chest. She glanced at Adri, who just stared at her, her red mouth open in a tiny circle.

"Stefania Francesca Scott," Ren said, folding their arms. Colorful scarves and swaths of fabric fluttered with the motion. "I swear to god."

"Leave her alone, Ren," Adri said.

Ren's eyes narrowed. "For real, Adri? You're that desperate to keep her under your thumb that you'd talk her out of—"

"I'm not talking her out of anything," Adri said. "I just said—"

"We know what you said," Ren said, "and I—"

"Shut up, both of you," Stevie said. Tears filled her eyes—embarrassment that her friends were having this conversation in front of their professor, shame that she couldn't just say yes like she knew she should. But that's what Ren never got—Stevie could always say yes to everyone, anything. It was always the easier path.

Except this one.

This *yes* came with consequences, a whole slew of actions and decisions that made Stevie feel like she was drowning.

And Adri . . . Stevie couldn't even look at her.

"Stevie," Ren said, "I'm just trying to help."

"Well, you're not," she said, tears spilling over.

"Okay, let's take a breath," Thayer said, who was well versed with Stevie's anxiety. Still, Stevie highly doubted the idea of an actor losing their shit over nothing on the Delacorte stage was appealing.

"I'm sorry, Dr. Calloway," Stevie said, then turned away, shoving open the doors that led into the lobby. She didn't slow down until she was outside, the late June sun too bright and strong, too sure.

She dropped the folder near the door and tried to breathe, but it felt like working to shove a ship down a drain. She heard her lungs rasping, passersby looking at her funny as they went on with their day. She waved off their concerned looks, retreated under the Empress's awning.

Breathe.

Fucking breathe.

Stevie closed her eyes, inhaled, but shit, she was spiraling. Full-on spiraling. She thought about calling for Ren, who knew how to help, but the idea just made the panic surge even more, because why the hell should Stevie be panicking this much about her friends pushing her into a once-in-a-lifetime opportunity?

Or not pushing, as the case may be.

But it wasn't that—it wasn't even Ren's insistence or Adri's clear reticence. It was how they spoke over her, as though she couldn't be trusted to do anything on her own.

And fuck, the idea of New York scared her so much, maybe she couldn't.

"Stevie?"

Iris's voice.

"Shit," Stevie managed to croak. She didn't want Iris to see her like this. She didn't want—

"Oh," Iris said as Stevie slumped against the Empress's facade. "Oh shit, okay. Um."

Stevie tried to wave a hand, communicate that she was fine, but she wasn't sure she was. Iris had done so much for her already, she didn't want Iris to regret it.

The thought was quick and cold, like ice flash-freezing over a lake.

She didn't want Iris to regret *her.* When this was all said and done, when they'd fake broken up, and Iris walked out of her life, Stevie didn't want . . . she didn't want Iris to—

"Look at me."

Iris.

Right in front of Stevie, so close, Stevie could see little gold flecks in her green eyes. Her hands were on Stevie's face, cupping her cheeks, eyes locked on hers.

"Look at me," she said again. "Focus on my freckles. You see them?"

Stevie managed a nod. She sounded like an asthmatic hippo right now, her breathing tight and raspy.

"Count them," Iris said. "Count my freckles. Start with that one under my left eye."

Stevie tried to swallow, tried to focus on the dots on Iris's face. She locked in on the freckle Iris was talking about and felt her attention snap in place. She recognized that freckle. "It's . . . it's blue."

Iris smiled. "Good. Do I have any other blue freckles?"

Stevie's eyes roamed Iris's face, searching. There were freckles in all shades of brown, from tan to dark espresso. They spilled over her nose, cheeks, over her eyelids and even dotted her lips.

They were beautiful.

But there was only one blue freckle, dark, like the deepest parts of the ocean.

"No," Stevie said, meeting Iris's eyes.

"You're right," Iris said softly. "It's one of a kind."

They'd stayed like that for a few minutes. Quiet and close. Stevie's heart still raced, her stomach like some creature stretching its wings, but soon her chest opened up, air flowing smoothly.

But Iris was still close.

So close.

And she smelled like orange blossom and mint, her hair so dark red it matched her ruby lipstick. A tiny braid twisted from her temple to loop over her shoulder, and Stevie had the urge to reach out and run her fingers down the plait.

So she did.

She took the braid in her hand, slid her thumb slowly down the silky strands. Iris's eyes stayed on Stevie's, the air between them tangling. Stevie's breath picked up again, but this time, it wasn't from panic. Her lungs were clear, her thoughts slowing down . . . down . . . until the only thing she could think about was Iris.

Right here.

So lovely and sweet. Stevie doubted Iris would ever use either of those words to describe herself, but she was. Iris, for all her bravado and boldness, was *sweet*. She cared for Stevie in a way Stevie had never really experienced, talking to her instead of at her. Letting her call the shots.

But that was all part of their deal.

Wasn't it?

"Stevie," Iris said softly. Her gaze slipped down to Stevie's mouth and back up, and that was all it took.

Stevie leaned in, inch by inch, waiting for Iris to pull away, but she didn't. And when Stevie slid her hands around Iris's waist and pulled her close, Iris released a tiny sigh that made Stevie feel wild and unhinged.

She pressed her lips to Iris's, softly at first, but her want soon took over. She opened her mouth and Iris opened back, her hands sliding from Stevie's face and into her hair. Their tongues touched, tangled, and when Iris pulled on Stevie's hair a little, Stevie let out a tiny moan that didn't even embarrass her. Iris tasted like citrus and cinnamon all at once, like summer and winter colliding. It was intoxicating.

She was intoxicating.

"Iris," Stevie said against her mouth. Just that. Just her name, because that was all she could think of right now.

"I know," Iris said, then kissed her again, tugging on Stevie's lower lip in way that made the space between her legs throb. She'd just slid her hands under Iris's tight black T-shirt, when she heard someone clear their throat.

They both reared back, eyes meeting in shock for a split second before turning toward the sound.

Adri stood there, her expression unreadable. "We need to get back to work," she said.

Stevie nodded, releasing Iris and straightening her own shirt. "Sure. Yeah. We'll be right there."

Adri smiled tightly, then disappeared into the theater.

Iris stepped back even farther from Stevie, then wiped a hand down her mouth.

"I guess we should get back inside," Stevie said.

Iris nodded. She wouldn't meet her eyes. "Yeah. Of course."

They started toward the door, and Stevie paused to pick up the folder Thayer had given her.

"What's that?" Iris asked, opening the door and holding it wide.

Stevie shook her head and tucked the folder under her arm. "Nothing. It's nothing at all."

CHAPTER

TWENTY-THREE

IRIS PUSHED OPEN Stella's giant oak door, scents of beer and sweat and perfume swirling around her as she and Stevie stepped inside.

Stella's was packed for its monthly line dancing night, but then again, it always was. A favorite among the small queer community in Bright Falls, the crowd was even more robust tonight, as the bar was one of the few businesses in town that actually decorated for Pride. Rainbow flags fluttered all around the large room, and the menu boasted special cocktails to represent the Pride flag, everything from mojitos for green and a color-changing martini for purple to something called Adios, Motherfucker, which was pretty much a blue Long Island iced tea.

"Iris!" Claire called from the back corner, standing up and waving. She had on a plaid flannel shirt tied at her waist and light blue denim cutoffs. "Over here!"

Iris slipped her hand into Stevie's and led her toward her friends. It was slow going, the press of bodies thick, and Iris took her time to smile at acquaintances and get herself in check.

She and Stevie hadn't talked much since their kiss at the Empress. They'd finished rehearsal—Adri had been in a particularly foul mood—and then Iris had pretty much run out of the theater and to her car, a quick *I'll see you tonight* her only goodbye.

When Stevie had arrived at Iris's apartment that evening, they'd only discussed how the flannel shirt Stevie had paired with a vintage Nirvana tee, black cutoffs, and black combat boots was the closest thing she had to anything country western. Iris had offered a cowboy hat to complete the ensemble and . . . well . . .

Stevie looked adorable.

Sexy, if Iris were letting herself think about the word, which she wasn't, because tonight was all about helping Stevie find someone to . . . well.

Iris took a deep breath, trying to smooth out the undulations in her stomach. Before they'd left Iris's, she'd thought about bringing up Stevie's panic attack at the Empress, what had put her in such a state. Iris was worried, sure, but she was also terrified that conversation would lead to what happened after, the kiss that still made Iris's knees feel weak when she thought about it.

The kiss that had nothing to do with putting on a show for Stevie's friends or practicing anything.

It was real.

Or was it?

Iris's brain couldn't make sense of it, couldn't figure out what she even felt about it. Stevie had been upset and Iris helped. Sure, they were attracted to each other. Of course they were. And of course, with all this time they spent together, they were getting to know each other better.

Care about each other.

Wasn't that to be expected? It didn't *mean* anything. Iris cared about a lot of people.

"Almost there," Iris said now as she looked over her shoulder at Stevie. Stevie smiled back at her, the straw-colored cowboy hat Iris had given her tilted over one eye, her shaggy curls coiling just over her shoulders.

Fuck, she looked cute.

Iris tipped her own dark brown hat at her—maybe *more* drama would simmer down her blood a bit. Hell, it had always worked in the past.

Iris is acting a bit emotional, oh shit, what do we do?

Iris always knew—more laughter, more jokes, more *Iris*. That was what everyone expected from her. Even Stevie, who laughed and shook her head, a beautiful blush creeping onto her creamy cheeks.

Iris squeezed her hand and broke through the crowd to where her friends were already a drink into the night.

"You both look amazing!" Claire said, reaching out for Iris and kissing her on the cheek.

"I know," Iris said, releasing Stevie and doing a little twirl, showing off her short, lace-ruffled skirt with the denim waist paired with a pair of authentic red cowboy boots and a red bandanna-patterned crop top.

"Don't give her another compliment, I beg you," Delilah said. She was lounging in the corner of the booth, dressed in her quintessential goth colors—a dark burgundy tank and black jeans.

"Shut it, Morticia," Iris said, flipping her off, but Delilah just smiled, tipping her bourbon in Iris's direction. Iris blew her a kiss.

"Stevie, good to see you," said Astrid, who was dressed in a vanilla-white tank and dark jeans, but at least she had on a cowboy hat.

"Hey," Stevie said. "Nice to see you all again."

"How's the play going?" Jordan asked. She had on a button-up with tiny green cacti printed all over it, one hand on the back of Astrid's neck, fingers playing in her hair.

"Good," Stevie said. "Iris is amazing."

"Of course she is," Claire said. "Sit, sit!"

"We're going to get a drink first," Iris said, "but here, honey, hold my purse." She tossed her fringed bag at Delilah, who caught it deftly, then looped it over her own tattooed shoulder.

"Finders keepers," she said.

Iris just laughed, then turned and guided Stevie toward the bar. She nearly took her hand again, but that might not prove a very wise move if every eligible queer person in Stella's thought she and Iris were together, so she settled for a gentle press between Stevie's shoulders.

"Club soda?" Iris asked once they reached the bar.

Stevie smiled at her. "Yeah."

Iris ordered Stevie's drink, along with an Adios, Motherfucker for herself, because why the hell not. Long Island iced tea was never a wise decision for anyone, in Iris's opinion, but tonight, she honestly didn't give a shit.

"Okay, let's strategize," she said once she had a drink in hand. She took a long pull, willing the liquor to fortify her for this. Maybe she'd even find someone she liked too—she hadn't had sex in way too long and god knew all this . . . whatever she and Stevie were doing had her sufficiently charged.

Granted, she knew every queer person in Bright Falls . . . all, like, ten of them, if you didn't count her own motley crew. Only a few who identified as women or nonbinary were even available in terms of couple-hood, and her eyes scanned the room for them.

"Okay, yeah," Stevie said, sipping her soda. Her voice trembled a bit.

Iris glanced at her. "You sure you want to do this?"

Stevie nodded vigorously, but her eyes were wide, her mouth shaking a little like she was working on her breathing.

"Stevie," Iris said, touching her elbow. "You don't have to—"

"Yes, I do."

Iris swallowed, something pulling tight in her chest. "Okay," she said softly. "Then let's do it."

Stevie met her gaze, both of them holding there for a split second before Iris forced her eyes away. A country song started up over the sound system and a squeal of excitement pulsed through the crowd. Out in the middle of the room, where tables had been pushed to the edges, dancers gathered on the dusty hardwoods, immediately falling into a line dance Iris recognized from the last time she'd come.

"Wow, everyone really knows how to line dance here," Stevie said.

Iris laughed. "Yeah, they take it pretty seriously. Small town, not a lot to do."

Stevie nodded, her amber eyes taking in the kicks and shuffles, the thumbs tucked into belt buckles. Iris saw Jordan and Astrid out there, Jordan really playing it up while Astrid, of course, performed a perfect routine. Iris made it her evening goal to get Delilah, whose New York City side refused to dance to country music unless it was a slow song with Claire, onto the dance floor.

Iris leaned back against the bar and was just about to suggest she and Stevie give it a try, just to loosen Stevie up a bit, when Iris saw her.

Jenna Dawson.

Jenna was pretty—had that small-town-girl air about her—with stick-straight, glossy brown hair that tumbled halfway down her back. She had on a blue-checked button-up tied at her curvy waist and cutoffs that showed off her lovely thick thighs. Jenna had moved to Bright Falls about five years ago and taught AP Chemistry at the high school, so she was smart *and* beautiful.

She was also extremely gay and single.

Iris watched her for a second, shuffling on the dance floor in a way that was both adorably clumsy and sexy. Jenna laughed with her best friend, Hannah Li—also super gay, but in a relationship—her demeanor sweet and approachable.

She was perfect.

Jenna was kind and patient—had to be to teach in public schools these days—and Iris knew Stevie would be safe with her . . . maybe even beyond a one-night stand, though Jenna wasn't one who turned up her nose at hookups. Iris had never made a move on Jenna herself—sleeping casually with Bright Falls residents was a recipe for disaster—but Iris had seen Jenna at Lush once or twice, both of them laughing across the room at each other as they hit on other people.

So, yeah, Jenna was perfect.

And yet, here Iris was, standing stock-still, her drink sweating in her hand, trying to get those exact words to settle on her tongue.

She inhaled, took another gulp of her Motherfucker. The alcohol zinged through her blood as she looked at Stevie, that open expression on her lovely face as she searched the room.

Stevie wanted this. For whatever reasons she'd kissed Iris earlier at the Empress, they didn't matter. Iris didn't want them to matter anyway . . .

She shook her head, took another large swallow of blue.

"Okay," she said, setting her drink on the bar, "let's go."

"Where are we—oh, okay."

Iris took Stevie's arm and pulled her out on the dance floor, weaving between everyone until she was next to Jenna and Hannah.

"Hey, you two!" Iris called over the music.

"Hey, Iris," Jenna said, smiling, then her eyes slid to Stevie, which was perfect.

It was perfect . . . right?

Everything was just perfect.

Iris's stomach clenched, but she forged ahead. "This is my friend, Stevie," she said. "She lives in Portland and is an actor. An amazing actor."

"Hey," Hannah said calmly, but Iris caught the nudge she gave Jenna's arm.

"Hey, Stevie," Jenna said. "I'm Jenna."

"Hey . . . hey," Stevie said. "I'm Stevie. But Iris already said that." Jenna laughed. "She did."

And just like the queer goddesses deemed it so, the quick-paced tune faded into a slow song, all mandolin and sultry twang. The crowd dispersed, coupling up, and Hannah drifted toward her partner, Alexis, by the jukebox.

"Ask her to dance," Iris said out of the corner of her mouth.

"What?" Stevie said, then startled. "Oh shit, right."

Jenna laughed again, and Stevie blushed, and it was all like something right out of a rom-com.

"I'd love to," Jenna said, before Stevie could even get the question out.

"Great," Iris said. "I'm going to get another drink." She nudged Stevie toward Jenna, then whispered in her ear, "You're in control, don't forget it."

Then she walked away, putting as much space between herself and the match she'd just made as quickly as she could. She didn't head to the bar though. Instead, she beelined for her friends, needing a minute of safe reprieve before she figured out what the hell to do with the rest of her night.

But once she fought her way through the happy couples, reprieve was most definitely not what she found. Instead, she faced a group of four queer women who were staring her down with incredulous looks on their faces.

"What?" she asked, plopping down next to Claire and guzzling half a glass of water. The Motherfucker was doing its work, but that work was a bit nauseating, if she was being honest.

"What the fuck was that?" Delilah asked, ever the subtle one of their group.

"What do you mean?" Iris asked.

"She means," Claire said, an appalled expression on her face, "why did you just set up your girlfriend with Jenna Dawson?"

"She's not my girlfriend," Iris said.

"Which is stupid," Claire said, the pitch of her voice rising. "You clearly like each other. She's all you ever talk about in the group chat."

Iris winced but smoothed it out quickly. "We're together all the time because of the play."

"Perfect situation to develop feelings," Jordan said.

Iris sighed. "Look, I'm helping Stevie, okay? She's a little nervous when it comes to hookups, so—"

"I don't think you're being honest with yourself, Iris," Astrid said.

Iris gritted her teeth. Astrid had spent years pretending her entire life was perfect, and ever since she liberated herself from a job she hated—not to mention her mother's expectations for what her life should look like—she had an extremely sensitive bullshit meter. Hardly anyone could pull a frown without Astrid probing them to be *honest with themselves.*

"I'm being perfectly honest," Iris said. "You all know I don't—"

"Date," all four women said in unison.

Iris pursed her mouth. "Good. We're all on the same page, then."

"What we don't understand is *why*," Claire said, then she scooted closer to Iris, that maternal look on her face she got whenever her daughter, Ruby, had a meltdown. "Honey, I know you've been hurt. You've had some real assholes in your life, but that's got nothing to do with you."

Iris laughed sarcastically, then grabbed Claire's wine and took a swig. She'd heard this all before. More than once in the last year, Claire had tried to have this conversation with her, sometimes with Astrid in tow, sometimes alone. But they didn't get it. They didn't understand what it was like to realize the common denominator to all her shitty relationships was, in fact, *her.*

It had everything to do with Iris.

"Claire, don't," she said. "Please. Just let me sit here and drink, okay?"

"Why do you feel the need to drink if you're fine with Stevie and Jenna?" Astrid asked.

"Seriously?" Iris said, looking to Delilah for support.

"Don't look at me," Delilah said, presenting her palms. "I'm on their side."

"So there are sides now," Iris said.

"In terms of you self-sabotaging everything good in your life, yeah," Delilah said.

Iris's mouth dropped open. She didn't fucking self-sabotage everything good. She worked hard. She loved her friends—well, maybe not so much right now, but usually. She'd built a business from the ground up and she was smart enough to know when it was time to walk away from that business. She put herself out there with her writing, and it had paid off. She was the lead in a play, and she was giving it her all. But now, just because she didn't want to lock herself into a relationship that would eventually end, she was self-sabotaging.

Well, fuck that.

"You know what?" she said, grabbing her bag from where Delilah had laid it on the booth. "I'm gonna go."

"Honey, no, don't," Claire said. "All we're saying is—"

"I know what you're saying," she said. "Loud and clear, okay?"

She got out of the booth before anyone could say anything else awful and shoved herself into the dancing crowd. She scanned the floor for Stevie, quickly finding her sitting with Jenna at a table, deep in conversation.

She watched them for a second and . . . yeah. All the signs were there. They were leaning close, only a few inches between their faces. Jenna's hands crossed the middle line of the table, well into Stevie's space, and every now and then, as though to emphasize something she said, Jenna placed a finger on Stevie's wrist.

And Stevie . . . she was smiling. Laughing, even. She looked relaxed and beautiful and perfect and something in Iris's chest started to ache.

Stevie looked up and caught her eye.

Smiled.

And Iris smiled back. She nodded toward the door, then offered Stevie a thumbs-up in question.

Stevie's smile faded, but only for a second. Iris watched her throat work and could almost feel Stevie's deep breath. But then Stevie nodded, presenting her own thumbs-up in return.

Okay, then, Iris thought. Mission accomplished.

And without another glance in Stevie's direction, she turned away, pushed open Stella's heavy door, and left.

CHAPTER

TWENTY-FOUR

STEVIE WATCHED IRIS leave, a sinking in her stomach she couldn't explain.

"Hey, you okay?" Jenna asked, one of her fingers tapping Stevie's arm.

Stevie looked back at her. She really was pretty. And sweet. So sweet. When they'd danced, she'd held Stevie tenderly, asked her questions about acting. It wasn't the wild first encounter she'd had with Iris, but that was probably a good thing, as that hadn't exactly turned out well.

No, Jenna was calm. She was slow and safe, and Stevie knew she was the perfect person to be with right now. Maybe even date. Stevie could see it—going to dinner with Jenna, holding hands in an ice cream shop, watching rom-coms on a rainy Saturday afternoon.

Jenna made sense.

"Yeah," Stevie said.

"Do you want to dance again?" Jenna asked as another slow song came on.

"Absolutely," Stevie said.

They stood and ambled out to the dance floor hand in hand. Stevie took a deep breath and pulled Jenna close. She led the dance, trailing her fingers up Jenna's back and down to her waist before settling on her lovely wide hips. Jenna rested her head against Stevie's, her fingers in her hair, pulling gently.

God, it felt good.

Stevie closed her eyes, her breath picking up, but not in a panicked way. She turned her head just a little, so Jenna's mouth grazed her cheek, then kept turning when she heard Jenna's own breath speed up.

"Okay?" she asked when their mouths were close, and Jenna nodded. Then Stevie kissed her. It was delicate and soft and perfect, and Stevie was absolutely not thinking about anyone else in this moment.

Not a wild redhead.

Not a loud and tender Beatrice.

Not a fake girlfriend with a single blue freckle.

"Do you want to go back to my place?" Jenna asked when they'd parted.

Stevie blinked, her stomach fluttering. But yes. Yes, of course she wanted to go back to Jenna's place. That's what all of this was for, and goddammit, she didn't want to face Iris at rehearsal tomorrow and tell her she'd chickened out. So she nodded and Jenna smiled and before Stevie knew it, the two were walking down a cobbled Bright Falls street holding hands, reaching Jenna's apartment in a couple of blocks.

"This is me," Jenna said, unlocking a unit on the third floor. The building was cute, only three stories tall, and was on the other side of Main from Iris's place.

"Great," Stevie said, stepping into the small space. It was clean and modern, all gray walls and furniture, bright splashes of coral and aqua pillows and artwork here and there. A calico cat rubbed against Stevie's legs.

"Oh, that's Nyla. You're not allergic, are you?" Jenna asked.

"No," Stevie said, leaning down to scratch the cat's head.

"Let me just feed her and then I'm all yours," Jenna said as she disappeared into the kitchen. "Want something to drink?"

"Water is fine," Stevie said, inching into the living room. Her palms were a little sweaty and she wiped them on the back of her shorts, then took off her hat and set it on the couch.

"Here you go," Jenna said, handing her a glass of water.

"Thanks." She took a single sip, eyes locked on Jenna, and then set the drink on an end table before reaching out and circling an arm around her.

"Oh," Jenna said, laughing, her hands going to Stevie's arms. "Down to business, then?"

"Yeah," Stevie said, her voice only a little shaky. "If that's okay."

"More than okay," Jenna said, then leaned forward and kissed Stevie.

Stevie gripped her hips and kissed her back. She tasted delicious, like wine and sun, and she definitely knew how to use her tongue. It was a perfect kiss, a kiss that promised other things. Stevie's stomach gave a tiny, barely-there lurch, so she focused.

She visualized what she wanted to do with Jenna, painted the picture in her mind, the slow peeling off of clothing, laying Jenna down on her bed and pushing her legs apart, pressing her mouth to the warmth between her thighs.

Making her pant and scream and come.

But in her mind, when she lifted her head to smile at her lover, it wasn't Jenna.

It was a wild redhead.

"Fuck," she said, pulling back.

"Are you okay?" Jenna asked, worry creasing her brows together.

Her fingers still rested on Jenna's hips. She squeezed her eyes shut and nodded. Tried to get back into this moment, not imagined ones.

"Hey," Jenna said softly. "It's okay. We don't have to do this if you don't want to."

Stevie shook her head, tears already swelling.

Fuck, fuck, fuck.

"We could just talk," Jenna said, so goddamn sweetly.

But Stevie didn't want sweet.

At least, not Jenna's kind of sweet. Maybe, at another time in her life, another world, Stevie and Jenna would've made sense. In fact, Stevie knew they would, even if just for one night.

"I'm sorry, Jenna," she said, dropping her hands from Jenna's hips and taking a step back.

Jenna's expression fell. "Oh."

"You're amazing," Stevie said. "You really are, but I have to go."

CHAPTER

TWENTY-FIVE

IRIS HAD JUST settled on her couch with a bowl of popcorn and a bottle of wine—no glass required, thanks very much—when a knock sounded on the door.

She groaned and let her head fall against the back cushion. Should've known her friends wouldn't let her get away with storming out of Stella's like a toddler.

Another knock.

She heaved herself off the couch. "You know, Claire," she called to the door, "sometimes, a good friend doesn't go after the recalcitrant redhead. Sometimes, you leave the recalcitrant redhead the fuck alone and let her—"

But her words were cut off when she flung open the door, ready to act like a real pain in the ass, to find Stevie in her hallway. She was out of breath like she'd run all the way here, her eyes glossy and locked on Iris.

"Stevie," she said. "What . . . are you okay? What happened?"

Stevie stepped into Iris's space, no hesitations, hands sliding over her hips. She kicked the door closed with her boot, pulled Iris closer.

"You happened," she said before crushing her mouth to Iris's.

Iris barely had time to be surprised, barely had time to think, before her body reacted. Her arms went around Stevie's shoulders, fingers sinking immediately into her hair.

And shit, she was tired of fighting it.

Tired to telling herself she didn't want this.

Stevie turned them around, backed Iris against the door, one thigh immediately slotting between Iris's legs. And fuck, Iris was already wet, her clit throbbing. Stevie devoured her mouth, pulling at her lower lip before dipping her tongue inside. She grabbed the bottom of Iris's crop top and lifted, exposing Iris's lacy bra to her hands.

"I fucking love your tits," Stevie said, and shit, all Iris could do was moan as Stevie's thumbs swiped over her nipples, seeking and pinching. Iris tugged at Stevie's shirt too, and soon half their clothes were on the ground. Stevie didn't have on a bra, and Iris was dying to get her nipples into her mouth, but Stevie would barely let her move, pinning her against the door with her thigh, hands sliding down Iris's ass and pressing her leg harder against Iris's center.

"Fuck," Iris said, the feeling zinging straight through her sleep shorts and underwear.

Stevie laughed against her shoulder, letting Iris go for a second. Iris whimpered in protest, but then Stevie pulled Iris's shorts down her legs, nudging Iris's feet to kick them free. Iris obeyed every request, already half dizzy when Stevie resumed her position, palming her ass again and grinding her thigh against Iris's pussy.

"Oh god," Iris said, tilting her head back. Stevie pressed her mouth to Iris's throat, teeth scraping her skin. Iris kept one hand deep in Stevie's curls, her other finding its way between Stevie's legs.

"Shit," Stevie said when Iris found her target, burying her face in Iris's neck. She ground Iris down on her thigh even harder, Iris pumping her hips for more friction.

Fuck, she was so close.

Stevie moaned as Iris pressed the heel of her hand to the seam of Stevie's shorts, moving her palm up and down, getting her fingers into the mix too. Stevie met her every thrust, and soon there was nothing but humping and moaning right there against Iris's front door.

"God, yeah," Iris said, free hand clawing at Stevie's shoulder. "Please."

"Please what?" Stevie said against her throat.

"Make me come."

"Beg me."

Stevie stilled her grinding and Iris practically went feral with need.

"Fuck, Stevie, please, make me come. Make me come now."

Stevie licked her throat then, pushed her own hips into Iris's hand, groaning as she fucked Iris with her thigh. Iris could feel how wet she was, soaking through her underwear and sliding over Stevie's skin. The smell of sex clouded between them, and Iris had never loved anything more.

She grunted in frustration, rolling her hips for a new angle, rotating her palm over Stevie. The feeling swelled, growing from her lower belly and spreading to her pussy, her fingers and toes.

"Oh my god, yeah," she said, her orgasm rushing through her. She cried out, gripping Stevie's hair and yanking, which seemed to be all Stevie needed too. Stevie locked up for a second, groaning into Iris's neck as she came, hips jolting against Iris's fingers.

They stayed pressed together for a second, both breathing heavily. Iris had just released Stevie, ready to laugh, and make some sort of sex joke, when Stevie laced her fingers with Iris's and started pulling her toward the bedroom.

"I don't think I'm done with you yet," Stevie said, and Iris was wet all over again.

"That wild frenzy back there wasn't enough?" Iris asked, tripping after Stevie as she all but ran into Iris's room.

Stevie pulled her around to face her, hands on her hips. Her eyes searched Iris's face, expression serious. "Not even close. I've wanted this since the moment I saw you. I've wanted it all along, I just . . . couldn't figure it out."

Iris's breath tangled in her throat, *Me too* on the edge of her tongue. She couldn't get it out though. Those two simple words felt huge, like a confession to some other life.

"Well, I guess you better take what you want, then," she said instead, smirking at Stevie.

Stevie laughed. "Gladly."

She kissed Iris once . . . twice, backing her toward the bed. Then Stevie slid her hands down the backs of Iris's thighs, lifting her in some sex-adrenaline-fueled show of strength. Iris gripped her shoulders as she moved them closer to the bed, then all but tossed Iris onto the mattress.

"Okay, wow," Iris said, laughing as she bounced and scooted toward the headboard.

Stevie grinned. "Yeah?"

"Very much yeah."

Stevie crawled onto the bed and slid up her body, straddling her hips and kissing her. She palmed Iris's tits, thumbs doing that evil pinching move, and Iris was already writhing underneath her.

"You have too many clothes on," Iris said, panting, pulling at the button on Stevie's shorts.

"So do you." Stevie reached behind Iris's back and undid her bra, nails scraping Iris's skin as she slid the straps down her arms.

They made quick work of the rest of their clothes and Stevie settled next to Iris, wrapping her arms around her bare waist and kissing her.

They stayed like that for a few minutes, just making out, hands roaming. Finally, Iris couldn't take it anymore. She needed her mouth on Stevie, on some part she'd never tasted before. She bent her head, tonguing one pink nipple before sucking it into her mouth.

"Shit," Stevie said, inhaling sharply. Her finger went to Iris's pussy, and Iris happily opened for her. "God, you're so wet."

"I've been wet for weeks."

Stevie laughed. "Me too."

She trailed her hand through Iris's folds, then brought her fingers to her mouth, sucking on them while looking Iris dead in the eyes.

Iris groaned. "Okay, so, you're a secret sex goddess, is that it?"

"You think so?" Stevie said between sucks.

"I mean, Jesus," Iris said, watching Stevie's mouth.

"It's easy with you," Stevie's expression going serious and soft. She leaned in and kissed Iris gently, arms wrapping around her waist. "It's so easy with you."

Iris laughed, but something went a little tight in her chest. She shook it off, focused on the feel of Stevie's mouth on her neck.

"You taste fucking amazing," Stevie said.

Iris could only fight to get enough air into her lungs, because goddamn.

"I need to taste more of you," Stevie said, inhaling deeply against Iris's neck. "Right now."

"Yeah," Iris said, head flopping onto her pillow. "Yeah, that'd be . . . that'd be—"

But she barely got another word out before Stevie rolled her onto her stomach, then straddled the backs of her thighs.

"Fuck, Iris," she said, fingers scraping down Iris's back to her ass. "I'm not the one who's a goddess here."

Iris grinned at her over her shoulder—a grin that promptly became a moan when Stevie's mouth touched between her shoulder blades, working her way down slowly. Her tongue was warm, wet, and Iris couldn't help undulating her hips, pressing her butt into the air, seeking more friction.

"Patience," Stevie said, her mouth reaching Iris's lower back. "God, your ass is a work of art," she said before her teeth scraped Iris's left cheek.

Iris sucked in a breath, hips swirling.

Stevie pushed Iris's legs apart, hands grabbing her hips to lift Iris up onto her knees. Then she pushed Iris between her shoulders so Iris's face rested against the mattress, her backside in the air.

"Okay?" Stevie asked.

"Fuck yes," Iris said, her voice pathetically breathy and needy. She didn't give one shit how desperate she sounded though. She'd never been this fucking horny in her life.

"Thank Christ," Stevie said, and then her mouth was on Iris again, tongue and teeth traveling over her ass cheeks, fingers massaging and spreading. As her lips got closer to Iris's center, Iris couldn't keep herself quiet. She panted, groaned, screamed *fuck, fuck, fuck* into her pillow, fingers curling around her sheets.

Stevie's mouth finally found its target, kissing Iris's pussy, then trailing her tongue upward along the seam in Iris's backside—just once, but it was enough to cause a flood to Iris's cunt, enough to pull more obscenities from her throat. After that, Stevie focused on Iris's sex, mouth kissing and tongue licking, swirling. She dipped a finger into Iris, then another, pumping them in and out while she sucked on Iris's clit for only a second before moving on to exploring Iris's folds.

"Oh my god," Iris said, her second orgasm building. "Fuck."

"Yeah?"

"Yes. Stevie, oh my god, yes."

Stevie spread her ass wider and sucked her clit hard into her mouth. "Do you need to come?"

"So badly. Oh my god," Iris said, but her voice was a squeal, bordering on a scream.

Stevie's tongue was wild now, impossible to track, slipping into Iris, then out, replaced with fingers, then swirling over her clit before her mouth closed over Iris's whole pussy. Iris was dizzy, sure she was about to literally pass out if she didn't come soon, so she begged, her voice almost unrecognizable to her own ears.

Please.

Yeah.

Now, please, Stevie.

And Stevie complied. She slid two fingers inside Iris again, curling them toward Iris's front in a move that had Iris slamming one hand against her mattress. Stevie fucked Iris with her fingers and her mouth, tongue circling her clit as her mouth sucked and sucked and sucked . . .

"Fuck, shit, oh my god," Iris screamed, face pressed into the bed as she yelled even more, wave after wave of pleasure cresting and crashing, only to crest and crash again.

It felt like forever before she came back to herself. Stevie kissed her center, gently, then her thighs and her backside, before Iris slumped down on her stomach, chest heaving for air.

"So," Stevie said, sliding in next to her. "I take it that was good?"

Iris rolled over to face her, laughing as she still struggled for air. "Are you fucking kidding me? Who the hell are you?"

Stevie laughed, her cheeks red, her mouth glistening with Iris's wetness. Iris leaned forward and kissed her clean while Stevie's hips circled against Iris's leg. Iris slid her hand between Stevie's thighs, relishing how soaked her curls were. Stevie grabbed Iris's wrist, pushing her hand to her pussy even harder.

"I got you," Iris said, dragging her fingers up Stevie's cunt, spreading her wetness to her clit. "Do you like penetration?"

"Yeah, sometimes. But I don't need it," Stevie said, her eyes closed, teeth biting her lip. "Just . . . just rub me, please."

"Happily," Iris said, spreading Stevie's legs wider for better access. Stevie lifted her arms above her head, moaning at the ceiling as Iris leaned in and closed her mouth around her nipple. She sucked as she played with Stevie's pussy, dipping her fingers into her wet folds, barely grazing her clit before moving away.

Stevie groaned, lifting her hips. "Iris."

"What? This torture is only fair," Iris said, swirling her tongue over Stevie's nipple. "Were you there for what you just did to me?"

"I was," Stevie said, her voice raspy. "And I'll fucking do it again."

Iris laughed, blowing a puff of air over Stevie's now damp peak. "I look forward to that, but for now, you get to beg me."

Stevie hissed a breath as Iris circled her clit, then dipped back into her folds, again and again and again until Stevie was practically whimpering.

"Iris, fuck, please," she said, her words barely audible.

Iris sucked at her nipple again, teeth and tongue, her fingers finally giving Stevie what she wanted. She kept her fingers on Stevie's cunt, pressing the heel of her palm down on her clit, rubbing harder and harder and harder until Stevie tensed and broke, hips reaching for the sky, the sexiest moan Iris had ever heard falling out of her mouth.

Iris waited until Stevie's body stilled, her fingers trailing lazily through Stevie's pussy until Stevie's breathing regulated. Then she settled at Stevie's side, arm slung over her bare stomach.

"Good?" Iris asked.

Stevie laughed, but it was a watery sound, and she swiped at her cheeks. Iris propped herself up on her elbow, peered at Stevie's face. Tears were definitely swelling into her eyes.

"Shit. Are you okay?"

Stevie laughed again, waved a hand through the air. "I'm fine, I promise. Take this as a compliment."

Iris frowned. "What?"

"Really good orgasms?" Stevie said. "They, yeah, sometimes make me cry. But in a good way. Like, in an overabundance of feelings way."

Iris's shoulders relaxed. "You're sure?"

Stevie smiled, and it was a real smile, crinkling the corners of her eyes and everything. She cupped Iris's face and brought her down to her mouth for a kiss. "I'm sure," she said against her lips.

"In fact," Stevie said, rolling Iris onto her back. "I'm already thinking about crying again."

Iris laughed, wrapped her leg around Stevie's hips, and didn't think about anything else but making this woman weep for the rest of the night.

CHAPTER

TWENTY-SIX

STEVIE WOKE SLOWLY, her body filled with that exhausted bone-less feeling she'd only experienced a few times with Adri. Outside, rain sluiced down the windows, turning Iris's bedroom cozy and gray and soft.

She turned to look at Iris, ready to fully watch her sleep now without any embarrassment attached, but Iris's side of the bed was empty. Instead, Iris was curled in the chair by the window, her iPad in her lap, stylus moving across the screen. Stevie watched her for a second, wondering what was on the page. She knew Iris drew, had even checked out her Etsy shop, but she'd never seen a full illustration, just tiny flowers and vines and other such doodles that filled her digital planners and stickers.

"Hey," Stevie said, and Iris startled.

"You're awake."

"Finally," Stevie said. "Sorry I slept so long."

"I exhausted you that much, huh?" Iris said, smirking.

Stevie laughed, but she didn't say anything. It was certainly true that they'd both worn each other out last night, but she didn't want sex jokes right now.

She wanted Iris in the bed, in her arms.

She wanted to kiss her good morning, make her come soft and slow, and then go out for brunch while holding her hand down the sidewalk.

The thoughts flipped through her mind like a picture book, one scene after another, quick and sure and surprising.

"What are you drawing?" she asked.

Iris clicked the iPad dark, slipped her stylus into its holder. "Nothing. Just . . . messing around."

Stevie patted the empty spot next to her. "Come back to bed, then."

Iris frowned, didn't move.

Stevie's throat went tight. "You okay?"

"Yeah," Iris said, then tilted her head at Stevie. "So . . . what happened last night? With Jenna?"

Stevie managed a smile. "I thought I already told you."

"No. You blasted into my apartment, said something super cheesy and romantic, and then fucked me sideways. Multiple times."

Stevie blushed, memories from last night rushing through her. "Not sideways. I distinctly remember your amazing body in various positions, but none of them sideways."

Iris laughed. "You know what I mean."

Stevie tucked a piece of hair behind her ear. "Jenna was nice. I knew I'd be safe with her, so you were right there. And, I don't know, maybe, if the timing were different, I'd be really into her."

Iris's brows pushed together, just a little. "But?"

"But I was in her apartment and I just . . . couldn't stop thinking about you."

"Really?" There was no sentimentality in the word. No excitement or happiness. Just wonder, as though Iris were waiting for Stevie to laugh and say, *April Fools.*

Stevie propped herself up on her elbow. "Really, Iris. Is that so hard to believe?"

Iris pressed her mouth flat, but then smiled. Laughed. "I mean, I am a pretty amazing screw."

Stevie frowned. "Don't. Don't do that."

"Do what?"

"Treat yourself like you're nothing but a piece of ass."

Iris's mouth dropped open, but nothing came out. She sat up, her iPad slipping to the floor, and rubbed her face. "Look, this was fun. Last night. And, clearly, it was a long time coming, but I have a few planner orders to fill and then have to do a shit ton of writing, so you should probably go."

She stood up, a satin lavender robe open and revealing her lovely body. She pulled it closed and secured the tie.

"Hang on," Stevie said, sitting up. "Iris, I—"

"I need you to go, Stevie."

She spoke the words firmly, a slight tremor to her voice as she started roaming around the room, picking up pieces of clothing here and there and tossing them into her laundry basket.

Stevie blinked at her, willing her to stop, to look at her, but she never did.

Stevie wasn't sure what she expected. A declaration of love? For Iris to write their love story like she was writing Tegan and Briony's? No, Iris had made it clear, on more than one occasion, that she didn't do love. She didn't do relationships.

But Stevie and her stupid romantic heart thought maybe this time—maybe Stevie herself—was different. Like a tornado forming over a field, quick and swirling and devastating, she realized she'd been hoping for that all along. In her desperation to move on from

Adri—a person who controlled their whole relationship, every move in bed, every show they watched and dinner they prepared—Stevie had convinced herself what she really needed was a random hookup. Sex, pure and carnal, a show of bravery and confidence.

But she'd been wrong.

So wrong.

She didn't want that at all.

She wanted Iris.

Maybe she'd wanted her from the moment Iris had tucked her into her bed that first night. Maybe it happened later, Stevie didn't know, but she knew it was true. She could see everything so clearly now. And fuck, she'd wasted so much time thinking everything she and Iris had done together in the past weeks was all about getting with some stranger, about Stevie proving something to herself.

But it was always about Iris.

And now Iris was asking her to leave.

She was saying *no*, and Stevie knew she had to respect it, but the panic flurried into her chest anyway.

"We're still good, right?" Stevie asked, desperate to get Iris to stop moving around the room. Look at her. "With our . . . our deal?"

Iris finally paused, finally put her eyes on Stevie's. She had her red bandanna crop top from last night in her hands. "Yeah. Of course. I wouldn't leave you out to dry like that."

"I know, I just . . . I didn't know if last night—"

"Last night was sex, Stevie," Iris said, all the warmth in her eyes and voice going cold again. Clinical. "And honestly, it was amazing, and I'd totally be down to fuck again." Here she smirked, that familiar flirty expression taking over her lovely features. "But last night doesn't change anything," she went on. "We're still good."

Stevie nodded, a knot in her throat. "Right."

"But I really need to get on with my day, so . . ."

Iris looked down at the shirt in her hands, cleared her throat.

"Right," Stevie said again. She pushed back the sheets, found her T-shirt on the floor, pulled it on.

"I'm going to jump in the shower," Iris said. "You good?"

Stevie's eyes filled, but she focused on her shorts. One leg in, now the other. "Yeah."

"Good. I'll . . . I'll see you at rehearsal on Monday."

Stevie could only nod and then Iris was gone. Down the hall, Stevie heard the bathroom door click shut, the shower squeak to life. She fought tears as she finished getting dressed, refusing to let herself have the relief of crying. Iris had never promised her anything—she'd only ever been herself.

Stevie stood up and started making the bed, just for something for her hands to focus on as she took deep breath after deep breath, trying to get herself under control. She pulled up Iris's mosaic duvet, grabbed her pillows from where they'd thrown them on the floor last night. As she reached for the last turquoise sham, her heel caught the edge of Iris's iPad still on the floor. She picked it up, and as she placed it on the nightstand, her thumb swiped the surface, the lock screen blooming to life.

It took Stevie a few seconds to realize the image on the iPad wasn't a wallpaper. It wasn't the lock screen at all. It wasn't even a background image on Iris's home screen.

It was Stevie's own face, a cowboy hat sitting crooked on her head, her mouth open in a laugh as she held Jenna's hand on the dance floor at Stella's. It was just a sketch, all black and white and rough lines, but it was definitely her.

Her heart drummed under her ribs as she navigated the program, finding other files with her name on it.

Stevie and Iris on stage at the Empress.

Stevie sitting alone on the beach in Malibu.

Stevie and Iris slow dancing in Iris's living room, candles all around, the colors in this one complete and dark and soft.

They were beautiful. Each illustration, each portrait, capturing Iris and Stevie's entire relationship. They were drawn with skill and talent, surely, but there was something else there.

Something real.

Stevie didn't know what to think or feel. These drawings, they felt warm. Careful and meticulous, every line thoughtful and purposeful. They didn't match up with the Iris who, for all intents and purposes, had just kicked Stevie out of her apartment after a hookup.

Nothing matched up whatsoever.

But before Stevie could think more about it, the shower turned off. She didn't want to still be here when Iris came back to her room—plus, she knew Iris expected her to be gone, and she had to respect that.

So she opened up to the file featuring Stevie at Stella's that Iris had been working on, clicked the iPad screen dark, and set it on Iris's nightstand. Then she pulled on her boots and found her bag on the floor in the living room and left.

RAIN PELTED STEVIE'S car, rivers of water washing down her windshield. She'd only made it two blocks from Iris's, but she could barely see and her anxiety had her heart sprinting against her ribs.

She pulled into a street parking space to catch her breath. She tried to think of what the hell she was going to do the next time she saw Iris. She tried to imagine everything between them going back to the way it was, which was clearly what Iris wanted, but the sheer thought of faking how she was feeling—how she'd *been* feeling—just made her lungs grow even tighter.

She leaned her head against the seat, wondering how long she was going to have to wait this rain out, when her phone buzzed. She dug it out of her bag, her heart swelling into her throat when she saw the notification for an email from Dr. Calloway. She tapped on it, words she wasn't sure what to do with springing into her view.

Hi Stevie,

It was so good to see you yesterday. Attached is all the information regarding the play. I do hope you'll consider it. Please know, I wouldn't cast just anyone—I have a lot at stake here, a lot to prove, and I don't gamble with my own career. I hope you won't gamble with yours. I'd appreciate your decision by September 1st.

Best,
Thayer

Stevie tossed her phone into the passenger seat, panic already starting to rise up like the tide. Her fingertips tingled, and she squeezed her eyes closed, focusing on the feeling of the seat's fabric under her legs, the weight of her body in the car, putting herself in the moment, using all five senses like her therapist suggested she do when she got overwhelmed.

New York City.

An actual, prestigious play in New York City.

She'd barely had time to process Dr. Calloway's offer, everything with Iris looming to the forefront of her mind since she saw her old professor.

She could barely make sense of it now—Stevie Scott on the Delacorte Theater stage.

Stevie Scott in New York City.

Alone.

She couldn't picture it, couldn't even fathom leaving everything she'd known and trusted for the last ten years, everything that kept her balanced and safe.

And now there were all these feelings for Iris . . .

Feelings Iris had zero interest in pursuing.

Her eyes were just starting to sting when the rain let up just enough for her to see the sign rocking in the wind just outside her window.

River Wild Books.

She took a deep breath and got out of her car, jogging to the cobbled sidewalk and hurrying under the shop's awning before she was completely soaked. A little bell dinged as she stepped through the door, and she was immediately hit with the smell of books, paper and glue and leather, a hint of coffee just underneath.

It was a beautiful store, all light wood shelving and soft lighting, a reading area in the center with dark brown leather chairs and a coffee table strewn with books.

"Can I help you with something?"

The voice startled Stevie and she turned around to face a young girl—no more than thirteen—smiling at her. She had golden brown hair shaved on one side and swooping past her shoulder over the other, hazel eyes, and a nametag that read *Ruby*.

"Oh," Stevie said. "Hi, um . . . I was just looking."

The girl nodded. "Let me know if you need help."

"Thanks."

The girl turned to head off, but then Stevie got an idea.

"Actually," she said, "can you direct me to the romance section?"

Ruby grinned. "For sure." She beelined through a maze of tables set with pyramids of books, until she stopped at a section of the built-in shelves full of colorful spines. "Here you go."

"Thank you."

"I recommend checking out our Pride display," she said, motioning toward a nearby table full of colorful paperbacks arranged in a rainbow. "It's July now, but read queer all year, right?"

Stevie smiled at the girl. "Yeah. Absolutely."

Ruby beamed and left her alone to explore. Stevie focused on the Pride table, picking up a yellow paperback with an illustration of a dark-skinned man holding a Black woman with pink hair in his arms. She sank down on the floor and started to read, soon lost in the world of two characters—one of them a bisexual woman—who started fake dating. She found herself suddenly ravenous for the sex scenes, the way the man clearly adored the woman even though she was terrified of commitment, for the ending that Stevie knew would be happy.

Before she knew it, she was crying on the floor in a bookstore. Actually crying. Snot ran out of her nose, and she wiped it on her own shoulder, and she wasn't sure if it was possible for her to be more pathetic.

"Stevie?"

She froze, snapping her head up to see Iris's friend Claire standing there with a few books in her hands, light brown eyes wide with concern.

"Honey, are you okay?" Claire asked.

And then Stevie burst into tears all over again.

"Oh goodness," Claire said, setting the books on the nearest table and squatting down in front of Stevie. "What happened? Can I get you something?"

Stevie waved a hand, trying to get *I'm fine* out of her mouth, but the tears kept flowing.

Okay, so *now* she couldn't be more pathetic.

⁀

CLAIRE SET A mug of peppermint tea in front of Stevie, who was now sitting in the shop's café area, hiccupping while she clung to the book she pulled off the Pride table like it was a lovey.

"I'm so sorry," Stevie said, sipping at the warm drink.

Claire waved a hand as she slid into the chair across from Stevie with her own mug. "I cry over a book at least once a week."

Stevie nodded, tapped the book's cover. "I'll buy this one. I'm pretty sure I cried on it."

Claire laughed. "I'd appreciate that."

"So . . . you own this store?"

Claire brought her mug to her mouth. "I do. Iris didn't tell you?"

"You could probably fill several of these shelves with all the stuff Iris doesn't tell me."

Claire pressed her mouth together. "Is that why you're crying in my shop? Iris?"

Stevie didn't say anything. She wasn't sure what the protocol was here. She and Iris were nothing, fake, a business arrangement, and Claire was Iris's best friend, not hers.

"I notice you're still wearing your line dancing outfit," Claire said. "Did you . . . did Jenna—"

"It's not Jenna," Stevie said. "Jenna is lovely, but I didn't . . ."

"Got it," Claire said. She tapped her nails on the table, a yellow diamond ring shining on a very important finger.

"That's a lovely ring," Stevie said.

Claire beamed down at her finger. "Thank you. Delilah did that all by herself. I was very impressed."

Stevie smiled, something Iris said a few weeks ago filtering slowly through her thoughts.

My best friend, Claire, is now engaged to the only person she's ever tried to have a purely sexual relationship with.

She took another sip of her tea, watched Claire fiddle with the ring, a little grin still on her face.

"Can I ask you something?" Stevie said.

Claire glanced at her. "Of course."

"How did you . . ." Stevie paused, half wondering if she should really be doing this, but she had to know. And there was no one else she could ask. All of her friends already thought she was with Iris.

"How did you know?" Stevie asked. "With Delilah. When you two first started . . . you know."

Claire laughed. "So Iris at least told you that story."

"No. Not all of it. Just that it started with . . . well, it started out as . . ."

"Sex?"

Stevie's face warmed. "Yeah."

Claire nodded. "And you're asking how I knew I wanted more."

"Yeah. I guess I am."

Claire inhaled deeply and sat back in her chair. "I just . . . knew. I couldn't stop thinking about her. Hated being away from her. And yeah, it was partly about sex, but it was more than that. I wanted to hold her hand. Make her laugh."

"Romance."

Claire smiled. "Yeah, I guess so. But it was deeper than just romance too. I wanted to be part of her life, the good and the bad, with all her snark and attitude and bluster. I didn't care about any of that. Or actually I did, but it didn't deter me. I wanted all of her."

Stevie's eyes stung, and goddammit, she was not going to cry again in front of this woman. Except she already was, her tears on a mission to humiliate her as they raced down her face.

"Oh, sweetie," Claire said, grabbing a café napkin and handing it to Stevie.

"Sorry, shit."

"It's okay."

Stevie wiped her eyes, the brown paper scratching at her tender lids.

"You like her," Claire said. "You *really* like her."

"Who, Delilah?" Stevie said, and Claire busted up laughing. Stevie laughed too, tears mixing with this brief moment of mirth, but then Claire reached out and squeezed her arm.

"You like her," she said again, "and she told you to leave this morning. Didn't she?"

Stevie lifted her thumb and forefinger into a finger gun. "You know your girl."

"I do," Claire said. "All too well."

"So I guess that's that."

Claire sniffed, eyes softly narrowed in thought. "You know, when you were dancing with Jenna last night, Iris was . . ."

Stevie's heart nearly stopped. "Iris was what?"

Claire tapped her fingers on her mug. "I could tell she didn't like it, I'll just say that. She didn't like it one bit."

Stevie thought back to their night together. She figured Iris had just gone home, forgotten about Stevie and Jenna, and simply been caught up in a moment of lust when Stevie showed up at her apartment.

But then Stevie's brain locked onto those illustrations—illustrations in complete dissonance with the way Iris refused to look at her while she picked up her room. Or even more, the way Iris *did* look at her— all smirk and flirt as she called herself an amazing screw.

An act.

A total show.

Stevie studied actors as part of her job. Dug into their performances, their methods, the way they created a persona, a character.

And Iris?

She was a fucking pro.

"Stevie," Claire said. "Iris has been through it—with relationships, I mean."

Stevie nodded. "I know."

"Do you?"

"She told me about Jillian and Grant. People from high school and college."

Claire blinked. "Iris doesn't usually tell anyone those stories."

"I'm not usual, Claire," Stevie said, feeling suddenly as bold and brash as Iris herself. Plus, she was right. There was nothing usual about Stevie and Iris. Nothing at all.

Claire watched her for a second before seeming to come to some conclusion. "No, I don't think you are. Does Iris know how you feel? Is that why she asked you to leave?"

Stevie laughed. "One doesn't just tell Iris Kelly that they like her, do they?"

Claire's mouth dropped open. "Wow, you sure do have her number."

"I don't," Stevie said, swiping a hand through her messy curls. "I have no idea what the hell I'm doing."

Claire's eyes narrowed in thought. "Well, Iris is . . . yeah, she's tough. Words are cheap to her. She's heard it all, both good and bad, and that's made her . . . skittish."

"Skittish."

"About love."

"Yeah, I see that," Stevie said. "So how do I convince her?"

Claire tilted her head, gaze spearing Stevie. "First, you make sure you want to. Don't jerk her around, Stevie."

"I'm not. I swear, I'm not. I . . ."

She couldn't say *love* to Iris's best friend. Iris deserved to be the first person who heard those words.

"I promise you, Claire," she said, "I'm very serious about Iris. And anything you can tell me to help me convince her how serious I am would be greatly appreciated."

Claire's brows lifted, a smile fighting to get through her pursed mouth. "Okay, then."

"Okay, then."

Claire's glanced around the store, then back to Stevie. "Iris responds to sincerity. Actions. She's a writer, yeah, but like I said, words are cheap when it comes to her own love life. But I think, with the right person, she'd believe they really cared about her if they *showed* her. Proved it, I guess. It's just that no one has done that in a long time, and she's been hurt by that."

Stevie nodded. All of that made perfect sense. She was sure Jillian uttered a lot of pretty words to get Iris in bed, then betrayed her at the first turn. Even Grant, who Stevie thought really loved Iris, left her in the end. He probably even said those exact words—*I love you, but* . . .

So it made sense that Iris needed proof, actions that spoke way louder than any words Stevie could rattle off. It was true, in the past few weeks, she and Stevie had been putting on quite a show for the world, for Stevie's friends, for themselves.

But what if that show were real?

What if, for all of Iris's scoffing at romance, that's what she really needed?

Really wanted.

Stevie smiled at Claire, an idea forming in her mind. "So I need to woo her."

Claire grinned. "Deep down inside, I think Iris really just wants to be swept off her feet, you know?"

Stevie grinned back, hope pushing out all her earlier despair. Iris wanted romance lessons? She wanted situations for her characters to fall in love?

That was exactly what she was going to get.

"Hey, babe."

Stevie glanced up to see Delilah coming into the café, wearing a black T-shirt and black jeans cuffed at the ankle.

"Hey," Claire said, tilting her head up for a kiss. "Is it lunchtime already?"

"Close enough," Delilah said, thumb sweeping over Claire's jaw. "I missed you."

All of Stevie's insides melted right then. Just a little.

"Hey, Stevie," Delilah said, nodding at her. "What's up? Iris here?"

"Um . . . no," Stevie said.

Delilah's gaze darted between Stevie and Claire. Then she closed her eyes. "Oh god."

"What?" Claire asked.

"I want no part of this," Delilah said.

"Part of what?" Claire asked innocently.

Delilah waved her finger between Stevie and Claire. "This little matchmaking thing you have going on."

Claire pressed a hand to her chest. "I would never."

"You would and you are and Iris will flay you alive when she finds out."

"Not if Stevie here gets the girl," Claire said, winking at Stevie over her own mug. Stevie smiled back, a confidence she would never have expected of herself filling her up.

Delilah pressed her thumb and forefinger into her eyes. "May the goddess have mercy on your souls."

CHAPTER

TWENTY-SEVEN

IRIS DIDN'T TALK to Stevie all weekend. Stevie didn't text, didn't call, and Iris didn't either. She didn't even think to. She also didn't stalk Stevie's social media. Stevie hardly ever posted on her Instagram anyway, not that Iris noticed.

Not that Iris was thinking about her at all.

Still, Sunday evening, after two days of relentless writing, her novel's word count finally creeping up to about the halfway mark, she sat in her living room drawing Stevie Scott.

Stevie Scott's mouth on Iris's neck.

Stevie Scott's hands on Iris's body.

Stevie Scott's eyes closed as Iris touched her, kissed her, made her—

"Fuck," Iris said as the definitely not-safe-for-work illustration came to life on her iPad.

She hadn't meant to draw their night together, but it was the next step, the next scene in her weird, true-story project, and now Iris couldn't stop thinking about how many times Stevie had made her come, the soft way she'd closed her body around Iris's once they were both finally spent.

How Iris had fallen asleep like that, the possibility of asking Stevie to leave in the middle of the night never even crossing her mind.

And Iris always asked her partners to leave.

And they always did, no questions asked.

Iris shook her head and swiped out of her drawing program. She just needed a distraction. She'd spent her whole weekend in her apartment, writing romance and *remembering*, and fuck, she needed to do something else.

Some*one* else.

Her hands shook as she pulled on a pair of high-waisted jeans and a yellow crop top, as she slicked on mascara and some sparkly coral lip gloss. Low blood sugar. That's all it was. She never remembered to eat when she was writing. In the kitchen, she dug into a box of crackers, then tapped out a text to the group chat, now named *Cheers for Queers*.

She tapped out Anyone up for Lush, but then hesitated before she hit send. She'd seen the way Claire had looked at her in Stella's the other night, the assumptions all of her friends were making about Iris and Stevie, even as Stevie danced with Jenna. Honestly, she didn't want to deal with their horror that Iris was looking for a random hookup.

She exited out of the group chat and tapped on Simon's name.

"You know, normal people text," he said when he answered her call.

"I'm not normal, Simon," she said. "Surely you know that by now."

He laughed. "Fair enough. What's up?"

"You in Portland?"

A pause, just long enough to make Iris ask if he was still there.

"Yeah, sorry, I'm here," he said. "And yeah, I'm in Portland. Why?"

"I need a wingman," Iris singsonged, grabbing her keys and bag.

"You don't," he said. "You really don't."

"What do you mean?"

"You honestly think I didn't hear about how you stormed out of Stella's after Stevie got with Jenna Dawson?"

"Oh fuck, not you too."

"I'm just saying, Claire would stick needles under my fingernails if she knew I took you out to get laid."

"It's not Claire's business."

"Okay, fine, but it is mine, since you're asking me to participate here, and I'm saying no."

Iris laughed. "Be serious."

"I am being serious, Iris," he said, his voice annoyingly soft and gentle.

"Okay, what is going on?" she asked, but her insides were starting to clench, her throat going thick.

Simon sighed. "Look, I don't want to tell you how to live your life."

"Then don't."

"But I love you. We all love you, and I just think that if you slowed down for a second, really thought about what you wanted, you'd see that—"

"No," Iris said, her throat full-on swollen now. "Hell no, Simon, you are not going to tell me what I want or who I do or do not want to sleep with."

"I'm not—"

"You are. And you can fuck right off, and yes, feel free to communicate my sentiments to everyone else."

"Iris, I—"

But she ended the call before he could get anything else out. Her hands were shaking, and tears swelled into her eyes. She knew it. She fucking knew it, all this time, that her friends thought she was screwing up her life, that to be happy, to be whole, she had to *be* with someone.

Well, fuck that.

"Fuck that!" she screamed to her empty apartment, her voice echoing off the walls. She swiped at her face, willing the tears to reverse their path. She pressed her palms to her kitchen counter, breathing in . . . out . . .

She was fine.

She was fucking *great*, and she didn't need a wingperson to have a good time. Granted, for safety reasons, she never went to Lush or any club by herself, but she didn't have a choice. She was not going to let her friends' small-minded views stop her from meeting her own needs.

She flung her bag over her shoulder and headed for the door. She wrenched it open, ready to hurl herself into the hallway, but her path was blocked.

By Stevie Scott.

Dressed in cuffed gray jeans and a black tank top, her curly hair brushing her shoulders, the slight mullet style making her look like she was about to step out on stage with a guitar.

"Hi," she said.

Iris stood there for a second, her chest heaving with adrenaline and anger.

Go away.

It was right there on her tongue—she needed someone else, not Stevie Scott, but fuck, even as she thought it, she felt herself reaching out, pulling Stevie inside by her waist and kissing her.

Hard.

She pressed her mouth to Stevie's, groaning into her mouth, tongue seeking contact. She slipped her hand up the back of Stevie's shirt, her skin so soft, so smooth. Iris squeezed her eyes closed, imagined herself as anyone, Stevie as anyone, two nameless women seeking comfort, sensation, and—

"Hey, hey, hey," Stevie said gently, pulling away and wrenching Iris out of her fantasy. "Slow down a sec."

Iris blinked at her, reality rushing back in. "Shit. Sorry. That was a little aggressive, huh? I should've asked."

"It's okay," Stevie said. She rested her hands on Iris's waist. "Seriously, are you all right?"

Iris waved a hand. "Fine. Just . . . turned on." She smirked at Stevie, all flirt and swagger, but Stevie didn't smile back. She just studied Iris in a way that made Iris want to scream.

Iris stepped back, causing Stevie's hands to fall away from her hips. Cleared her throat. "I was just on my way out."

"I see that," Stevie said.

"Did you need something?"

Stevie smiled. "Actually, yeah. I was hoping you'd go somewhere with me."

Iris frowned. "Where?"

"That's a surprise."

"What?"

Stevie ran her hand through her hair, laughed a little nervously. "I was at home, thinking about you, and I realized we hadn't had a true romantic date yet."

"A date."

"Our deal is still on, right?" Stevie said. "You've held up your end, but I've been a pretty horrible teacher to you."

Iris sighed. "Stevie, you don't have to do that."

"Is your book finished?"

"No, but . . ." She trailed off, because despite Stevie's claims, Stevie had actually helped Iris a lot, igniting every dormant romantic bone in Iris's body. Tegan and Briony's enemies-to-lovers story was flowing from her like a chocolate fountain at a wedding. Iris had even sent the first fifty pages to her agent last week, who loved them and encouraged her to keep going.

So Iris had, writing as if in a fever dream in the mornings and late into the night after play rehearsal.

Writing and drawing.

Drawing Stevie.

Stevie and Iris.

She shook her head, determined to tell Stevie no, she wouldn't go with her.

Couldn't.

But as Stevie tilted her head, that soft smile on her mouth, Iris found she was curious about this surprise, curious about what Stevie had planned for this next romance lesson.

And, if she was being honest with herself, she wasn't actually sure she was in the mood for Lush, for searching for someone to fuck in a sea of nameless faces.

She didn't really want *nameless* tonight.

She wanted a friend. The kind of friend who wouldn't ask her about her love life or give her *I actually know what's best for you* looks like Claire had been doing lately.

And Stevie was just such a friend.

If they ended up having sex at the end of this fake date, then so be it. Iris certainly wouldn't say no to that. She'd never admit it to Stevie—and definitely not to Claire or Astrid or even Simon—but her night with Stevie was the best sex Iris had ever had.

"Okay," Iris said. "Fine. What's this surprise you have up your sleeve?"

TWENTY-FIVE MINUTES LATER, they turned into a driveway with a sign welcoming them to Woodmont Family Farms. The sun was

just starting to dip below the trees, turning everything golden and
soft.

"We're . . . going . . . strawberry picking?" Iris asked.

"Not quite," Stevie said, smiling as she parked next to a tiny
house with a sign on the front porch that said *Farm Office.* "Ready?"

"I'm not sure," Iris said, laughing.

Still, she got out of the car and let Stevie take her hand—this was
a romantic date, after all, so what the hell—and they walked along
a dirt path through a copse of trees. Iris continued to guess at what
they were doing.

"Scavenger hunt?" she asked.

"No."

"Vampire hunting."

Stevie laughed. "Intriguing, but nope."

"Damn. I've always wanted to fall madly in love with a vampire."

"I'll do some research for next time."

"You're pretty confident I'll say yes to a second date," Iris said.

Stevie just smiled at her. Soon, the trees thinned, and they broke
through to a field, an endless swath of summer green.

And there, about a hundred feet away, a woman in a pair of dusky
rose-colored coveralls stood next to a hot-air balloon.

"Oh my god," Iris said, neck craning to take in the giant inflat-
able. It was huge, much bigger than she'd ever imagined a hot-air
balloon would be, the body a beautiful rainbow of colors.

"Surprise," Stevie said softly as Iris gaped.

"I'd say so," Iris said, then turned to look at Stevie. "For real?"

"For real. Have you ever been on one?"

Iris shook her head. "I've always wanted to though."

"Same." Stevie squeezed her hand.

Iris grinned at her, her foul mood from earlier evaporating like
fog under the sun.

"Stevie Scott?" the woman asked as Stevie and Iris approached.

"That's me," Stevie said. "And this is Iris. Are you Laney?"

"I am," Laney said. "Welcome to Woodmont. You two ready?"

Iris swallowed. "I think so?"

Laney smiled. "It's natural to be nervous, but you're safe, I assure you. Go ahead and step into the gondola while I get things ready on the ground."

"Thanks," Stevie said, then pulled Iris toward the balloon's gondola, which was truly just a giant wicker basket, a propane tank on top, flame filling the balloon.

They stepped inside, Stevie keeping hold of Iris's hand even once they were situated in a corner. They didn't talk—Iris found she was actually speechless. She'd never done anything this extravagant on a date before. Grant liked to wine and dine, but he took the term literally, and his idea of a perfect date was a night out at a nice restaurant and an expensive bottle of pinot noir.

"I mean, wow," Iris said as Laney finished whatever she was doing and the basket lurched a bit.

Stevie laughed. "I know, it's a bit over the top. But I figured, if a character in a romance novel was trying to woo another character, they'd probably do something a bit more dramatic than dinner and a movie."

Iris laughed. "True. And Briony *is* chasing Tegan at this point."

"See?" Stevie said softly, smiling at her. "Perfect."

She held Iris's gaze for a second before looking out over the field, and Iris felt suddenly off-balance. Then again, Laney had just stepped into the gondola, causing it to rock a little side to side.

"Okay, here we go," Laney said as she fired up the tank even more, then pulled in the weighted bags holding the basket down. Soon, they were lifting into the sky, and Iris couldn't help but squeal a little and grip the sides of the basket. The ground got smaller and smaller, the trees, the crops, the white farmhouse.

"Oh my god," Iris said, watching as her entire world turned on its head. "This is amazing."

"It really is," Stevie said. She let go of Iris's hand, then moved behind her, caging her in between her arms as she rested her hands on the basket's sides. She set her chin on Iris's shoulder, and Iris leaned her head against hers. She couldn't help it. It felt so natural, so . . . normal.

"A-plus on the romance," she said, her words a little shaky as they ascended higher into the sky.

"Oh, I'm just getting started," Stevie whispered, her breath tickling Iris's ear.

Iris shivered, shook it off. "You're not proposing, are you?"

"I wouldn't do that to you."

Iris turned to look at her, that simple declaration nearly knocking the wind out of her, like she *saw* Iris and what she saw was . . . okay. It was great, even. Suddenly, her joke felt all too real, as did Stevie's response, and she wasn't sure what to say.

"But I am going to ask you to dance," Stevie said.

Iris blinked. "What?"

"Well, we've danced in your living room. In the rain on the beach. If this is Tegan and Briony's quirky romantic thing, I think dancing while in a hot-air balloon is the next logical step."

"Upping your game, are we?"

"Absolutely."

Iris laughed and turned in Stevie's arms, her hands coming to rest on her shoulders, Stevie's own fingers curling around Iris's waist.

"Okay," Iris said. "I accept."

Stevie smiled, then pulled Iris even closer, her cheek pressing against Iris's head. They swayed in the air, staying close to the edge so they could see the Willamette Valley spread out below them. Iris tried to imagine how she could work this into her book, but she couldn't hold on to a single thought. She was full of other things—the way Stevie's hair smelled like grass and summer, the feel of her fingers trailing up and down Iris's back.

The way Iris's heart suddenly felt huge, too big for her own chest, sending blood rushing to her head and making her a little dizzy.

"Can I ask you something?" Stevie asked as she twirled them in a small circle.

"Sure," Iris said.

"Why did you kiss me? When I came over tonight?"

Iris swallowed, unsure of how to respond. Finally, she settled on the truth. "I don't know."

Stevie pulled her tighter and Iris suddenly felt like crying. She couldn't explain it. She'd spent the better part of fourteen months running from this exact feeling, making sure she never got this far into her emotions, yet here she was, dancing with a woman who'd puked on her during a hookup, her heart lodged in her throat. She both hated and loved it, this romance, this feeling like she was falling, only to have Stevie reach out and catch her.

It was ridiculous.

It wasn't real. Couldn't be.

But fuck, it felt so, so good.

She could at least admit that—romance was *nice*, and Stevie was a goddamn expert.

So she let herself feel it, all of it, the falling and catching and comfort, pushing away the panic she knew would catch up to her sooner or later.

For now, she simply closed her eyes and danced, floating through a golden sky.

~

AFTER THE BALLOON ride, Stevie and Iris drove back to Bright Falls and ate at Moonpies, gorging on veggie burgers and fries and, of course, homemade moon pies in various flavors. They talked about growing up in small towns and coming out and college and all the stories Iris wanted to write, all the plays Stevie had done.

"What was the worst performance you ever had?" Iris asked, pushing the remnants of her strawberry shortcake moon pie around on her plate.

Stevie looked affronted. "Worst? What makes you think I've ever had one of those?"

"Okay now, I see my confidence lessons have gone a step too far," Iris said. "I'll have to reevaluate my curriculum."

Stevie laughed, popped a fry into her mouth. "I've had plenty of horrible performances. Worst? Probably the first play I ever did at Reed. I was so nervous—our director was amazing, really demanding—so Ren, in their infinite wisdom, gave me a weed gummy about half an hour before curtain."

"Uh-oh."

"Yeah. A whole one too, not even a half. Let's just say that interpretation of *And Then There Were None* had never been quite so giggly."

"Ah, so you laugh a lot when you're high."

"So much, oh my god. I managed to get it together after a few scenes, but Dr. Calloway was furious." Stevie's gaze went a little dreamy, her fingers playing with her napkin. "I'm amazed she even . . ." She trailed off, cleared her throat. "Anyway, needless to say, I swore off recreational substances to help me deal with stage nerves."

"Probably wise. Though it doesn't seem like you need them these days."

Stevie shrugged one shoulder, her expression going playful. "Hard to be nervous when you're this good."

Iris knew Stevie was joking, but she didn't laugh. "Yeah. Exactly."

Stevie rolled her eyes.

"You never thought about going somewhere else?" Iris asked.

Stevie frowned. "What do you mean?"

Iris speared her last strawberry with her fork. "Isn't New York the theater capital of the world?"

Stevie licked her bottom lip, looked out the window. "Ren's always pushing me to move there. Or somewhere. But . . . I don't know."

"That's a big step," Iris said.

"Yeah," Stevie said, turning to look at her. "It is. Maybe too big for me."

Iris frowned. "I don't think so. I think you could—"

"Can I have a bite of your moon pie?"

Iris nodded, then pushed over her plate. She took a bite of Stevie's chocolate mint moon pie, and soon they were on to other topics, other things that were clearly easier to talk about for both of them, which was exactly how Iris liked it.

She had to admit, it was a perfect date.

A date she wasn't sure she could actually re-create on paper, because she could barely make sense of it herself. As they walked back to Iris's apartment, she felt overwhelmed, like she needed to cry or scream or pull Stevie immediately into her arms and kiss her senseless.

When they reached her apartment door, she settled on the last option. She needed to un-romanticize this night a little, help her heart return to its usual rhythm. Sex would do the trick, and Iris would be lying if she said she hadn't imagined getting Stevie back into her bed a million times in the last couple of days.

So she kissed Stevie at her door.

Pulled her into her arms and slid her hands down Stevie's ass, pressing her leg between her thighs so Stevie would know exactly what she was thinking.

But Stevie pulled away, resting her hands on Iris's hips.

"Still too much?" Iris asked, looking up at Stevie through her lashes.

"That's not what tonight was about, Iris," Stevie said, her expression soft yet serious.

"I know that," Iris said, laughing. "But don't most romantic dates end with a nice round of fucking?"

Stevie flinched, but just barely. In fact, Iris thought maybe she'd imagined it as Stevie's expression smoothed out, head canted as she watched Iris. Finally, she smiled, leaned in, and kissed Iris lightly on the mouth—once . . . twice—before stepping back and shoving her hands in her pockets. She walked backward toward the stairs.

"Good night, Iris," she said, then turned around and was gone.

CHAPTER

TWENTY-EIGHT

IRIS KELLY WAS at the end of her rope.

For the last two weeks, she had gone on more "dates" with Stevie than Grant had taken her on the entire last year they were together.

They went to dinner in Portland.

They went to brunch in Bright Falls.

They went to a winery in the Willamette Valley, a day trip that ended with Iris so sloshed, she didn't even remember how she ended up tucked into her bed.

They played boozy mini-golf at Birdie's with her friends.

They took a hike through Lower Macleay Park to the Pittock Mansion, Stevie's legs completely covered in bug bites by the time they reached their destination.

Most recently, Stevie had shown up at Iris's apartment at ten o'clock at night, blankets and pillows in her hands, so they could watch a lunar eclipse from the roof of Iris's building.

And after each and every date, Stevie kissed Iris on the mouth and said good night.

That was it.

She never even tried to slide into second base, much less cop a feel below the waist. By mid-July, just two weeks before *Much Ado* opened at the Empress, Iris was ready to pull every single hair out of her body. She had more than enough content for her book, her progress with her cranky vintner and cinnamon roll wine critic inching toward the last act at this point. Still, Stevie kept asking her out, kept driving her crazy with slow dances in the middle of the forest and on hole eighteen.

And Iris, inexplicably, kept saying yes.

"Winner!" a man cried from inside a lit booth, plucking a plush purple frog from the row of stuffed animals and handing it to Stevie.

They were at the Bright Falls Summer Fair, an annual event that included a fluorescent Ferris wheel and a rickety Tilt-A-Whirl, games and cotton candy and corn dogs, vendors selling local honey and handmade jewelry and art out of cloth-draped booths.

"For you," Stevie said, presenting the frog to Iris. She'd just looped three rings in a row around old 7-Up bottles, winning Iris the prize.

"Forever grateful," Iris deadpanned, taking the frog. "What should I name her?"

"Peppa."

"I think that's a pig."

"Okay, Wilbur."

Iris laughed. "She's a frog."

Stevie laced their fingers together, kissed Iris on the back of the hand. "Says who? Her identity is her own."

Iris smiled and stuffed the frog under her arm. They walked along the crowd, people waving at Iris every so often, and a silence fell over them that caused Iris's heart rate to pick up.

This had been happening a lot lately, the closer they got to *Much Ado*'s opening night. The play would run for the month of August, and then . . .

Her deal with Stevie would be done.

They'd have no reason to keep up their charade, and Iris didn't think she could take many more of these dates anyway. They were fun, sure, but they were also confusing, leaving Iris scribbling out each encounter on her iPad late into the night, analyzing every word the next day, tormenting herself over why Stevie didn't seem to want to sleep with her again.

She knew she had to bring up their inevitable end. They had no exit strategy so far, no plan for how they'd break up their fake relationship for Stevie's friends and the play's cast and crew. She knew Stevie always did better with a plan, even if the idea of everything just stopping made Iris uncomfortable in a way she couldn't explain.

"Hey, you two!" Claire called from River Wild's booth. She and Ruby were working, selling the summer's hottest reads for the store. Delilah was around here somewhere, taking photos for a National Geographic project she was working on—a book about liberal small towns—and Astrid and Jordan were both working at the Everwood Inn tonight, as they were fully booked with visitors for the fair.

"Hey," Iris said, pulling her hand away from Stevie's and kissing Claire and then Ruby on the cheek. "Selling a lot?"

"Oh, yeah, summer romances," Claire said holding up a yellow paperback. "This one's about fake dating and a bisexual disaster. Selling like hot cakes." Here she winked at Stevie, a move she didn't even try to hide from Iris, and Stevie cleared her throat, making a pretty huge show of inspecting a book on the flora and fauna of Central Oregon.

"Okay," Iris said. "What am I missing?"

"Nothing, nothing," Claire said, waving a hand.

"I think she's calling you a bisexual disaster, Aunt Iris," Ruby said.

Stevie choked, hitting her chest with her fist, and Iris popped her hands on her hips.

"Oh, your mother is one to talk," she said to Ruby. "Let me tell you a little story about a cranky photographer and a little bet that she—"

"Okay, okay," Claire said, literally pressing her hand to Iris's mouth. "She knows the story."

"Clearly not," Iris said when Claire released her.

Claire just shook her head.

"Isn't Stevie your fake girlfriend?" Ruby asked.

"Yes," Iris said, pulling Stevie in close. "Yes, she is."

Ruby just frowned, those hazel eyes she got from her father, Josh, narrowing in on Stevie. "Still? Even after—"

"Ruby, honey," Claire said, "text your dad for me, will you? See if he's still coming to pick you up tomorrow at nine."

"Hang on," Iris said, glancing at Stevie before frowning at Ruby. "After what?"

Ruby just shrugged. "Like, you know, all the wooing and—"

"Ruby," Claire snapped. "Go. Text. Your father."

Ruby rolled her eyes, then stomped off to the back of the booth, her phone in her hands.

"Teenagers," Claire said, laughing, but Iris wasn't looking at Claire.

"What is she talking about?" she asked Stevie. "Wooing?"

Stevie and Claire looked at each other, a quick glance and then away, but it was enough to set Iris on edge.

"Okay, someone better tell me what the fuck is going on right the hell now," Iris said.

"Iris," Stevie said. "It's nothing. I—"

"Ruby doesn't fucking lie," she said. "And Claire, goddess bless her, is horrible at lying. Her face turns beet red and she chews her lower lip to shreds"—here she pointed at Claire—"just like that."

Claire's teeth released her lip.

"Iris," Stevie said, taking her hand. "Let's go talk, okay? It's my story to tell, not Claire's."

Iris's shoulders released a little, but her breath still felt tight, her jaw locked up and tense. "Fine."

Stevie led her away from the booths and toward the water. The fair was set up in a park at the edge of town, Bright River rushing along to the east. Stevie kept walking until they reached one of the small docks, the fair's crowd just a gentle hum behind them. A single lamppost in the grass turned the area golden, but the farther they walked out on the dock, the darker it got. The world was quiet, the stars above a brilliant silver.

"If you fucking say this is romantic, I will hurl myself into this river," Iris said. She set her purple frog at her feet, then rested her forearms on the wooden railing, eyes going glassy on the water.

"I wasn't going to say that," Stevie said, coming to stand next to her.

Iris turned toward her. "Well, you better say something, Stevie." Her throat tightened, but she swallowed around it. "What was Ruby talking about back there? What is all this? These ridiculous dates. What are we doing? Because it's not for my book, and it can't be for you, because you barely touch me."

"I barely touch you?" Stevie said. "I hold your hand all night. I kiss you when we say goodnight, and—"

"Yeah, a single kiss, how exciting. We haven't slept together since Stella's."

"So, sex equals . . . what? Proves what?"

Iris scraped a hand over her tangled hair. "I don't even know what that means. What are you *trying* to prove, Stevie? We're fake dating and we were fucking—which we're clearly not doing at all anymore— and now Claire's thirteen-year-old seems to know something I don't, so tell me what you want, Stevie. What is all this for? What the hell do you—"

"I want *you*."

She said it so quietly, Iris almost didn't hear her. Stevie's eyes were fixed on Iris, the moon glinting off that light amber color, turning it into bronze.

"What?" Iris asked, her own voice a whisper.

"I want you," Stevie said again.

Her eyes filled, and Iris could tell she was shaking, but still, she didn't look away from Iris. Didn't even blink.

"I know you may not believe me," Stevie said. "But the night we slept together—actually, before, when I went home with Jenna—I realized I didn't want some stranger. I never really did, I just told myself what I thought I needed so I could be . . . I don't even know. An adult? A person who controlled her own sex life? But I didn't want just anyone. And I sure as hell don't want to have sex with just anyone. I want *you*. Everything changed that night we went to Stella's. It was like waking up from the longest sleep of my life. But then the next morning, you . . ."

She paused, took a deep breath. Iris couldn't even get a sip of air, her entire body locked up and on alert.

"You asked me to leave," Stevie went on. "And I didn't know what to do. I ended up at River Wild Books and I was a mess. Ruby was there. So was Claire, but I didn't know it was her store. She found me and just . . . gave me some tea. That's all."

"That's all?"

Stevie sighed. "I might have confessed a few feelings to Claire. I guess Ruby overheard."

Iris's own eyes stung, a pinch in her heart she couldn't parse as she processed this information. "And this . . . these dates. This was all for me?"

Stevie shrugged. "Ruby was right. I was wooing you."

"Wooing me."

Stevie closed her eyes, inhaled deeply. When she opened them again, she took a step closer to Iris. "I know you've had some shitty people say they love you. I know you don't think you're built for dating and relationships. And if you truly don't want that in your life, fine. I won't argue with you. But I wanted you to be sure. I wanted to show you."

Tears spilled down Iris's cheeks. "Show me what?"

Stevie took another step closer. Iris didn't move back. She couldn't. There were only inches between them now and it felt like too much.

"Show me what, Stevie?" she asked again.

Stevie rested her hands on Iris's waist, tentatively, as though waiting for Iris to stop her. She didn't. Instead, she gripped Stevie's forearms, her breathing loud and heavy. She felt herself fading, disappearing, the strong, secure, confident, no-bullshit Iris Kelly vanishing right before her eyes. In her place was a woman whose heart felt tender and raw. A woman who was tired, so fucking tired of fighting the way Stevie Scott made her feel.

Because Iris could see it now—these dates, every move Stevie had made since they embarked on this whole ridiculous deal together, it had all been chipping away at Iris's icy heart, bit by bit, showing her that she . . . that Stevie . . . that Iris . . .

"Show me what?" she asked one more time. "Stevie."

Stevie pressed her forehead to Iris's. "That you're worth loving."

It was so simple. Just four words, barely whispered, but they felt like a bomb landing right on its target. Iris exploded—her heart, her mind, her skin. She was just a shell of the person she was even seconds ago, and she didn't know how to put herself back together, how to do anything but simply dive into the explosion, join it, become one with all the shrapnel.

"Well, it fucking worked," she said, her voice shaking as she slid her hands into Stevie's hair and pulled her in for a kiss. And this time, Stevie didn't settle for a single press of their mouths. She opened her mouth to Iris's, wrapping her arms around Iris's waist, hands trailing up her back and into Iris's hair to her shoulders, then curling around her neck to cup her face, thumbs swiping at her cheeks.

Stevie held her like that, tongue exploring Iris's, her mouth sliding to Iris's ear, her neck, all the while holding her face like Iris was some kind of treasure Stevie had been searching for and had finally, finally found.

Iris breathed her in, all summer nights and grass, slid her hands under her navy T-shirt, fingertips gliding over her soft skin. God, she wanted this woman. Wanted all of her, and she didn't know what that meant, or how she'd face the fear that she knew was still lying dormant in her heart.

All she knew was that she couldn't say no.

She didn't want to.

For the first time in over a year, maybe even since Grant or before—maybe for the first time in her life—she wanted to say yes, to everything, every word and every question and every quiet look.

Yes, yes, yes.

"Stevie," she said against Stevie's mouth.

"Yeah," Stevie said, her breath beautifully labored.

"Can I ask you a question?"

"Anything," Stevie said, pressing a kiss to Iris's temple. "Ask me anything."

"Will you take me home?" Iris framed Stevie's face in her hands, tucked a curl behind her ear. "Take me home, Stevie Scott, and take me to bed."

CHAPTER

TWENTY-NINE

IT TOOK THEM forever to get back to Iris's apartment.

Stevie had never experienced a panic attack caused from sheer happiness, but she was pretty sure she was on the verge. She could barely breathe as they rushed through the fair and onto Bright Falls' cobbled sidewalks, and she kept getting distracted by Iris's scent, her laughter, the way she tasted when Stevie pulled her into the alley between the bakery and the post office, kissing her against the brick wall until they were both moaning.

"We need a bed," Iris panted into her mouth.

"I'm working on it," Stevie said, then kissed her again, hips pressing into hers, Iris's finger digging into Stevie's shoulders.

"Are you though?" Iris said, laughing.

"I mean, you're making it really hard to focus."

"I'm just a girl standing in front of another girl, asking her to fuck her senseless."

"Exactly," Stevie said, burying her face in Iris's neck. "I can barely walk just thinking about it."

Then Iris bit Stevie's earlobe, and Stevie's entire body broke out in goose bumps.

"Not helping," she said.

Iris grinned evilly and Stevie pulled them back onto the street, not slowing down, not even glancing Iris's way until they were inside Iris's building and climbing the stairs to her unit.

But then there was the door to contend with, and Stevie couldn't resist pressing her body against Iris's back as she dug into her bag for her keys, sliding her hands around her hips and down to that delicious warmth between her legs.

"Fuck," Iris said, ass pushing against Stevie's thighs. She finally got the key in the door and was in the process of turning the lock when Stevie remembered.

"Oh shit," she said, covering Iris's hand on the doorknob with her own.

"What's wrong?" Iris asked, then laughed. "I need to get you inside right the hell now."

"Okay, yes, but . . ." Stevie said. "I sort of forgot that I had something delivered to your apartment this afternoon when you were writing at the coffee shop."

Iris froze, turned to look at Stevie over her shoulder. "For real?"

Stevie just grinned. "Wooing, remember?"

Iris's eyes searched hers, her expression nothing less than wondrous. She leaned in and kissed Stevie softly. "I love it."

"You don't even know what it is yet," Stevie said.

"I don't care. I still love it."

Stevie kissed her, then let her open the door. They stepped into Iris's dimly lit apartment, and the smell hit them first.

Sweet and organic. Earthy.

"Oh my god," Iris said, clicking on the lamp she had on the console table in the entryway for more light.

Color exploded throughout the living room and kitchen, at least ten Mason jars full of purple flowers covering the space.

"Purple bearded irises," Iris said, picking up a jar and pressing her face into the flowers. "How did you know these are my favorite?"

Stevie shrugged. "Lucky guess? They're all over your planners. Also, the name. I figured you'd love the name."

Iris laughed, plucking a single blossom from the jar and twirling it in her fingers. "I do. Plus, they look like vulvas, which I'm all about."

Stevie threw her head back and laughed. "You are a true romantic, Iris Kelly."

"Look at them!" Iris thrust a flower toward her. "You can't deny they look like puss—"

"Okay, flower girl," Stevie said, taking the iris from her and holding it to her nose. Then she tucked it behind Iris's ear and pulled her close. "Full disclosure, Claire might have let the florist in."

Iris pressed her mouth flat, but Stevie could tell she was fighting a smile. "Claire."

"She's a romantic like me."

Iris shook her head, but she pulled Stevie closer. "I love this surprise." Her breath fluttered against Stevie's mouth.

"You already said that."

"Yeah, but now I really, really love it."

Stevie smiled, her heart buoyant and strong under her ribs.

"What's your favorite flower?" Iris asked.

Stevie gazed at all the irises. "Tulips. Yellow ones."

"Why?"

Stevie shrugged. "I don't know. They're simple, but strong, you know? Like, their petals are really thick and sturdy. I like that, withstanding wind and weather."

Iris smiled, then sighed as she looked around the room. "How did you afford all this? Flowers are expensive. And the hot-air balloon, and the winery—everything we've done over the last couple of weeks. It's too much, Stevie."

Stevie swallowed but shook her head. "Nothing is too much for you."

Iris just stared at her for a few seconds, her chest moving up and down rapidly. Then she smoothed Stevie's hair back, slipping her fingers into the curls and cradling Stevie's head. "Take me to bed right now."

"As you wish," Stevie said, feeling both cheesy and romantic and wild with desire all at the same time. She decided to lean in to it, and promptly scooped Iris into her arms in a bridal carry.

Iris laughed as Stevie walked them down the hallway. "Oh my god, who are you, Wonder Woman?"

"I'm skinny but wiry," Stevie said, angling them into Iris's room.

"Hot as fuck," Iris said as Stevie set her down near the foot of the bed.

Stevie expected them to go at each other then, the wildness from earlier in the night finally overtaking them, but they both just stood there, watching each other, breathing heavily. It was erotic and sweet all at once, the way Iris looked at her, and she never wanted it to end.

She stepped closer, then bent down, lifting Iris's knee-length sundress to her hips. She had on a pair of plain sky-blue cotton bikinis, and Stevie had never seen anything so sexy.

"Hold this," she said, taking Iris's fingers and wrapping them around the hem of the dress. Then she sank to her knees, knocking Iris's legs apart, hands sliding up her smooth thighs. She put her mouth on her, right over her underwear.

"Oh god," Iris said, her head falling back. "Fuck, Stevie."

Stevie kissed her, nipped with her teeth, tongue swirling over the wet spot at her center and tasting her through the cotton.

Iris's free hand dived into Stevie's hair, clenching tight around the locks as she gasped more obscenities. Stevie lapped at her, ready to make her come right there, but when she pulled Iris's underwear aside, her tongue licking up her bare pussy, Iris's grip tightened, and she pulled Stevie's mouth free.

"Wait, wait, wait," Iris said, urging Stevie to stand.

"You okay?" Stevie asked.

"Yeah," Iris said, letting her dress fall so she could pull off Stevie's tank top. "But I want something else first."

Stevie grinned as Iris pulled at Stevie's bralette too, fingers brushing her small breasts. "Anything."

"Good girl," Iris said, grinning as she dipped her head to suck one of Stevie's nipples into her mouth.

Stevie hissed a breath, arching her back to give Iris better access. Iris unbuttoned Stevie's jeans, sloughing them off her legs. Stevie's foot got stuck for a second, and they both laughed as she collapsed onto the bed, feet kicking at the infernal garment.

"Much better," Iris said, hurling her own dress into a dark corner and unhooking her bra.

"Efficient," Stevie said, eyes scanning Iris's goddess-like tits. "I like it." She pulled Iris down onto the bed, then slid her underwear down her legs. Stevie's own boxer briefs soon followed, and she braced herself above Iris, kissing her stomach, tongue gliding upward to her breasts, nipples already hard for her.

"You taste so good," she said, hands palming Iris's tits as she lapped at her peaks. "Tell me what you want."

Iris didn't answer right away, her own hands trailing down Stevie's stomach to her pussy, fingers exploring through damp curls and into her folds.

"Fuck," Stevie said, pressing her forehead between Iris's breasts.

"I want you to fuck me," Iris said, even as she pressed her fingers even harder into Stevie, making her wild with want.

Stevie managed to lift her head. "There's no doubt about that." She removed Iris's hand from between her legs, licking them clean.

"Jesus," Iris said, her pupils blowing wide.

"Tell me," Stevie said between licks, "what you want."

Iris laughed. "You're definitely a switch—you know that, right? The top energy coming off of you right now is about to make me come right here."

Stevie's grin was so wide, her cheeks ached. She wasn't sure why, but Iris seeing this, seeing *her*, after so many years of Adri not seeing anything, was the definition of happy.

"Okay," Stevie said, kissing her sternum, eyes still on hers. "Then my top side is ordering you to tell me what you want. Now, Iris."

Iris squirmed underneath her, laughed. "Have you ever worn a strap-on?"

Stevie paused, lifted her head. Adri had worn one, of course, and Stevie always enjoyed it, but she'd never worn one herself. Adri usually took charge in bed, and Stevie came every time, so she never complained, hardly even thought about it. Now, though, with Iris looking down at her, that impish gleam in her eyes, her hips circling underneath her, Stevie was instantly soaked at the thought of pushing into Iris, making her scream and pant like that.

Of being the one in control.

"I haven't," Stevie said. "But I really, really want to."

Iris's brow lifted. "Good." She nudged gently at Stevie, who released her so she could get up. Then she opened her bedside table and took out a black nylon harness and a sparkly red dildo. It was smooth, curved just slightly at the tip, and made Stevie immediately clench her legs together.

"That's . . . large," she said.

Iris laughed. "Are you okay wearing the harness? Everything's clean."

"Yeah," Stevie said, getting up onto her knees and scooting to the side of the bed where Iris stood. "Though you'll have to show me how to put it on." She rested her hands on Iris's hips and pressed their mouths together.

"I can do that," Iris whispered between kisses.

They stayed like that for a second before Iris fit the dildo's flat circular base into the O-ring, then helped Stevie step through the leg straps.

"This is for you," Iris said, brandishing a small mint-green bullet vibrator.

"Oh?" Stevie said.

Iris giggled. "Oh, indeed." Then she slipped the bullet into a little pocket inside the harness, which would rest right near Stevie's clit. Stevie sucked in a breath when Iris's finger grazed her pussy and again when Iris flicked the device to life. A gentle vibration rolled over Stevie's center and down her legs. Iris kissed her, swallowing Stevie's whimpers as she tightened the harness's waistband on Stevie's hips.

"I need you inside me," Iris said against her mouth, then trailed her fingers over the length of the red cock.

"Do . . . do you need lube?" Stevie asked, trying to breathe normally.

Iris shook her head. "I'm wet enough. The only thing I need is you."

Stevie gripped Iris's hips then, pushing her back onto the bed. She followed after her, eyes never leaving Iris's.

"God, you're pretty," Stevie said, hands trailing down Iris's torso, drinking her in with her fingers.

Iris just smiled, then let her thighs fall open. Her pussy was just as gorgeous, wet and ready, and Stevie couldn't resist a taste. She leaned down, kissing right where her leg met her hip on one side . . . then the other. Iris made a noise not unlike a growl, back arching, and Stevie slid her tongue up her cunt before closing her mouth around her, kissing and sucking.

"Jesus, Stevie," Iris said, fisting her hand into Stevie's hair. "Please."

"Please, what?" Stevie asked, lifting her head.

"Fuck me now. Please," Iris said, her eyes squeezed shut, teeth dragging over her bottom lip.

Stevie kissed her once more before sitting up and settling between her thighs. She spread Iris with her fingers, and the sight of her was so goddamn beautiful she nearly came right there. The bullet continued its work, working Stevie into a slow-building frenzy as she trailed her fingers through Iris's folds.

"You're so wet," she said, thumb dipping into her heat and then out again.

Iris's hips lifted toward the ceiling, and she laughed. "I told you I was. I want you so bad, Stevie."

Stevie positioned the head of the dildo at Iris's entrance, leaning down to kiss her.

"You have me," she said against Iris's mouth.

"Then fuck me," Iris said. "Fuck me with your cock, please."

Stevie leaned up again to focus, relishing the view of the red dildo sliding into Iris's wet warmth.

Iris moaned, lifted her arms above her head.

"Like this?" Stevie asked.

Iris nodded, whimpered. "More."

Stevie thrust deeper, a little harder, until Iris arched her back and groaned, "God, yeah. Just like that."

Iris opened her eyes, her breathing impossibly fast, and grabbed Stevie's waist.

"Come here," she said, pulling Stevie fully on top of her. Stevie braced herself on her forearms, kissed Iris as she pumped her hips slowly, loving the feel of Iris's legs clenching around her waist, of Iris panting into her mouth.

"You like that?" Stevie said, rolling her pelvis upward. "You like my cock inside you?"

Iris bucked her own hips, wordless moans and whimpers spilling from her gorgeous mouth. "Yeah," she finally managed to say. "Yeah, like that, fuck me, oh my god."

Stevie worked faster, sweat beading on her forehead, the bullet shoving her toward her own edge as she buried her face in Iris's neck, between her tits, kissing her mouth as she drove into Iris harder, giving her everything she asked for.

"Oh . . . fuck . . . yeah . . ." Iris said. "I'm going to come."

"Do it," Stevie said, so close herself. "Come on my cock."

"Fuck, Stevie, I . . ."

Iris's entire body clenched and then shuddered as she yelled at the ceiling as she came, fingernails digging into the skin at Stevie's hips. Stevie kept pumping, fucking Iris until Stevie's legs started to tremble, her own orgasm rushing toward her like an ocean wave in a hurricane.

"Shit," she said, pressing her face to Iris's neck, fingers curling into the sheets as she broke against Iris, vision going dark for a split second as she groaned.

Still, neither of them slowed their pace. Iris's thighs viced around Stevie, her hands gripping Stevie's ass and shoving her up and down, deeper into Iris, harder onto Stevie's bullet.

"Don't stop," she said, so Stevie didn't. She kept moving, kept fucking, until they both came again in a string of swears and moans. Stevie bit down on Iris's shoulder hard enough to leave a mark, and Iris rasped out her name, the most gorgeous sound Stevie had ever heard.

"Holy fuck," Iris said, her voice barely audible as her lungs heaved for air.

Stevie just pressed her face against Iris's damp throat. She didn't think she could speak, let alone move. Iris's hand squeezed her ass once before moving upward, fingertips drifting over her back and neck and into her hair.

"I think I'm dead," Stevie finally managed to say. "You killed me, Kelly."

Iris laughed, hooked her leg higher on Stevie's hips. "Death by dildo. Not a bad way to go."

Stevie lifted her head, kissed her once. "Not a bad way at all."

She slid out of Iris, then unbuckled the harness and turned off the bullet before dropping everything on the floor so she could wrap Iris in her arms.

"I hope my neighbors aren't home," Iris said, settling against her, sighing happily as she hooked one arm around Stevie's waist.

"Oh my god," Stevie said. "If they are, they just got an auditory show."

"Hell yeah, they did," Iris said, grinning. "It's a couple. Sweet, in their mid-forties, I think."

She leaned in to kiss Stevie. They stayed like that for a while, chest to chest, just kissing and touching. Iris had just rolled on top of her, whispering in her ear how much she wanted to taste her when they heard it.

The distinct sound of a headboard slamming rhythmically against a wall, the muffled moaning of a woman in the throes of pleasure. They both froze, eyes wide on each other as Iris's neighbors—whose bedroom must align with Iris's—had very loud sex.

"Oh my god," Iris said, covering her mouth as she and Stevie both busted up laughing.

"I guess that answers the question of if they heard us or not," Stevie said.

"I bet we can out-moan them," Iris said, one eyebrow raised.

Stevie grinned. "Oh, hell yes we can."

And they spent the next hour proving it.

LATER, AFTER THEY had slow, languid sex on Iris's living room couch, popcorn abandoned on the coffee table and *13 Going on 30* playing unwatched on the TV, they laid curled together in Iris's bed.

Stevie was the little spoon, just like she liked. She loved the feel of another person—of *Iris*—surrounding her, hemming her in. But as the minutes ticked by and she felt Iris grow heavy with sleep, she couldn't seem to quiet her brain down.

Anxiety spilled in, everything that had happened that night running through her mind like a movie. It had been amazing, but so had that night after Stella's.

What if . . .

Did Iris really . . .

How would Stevie handle . . .

The questions swirled, raising her heart rate, drying out her mouth.

"Iris?" she whispered.

She was sure Iris was asleep, so she was surprised when Iris nuzzled against the back of her neck and said, "Hmm?"

Stevie exhaled, then turned in Iris's arms so they were facing each other. Iris looked beautiful, sleepy.

Happy.

"You okay?" Iris asked.

Stevie didn't answer for a second, but then asked the main question that was keeping her awake. "You . . . you're not going to ask me to leave in the morning, are you?"

Iris shoulders tensed, just a little, just enough.

"It's okay if you're scared," Stevie said. "Just don't hide that from me. I'm scared too."

Iris closed her eyes for a second, body loosening. Stevie traced a finger along her jaw.

"I'm not going to ask you to leave," Iris said. "I promise."

"Is that what you want?"

"Yeah," Iris said, then laughed, her voice a little shaky. "I want you here tomorrow. And the next day. Maybe even the next."

Stevie laughed, relief like she'd never known making her fingertips tingle. She knew Iris wasn't lying—Iris never lied about this sort of stuff, never did anything she didn't want to do.

"I can handle that," Stevie said. "Though I do have a Bitch's shift on Monday."

Iris leaned in to kiss her. "I'll take every second I can get."

CHAPTER

THIRTY

THREE DAYS LATER, Stevie left Iris's apartment in a haze of sex and delivery food, Iris's scent still on her skin even after a shower. She didn't bother going by her apartment before her shift at Bitch's, instead opting for her own jeans—which she had included in a load of laundry at Iris's—and one of Iris's tank tops. The shirt hung on her a bit, a size too big and revealing the rainbow band of her black sports bra, but she didn't care. Anything went, really, at Bitch's, and she loved the idea of wearing Iris's clothes . . . which meant she was really and truly gone for this woman.

She smiled to herself as she pushed open Bitch's heavy wooden door.

"Oi," Effie snapped from behind the bar, tamping down a shot of espresso. "You're late."

Stevie glanced at her phone. "By two minutes."

"That's two minutes I should've been in my office doing payroll for you wankers, so hurry up and clock in."

"Always good to see you, Eff," Stevie said, smiling.

Effie all but snarled at her, and Stevie just laughed as she passed her on her way to the back room.

She clocked in and was just putting her bag in one of the tiny lockers when her phone buzzed. She fished it from her back pocket, already looking forward to a text from Iris.

But it wasn't Iris.

Ren: You're avoiding me

Stevie sliced a hand through her hair, then tapped out I am not.

Except she sort of was. In the weeks since Dr. Calloway's visit and subsequent offer for Stevie to play Rosalind, Stevie had done her level best to avoid the entire situation.

That included Ren and Adri, as they both knew about the offer and had already made it quite clear—Adri's silence and Ren's overbearing insistence that Stevie blow up her entire life and move to New York—how they felt about it. Adri was in crisis mode with the play, constantly busy with details for the fundraiser dinner that would follow the show on *Much Ado*'s closing night, so she was easy enough to avoid. Ren was trickier, but they were also pretty wrapped up in costumes whenever they were at the Empress, and their day job took up plenty of their time as well.

Granted, there might have been texts—okay, a lot of texts—that Stevie simply hadn't answered lately, but in her defense . . . well, *Iris*.

Stevie stuffed her phone in her back pocket and took Effie's place behind the bar, losing herself in steaming milk and creating leaves and flowers in the foam of her craft beverages. For all its drudgery, she actually liked making espresso drinks. It was fast-paced and fun, and Effie paid her well over minimum wage.

"Thanks, Tim," she said, her phone buzzing again as she handed over a dry cappuccino to one of their regulars.

"Take it easy, Stevie," he said, his handlebar mustache twitching as he spoke.

She nodded, then wiped her hands on a towel so she could check her texts.

Ren: Are you at work? I was thinking of stopping by

Stevie's thumbs hovered over the screen. She didn't often lie to Ren—in fact, with the exception of dating Iris, Stevie couldn't think of a single lie she'd ever told her best friend—but she also didn't want Ren's *I know what's best for you* attitude to spoil her good mood right now.

Stevie: No. Running errands. Talk later?

"I know you didn't just fucking lie to me."

Stevie yelped, her phone flying into the air and landing with a crack on the stainless steel bar.

"I hope it's broken," Ren said. They stood at the bar just a little to the left of the espresso machine where Stevie hadn't noticed them. "I really, really do."

"Ren, Jesus." Stevie grabbed her phone, thankful to see the screen was still whole. She stuffed the device in her back pocket and got to work on her next order. "What are you doing?"

"*I* am being a faithful friend." They shifted and settled on a barstool. "What are *you* doing, Stefania?"

Stevie finished up the last drink in her line of orders and set it on the serving counter. "Look, I'm sorry. I've been busy."

"Busy."

"The play. Work."

"Iris."

"Well, yeah." Stevie couldn't help the grin that settled on her mouth. "I like her."

"Okay," Ren said. "Fine. What about New York?"

Stevie sighed. Ren always did get right to the point. "I don't know."

"How can you not know? Stevie. It's the Delacorte. It's Thayer Calloway. It's the *Delacorte*."

Stevie braced her hands on the bar, focused her gaze on the drops of spilled milk and espresso. "I know that."

"Do you?" Ren asked, their brows lifting into their swooping hair. "Because it looks like you don't know shit. This is your dream, Stevie. For the last, what? Five years? You've talked about how you need to up your game, you need to expand your craft, you need to get the hell out of the Pacific Northwest and into a place where you can act full-time."

"I've never said I wanted to get out of the Pacific Northwest."

"Well, fine, I said it and you know it's true."

"Plenty of people act full-time in Portland, Ren. Look at Adri."

Ren laughed, but it wasn't a mirthful sound. "Adri is one dropped donor away from having a heart attack at age twenty-eight. You really want that kind of stress?"

Stevie scoffed. "You think I won't live paycheck to paycheck if I *did* leave Bitch's and tried acting full-time—and in New York of all places? I'm already barely making ends meet. There are no guarantees with this kind of life, Ren."

"Then why the hell do you keep doing it?"

Ren's question settled between them, Stevie's breathing and heart rate already elevated. She just stared at her friend, no answer on her tongue.

"Yeah," said Ren, who always seemed to have an answer. "You do it because you love it, and you're fucking great at it. Better than anyone I've ever seen on stage, and I'm not just saying that. Stevie. Come on. What are you so scared of?"

Stevie shook her head, looked away. Ren's question had infinite answers, everything from the mundane to existential. Failing. Being alone. Navigating the New York subway system. Running out of money. Auditioning and auditioning and auditioning with no callbacks. Letting Dr. Calloway down. Acting on stage next to a legitimately famous actor and making a fool of herself. Rats. Not being able to afford her medication.

You name it, Stevie was probably scared of it.

And then there was—

"Is this about Iris?" Ren asked.

Stevie's head snapped up. "What?"

"It is, isn't it? At least partly."

"It's not—"

"I've seen you, Stevie. Both of you. You're totally caught up with this woman, which, fine. Not exactly what I had in mind when I suggested you needed a few hot hookups to wash Adri out of your system, but fine. I'm happy for you. She's nice and I can tell she's pretty bonkers for you too."

A tiny smile settled on Stevie's mouth—a smile Ren absolutely noticed, because they rolled their eyes.

"But tell me you're not turning down this life-changing, once-in-a-lifetime opportunity for a girl?" Ren said. "Tell me that is not what's happening."

Stevie rubbed her temples, didn't look at Ren. "Look, I haven't given Dr. Calloway my answer yet because . . ." She trailed off, because she didn't know how to finish that sentence, and they both knew it. Fear, sure. But there were a thousand other factors here, factors Stevie didn't know how to tackle.

"What does Iris say about it?" Ren asked.

Stevie's mouth hung open for a split second before she snapped it closed.

Ren's eyes went wide. "Holy shit. You haven't told her. Have you?"

Stevie scrubbed a hand down her face.

"I don't believe this," Ren said. They took a deep breath through their nose. "Okay. I'm just going to say it, Stevie. You're not going to like it, but here it is—my tough love. You ready?"

Stevie folded her arms, looked down at the floor.

"Okay," Ren said. "Here we go. You've spent the last ten years ordering your life around Adri Euler."

"I have not—"

Ren held up a hand. "Let me get this out. Then you can avoid me all you want."

Stevie pressed her mouth closed, eyes already starting to sting.

"You have spent the last ten years ordering your life around Adri Euler," Ren said again, their voice quiet and shaky. "You followed her around, did whatever she asked, and I get it. She was your first love, and she's a strong personality. Fine. But you know what? When you two broke up, I was relieved. I love you both, but you're toxic together, and I was glad she finally had the guts to end it, because I worried you never would."

Stevie frowned, her chest tightening at Ren's lack of faith. Still, she couldn't really deny it. She knew Ren was right—Stevie hadn't been able to see Adri clearly for a long time.

"Then she wrapped you up in this play again, and it pissed me off to no end," Ren said. "But then Iris came along. And I thought, hey, maybe she'll be good for Stevie. A new start. A fresh perspective. But you're just back to exactly where you were with Adri."

"Iris is *not* Adri," Stevie said. "I get what you're saying, Ren. I do. Adri was controlling. I see that now, okay? I let her call the shots, yeah, but Iris is not like that. She gives *me* control. She talks to me, works through my anxiety with me. She's not like Adri at all."

Ren nodded. "Okay. Fair enough."

Stevie exhaled, hoping this whole horrible conversation was coming to an end. But then Ren leaned their forearms on the bar, head tilted and that scary, no-bullshit expression in their eyes.

"But if all that's true," they said, "if you're not wrapping your entire life and self-worth around a woman you're clearly in love with, why haven't you told her about New York?"

Stevie stared at her friend. Dozens of excuses filled her mind— she hadn't had time to tell Iris, hadn't decided what she wanted to do, hadn't wanted to ruin their dates—but deep down inside, she knew the real answer.

She was scared.

Scared Iris would tell her to go . . . and scared Iris would ask her not to.

Ren just nodded, took a deep breath. "I've got to get back to work."

"Yeah," Stevie said. "All right."

"Hey," Ren said, reaching over the bar and grabbing Stevie's hand. "I love you. You know that, right?"

Stevie could only bob her head, tears close to breaking free as Ren walked out the door.

CHAPTER

THIRTY-ONE

IRIS KELLY HAD become her own worst nightmare.

Since the night of the fair over a month ago, Iris couldn't stop thinking about a curly-haired lesbian. She couldn't stop texting that curly-haired lesbian that she missed her. And she couldn't stop constantly fucking grinning when she and the curly-haired lesbian were together.

Barely forty days into her and Stevie's official and very *real* dating relationship, and Iris was already a complete disaster.

Her friends, of course, loved it. Claire especially. Iris had deigned to go on several octuple dates with everyone, Simon and Emery included, and she had to admit it was nice having a hand to hold. Not just any hand though—Stevie's hand was soft, and a little calloused from her work at Bitch's Brew, and fit inside hers perfectly.

She'd even told her parents about Stevie, though she refused to let them meet her until her book launch for *Until We Meet Again* at River Wild in October. At least there, they'd be surrounded by her friends, making it nearly impossible for Maeve to show Stevie all of Iris's baby pictures she'd undoubtedly bring with her and drop endless hints about rings and wedding dresses.

Despite all of this disgusting romantic bliss, every now and then, Iris would have a flash of a memory—Jillian or Grant or some asshole from college. She'd lock up, freak out for a few seconds, but fuck if Stevie Scott wasn't an expert in calming her down. All the woman had to do was look at Iris and know, then take her into her arms and start swaying to some unheard slow song. They'd danced everywhere by now—restaurants, bowling alleys, grocery stores, the Urgent Care center in Bright Falls when Iris woke up one morning at the end of July with a fever and a sore throat.

They'd even danced on stage, in the middle of a live performance of *Much Ado*. They were on the scene where Benedick and Beatrice confess they love each other, and one night last week, Stevie had really played the scene up, taking Iris in her arms and circling her across the stage while all but yelling, *"By my sword, Beatrice, thou lovest me!"*

Iris had laughed, kissed Stevie right there on stage, whispering, *"Do not swear and eat it"* against her mouth. The audience had fucking loved it, and so had Iris. Stevie was magnetic on stage, pure magic, and Iris couldn't take her eyes off of her, even as she waited in the wings, watching a scene that didn't feature Beatrice at all.

The play was going well, a nearly packed house every performance since they opened at the beginning of August. Now, as the weather grew cooler and cooler and they neared the end of the show's run, getting ready for closing night and the fundraiser dinner and auction to follow, Iris was completely exhausted. This was tough work, acting in a show four times a week for a month, and she was wrapping up her agent's edits on her second book in her free time as well. Still, it was a good tired, a productive one, and Iris felt a pang of sadness about her time at the Empress ending.

"It doesn't have to end, you know," Stevie said now, wrapping her arms around Iris and kissing the back of her neck. They were in Stevie's bed, the morning of the last show, and Iris laughed.

"Right," she said. "Even if I did have time to do another play, working under your ex isn't exactly my dream scenario."

She felt Stevie smile against her skin. "She hasn't been too bad lately."

"Only because she's too busy planning for tonight. Last week, she told me my Beatrice was too sentimental. Can you believe that? I, Iris Kelly, have never been accused of such crimes."

Stevie squeezed her tighter, slid a hand up to cup Iris's bare breast. "Well, maybe my dashing and irresistible Benedick is having more of an effect on you than you thought."

Iris turned in Stevie's arms, tucking a wild curl behind her ear. "Maybe."

"There are worse things in the world."

"There are." Iris leaned in to kiss her.

The kiss soon turned heated and desperate, and within fifteen minutes, they were gasping every breath, whispering *yeah* and *fuck* and *god* as their fingers rubbed each other's centers until they both came fast and hard.

"Jesus, woman," Iris said as she returned to herself. "I think I've lost five pounds since we started all this, just from the sex alone."

Stevie laughed, sliding a hand down the outside of Iris's soft thigh. "I'll have to feed you some cake, then."

"Astrid is a great baker, and my favorite is her caramel dark chocolate seven-layer."

"Noted."

Iris smiled, then grabbed her phone and glanced at the time. "Shit. What time did you tell Adri?"

Stevie groaned and flopped back on her pillow. "Noon. What time is it now?"

"Nearly eleven."

"Yeah. I need to go pretty soon."

Stevie had promised Adri that she'd help set up for the night's dinner and auction, which was taking place in the private back room of Nadia's, a swanky, queer-owned Portland restaurant not even a block from the Empress. Iris would join them later, but her deadline for Fiona's edits was in two days, and she had to work a little this afternoon before heading over for the show.

"Hey," Iris said before Stevie could escape the bed. "What's next for you? I've been meaning to ask you."

Stevie's eyes went a little tight. "Next?"

"Yeah. After tonight, *Much Ado* is finished. Do you have any auditions lined up or plays you know are happening around the city?"

"Oh," Stevie said, then pressed her mouth together.

"I know you don't want to do community theater again," Iris said, then nudged Stevie's arm. "You do need to get paid."

Stevie nodded, but just blinked up at the ceiling. She'd been doing this a lot lately, or at least, anytime they talked about the play, or the plays Stevie had done in the past, her dream roles and goals for the future. Iris was always the one to bring up Stevie's career, and Stevie was usually the one to shut it down. Iris let her, because she understood the uncertainty of your next step—in the few months after closing down Paper Wishes, before she decided to give writing a try, she'd burned through her savings, a constant panic simmering just under her skin. Sure, Iris knew Stevie needed a plan, but she certainly didn't want to insult Stevie's abilities to figure out her own shit.

"I don't know," Stevie said quietly. "I guess we'll see." She heaved herself out of the bed, turned to kiss Iris on the forehead, then headed toward the shower.

IRIS WAS SITTING cross-legged on Stevie's bed, completely entrenched in Tegan and Briony's world, trying to figure out how to address Fiona's note about Tegan's too-weak motivations in the third act breakup, when there was a knock on the door.

At first, she ignored it. This wasn't her apartment, and her brain was right on the cusp of a breakthrough, she could feel it. She knew not all romance readers liked the quintessential third act breakup, and Iris had read her share of novels that didn't feature it and enjoyed the change immensely, but for her, she loved that drama-filled split. She loved the pain of it, the emotions, the obstacles the characters had to face in themselves and their relationship to truly be together, all of this followed by the couple's blissful reconciliation.

She'd just started to type, planning on adding to Tegan's interiority, when the knock sounded again.

"Iris?"

Iris froze at her name.

"It's Ren," the person said.

Iris closed her laptop and hurried toward the front door. "Sorry," she said when she unlocked and opened it, revealing Ren in a slim gray suit, black dress shirt and tie, and bright red heeled oxfords. "Shit, you look amazing."

Ren smiled. "Thanks. Big night and all."

Iris nodded as Ren stepped inside. "Stevie's not here."

"I know."

Ren walked farther into the apartment, their hands in their pockets.

"Oh," Iris said. "You're here to see me, then?"

Ren turned to look at her, their heavily lined eyes a little glassy. "Yeah."

"Is everything okay?" Iris frowned. "Oh god, is Stevie all right?"

"No, she's fine."

"Okay, so . . ."

"Can we sit down?" Ren asked.

"I'd rather just get on with it," Iris said. Everything in her was on high alert and she folded her arms.

"Fair enough," Ren said, then sighed. "Look, I just need to ask you a question."

Iris lifted her brows, waiting.

"Has Stevie told you about New York?" Ren asked.

Iris blinked, processing Ren's words. "New York."

Ren closed their eyes. "I'll take that as a no."

"Ren, what are you talking about?"

Ren shook their head, sunk down onto the couch. Iris stayed put, her heart thrumming too fast despite her attempts at deep breaths.

"I didn't want to do this," Ren said. "I kept watching for signs that she'd told you, but it's obvious she hasn't and I didn't know if I'd see you again after tonight. Then it'd be too late."

"What would be too late?" Iris said, her voice razor-sharp. She got bitchy when she got anxious, she knew, but she couldn't seem to help it right now.

Ren tented their fingers between their splayed legs. "Stevie's been asked to play Rosalind in *As You Like It* next summer in New York."

Iris blinked. "She . . ."

"For Shakespeare in the Park at the Delacorte Theater."

A buzzing sounded in Iris's ears, like a tiny bomb exploding.

"September first is the deadline to accept," Ren said. "I don't have to tell you what a huge deal this is."

"September first," Iris said. She suddenly didn't recognize her own voice. It had gone feathery, barely solid.

Ren nodded. "Two days from now."

Iris all but fell onto the pilly gray chair across from the couch. "How . . . She . . . Why didn't she tell me?"

Ren tilted their head. "She'd have to live in New York, at least from January when rehearsals start through the end of July. She'd have to leave everything. Everyone."

Iris dropped her head into her hands, mind swirling at everything Ren seemed to be implying.

"When," she asked, not looking up.

"When what?"

"When was she asked."

Ren was quiet for a second. "Last month. That Black woman who was at the Empress a while back? That's Thayer Calloway, Stevie's favorite professor at Reed. She's the one directing at the Delacorte next summer."

That was the day they'd first slept together, after line dancing at Stella's and Jenna. Stevie had known this for nearly six weeks and hadn't said a damn thing. A myriad of emotions spilled into Iris's chest. Hurt, anger, excitement, fear, pride—a confusing blend she couldn't even begin to parse.

"Anyway," Ren said. "If I were in your position, and a person I loved got a life-changing opportunity, I'd . . . well, I'd want to know."

Iris looked up, that one word hooking around her lungs.

Love.

Shit.

Did she . . . Did Stevie . . .

She swallowed around the knot in her throat and nodded. "Yeah. Thanks for telling me."

"I'm sorry the timing sucks."

Iris waved a hand. She needed Ren to leave. She needed to think, to cry, to fucking scream until the neighbors banged on the wall for her shut up.

"I'll see you in a few hours?" Ren asked, standing up.

And Iris could only nod as Ren left, wondering what the hell she was going to say to Stevie when she saw her, how she was going to look her in the eyes.

She wandered back to the bed, staring down at her laptop, all thoughts of Tegan and Briony like nebulous vapor right now. No way she could get back to writing. She could barely even breathe.

Love.

She squeezed her eyes shut, a familiar hurt crowding around her heart. Because now that she knew about Stevie's offer, she couldn't unknow it. She couldn't ignore it, and neither could Stevie.

New York.

Three thousand miles away.

But *New York*. The Delacorte. Even Iris knew that was huge.

Life-changing.

And Stevie . . .

Iris didn't know what to think or feel. Instead of trying to figure it out, she dug into her overnight bag and pulled out her iPad, crawling back to her spot on Stevie's bed. She opened up her "S & I" folder, then tapped on a blank file. For the next two hours, until she had to start getting ready for the last time she'd ever play Beatrice on stage, she drew.

She drew a curly-haired woman, amber eyes bright, arms outstretched and a beatific smile on her face, standing alone on a New York City street.

CHAPTER THIRTY-TWO

THE EMPRESS WAS packed tonight. Adri had agreed to sell extra tickets, bringing in more chairs to line against the back wall, and Stevie could feel the cast's energy the second she stepped into the dressing room backstage.

"Listen to this," Jasper said, dramatically flipping a newspaper in his hands. Stevie saw *Seattle Times* written across the front page.

"'With a diverse and queer cast that thrusts the Shakespearean classic into a new and erotic light,'" Jasper read, then flicked his eyes to Stevie, "'it is Stevie Scott as a secretly tender and wounded female-identifying Benedick that sets this interpretation apart. Alongside newcomer Iris Kelly as Beatrice, the couple emanates a nearly orgasmic tension on stage.'"

"Let me see that," Stevie said, grabbing the paper from Jasper. She reread the review, which also had lovely things to say about the direction, as well as several other principals' performance. Still, her cheeks warmed, seeing her and Iris's names side by side in the *Seattle Times*. She'd been reviewed in papers before, but this one felt particularly glowing. She couldn't wait to show Iris.

"Can I have this?" she asked Jasper.

"Yes, fine, take it to your girl," he said.

"Nearly orgasmic?" Peter said, slicking mascara onto his lashes. "Just once I want to be described that way."

"Can't bring it to the finish line, huh, Peter?" Zayn said, pursing their lips.

Peter flipped them off. "I mean my stage performance, asshole."

"Uh-huh, sure."

They were still bickering back and forth when Iris finally stepped into the room. Stevie felt her entire body relax a little at the sight of her.

"Hey," she said, working her way toward Iris. The dressing room was small, and every chair was already taken.

"Hey," Iris said, but her smile didn't reach her eyes.

Stevie frowned. "You okay?"

Iris nodded, set her bag on the couch. "Just tired. I worked this afternoon."

"Did you get a lot done?"

Iris nodded again, not meeting Stevie's eyes. Stevie's stomach immediately clenched up, worry fizzing into her fingertips. "Are you sure you're okay?"

Iris looked at her then. Stared, really. She canted her head and narrowed her eyes, as though waiting for Stevie to answer her own question.

"Yeah," Iris said finally. "I'm fine. Just nervous."

Stevie squeezed her arm. "Well, take a look at this." She handed the paper to Iris, pointing at the review for their *Much Ado*.

Iris's eyes scanned the words, a small smile on her mouth as she read. She glanced up, meeting Stevie's gaze.

"'It is Stevie Scott as a secretly tender and wounded female-identifying Benedick that sets this interpretation apart,'" she said out loud, her voice small, almost awe-filled.

Stevie waved her hand. "It's one review."

"It's amazing, Stevie. *You're* amazing. You know that, right?"

She said it so quietly—almost sadly—that Stevie frowned. "I think I—"

"No," Iris said, grabbing Stevie's hand. "You're incredible, full stop."

Stevie searched Iris's eyes, which were a little glassy-looking. "Are . . . are you sure you're okay?"

Iris inhaled deeply then smiled. And right there, Stevie saw it—that mask Iris wore, the one Stevie hadn't seen in over a month, slide over her girlfriend's expression.

"Well," Iris said, all smirk and flirt, "I'm incredible too, so, yeah, I'm great."

Then Iris turned away and went over to where Satchi was peering into a lighted mirror, asking to share the space. Soon the two were laughing and joking as Iris put on her makeup. Stevie kept eyeing Iris as she got ready herself, wondering what she was missing, but Iris never let that mask slip again.

———

THAT NIGHT'S PERFORMANCE was their best yet.

Everyone said so.

But Stevie didn't feel it. Iris was lovely on stage. She was flirty and sly and vulnerable, but something still felt off about the whole production, every time Benedick and Beatrice interacted—a stiffness to Iris's expression Stevie couldn't seem to break through.

Now, in the private backroom at Nadia's, champagne flowing and the lights dim, art donated by local artists on the walls and up for auction, Stevie couldn't even find her girlfriend.

"What a night, huh?" Adri said, coming up next to Stevie. She looked gorgeous, dressed in a strapless black bandage dress, her mermaid hair pinned back on one side.

"Yeah," Stevie said, taking a sip of her club soda. "You really pulled it off."

Adri smiled, nudged her arm. "*We* pulled it off. That *Seattle Times* review sold all the tickets for this dinner, I'm pretty sure."

Stevie shook her head. "It's one person's opinion."

Adri nodded, eyes scanning the buoyant crowd. "Where's Iris?"

Stevie finally spotted her across the room, standing with Claire and Astrid and looking gorgeous in a grass-green dress, straps as thin as thread hooked over her shoulders. Her entire friend group had come tonight, and Stevie saw Delilah wandering the room with Jordan, checking out the art. Simon, of course, was part of the company, so he was around here somewhere too.

"She's with her friends," she told Adri, then glanced at her ex. "Where's Van?"

Adri's expression slipped for a second. "She's around."

"You two okay?" Stevie asked.

Adri sighed. "I think so. I just . . . I've been a bit of an idiot."

Stevie said nothing to that. She and Adri hadn't really talked outside the play since Adri's power moves in Malibu, and Stevie wasn't sure she wanted to go there. Not tonight.

"I'm going to talk to Iris," she said, then walked away before Adri could say anything else.

She wove through the crowd, nodded at Ren who was chatting with Nina and Satchi, not slowing down until she reached Iris's side.

"There she is," Iris said, her voice a little slurred as she looped her arm through Stevie's. Her champagne glass was half full, but she still managed to slosh a bit over the sides.

"Okay, you're cut off," Astrid said, taking Iris's glass.

"Ever the proper lady," Iris said, wrinkling her nose at Astrid.

Stevie frowned. "Are you drunk?"

"She's very drunk," Claire said. "Sorry, I think she'd already downed like two glasses by the time we got here."

"Sorry?" Iris said, brows shoved together. "I'm a grown-ass woman, Claire. I can get drunk if I want."

"I know, honey, but—"

"No," Iris waved a finger. "*I* am nearly orgasmic. *Seattle Times* says so."

Claire and Astrid shared a look over Iris's head, clearly befuddled by that proclamation.

"Baby, let's get you some water," Stevie said, trying to lead Iris to the table full of sparkling water in crystal glasses.

"Baby," Iris said, narrowing her eyes at Stevie. "I bet you call all the girls *baby*."

"What girls?" Stevie asked.

"All of them. The ones in New York," Iris said. She swayed a little on her feet. "I need another drink."

"Yes, water," Stevie said, then pulled Iris toward the table. Iris went, but only because Stevie yanked her pretty firmly. They were halfway across the room, Stevie's heart pounding, when she saw her.

Thayer Calloway.

Right there, smiling at Stevie from five feet away, resplendent in a black suit and silver tie.

"Stevie," Thayer said. "I was hoping to catch you."

Stevie swallowed, glanced at Iris, who regarded Thayer with a mixture of swaying curiosity and suspicion.

And she was right to be suspicious. Stevie could at least admit that, even if she was terrified to face every other truth she hadn't said yet. This morning, after Iris had asked her about her next steps, Stevie had lied. She'd told Iris she didn't know, and she felt horrible about it. Because just the night before, after Iris had fallen asleep, she'd sent Thayer Calloway an email.

Thank you so much for your offer. I can't tell you how
honored I am that you'd think of me for this role. I'm thrilled

to accept. Please let me know next steps when you get a
chance.

It had taken her six weeks to get to this point, to get to this *yes*,
then another ten minutes to hit send on the email that would seal it.
And all the while, Iris slept next to her, oblivious. Stevie had wanted
to talk to her about it, but her courage only went so far. In truth, part
of Stevie had always known she was going to accept Thayer's offer—
she'd known it the moment Thayer had asked her to be Rosalind.
There was no way she could ever say no, no way she could ever live
with herself if she passed up this chance. She was scared shitless, but
she felt strong too. She knew she was good, knew she needed to take
a chance if she was ever going to turn acting into a lasting career.

And being with Iris these last several weeks . . . she felt even
stronger. More capable. More ready.

But she also had even more to lose. Her decision affected Iris too,
she knew, but she also knew Ren was right—she couldn't make her
choice based on this relationship.

She had to choose herself and hope to god Iris understood.

This morning, she'd had every chance to tell Iris about the role,
that she'd accepted it, but she chickened out. She told herself she was
simply waiting until the play was done, the final night, so they could
both enjoy it without New York hanging over their heads. She'd been
determined to tell Iris tonight, once everything at the Empress was
done, and she and Iris were tucked into bed together, close and intimate and safe.

But now, with Thayer right here and Iris drunk and acting so
strange even before the play, Stevie was questioning every decision
she'd made since hitting send on that email.

"Dr. Calloway," Stevie said, her heart fully in her throat now. She
had no idea that her professor would be here, but now that she
thought about it, she should've prepared for this. Thayer was a big

supporter of the Empress, financially speaking, and she wouldn't miss a chance to bolster a queer theater in her own hometown.

"Excellent performance, as always," Thayer said, then her eyes flitted to Iris. "And this must be Iris Kelly. I greatly enjoyed your Beatrice."

Iris pursed her mouth, eyes glassy, and panic crowded into Stevie's chest.

"I *am* Iris Kelly," Iris said, words a little slurred. "And *you* are Thayer Calloway. You're Stevie's favorite professor."

Thayer smiled brightly at Stevie, but Stevie frowned. She'd never told Iris that. She'd never told Iris anything about Dr. Calloway.

"A high compliment," Thayer said.

"And you're directing *As You Like It* next summer," Iris said, jutting a wobbly finger toward Thayer.

Stevie froze.

"I am," Thayer said, frowning a bit at Iris's thick consonants. "And I'm so excited that Stevie here is joining me."

A horrible silence spilled in between them. A silence Thayer clearly didn't understand, her head tilted toward Stevie in question.

"Yeah," Iris said, her voice even and quiet. Too quiet. She blinked heavily. "We're all so excited."

"I really need to get her home, Dr. Calloway," Stevie said. Dread coiled in her stomach.

"Of course," Thayer said. "I'll be in touch."

"Great," Stevie said, then started to pull Iris away.

Iris, however, dug in her heels. "Stevie's amazing, right? Totally belongs in New York. She's a star. So big a star, she shouldn't even think about anyone else, right?"

Stevie couldn't breathe. Could barely think.

"I'm not sure what you mean," Thayer said, but she was clearly caught off guard by Iris's behavior.

"Well, let me explain," Iris said, clapping her hands together, but

Stevie knew whatever Iris was about to say, Stevie couldn't bear to hear it in front of her future director. She wasn't sure she could bear to hear it at all.

Because in this moment, Stevie realized she had right and truly fucked this up.

"Dr. Calloway, I'm sorry, please excuse us," Stevie said, and finally managed to haul Iris away, one arm tightly hooked around her waist. Partygoers looked their way, amused expressions on their faces as a drunk Beatrice stumbled through the room.

Stevie managed to find a bottle of water and tucked it under her arm, never letting go of Iris for a second. She got them outside, the air warm and breezy, and nearly ran to get Iris to Stevie's car.

"I'm not ready to go home," Iris said, but she didn't resist as Stevie tucked her gently into the passenger seat and buckled her in. Iris flopped her head against the headrest, and Stevie opened the water, placing both of Iris's hands around the cool plastic.

"Drink, please," she said.

Iris did, but she watched Stevie as she gulped, an unreadable look in her eyes.

Stevie drove them to her apartment. Neither of them spoke and Stevie was glad. She had no clue what to say, what to do. Plus, Iris was drunk, and she felt like whatever conversation they were about to have, they both needed to be clearheaded.

Once inside her place, she put on a pot of coffee and got Iris another glass of water. Iris downed it, her hands shaking as she did. Once she finished it, she simply stumbled off toward the bathroom, mumbling something about a shower.

Stevie sat outside the bathroom door to make sure Iris didn't fall or hurt herself in some way. And there, underneath the gentle hush of the water, came a sound Stevie had never heard before—a sniff and a hiccup, a wordless hum.

Iris Kelly was crying in Stevie's shower.

CHAPTER
THIRTY-THREE

FUCK, SHE WAS crying in Stevie's shower.

Iris sunk down into the tub, sitting on the porcelain with her forehead pressed against her knees, letting the cold water beat down on her back.

She should've known that first glass of champagne was a mistake. She hadn't meant to get drunk, not really. But once the performance was over and she and Stevie had changed and walked down to Nadia's hand in hand in silence, an awful silence full of questions Iris didn't know how to ask, she'd immediately reached for a glass when they'd walked in the door. Stevie had been pulled away by some adoring donor, and goddamn if the cool bubbles hadn't made Iris feel a little calmer, a little clearer.

But then Stevie didn't return, and one drink became two, which soon turned into three, and she was already laughing at nothing and everything by the time Claire and Astrid found her.

The rest of the night was a bit hazy, lucidity returning only when Thayer Calloway had announced Stevie was heading to New York.

I'm so excited that Stevie here is joining me.

Like a cymbal crash.

That's what it had felt like in Iris's head—a loud, nearly incomprehensible noise, followed by a clear ringing in her ear.

Ren's fears had been unfounded, all their worry—*Iris's* worry since Ren's visit—that Stevie would give up such a chance for *her* . . .

Well.

Iris sob-laughed against her knees and spent the next half an hour in the shower, wondering how the hell she got to this point with Stevie. She went through every detail of their relationship, trying to figure out when she fell, when she became this person she barely recognized.

As the old Iris, Ren's news about New York would've landed differently. Iris would've been surprised that Stevie hadn't told her, but then she would've shaken it off, known Stevie had her reasons. They'd had fun while it lasted, time to move on and all that.

As the old Iris, Stevie's acceptance of Rosalind, this life-changing role in New York, would've landed differently too.

Iris would've been happy.

She would've fucking rejoiced, because Stevie deserved this, she deserved to be a star, Iris knew it. And even as this new and pathetic Iris, part of her *was* excited for Stevie.

The part that loved her.

But that was the tricky thing about love—it was selfless and also needy; generous, but greedy and desperate too. It was *everything*, and she hadn't even noticed it sneaking up on her, tangling her together with Stevie so tightly she now found herself sitting in a dingy shower, wiping tears off her face, wondering why she *couldn't* rejoice, why her heart felt like it was splintering, why she couldn't shake off this sad, old, familiar feeling of being disregarded.

Of being left behind.

Always good for a nice fuck, that Iris Kelly.

"Shit," she said, slicking her wet hair back. She took several deep breaths and stood up, turning the shower off. She took her time drying, then put on the tank top and sleep shorts from last night she'd left in the bathroom earlier that day. She plaited her wet hair into a single braid, brushed her teeth, and packed all of the toiletries in her bag.

Her hand hesitated on the doorknob so long the metal grew warm under her fingers. Then she rolled her shoulders back, set her face to a neutral expression, and went out into the main room.

Stevie was on the bed and bolted to standing as Iris emerged. Iris tossed her toiletry bag toward her larger overnight bag, Stevie's eyes following the movement.

She sat back down.

"You're not staying the night?" she asked, her voice small.

Iris didn't answer. She just sat down in Stevie's desk chair across from the bed, pulled her knees to her chest.

"When?" she asked.

Stevie's throat worked. "When . . . when what?"

"When did you tell your professor you'd do it?"

Stevie sighed, swiped her curls back. "Last night."

Iris nodded, didn't say anything.

"I was going to tell you tonight," Stevie said.

Iris laughed. "That's easy to say now that I know, isn't it?"

"Iris, I . . . I'm sorry, okay? I thought I was going about this the right way. Taking my time, thinking it through, but—"

"And you couldn't bring me into that?" Iris asked. *You didn't think about me at all*, her brain said next, but she couldn't get it out of her mouth.

"I . . . dammit," Stevie said. "I did. I swear to god, Iris, I did think about you. But we were so new and I . . . I was scared."

"Scared."

"Yes, scared."

"Of what?" Iris asked. She shocked herself by how much she

wanted to know, how much she wanted to feel *not* alone in this terrifying space.

Stevie didn't answer for a few seconds. They ticked by, turning into minutes, Stevie staring down at the sleek black pants she'd adorned for the fundraising dinner.

"I was scared," she finally said, "that you'd tell me to go."

Iris frowned, Stevie's small tone slipping another splinter into her heart.

"Of course I would've told you to go," Iris said.

Stevie's eyes met hers, wide, shining.

"This is . . . it's New York, Stevie," Iris said. "And you deserve it. You belong there. I would've never held you back from that."

Stevie nodded, a tear slipping down her cheek. Iris curled her hands into fists, fighting the urge to wipe it away.

"But you didn't even give me the chance," Iris said. "You cut me out of the decision, you cut me out of being happy for you, of celebrating—"

"I didn't want you to celebrate it," Stevie said, her voice suddenly firmer, stronger. "I wanted you to ask me to stay. Even if I knew I couldn't, I wanted you to *want* me to. Or at least . . . I don't know. Show some emotion that I might be moving three thousand miles away. And I was fucking terrified that you wouldn't. That you'd treat this"—she waved her hand between them—"like it was nothing."

Iris shook her head, fresh tears welling into her eyes. God, she hated this. She hated this feeling, the empty hollow all these splinters were carving out in her heart.

"You're the one who treated this like it was nothing, Stevie," she said softly.

Stevie swore under her breath, shoved her hands into her hair and left them there, her shoulders undulating up and down. Iris watched her, uncertain what else there was to say.

Finally, Stevie stood up, presenting her palms. "Okay. Okay, I know I fucked up, that not telling you was the wrong move and maybe the worst thing I could've done. I'm so sorry. But I swear, Iris, I didn't cut you out of this. I thought about you every second. I thought about how—"

"Stop," Iris said, shaking her head. She stood up too, but only so she could grab her duffel, loop it over her shoulder.

"Are you fucking serious?" Stevie said, her mouth hanging open. "You're leaving? Just like that?"

Iris felt the color drain from her face, but she didn't flinch. "What else is there to say?"

"Are you . . ." Stevie blinked, her face just as pale as Iris's. "There's a shit ton to say."

Iris sighed. "Like what?"

Stevie stared at her, jaw working. "Like the fact that I love you."

Iris didn't move.

"Like the fact that, yeah, I fucked up," Stevie said. "I was scared. I'm still scared, okay, but I don't want you to leave. I want you to forgive me and talk to me and let us figure out what the hell to do."

Iris shook her head. "You already decided, Stevie."

"I decided on *me*," Stevie said, her voice nearly a shout. She slapped at her chest, the sound echoing through the room. "I picked *me*, Iris, the exact thing everyone in my life has wanted me to do for years, and you know that's not easy for me. You know it's not, but I did it, because yeah, I want this. I want to play Rosalind in New York. But that doesn't mean I don't want you."

Iris closed her eyes, tried to let Stevie's words break through the protective layer already sliding over her tender heart. She thought about the last two months, how every day with Stevie had felt . . .

Different.

It hadn't felt like Grant. It hadn't felt like Jillian. It hadn't felt like a fling or fake or purely educational or any of the things they'd both told themselves it was for so long.

She tried to let it all in, but now, in this moment, with Stevie leaving to start a whole new life—a life she *should* lead, a life she deserved—Iris felt . . .

Nothing.

Her heart had already closed up, surrounded in that protective layer she'd spent the last year building back to its full strength, shoving out all the splinters, keeping her safe.

Keeping her whole.

"Stevie," she said, "this was fun, okay? But I can't let you break your back trying to work me into your plan, all for a relationship that will only—"

"Don't," Stevie said. "Don't you fucking dare."

"What?"

"*This,*" Stevie said, her teeth gritting.

Good. Let her get angry. It would probably make this whole thing easier.

"The exact thing you said I was doing," Stevie said, "trying to tell me this is nothing. You're trying to tell me you're not worth considering. Not worth factoring into my life. Again. Why do we always fucking come back to this?"

"Because *you* didn't factor me, Stevie," Iris yelled back. "And you know what? You shouldn't. You were right to pick yourself. Because if you'd told me about New York a month ago, god knows what sort of mess we'd be in right now."

"Mess? What are you talking about?"

"I'm talking about us, Stevie. We'd be the mess. The ticking time bomb, trying to do long distance and burning through our savings on plane tickets, driving ourselves crazy wondering how long it would last, how long before someone else came along, how long before you realized I was just—"

A sudden swell of tears cut off her voice. She swiped them away, furious at her own emotions.

"At least this way," she finally said, "we know you and I were nothing but brain chemicals and sex."

It was like dropping a nuclear bomb—a huge explosion followed by . . . nothing. Silence. A complete lack of air and light and life.

Stevie stared at her, tears tracking silently down her cheeks. Finally, Iris managed to turn away from her, legs shaking, hoisting her bag higher onto her shoulder. She started to move, one foot in front of the other, one step at a time that would eventually get her out of this apartment and to her car, to her own home, to her bed where she could finally fall apart.

She was nearly to the door when Stevie spoke.

"Bullshit," she said.

Iris turned. "What?"

Stevie faced her, fists clenched by her sides, her face a ruin of tears and pain. Iris's heart broke, right there, but she knew she couldn't take any of it back.

She wouldn't.

"I said bullshit," Stevie said. "You're lying. You're lying to protect yourself, to protect me, and it's bullshit, Iris."

Iris shook her head, but Stevie was already crossing the room to her. Iris braced herself for her touch, trying to work up the courage to push her away, but Stevie didn't even try to pull her into her arms. Instead, she dipped her hands into Iris's open bag and brought out her iPad.

"What are you doing?" Iris asked.

Stevie tapped on the screen. The home screen came to life and Stevie's eyes scanned Iris's icons.

"What the hell are you doing?" Iris asked.

Stevie turned the iPad to reveal a drawing of Iris and Stevie standing by Bright River the night of the summer fair. Iris had already added color to this illustration, and they were bathed in silvery starlight. In the drawing, Iris's hands were in Stevie's hair, Stevie's arms around her waist, and their mouths were a centimeter from touching.

That moment right before they kissed.

Right before they fell into each other for real, all of their lessons and fake dating and Stevie's wooing falling away, leaving nothing but them.

Iris's heart galloped against her ribs. "How . . . how did you know about my drawings?"

"I saw them the day you kicked me out after Stella's," Stevie said.

"Stevie, I—"

"It doesn't matter, Iris. What matters is that you drew them. And you drew them like *this*." She flipped to another drawing, and another and another—Iris and Stevie dancing in the grocery store, Iris and Stevie laughing at boozy mini-golf, Iris and Stevie tangled together in bed. "You drew us, Iris. Because you love me. You fucking love me and you have for a long time."

Iris closed her eyes, shook her head as she took the iPad from Stevie and stared down at the image on the screen. "I . . ."

But she didn't know how to finish that sentence, because Stevie was right. And it was so obvious in every single one of these illustrations, how gone she was on this woman, how wrapped up.

How in love.

She shook her head, ready to protest a bit more, but suddenly, Stevie's hands were on her face, cupping her cheeks and tilting her head up to meet her eyes. Iris's heart swelled into her throat, tears flying down her cheeks.

"Come with me," Stevie whispered against her mouth.

Iris froze. "What?"

"Come with me, Iris. To New York. Come with me. Live with me. I love you, okay? I am wildly, stupidly in love with you. Yes, I messed up. Yes, I chose me, but I choose you too. That's what love is, right?

I want both, and I know you do too. We can figure this out, we can. Just say yes."

Iris squeezed her eyes shut, but Stevie didn't back away. She didn't take it back. She just kept whispering, "Come with me," while her thumbs swiped Iris's tears away.

And fuck, Iris wanted to say yes. She wanted it so badly, her fingers tingled, her heart beat as though jolted with a shot of electricity. She could see it—her and Stevie on the streets of New York, holding hands in Central Park, Stevie glowing on stage with Iris in the front row with a bouquet of yellow tulips for her star, kissing in their bed, their apartment, their own private universe, the city sounds like music on the street below.

It was a beautiful vision. A dream. But that's all it was. Because even as Iris wanted to say yes, that old fear crept up her throat like a poison, that armor around her heart tightening its locks, bringing with it the understanding that, eventually, Stevie would change her mind. Or she'd push to get married or have babies or some other thing Iris simply didn't want. And then she'd look at Iris like Grant had, like Jillian had, like she wasn't . . .

Enough.

And Iris couldn't bear it. She couldn't bear for Stevie, her Stevie, to ever look at her like that. She couldn't give everything away—her entire life in Bright Falls, her friends, her family—for a person who would eventually see Iris for exactly who she was.

"Look," Stevie said, taking the iPad out of Iris's hands and flipping through Iris's illustrations again. "Let's make a new drawing. You and me, right now, in New York."

"Stevie," Iris said.

Stevie shook her head, fingers trembling as she flipped through drawing after drawing. "We can do it, okay? How do I get to a blank page?"

"Stevie," Iris said again.

"No, Iris." She kept flipping. "Just think about it, okay? We can—"

She stopped, her mouth open, gaze reflecting the screen.

Iris closed her eyes, knowing exactly what drawing Stevie had finally landed on, the one Iris had just sketched this morning—Stevie, arms outstretched in the middle of Times Square, a lovely smile on her face.

Alone.

Stevie blinked down at the black-and-white drawing. It was good, if Iris did say so herself, capturing all of Stevie's strength and fear and determination.

Slowly, Iris pulled the iPad from her hands, slipped it back into her bag. Stevie let her, a shocked expression on her face.

"I can't," Iris said simply, and left it at that. She opened Stevie's door, stepped through it.

"You know," Stevie said as Iris's feet hit the hallway.

Iris froze, but she didn't turn around.

"Ever since we met, I thought I was the one who was scared," Stevie said, her voice low and quiet. Steady. "*I'm* the one who needed confidence. *I* needed to take a chance. *I* needed to be brave. But really, all this time, it was you. You're the real coward, Iris. Aren't you?"

Iris's chin trembled, the truth of Stevie's words closing around her like a second skin.

But she couldn't do this again—this moment, after only six weeks together, was already enough to crush her lungs. What would six months do to her?

Six years?

So she didn't answer. She didn't say anything at all. Instead, she simply walked away, leaving the woman she loved crying in her doorway.

Just like the coward they both knew she was.

CHAPTER

THIRTY-FOUR

STEVIE SAT ON the couch in her and Adri's old apartment.

There were touches of Vanessa everywhere—new potted plants to join Adri's ferns on the balcony, aqua- and coral-colored pillows strewn throughout the living space, vibrant art by Latin American artists on the newly painted mustard-colored walls. The place looked homier than it ever had with Stevie as half its decorator, Stevie who favored neutral colors and brain-calming gray walls.

The apartment was crowded tonight, full of friends and actors from the Empress, even a few actors from other local plays in which Stevie had acted. Everyone was here for her goodbye party, but she felt oddly disconnected from the whole event. Still, she smiled as people squeezed her shoulder, told her congratulations, stopped her to chat about New York as she moved through the room, looking for a redhead she knew she wouldn't see.

It had been two weeks since she and Iris had broken up, since she'd emailed Dr. Calloway with trembling fingers and accepted the role of Rosalind in *As You Like It*. Two weeks since that simple message had turned her entire life upside down.

Even though rehearsals didn't start until January, Dr. Calloway had mentioned that she'd love to have Stevie's input on auditions—along with the couple of other principals Thayer had already cast, actors whose well-known names Stevie couldn't even fully comprehend right now—which started in mid-September.

Details fell into place easily—so easily, Stevie barely felt like she was a part of it all, struggled to remember this was actually happening to *her*. Thayer had arranged an apartment for Stevie, a tiny, one-bedroom flat in Williamsburg that Thayer's wife's family owned and never used. She told Stevie to leave her car behind, bought her an annual MetroCard on the theater's dime, and even sent her the link to a New York subway app so she could prepare herself to navigate the city.

Her professor—her *director*—knew Stevie well, knew her disorder necessitated planning and practice, and Stevie had to admit that all of Thayer's help went a long way to calming her constantly frantic heart.

Still, the days passed in a blur, her phone lighting up regularly with texts and emails from Ren and Thayer and Adri and her mother, the latter of whom was already planning Christmas in New York, ecstatic that Stevie was *leaning into life*.

But Iris never called.

Never texted.

Never emailed.

Stevie told herself she wouldn't check Iris's Instagram, an account with tens of thousands of followers due to Iris's popular planners, but she couldn't seem to stay away either. In the end, it didn't matter, as the last picture Iris had posted was a selfie of Iris kissing Stevie's cheek as they sat on the edge of the Empress's stage after a show, the soft theater lights turning the whole shot golden.

It was dated two days before they'd broken up and had over ten thousand likes, the comments seemingly endless and effusive.

Cutest couple!
Omg wlw goals!
Where can I get a gal like Stevie?
Iris, your freckles are GORG!
You two are so in love it makes me sick! Except
    not lol!

Stevie had made a habit of staring at the picture late at night, then promising herself she'd never look at it again, only to cave again twenty-four hours later, scouring Iris's expression for some hint of what was to come two days after snapping this photo.

But all she saw was her girlfriend, smiling mouth pressed to Stevie's cheek, eyes scrunched up with happiness and contentment.

"Jesus, will you put that away?" Ren asked, coming up behind Stevie and leaning their arms on the back of the couch.

Stevie clicked her phone dark, Iris's beautiful face disappearing. She sighed, took a sip of her club soda. Ren squeezed her shoulder and Stevie smiled up at them. She and Ren had made peace—after a complete blowout that involved Stevie totally losing her shit about Ren minding their own business, followed by a full forty-eight hours of the silent treatment, which was only broken when Ren showed up at Stevie's place with curry from Stevie's favorite Thai place and a huge Thai iced tea. Stevie knew Ren loved her, knew they were just looking out for her. Stevie knew she was an infamous chickenshit. Still, even though Stevie's plan to tell Iris about New York was ill-conceived and backfired spectacularly, Ren had crossed a line by talking to Iris, and Stevie made sure they knew it.

"Come on, let's get some air," Ren said, tugging gently on Stevie's arm.

Stevie acquiesced—it didn't really matter if she brooded on the couch or on the balcony—and followed Ren outside. Adri and Vanessa were already out there, pressed together against the railing, Portland glittering behind them.

"Hey, you," Van said, holding out her hand to Stevie. "How are you feeling?"

"Dizzy," Stevie said, and laughed, but it was true.

Van nodded. "You're going to be amazing. Adri and I are already planning our trip out to New York for opening night."

Stevie smiled, glanced at Adri, who just tilted her head at Stevie, an unreadable expression on her face.

"I, for one, will be out there way before that," Ren said. "I can totally write it off as a work trip."

"You're welcome anytime," Stevie said, but then her throat went thick at the thought of being away from these three people. They'd been her best friends for ten years, walking with her through her anxiety, through her acting ups and downs. Through Adri herself. She and Adri may be complicated, but Stevie would always love her.

As she looked at her now, her green hair fading more and more into her natural dark brown, Stevie felt nothing but grateful. She reached out and squeezed Adri's hand. In turn, Adri smiled sadly at her, then winked. It was such a small gesture, but it felt huge to Stevie's heart.

A letting go.

An accepting.

She nodded, squeezed Adri's hand one more time, then released her, turning to face the city she'd loved for so long. The air was cool, that September promise of fall, of sweaters and scarves and rain boots. Stevie breathed it in, tried to visualize herself on that airplane tomorrow morning, three full duffels checked and stowed underneath.

"I invited her," Ren said, coming up next to her, shoulder pressing close. "Texted her the details."

Stevie frowned. "Invited . . ."

"Iris, of course," Ren said, rolling their eyes.

"Oh," Stevie said, gazing back out at the city. "Right."

"She didn't respond. Not even to decline."

Stevie nodded, then shrugged. She couldn't imagine leaving Oregon without telling Iris goodbye. Then again, she supposed they'd said all there was to say two weeks ago.

"I'm sorry, Stevie," Ren said, leaning their head on Stevie's shoulder. "I know you liked her."

Loved, Stevie's brain supplied, but she shoved the word away. Love had nothing to do with her and Iris. Nothing at all. She breathed in her anger at Iris's cowardice and denial of what they had, letting it push out the ache in her heart. Anger was easier. Anger was fire, cleansing and overpowering.

"It was fake," Stevie said. She felt Ren's attention, Adri and Vanessa's, snap to her.

"What?" Ren said.

"Me and Iris," Stevie said, taking a deep breath. "It was all fake. We did meet at Lush, but then . . . god, I won't even go into the details about that night, but it didn't go well. I let you all believe it had. And then she showed up at the Empress and . . . I don't know."

"You . . . made up your relationship?" Adri asked.

Stevie met her eyes, nodded.

"Why?" she asked.

"Fuck," Ren said, shaking their head. "Adri, you know why."

"Oh, Stevie," Van said, her lovely face crumpling.

"Okay, stop," Stevie said. "I didn't do it only because of you two. And Ren, honestly, you didn't help."

"Me?" Ren asked.

"You. Look, I know you all love me. I do. But sometimes . . . you assume you know what's best for me before even giving me the space to figure it out myself."

Ren had the self-awareness to look away but said nothing.

"Iris agreed to go along with the whole thing to give me some space. Some time, I don't know, to figure myself out without Adri and Van constantly feeling guilty about getting together and without Ren's nagging me to move on. I needed time to be *me*."

"Stevie," Ren said. "I'm sorry."

Stevie shook her head. "I get it. Really, I do. But I need you all to understand that just because I have an anxiety disorder, it doesn't mean I don't know how to take care of myself. I *do* need you. I need you all so much, but part of that need is you having a little fucking faith in me."

They were all silent and Stevie turned back toward the city, letting her words sink in. Her heart was racing, but god it felt good to finally say it.

Adri broke the spell first. She reached out and took Stevie's hand again. Stevie let her, because she knew everything she needed from Adri she'd already given to herself.

"I love you," Adri said.

Stevie smiled. "I know you do."

She nodded, then let Stevie go, kissing Vanessa's cheek before she excused herself and went back inside. Vanessa hugged Stevie once, then followed her, leaving only Ren.

"I take it the fake relationship eventually turned pretty real," they said.

Stevie just laughed. "Real as it gets."

Ren nodded. "I'm sorry. For putting you in that position."

"I'm not," Stevie said, shaking her head. "I mean, yeah, it's true you get a little overbearing—"

"Fair."

"—but I don't regret meeting Iris," Stevie finished, then smiled at Ren, a lump in her throat. "Not one bit."

Ren turned around so they were facing Adri's apartment windows, leaning their elbows on the railing. "I can see that."

Stevie looped her arm through theirs, leaned her head on their shoulder. They stayed like that for a while, then Stevie felt Ren tense up.

"What is it?" Stevie said, turning to look at whatever had caught Ren's attention.

"Isn't that . . ." Ren asked, squinting and pointing to someone inside.

Stevie's heart betrayed her, all anger flooding out of her system. She swallowed, her mouth immediately dry, eyes searching for red hair and freckles.

". . . Iris's friends?" Ren went on. "What are their names? The one with the tattoos and her fiancée who owns the bookstore?"

Stevie couldn't breathe, her chest completely locked up. She spotted Claire and Delilah weaving through the crowd. "You invited her whole crew?"

Ren shook their head. "Just Iris."

Stevie watched as Claire spotted her, waving and leading Delilah—who paused by the bar Adri had set up and grabbed two glasses of wine—in Stevie's direction.

"Hey, Stevie," Claire said, smiling sweetly.

"Um. Hey," Stevie said, frowning. "Is . . ."

Claire shook her head.

Stevie exhaled audibly, pressing a hand to her chest. She didn't mean to be so dramatic, but it felt like she hadn't taken a breath in about an hour.

"I'm sorry," Claire said.

Stevie waved a hand, swallowed around the balloon in her throat.

"So . . ." Ren said. "Okay, I'm going to go check on the food."

They kissed Stevie on the cheek, then left Stevie on the balcony with her ex-girlfriend's best friends.

"Does Iris know you're here?" she asked.

"Are you kidding me?" Delilah said, sipping on her red wine. "She'd slip arsenic in our drinks first chance she got."

Stevie sighed. "Then—and sorry if this is rude—but what are you doing here?"

"My fiancée is a hopeless romantic?" Delilah said.

Claire smacked her lightly on the shoulder. "Babe."

"I didn't say I don't like it," Delilah said, leaning close and kissing her on the neck, just once, but it was enough to make Stevie's heart clench.

"I'm sorry to just show up," Claire said. "But Iris mentioned Ren had invited her to your going-away party and I—"

"She did?" Stevie said.

"She didn't mean to," Delilah said. "She was drunk."

Stevie closed her eyes, shook her head. "Oh."

"She's hurting, Stevie," Claire said. "I know she is."

"She said as much?" Stevie asked.

"Not in so many words. You know Iris."

"I'm not sure I do, actually," Stevie said, folding her arms. Even now, after everything that had happened, it felt like a lie.

Claire nodded. "I know she hurt you. But she's just scared. I didn't want you to leave without making sure you understood that."

Stevie looked away, her eyes already starting to sting. But underneath her sadness, her heartbreak, there was also that anger. She leaned in to it. She needed it to keep her upright, to keep her going.

Because at the end of the day, it didn't matter how scared Iris was. Stevie was scared all the fucking time, but she was ready to *try*. To take a chance with her career and her heart.

"Claire," she said, "I get that you love her and you want what's best for her. But look around you. She's not here."

Claire pressed her mouth together. Delilah looked down at her wine.

"I already told Iris everything she needs to know," Stevie said, a confidence she didn't realize she had flooding into her veins—or maybe she had known it all along, she just hadn't trusted it before now. "And she said no. Didn't even want to talk about it with me. It no longer matters why."

Claire swallowed, and she nodded. "I get that."

"Good," Stevie said. Her hands were starting to shake, but she shoved them into her pockets, a show of strength and resolve. "I'm glad to see you both so I could say goodbye. And I really appreciate all of your support, but Iris and I are over."

Claire nodded again, and Delilah laced their hands together, kissed the tips of her fingers.

Stevie stepped forward and hugged them both—they were good friends, she could see that, and in another life, she would've loved being part of their lives.

But this wasn't that life.

"I wish you both all the best," she said as she released them. They smiled at her, offered her the same, and then she excused herself.

Once inside, she wove through the crowd, the well-wishers, the friends and colleagues she was leaving behind, and found her way to the bathroom. Thankfully, it was empty. She locked herself inside and sank down against the door, a sob escaping from her chest as she hugged her knees close, letting herself finally fall apart.

Ten minutes later, her body like an empty husk, clean and ready for something new, something real, she stood up. She wiped her face, blew her nose, smoothed her hair back as much as she could.

Then she went back to her party, ready to say goodbye to her old life, finally ready to welcome in a new one.

CHAPTER

THIRTY-FIVE

OCTOBER IN BRIGHT Falls was truly a sight to see.

The trees were a riot of color, all reds and yellows and purples. When Iris was a kid, she and her siblings would trounce around the backyard, trying to find a dying leaf whose shade exactly matched their hair.

As an adult, she still couldn't resist the tradition. As she stood in River Wild Books, the shop crowded with her friends and family, Bright Falls residents with Iris's debut romance novel in their hands, ready for her to sign their copy, her hand played in the pocket of her teal maxi dress, fingers sliding up and down the smooth red leaf she'd found on the sidewalk before her event started.

"Quite a turnout," Astrid said from next to her, a glass of champagne in one hand, Jordan's fingers tangled in the other.

"You sound surprised," Iris said, smiling over her own glass of bubbly.

"Not at all," Astrid said. "I knew your book would be a hit."

"I think this is more of a *We've known Iris since she had braces* kind of crowd, as opposed to actual romance fans," Iris said.

"Fair," Astrid said, "but all they have to do is read the first page and they'll be hooked for life."

"Agreed," Claire said, winking at Iris through her glasses.

"I'm incredibly jealous of this launch party," said Simon, who'd come alone, as Emery was traveling for work. He pulled her in for a hug. "Proud of you," he said into her hair. She squeezed him close, let herself be held for a few seconds before she pulled back.

In the last several weeks, Iris's friends had been nothing but supportive of her. Gentle. Calling and texting her, stopping by her apartment with her favorite delivery foods, trying to get her to talk about how she felt. Iris let it all wash over her—though she refused to get into any lengthy discussions about Stevie—and appreciated her friends' very obvious love for her. By all accounts, she had everything she needed to be happy.

And she was, but . . .

Well, she didn't want to think about that *but*. Every morning, she woke up, ready to feel free of this whole ridiculous thing. It had been over a month since Stevie left for New York. In the last few weeks, Iris had finished revising her second novel, turned it in to her editor. She'd done interviews for her debut, recorded publicity videos for her publisher, received good reviews from trade publications, and she'd introduced a new digital LGBTQIA+ planner in her Etsy shop that her fans were losing their minds over. She'd even had an offer from a local theater in Seattle to audition for their upcoming production. She'd turned it down, but still. It was pretty amazing just to be asked.

So, yeah, Iris was doing great.

She was thriving.

So the fact that she still woke up every morning with a curly-haired thespian lingering in her brain from her dreams was simply a temporary annoyance. The fact that she looked around right now at her launch party—her *success*—and felt completely alone? That was just a byproduct of everyone in her life being coupled up. It was natural to feel a little alienated in these situations. Nothing she couldn't handle.

Because she *was* happy.

She was Iris-fucking-Kelly, and she was goddamn euphoric.

"Sweetheart, this is amazing!" Her mother appeared next to her, red-and-gray curls bouncing as she pulled Iris's father along by the hand.

Her friends widened their circle to make room.

"Thanks, Mom," Iris said, leaning in to kiss her cheek. "And thanks for coming."

"Of course, honey. We're so proud of you."

Iris smiled, decided not to bring up the fact that just last week Maeve has asked Iris on the phone if she had decided to get a "real job" yet.

"Seems like the whole town is here," her dad said, gazing around at the crowd.

"Yeah, well, everyone likes reading about sex." This from her brother, Aiden. Addison stood next to him, regal in a mustard-colored bandage dress, wrinkling her nose at her husband.

"Who doesn't?" Delilah asked, and god, Iris loved her.

Aiden winced. "That sounded condescending, didn't it?"

"It sure did," Addison said.

Iris just sighed and waved a hand through the air, avoiding Claire's concerned gaze. At least her brother and parents were here. Her younger sister, Emma, hadn't even bothered to show up, claiming Christopher had a fever and she couldn't possibly leave him with a babysitter. Which, fair enough, but she *could* leave him with Charlie and come to Iris's launch party on her own, as Iris knew Charlie was a more than capable father.

But no.

Emma had to control everything, including making Iris feel like nothing she did was ever good enough for her perfect baby sister. Iris tried not to let it ruin her night—this was the event she'd been waiting on for over a year; longer if she counted all the time she spent dreaming about writing her own romance novel since she started reading the genre as a teenager—but Emma's absence only threw other absences into stark relief.

Well.

Just *one* other absence, really.

Iris squeezed her eyes closed for a second, concentrated on the leaf's waxy surface under her fingers.

"I can't wait to read it, honey," Maeve said, grabbing a copy of Iris's book from a nearby table and smiling down at the colorful cover.

"Gross," Aiden said.

"God, what now?" Iris said, folding her arms, the leaf tucked into her palm.

"Sorry, sorry, just, the idea of our mother reading your sex scenes is . . ." He shuddered dramatically, making Addison laugh.

"I'm no prude," Maeve said, a fact she emphasized by slapping Liam on the butt.

"Oh, lovely, nice, thank you for that," Aiden said.

Maeve just laughed while Liam's cheeks turned pink.

"Anyway," Maeve said, glancing around. "Where's this famous Stevie we've heard so much about?"

Iris's stomach turned over. Her friends all froze, eyes wide like they were teenagers and they'd all just been caught sneaking out of the house in the middle of the night.

In her mother's defense, Iris *had* told her family that they could meet Stevie at her launch. And Iris hadn't been exactly forthcoming in her recent conversations with her mother about her and Stevie's breakup. She hadn't really thought through the consequences of that decision, that she'd have to explain the whole split *in person,* and at her own book launch no less.

"She's not here" was the excuse Iris went with, hoping her mother would settle for the paltry non-explanation.

Which, of course, she didn't.

"Not here?" Maeve said, frowning. "She's your girlfriend. Shouldn't she be at your book flight?"

"Book *launch*, Mom," Aiden said.

"Whatever," Maeve said, her eyes on Iris. She smelled blood in the water, and Iris could see the second her mother realized Iris was full of shit.

Maeve sighed, pursed her mouth. "I see."

"Mom, please don't," Iris said. "Not tonight."

"Don't what?" Maeve said. "Express concern that my beloved daughter keeps running away from her own life?"

Iris gritted her teeth. She heard Delilah whisper a quiet "Oh shit."

"Mom," Aiden said, but Maeve could not be stopped.

"I'm just curious," she said. "What happened, Iris?"

Iris pressed her fingers into her eyes. "Nothing. Just . . . nothing, okay?"

"Oh, you don't want to talk about it," Maeve said, folding her arms. "You never do, do you? I wish you would've told me before this, I would've invited Shelby."

"Shelby," Iris deadpanned.

Maeve smiled. "I went to the dentist last week. She's a new hygienist. Cute as a button and she had on a rainbow pin, so I asked her if—"

"Stop," Iris said. "Mom, please, just *stop.*"

Maeve frowned. "Sweetie, if you don't care about dying alone, I'll have to care enough for the both of us."

"Mom, Jesus, dramatic much?" Aiden said.

Maeve just laughed. Aiden laughed. Addison laughed. Only her friends didn't, their eyes on Iris, wide with concern. Iris could tell Astrid was a split second away from saying something, her fists clenched, jaw tight.

Iris shook her head slightly.

It wasn't worth it.

"Excuse me," Iris said, then turned and all but flung herself into the crowd. She lost herself for a while, accepting congratulations, talking about her publishing journey for those who were curious. She even spoke with Jenna for a few minutes, though neither of them mentioned Stevie.

"Sweetie?" Claire asked, finding her in the children's section, where Iris had been hiding for a good ten minutes just to get her breath back under control.

"Hey," Iris said.

"You okay?"

Iris shrugged. "Same old shit."

"I'm sorry. Your mom . . . I know she loves you."

Iris nodded. She knew her mom loved her too. She was just very sick of Maeve's kind of love. The kind that constantly tried to fix her. Granted, it wasn't anywhere near Isabel Parker-Green's kind of molding, but it still stung.

"If it helps, she looked pretty horrified after you stomped off," Claire said.

Iris cracked a smile. "It does. A bit."

Claire smoothed her hand over Iris's hair, and Iris leaned into her touch. It was comforting—her friends usually were—but she still felt itchy, unsettled. She wished she could blame her mother, even Emma's absence, but if she was being honest, she'd felt like this for the better part of a month.

"Hey," she said, an idea forming in her head. She took Claire's hand. "Can we go to Lush tonight? All of us. To celebrate. Ruby is staying at Josh's, right?"

Claire's mouth dropped open. "Oh. Um . . ." Lush wasn't exactly Claire's scene. It wasn't any of Iris's friends' scenes, not anymore, though occasionally Delilah had gone with her to the bar, then spent the entire time snapping photos of all the writhing bodies and sipping bourbon like a barfly. The mere idea of Astrid Parker in a place like that was nearly comical—all the more reason for Iris to push it.

Plus, she hadn't been since she'd met . . .

Well.

It had been a while, and she missed her old haunt. She missed the noise, the smells, the crowd. She missed the people, the game of finding that one person who caught her eye more than most.

She missed the distraction, the sweet oblivion of someone other than herself in her bed.

I'm Stevie. Shit. I mean, I'm Stefania.

Iris shook her head, squeezed Claire's hand. "Please? I need to let off some steam after all this buildup to publication."

Claire smiled, tilted her head. "Is that the only reason?"

Iris knew what she was getting at—*who* she was getting at—but she refused to bite.

"Of course," Iris said, displaying her best smile. "I just want to celebrate with my friends."

Claire kissed the back of Iris's hand. "Okay. I'll talk to everyone about going."

Iris's shoulders literally slumped in relief. "Thank you."

"Now, are you almost ready to start?" Claire asked. "I can give you a few more minutes if you need it."

"No," Iris said, smoothing her dress. "I'm ready."

"Great," Claire said, then hooked Iris into her arms, squeezing her tight. "You know, I think she'd be really proud of you."

Iris pulled back. She didn't need to ask who Claire was talking about. She also knew Claire was full of shit.

Stevie Scott was anything but proud of Iris Kelly.

"Let's get this show on the road," Iris said.

Claire nodded, then headed toward the event space in the middle of the store, currently set up with at least a hundred folding chairs.

"Good evening, everyone, and welcome to River Wild Books," Claire said into the microphone at the podium. "If you'd please take your seats. It's my pleasure and my privilege to introduce to you our author for this evening. Iris Kelly is . . ."

Iris stood behind her, mind wandering as Claire read out her bio. She'd flitted her gaze halfway through the room when she realized she was looking for curls, for an almost-mullet that always reminded Iris of a pop star, a kid's T-shirt most likely bought in a thrift store.

Which was ridiculous.

She sniffed, focused.

". . . please welcome Iris Kelly, author of the critically acclaimed novel *Until We Meet Again!*"

The audience clapped and hooted, and Iris stepped up to the podium. Claire kissed her cheek. Iris smiled and took a deep breath. She rolled her shoulders back and became author Iris. A role—a real one, but a role, nonetheless. This Iris was elegant, graceful, and in no way looking for a woman who lived three thousand miles away to show up at her event with some grand gesture to sweep Iris off her feet.

Because wouldn't that be silly?

AFTER HER READING, the audience queued up so Iris could sign their books. It took a while to get through everyone, some wanting a photo, some wanting to chat about how far Iris had come, particularly a few of her high school teachers, who undoubtedly remembered Iris as a solid B student in too-short skirts who frequented detention.

Iris took it all in, tried to stay in the moment.

"Here are some preorders for you to sign," Claire said when

they'd made it through everyone in person, partygoers now mean-dering through the store and finishing the champagne. Claire set a stack of books on the table, while Brianne, the shop's manager, opened each one for Iris so she could see the pink sticky note inside with the buyer's name. *Ivy. Mara. Grace. Sunny. Luca.*

Iris signed them all, looping her name with a flourish on the title page, along with a little message for each reader—*Make your own happily ever after.*

She'd thought long and hard about what she wanted to write when asked to sign her book. It had to be sincere, honoring romance readers and who Iris was herself. This message felt right, felt like something everyone could stand to hear.

The stack dwindled, Iris's hand just starting to cramp, and they were nearly to the end when Brianne opened a book to a name that froze Iris's heart in her chest.

Stevie.

She blinked down at the bright pink sticky note.

"Everything okay?" Brianne asked.

Iris nodded but called Claire's name.

"Yeah, hon?" Claire asked, a stack of already signed books in her hands.

Iris just blinked down at the name. Claire followed her gaze, sucking in a soft breath. It wasn't a very common name. Still, Iris supposed it could be someone else . . . someone different . . .

"Oh, sweetie," Claire said.

"Is it . . . ?" Iris asked.

"I don't know," Claire said, then looked at her manager. "Brianne, do you have the order invoice for this one?"

Brianne nodded, pulled her phone out of her back pocket. "Yeah, let me look it up."

Iris sat there while Brianne tapped on her screen, her fingers in a knot around her Sharpie.

"Here it is," Brianne said. "Um . . . Stevie Scott. She lives in New York?"

"When . . . when did she order it?" Iris asked.

Brianne frowned, eyes on her phone. "She placed the order . . . two days ago?"

Claire's hand closed around her shoulder, squeezed, but Iris barely felt it. She smoothed her hand over the title page, poised her Sharpie to sign her name.

To write Stevie's name.

To write *Make your own happily ever after* to Stevie Scott, the woman Iris had rejected, refused, lied to. The woman Iris was too fucking scared to make any kind of *ever after* with. The woman who, after all that, still preordered Iris's book from Claire's store, wanted Iris to sign it.

"Fuck," she said, her eyes starting to sting.

"Oh, honey," Claire said.

"I'm fine, just . . ." She shook her head, forced herself to think of something else, anything else, any*one*. She closed her hands into fists, squeezing until she felt the sting of pain from her nails.

Nothing helped though.

Stevie . . . make your own happily ever after.

The inscription felt like a jab, a cruel joke, and she knew she could never write that to Stevie. She couldn't imagine writing anything.

She stood up suddenly, taking Stevie's book with her. "Can we go? I'm ready to get out of here."

Claire frowned, eyes flicking down to Stevie's book in Iris's hand. Iris crushed the book to her chest, and Claire glanced at Brianne, shook her head slightly. Iris didn't comment on it, she just needed to leave. Now.

"Claire."

"Okay, yes," Claire said, but she sounded anything but excited about the whole thing. "Brianne, you're okay to close up?"

"Of course," Brianne said, her pink bangs in her eyes. "Congratulations, Iris."

"Thanks," Iris said. "And thank you for a wonderful event." Her voice shook, her fingertips fizzy as she slipped Stevie's book into her bag. She'd figure out what to write to Stevie, mail it off herself.

"I hear we're heading into the den of iniquity?" Delilah said, walking toward her. Astrid and Jordan hovered by the door with Simon, their heads close together as they talked, glancing at Iris with worried expressions.

"Yes," she said firmly, chin up as she looped her arm with Delilah's and spun her around, looking at each of her friends right in the eye in turn. "It's time to celebrate and I'm looking for the hottest piece of ass I can land."

CHAPTER

THIRTY-SIX

IRIS WAS SURROUNDED by dry humping.

Literally, it felt like everyone in this bar was coupled up and grinding on each other. But then again, she supposed that was the point of a bar like Lush, which was crowded tonight, with dim lighting, custom fall-themed cocktails, and music that felt like it was written for sex.

It was the perfect place to get lost in. Iris looked around, looking for anyone who might be looking back. She leaned against the bar, hip out, martini glass half full and held lazily in one hand. All the nonverbal cues for *I'm down to fuck.*

Only problem was, Astrid was sticking by her side like glue while Jordan and Simon had some serious conversation at the end of the bar. Claire and Delilah were . . . well, they were part of the dry-humping scene on the dance floor, which was a little disturbing and also a complete delight.

"This is . . . interesting," Astrid said, clutching her bag to her chest with one arm, a glass of white wine in the other. She was very obviously trying not to look at Claire and Delilah.

"Oh, baby's first queer bar," Iris said, petting Astrid's blond hair.

Astrid rolled her eyes and batted Iris's hand away, but a small smile settled on her mouth before she went back to watching everything with a slightly stunned expression. She'd worn three-inch heels to the bar, pairing them with cuffed jeans and a fitted navy blazer. She was like a queer Ann Taylor.

Iris laughed when Astrid's mouth dropped open as two men whipped off their shirts and then continued their grinding.

"Well," Astrid said, sipping her wine.

"Welcome, my darling," Iris said, and Astrid grinned, clinking her glass with Iris's. The current song ended, drifting into another, but Claire and Delilah headed toward them at the bar, laughing and holding hands.

"I forgot how much I love dancing!" Claire shouted over the noise.

"I can't believe I've never brought you here before," Delilah said, her arms wrapping around Claire's waist from behind. "All those times Iris dragged my ass here, I could've been . . ." She trailed off and whispered something in Claire's ear, something that turned Claire's face bright red—visible even in the dim light—and made her giggle.

"Jesus, you two," Iris said.

"Oh, they're cute, leave them alone," Astrid said as Jordan came up silently behind her, slipping a hand around her waist. Simon ordered a beer and sat on a stool.

"Okay," Iris said. "Who do we see?"

Her friends just blinked at her then glanced at one another.

"What?" Iris said.

"Who are you in the mood to see?" Delilah asked slowly.

Iris frowned. "Um, literally anyone."

"Are you sure you don't just want to dance with us?" Claire asked. She reached out and took Iris's hand. "I'll dance with you."

"Not in the way I'd prefer," Iris said. She wanted the press of bodies, sweat and alcohol, someone's thigh between hers, nearly making her come right here in the middle of Lush.

Her stomach fluttered at the thought, a rare roll of nervousness.

"Honey, are you sure?" Claire asked.

Iris froze, looking at each of her friends. "What do you mean?"

"She means Stevie," Delilah said, ever straight to the point.

Iris clenched her jaw.

Make your own happily ever after.

She shook her head, trying to dislodge the phrase, but she couldn't get it out of her mind. Granted, she'd written it about a hundred times tonight. It made sense it would be stuck on a loop.

Total, perfect sense.

"Iris, have you even talked to her?" Astrid asked softly, squeezing her shoulder.

Iris shook her off.

Of course she hadn't talked to her. She couldn't. What the hell would she say? Iris didn't even know how to explain what had happened between her and Stevie to her best friends, to her own heart, how could she offer an apology for it?

If she even wanted to apologize at all.

Which she didn't.

She and Stevie were over. Stevie had left and Iris hadn't gone after her and that was that.

Make your own happily ever after.

"I'm going to dance," she said, pushing off the bar and plunging into the sea of writhing bodies before her friends could stop her. She closed her eyes, lifted her hands and moved. She spun and twirled until everything was a blur.

Until she felt a hand on her shoulder.

She opened her eyes to see a dark-haired woman, all hips and ass, a total goddess, standing in front of her.

"Hi," the woman said. She had on a dark purple dress, which clung to every curve perfectly.

Iris smiled. "Hi."

"My name's—"

"I don't care," Iris said, hooking her arms around the woman's hips and pulling her close.

The woman laughed, revealing lovely white teeth, gold earrings dangling with her movement. "Fair enough."

Iris pulled her closer, the woman wrapping her arms around Iris's shoulders, hip-to-hip. She looked Iris in the eyes, smiled. She was so—

"Pretty," Iris said.

"You . . . you too."

Iris laughed. Fucking. Adorable. "I meant your name, but I'll take that compliment."

Iris closed her eyes, felt the curve of the woman's waist, moving them to the music, a frantic beat that felt like the entire room was building to climax.

This was what Iris needed.

This was what she wanted.

"You're good at this," the woman said.

Stefania rubbed her forehead. "God. I'm terrible at this."

"Maybe," Iris said. "But it's working for me."

Iris said nothing. She pulled the woman closer, grazed her mouth along her bare shoulder, breathed her in. Flowers and vanilla and sweat. Lovely and . . . different.

"Do you live nearby?" the woman asked.

Iris pulled back, met with a pair of ice-blue eyes. "I don't."

"I do. Very close, in fact."

Iris knew her next line. A flirty *Interesting.* Or maybe just a smirk, followed by a slow lean-in for a kiss. Even a coquettish *That's very good to know.*

But she couldn't get anything off of her tongue. She couldn't get her face to even move. She simply stared at the woman—this gorgeous person who wanted Iris, wanted to give Iris everything Iris had come here to find.

The woman's smile faltered. "Are you okay?"

"Yeah," Iris said. Maybe a name *would* help. Make it a little more personable. "I'm Iris."

Her partner smiled. "Beatrice."

Iris's heart beat everywhere—her throat, her fingertips, her stomach.

By my sword, Beatrice, thou lovest me!

Iris shook her head, whispered, "I don't."

Beatrice—the real one, the flesh-and-blood one—frowned. "What?"

"I . . ." Iris dropped her hands, backed up. "I'm sorry . . . you're perfect, but . . . I'm sorry, I just . . ."

She turned and headed back toward the bar without another word, leaving Beatrice behind. Her friends all watched her, parting to make room for her in between them. She rested her hands on the smooth lacquered surface of the bar, knocked back the rest of her martini.

Then she laughed.

It started as a snort, an incredulous, sarcastic sound, but it soon turned into something more. Something bone-deep and raw, so forceful her stomach muscles ached, tears springing into her eyes. She dropped her head into her hands and laughed and laughed until she couldn't tell if she was actually laughing or crying.

"Um . . . honey?" Claire said.

Iris just shook her head, kept laugh-sobbing. "I'm broken," she said between hiccups. "I'm fucking broken. She broke me."

This was what Iris *did*. She hooked up. She had fun. She flirted and danced and fucked and that was what everyone expected of her.

That's what she expected of herself.

It was what she wanted, but now, here she was, unable to do any of that. Here she was, crying in her favorite bar, after having walked away from one of the hottest people in this whole place.

She felt a hand on her back, soothing circles. She didn't shrug off the touch. She didn't look up to see who it was, she simply stood there, her fingers wet from her tears, her throat raw, and she . . .

She . . .

She wanted to tell Stevie about it. She wanted to laugh-sob with Stevie. She wanted to dance with Stevie, flirt with Stevie, touch and kiss and hold Stevie. She wanted to sleep with Stevie and wake up with Stevie, and goddammit, she didn't want to write *Make your own happily ever after* in Stevie's book.

I am your happily ever after.

The phrase came so easily, just a simply exchange of letters and words, but it fit. It was perfect. Cheesy and ridiculous and something right out of the romance section at River Wild.

And it was true.

Goddammit, it was true, if not for Stevie—who Iris wasn't sure would ever forgive her for being such a coward, such a selfish idiot— it was true for Iris.

Stevie was who Iris wanted.

Stevie was Iris's HEA.

Even if everything between them went badly. Even if they broke up in six months or six years. Even if Iris sometimes doubted Stevie really wanted her.

Even if Stevie didn't want her at all.

Maybe Iris wasn't broken after all. She was just . . . different. Changed by a person who'd finally gotten under her skin, under her heart, and made her so desperate to belong to someone, she barely recognized herself anymore.

No, Iris wasn't broken.

Iris Kelly was in love.

She lifted her head, grabbed a cocktail napkin, and wiped at her face. She felt her friends on either side of her, gentle hands on her back, waiting for her.

Loving her.

Because Iris Kelly was worth loving.

And she always had been.

She turned around, smiled at them.

"I need to go to New York."

CHAPTER

THIRTY-SEVEN

NEW YORK CITY looked like fire in October.

Stevie would never cease to be amazed how much green space wove throughout the buildings and sidewalks, the florescent lights and vendors and cars. When she'd first arrived in the city last month, it had overwhelmed her, how New York could feel so vast, like a country in and of itself, but so small at the same time. In the beginning, she could barely step out of her Brooklyn building—an apartment for which she paid Thayer and her wife a pittance—without having difficulty breathing. She lived on the subway app, talked to both her mother and Ren every single day so they could in turn talk her out of coming home, and cried herself to sleep for a solid seven nights.

Now, though, a few weeks into her new life, she felt a bit more settled. She still lived on the subway app. She still talked to Ren every day. And she still cried herself to sleep sometimes. But she also loved it here—the way her neighborhood smelled like bread and coffee and earth in the mornings; the bustle of the theater district, the city streets full of so many people, each with different dreams and fears and loves; the trees lining her street, the leaves like flames licking at the branches, a bit of purple shining through here and there.

It felt right, being here in the fall, when everything was dying so it could be reborn. Every day she felt stronger. Every day, she took her medication, prepared herself for what lay outside her door as best she could, and was still lambasted by a brusque stranger here, an attempted grope in the subway there. The mere fact of simply walking down the street still overwhelmed her, stole her breath.

But she handled it.

She freaked out sometimes, but she got through it, so even when tears did soak her pillow a little, she still felt . . . proud. That's what it was. She was proud of herself, for leaping, for jumping, for taking the plunge, and every other cliché saying she could think of for how she'd changed her life.

How she'd chosen herself.

I chose me, but I choose you too.

Stevie stared down at her script as she sat in Devoción, her favorite coffee shop on Grand. She sipped a flat white, tried to focus on Rosalind's motivations, reasons, fears, but suddenly all she could think about was that drawing Iris did the morning they broke up.

Stevie. Alone. In New York City.

Turns out, Iris was a bit of a psychic. Stevie was alone. She was in New York City.

And . . . Stevie was okay.

If there was one thing that drawing emanated—Stevie's arms spread, head tipped up to the sky—it was that. Stevie was okay.

"Hey, hey, sorry I'm late," a voice said.

Stevie looked up to see a young white woman with shoulder-length pink hair and blunt bangs skirting around the café's greenery then plopping down on the tufted brown leather couch where Stevie sat.

"The Q was down again," Olivia said, huffing out a breath that ruffled her fringe. She wore gray leggings and a heavily patterned sweater that looked like it might have belonged to her dad in the seventies, but that she somehow made work.

Stevie waved a hand. "No worries."

Olivia smiled at her, and Stevie smiled back. Olivia was young—twenty-five, though that was only three years younger than Stevie herself, but Olivia had such a hopeful, innocent air about her, she felt younger. She was an actual graduate of Juilliard, so she was a ridiculously talented actress and was playing Celia, Rosalind's cousin and dear friend in *As You Like It*. She and Stevie had met during the auditions Thayer had invited Stevie to attend her first week in New York. Olivia was there too—she knew Thayer from some off-Broadway play they had both worked on last year—and her naturally open and bubbly personality made it easy for Stevie to relax around her.

She was also pansexual, and Stevie always felt safer, more herself, around other queer people anyway.

"What scene are you on?" Olivia asked, scooting close to Stevie and peering down at her script.

"Did you forget your copy again?" Stevie asked.

Olivia laughed, her clearly-false-but-still-gorgeous lashes fluttering against her cheek. "You know me. Last week, I lost my keys. Guess where I found them?"

"Let me guess. Your cat's litter box?"

"Nope, that was last month. In the oven." Olivia made a face. "Like, I don't even use my oven. I keep my emergency stash of dark chocolate–covered almonds in there and—oh, oh, I see what I did now."

Stevie smiled and shook her head. "You need a key hook. Right by your door."

"I have one."

Stevie laughed, then moved her already heavily marked-up script so it rested between them. "Act 1, scene 3."

Olivia scooted close, her slim leg pressing against Stevie's, and soon they were lost in the scene, whispering the lines to each other so they didn't bother the other patrons, pausing so Stevie could mark something in her script or Olivia could tap out a note on her phone. It was exciting work, Stevie's heart beating faster at the idea of performing this at the Delacorte under a July sky, the crowd happy and summer-soaked and beautiful.

"You're really good," Olivia said when they'd finished the scene, nudging Stevie's shoulder.

Stevie smiled. She was learning not to brush off compliments—especially coming from someone like Olivia, someone who'd already been a part of New York's theater scene for a few years. Stevie knew her words weren't empty.

"Thanks," Stevie said. "You too."

Olivia smiled, fluttered her fingers down her face. "I know."

Stevie laughed, then flipped through the script for another scene between Rosalind and Celia. Olivia waited patiently, her arm still warm against Stevie's.

"You know," Olivia said, "we should go out sometime."

Stevie's fingers froze on a page. She glanced at Olivia, who was looking at her with softly narrowed eyes, head tilted as though the idea had just occurred to her.

"Like . . ." Stevie said but trailed off.

Olivia just grinned. "Yeah, like . . ."

Stevie forced herself to keep eye contact. God, Olivia was pretty. Sweet. She understood theater life, had already helped Stevie navigate so much in New York, from where to get the most delicious bagels to the best little-known indie bookstores in Brooklyn.

She checked in with herself, gauged her breathing, her thought process, felt her legs pressing into the couch's worn leather, all things her therapist encouraged her to do when faced with a new situation.

She wasn't nervous—or at least, not in a way that crippled her, made her feel helpless and paralyzed. Her stomach fluttered a bit, but that was normal for Stevie, as was the warmth rushing into her cheeks right now.

"Oh, that is adorable," Olivia said, laughing.

"God, sorry," Stevie said, pressing her palms to her heated face, but she laughed too, the embarrassment easy and light, like a joke between friends.

And Stevie realized she wanted to say yes to Olivia. She had zero reasons not to, other than potential awkwardness during the play, but they were both professionals. Adults. And theater would hardly be theater if actors didn't connect in these ways during productions. Olivia was safe, made Stevie laugh. She was lovely. She was perfect, really.

So . . . why couldn't Stevie get that *yes* off her tongue?

She even opened her mouth, ready to take the chance, ready to try, ready to *date*, but all she could see in her mind—all she could *feel*, right there under her skin—was Iris.

Stevie exhaled, and Olivia saw it happen, that subtle droop of Stevie's shoulders.

"It's okay," Olivia said.

"I want to say yes," Stevie said. "I do. But I . . . I just got out of something, right before I moved here."

Olivia nodded, waved a hand. "Totally fine. I get it."

Stevie watched her, and she really did look fine, her smile just as real, just as eye-reaching. "I think I could really use a friend though. If you're in the market."

Olivia grabbed Stevie's hand and pressed a kiss to her palm, a loud, friendly smack. "Already done."

Stevie smiled, squeezed her hand, and then they got back to the script. Just like that. No awkwardness, no hurt feelings. It was amazing, really, the fucking maturity of it all. It took a while for Stevie's heart to slow, for her fingertips to feel like they weren't fizzing with adrenaline, but soon, she was back to normal, sitting in a Brooklyn café with her co-actor and friend.

Still, as the sun moved west across the sky and Olivia stood up, declaring she had to meet her two roommates for a house meeting about how one of them kept clogging the toilet and very pointedly not *un*clogging it, Stevie wished she could change her mind.

She wished Iris wasn't still with her, hovering like a phantom, making her unready for someone as great as Olivia. As she walked back to her apartment, the dying light spreading gold over the city, she forced her mind to think of other things—the cup of tea she planned to make when she got home; her virtual therapy appointment in two days; Thayer's most recent email updating her on the cast, which included the man who would play Orlando, an up-and-coming and publicly out gay actor who'd just finished a press tour for his first feature film.

All of these thoughts, from the mundane to the nearly fantastical, should've done the trick. They should've shoved a wild redhead right out of her mind, forcing Stevie into her life *now*, her reality *now*, her heart and feelings and needs *now*, but they didn't.

They rarely did.

She knew from experience she probably needed a bit more than thoughts—she needed some intense distraction, like a movie or more work on her script. She could always work on her role, weaving together a Rosalind who was fresh and intoxicating and vulnerable.

She entered her building, picked up her mail, and had just arrived at her apartment on the third floor when she saw a manila bubble mailer leaning against the door. She didn't remember ordering anything, but it had her name on the front, so she scooped it up, stuffing it under her arm as she struggled to get keys out of her bag.

Once inside, she dumped everything onto the quartz kitchen counter, then stood for a second with her hands on her hips. Thayer's wife, an independently wealthy gallery owner named Danielle, had clearly decorated the open space, all cool grays and blues, modern lines, and expensive art on the walls. Stevie liked the neutral palette, but the rest wasn't exactly her taste—she preferred more coziness, more clutter and life—but as Danielle barely charged what Stevie's shitty Portland apartment had cost her, Stevie didn't complain.

She filled the kettle in the polished silver-and-gray kitchen, then flipped on the burner before she changed into a pair of sweats and one of her mom's old cardigans, as the chilly October day had turned into a cold night. She had just settled on the couch with a cup of minty green tea and her script in her lap when she remembered the package. She stood up, found the envelope on the counter among the junk mail, and inspected the front.

Stevie Scott.

Goose bumps rushed over her arms as she lifted it into her hands. It was heavy, something rectangular and thick inside. Fingers trembling for reasons she couldn't quite explain, she ripped the top open, dipped her hand inside. It was glossy-paged paperback book.

She wasn't quite sure what she was expecting to see on the cover, but it sure as hell wasn't her own face, drawn with such intricacy and care, a woman with brown curls and low-hanging jeans, her forehead pressed against another woman's, their hands tangled together between them.

A redheaded woman.

A redheaded woman who chased Stevie in her dreams at night, followed her down the Brooklyn sidewalks.

There was a title too, slashed across the lower half of the cover in a messy handwriting font.

The Truth About You and Me

Her heart felt huge, pounding everywhere at once, tears swelling into her eyes before she even processed what she was looking at, what she was holding in her hands.

What it might mean.

She sunk onto the hardwood floor and flipped through the heavy pages, printed professionally and bound, just like a graphic novel Stevie might pull off the shelves in a bookstore. She saw images she recognized, all of them now in full color—Iris and Stevie meeting in Lush; Iris tucking Stevie into bed; Stevie sitting alone on the beach in Malibu; the two of them at rehearsal for *Much Ado*; Stevie pressing Iris against her apartment door, her thigh between Iris's legs.

Page after page, scene after scene, Stevie and Iris's romance unfurled onto the page. Because it *was* a romance, colorful and wild and terrifying and beautiful, every moment pushing them to each other, the fabrication they both claimed in the beginning fading with every kiss, making way for something new and authentic and perfect.

Tears tracked down Stevie's cheeks, a month's worth of feeling brave and bold and *okay* spilling out as she sifted through the scenes. Her stomach coiled when she turned a page and took in their breakup, the way Iris captured the emotions on both of their faces. It was so raw and real, Stevie had to put the book down and just breathe.

After a few seconds, though, she went back to the story, desperate for the ending, even though she already knew it. She flipped the page, blinking down at herself, that same illustration she'd seen the day she and Iris broke up—Stevie in New York City, arms flung wide, head tilted to the sky.

It was beautiful.

It was true.

But there were more pages under Stevie's fingertips, more to the story, the thickness of the next few sheets like an electric shock to Stevie's nervous system.

She crushed the book to her chest, her throat so tight, she nearly couldn't swallow. She stood up, then grabbed the padded envelope again.

Stevie Scott.

Iris's handwriting. She recognized it from Iris's digital planners, as a lot of the designs were replications of Iris's own handwritten text, a neat and elegant blend of cursive and print. But Stevie's name was the only thing written. There was no address. No postage. No return address.

She set the envelope down, looked around her apartment. Her pulse was in her throat, her ears, and she half expected Iris to reveal herself like a bouquet of flowers. But the space was quiet. Stevie took out her phone, wondering if maybe Iris had texted her, but there was nothing, just a blank screen featuring the photo Stevie had taken of the Delacorte her first week in New York.

Her fingertips whitened on the book. She wasn't sure what she wanted these last pages to show, how she wanted this story to end. Or rather, she was very sure, had never been more sure of anything in her life, but her protective strategies were sliding into place, lies she'd convinced herself were true to keep her heart from shattering more than it already had.

I'm over her.

I'm happy without her.

I don't want her anymore.

I'm just lonely.

But she knew none of those things were true.

So she turned the page.

It took a few moments for Stevie to register what she was seeing. Iris had drawn herself standing on a street in front of a red brick building, her back to the viewer. Her hair was dark in the dim light, long and wild, and she wore jeans and heeled brown boots, a grass-green pea coat.

And in one hand, held loosely at her side, was a single yellow tulip.

Stevie stood up, her limbs shaky and fizzing with adrenaline. Her eyes roamed the page, desperate for every detail . . . for why . . . what . . .

She sucked in a loud breath.

Iris was standing at the bottom of a set of stone steps.

Familiar steps.

Familiar double glass doors at the top.

Familiar decorative cornices around the windows.

"Oh my god," Stevie said, pressing one hand to her mouth. She only hesitated a moment before shoving her feet into a pair of boots and then closing her fingers around her doorknob, flinging the door open with such force, it smacked loudly into the wall. She flew down the stairs, the book pressed against her chest. Her eyes stung, tears already forming, and goddammit, she tried to hold them back, tried to prepare herself if she was wrong, if she'd misinterpreted that drawing, if Iris wasn't really . . . if she didn't actually . . .

Stevie burst out of the building, her lungs working so hard to keep her upright she felt a little dizzy. Her eyes strained to adjust to the growing dark, the cool fall air hitting her like a slap, desperate to see—

Wild red hair.

A green pea coat.

A single yellow tulip.

Stevie didn't say anything. Couldn't. She didn't even remember getting down the steps, but suddenly she was standing in front of Iris, breathing the same autumn air, her ginger and citrus scent like a drug, and the only thing Stevie could do was stare at her, starving for her face, her mouth, that blue freckle right under her left eye.

"Hi," Iris said, and Stevie's knees nearly buckled, that voice curling around her like a warm coat in the middle of winter.

"How long have you been out here?" Stevie said, wrapping her cardigan tighter around her torso, book to her chest. "It's freezing."

Iris shrugged, laughed. Her nose was red from the chill and Stevie wanted to kiss it. Kiss *her.*

"A while?" Iris said, then motioned to a bench half a block down the sidewalk. "I've been sitting over there for about two hours. Before you came home."

"You . . . you saw me?" Stevie said. "Why didn't you—"

"I didn't want you to feel like you had to talk to me," Iris said, stepping closer. "I wanted it to be your choice."

"When I saw the drawing," Stevie said, hugging the book even closer.

Iris nodded. "When you saw the drawing."

"How did you know I was here?" Stevie asked. "How did you *draw* my building and put it in a book?"

Iris bit her lip. "Well, Claire wouldn't give me your address from when you ordered my book. Ethics or some shit."

Stevie laughed.

"So I called Ren," Iris said. "And it's amazing the details you can get from Google's street view."

Stevie could only stare at her, awed at the effort Iris had gone through, the time she'd spent, the things she'd created just to give Stevie a story.

No. Not just a story.

Their story.

"You're here," Stevie said, the fact of it finally settling around her heart.

Iris smiled, but it was small, nervous, and it was the most beautiful thing Stevie had ever seen.

"I am," Iris said. "I'm sorry it took me so long."

Tears spilled down Stevie's cheeks, because this.

Iris.

In New York, wooing Stevie with art and flowers and romance.

For the last month, Stevie had been okay. She was still okay, and she'd be okay if she'd never seen Iris again. She knew that, without a doubt—she was capable, she had friends and family who loved her, who supported her, who would help her when she fell apart.

Yes, Stevie Scott would be just fine without Iris Kelly.

But she wouldn't be *this.*

Completely alight with this woman who was wild and unpredictable, soft and vulnerable and sweet, so beautiful Stevie sometimes couldn't look directly at her, like she was staring at the sun, dizzy and terrified and euphoric.

Seeing her now, here, flesh and blood, Stevie felt a tiny corner of her heart she'd convinced herself she could live without spark to life, enervating her blood, her bones, her skin. Stevie wanted Iris, and she didn't care why it took Iris so long to get to this point, she didn't care about anything except the way Iris was looking at her right now, her eyes wide and hopeful and scared, and Stevie couldn't do anything but frame her face in her hands, swipe her thumbs over her cheeks.

Iris inhaled sharply, her eyes fluttering closed as Stevie pressed their foreheads together.

"You're here," Stevie said again.

Iris laughed, a watery, relieved sound, gripping Stevie's hips with that tulip still in her hands. Stevie kissed her eyes, her temple, her cheeks, trailing down until their mouths met, a desperate press, tears and teeth and tongues.

"I'm so sorry," Iris said, pulling away enough to look Stevie in the eyes. "I am *so* sorry, Stevie, and I—"

"Shh," Stevie said. "I know."

"No, you don't." Iris shook her head and gripped Stevie's wrists, her beautiful green eyes dark and shiny. "But I want you to. I want you to know that I love you. I do. I'm sorry I lied. You were right—I was a coward, but I was . . . god, Stevie, I was scared. So fucking scared, and I'm pretty sure I still am, and I might need you to be patient with me, but I can't . . . I have to try. You were so brave for me, and I want to do the same. I want to be brave for you."

She took a deep breath, her exhale so shaky, Stevie just wanted to kiss her, quiet her, but she knew Iris needed to get this out.

"I spent a lot of time," Iris went on, "convincing myself I wasn't built to last, wasn't built for romance, for love. But maybe . . ." Tears bloomed into her eyes. "Maybe I was just built for you."

Stevie's heart swelled—that's what it felt like, her chest expanding, making more room—and she smiled. She held Iris's face and kissed her once . . . twice . . . then whispered against her mouth. *"What offense, sweet Beatrice?"*

Iris laughed, pulled Stevie closer, tighter, one arm around her waist and the other holding her hand, the tulip now tangled in both of their fingers. She danced Stevie in a circle, pressing her mouth to her ear and whispering, *"You have stayed me in a happy hour. I was about to protest I love thee."*

"And do it with all thy heart," Stevie said, sliding her nose along Iris's throat.

Iris arched her neck, giving Stevie more access, but then she straightened, took Stevie's face in her hands, locked their gazes in a way that made Stevie's breath catch, made her heart settle and soar all at once.

"I love you with so much of my heart that none is left to protest," Iris said.

And as they danced, held each other and laughed, whispered and kissed and touched, right there in the middle of a Brooklyn sidewalk, Stevie knew Iris Kelly was finally telling the truth.

CHAPTER

THIRTY-EIGHT

SIX MONTHS LATER

THE EVERWOOD INN at springtime was a riot of color. Red, pink, and yellow tulips flourished, bordering the walkway to the front door, while fuchsia rhododendrons and wildflowers encircled the backyard where a gauzy tent laced with fairy lights arched under the oaks.

Iris felt herself exhale as she walked into Claire and Delilah's wedding space—underneath the tent, it was golden and green, candles already lit on the ten circular wooden tables. The event would be small, but perfect, Iris had no doubt, as Astrid Parker stood near the center of the tent with her iPad, dressed in a black tea dress, ruling the world.

Iris watched her for a second, this first in-person glimpse of her friend since she moved to Brooklyn four months ago like a cooling sip of water on a July afternoon.

"She looks good," Stevie said, her fingers tangled with Iris's.

Iris smiled. "She always does."

"Don't you want to say hi?"

Iris nodded but didn't move. In all honesty, her heart felt huge in her chest, her eyes stinging slightly. God, she'd missed Astrid. She'd missed them all, but she knew that was part of the deal when she decided to move across the country to be with Stevie. It was the right choice. Iris loved New York, loved Brooklyn in particular, and there was nothing like waking up next to Stevie Scott every morning, kissing her to sleep every night.

Iris was happy, hard at work on her third novel, partnered with the most beautiful person in the world.

But god, it was nice to be home.

"You okay?" Stevie asked, sliding a hand down Iris's hair.

Iris nodded, pressed her nose to her girlfriend's neck. Even six months after their reconciliation outside of Stevie's apartment in Brooklyn, after the long discussion they had afterward about next steps, after two arduous months where they did long distance before Iris moved to New York, she still couldn't believe she got to kiss this woman every day. Touch her, hold hands while walking down the street. Even more, she couldn't believe how much she loved doing it—all the relationship things she'd convinced herself for too long she wasn't built for, didn't want.

Turned out, Stevie Scott had transformed Iris into a *partner*, and Iris was grateful for every second.

"Just happy to be here," Iris said against Stevie's skin. Stevie's arm circled her waist, pulled her close, and they stood like that for a second, Iris mentally preparing herself for this wedding. About two months ago, Claire and Delilah had set up a Zoom call with Astrid and Iris to go over some wedding details, at the end of which the brides had requested that Iris and Astrid walk them down the aisle, all four of them at once. Iris had been floored, honored beyond meas-ure, and then spent the rest of the evening in tears with her head in Stevie's lap, missing her friends so much there was a physical ache in her chest.

"Me too," Stevie said now into Iris's hair. "Why don't we go say—"

"Iris!"

Claire's voice cut Stevie off, as bride number one strolled into the tent, her hair already done up in a gorgeous twist, her makeup perfect. She wore a button-down and denim shorts, and she looked beautiful.

Iris's eyes welled—she couldn't help it, they filled on their own, tears already tracking down her cheeks as Stevie released her and she made her way toward her best friend. They collided, arms and hands and laughter, trying to squeeze four months' worth of hugs into a single embrace.

"Claire, don't you dare cry," Astrid said as she headed their way.

Iris pulled back, but only so she could gulp Astrid into her arms as well.

"Iris is!" Claire said, laughing.

"Yeah, but I'm not a blushing bride," Iris said, still holding on to Astrid while she reached out and wiped gently at Claire's cheeks, then cupped her face. "You look fucking hot."

Claire smiled. "Thank you. I've missed you."

"Me too," Iris said. "I've missed you both so much."

"I barely noticed you were gone," Delilah said as she strolled into the tent, her hair loose and wild. She had on her customary black tank top and dark gray jeans, all of her tattoos on display.

"Bitch, who could miss this much attitude?" Iris said, but she grinned and yanked Delilah into her arms. Delilah laughed and held her close, kissing Iris on the side of the head. Iris leaned into her, one arm wrapped around her waist, when she noticed three birds inked onto Delilah's chest, right above her heart.

"What is this?" Iris said, grabbing Delilah's arm and pulling her closer. "New ink?"

Delilah met Claire's eyes. Smiled. "Very new. Just got it a few weeks ago." She pulled her tank strap down a little, revealing the full art. Three birds—swallows, Iris thought—faced one another in a triangle shape, all of their wings in different positions.

"If you tell me these beautiful birds on your skin represent you, Claire, and Ruby," Iris said, "I'm going to faint right here. Might literally die."

Delilah shrugged. "Okay, I won't tell you that, but only because I'd rather your violent death not mar my wedding to the love of my life."

Claire laughed, laced her fingers with Delilah's before tangling her other hand with Iris's. Iris reached out to take Astrid's hand, her chest opening up at their little foursome. It was nearly three years ago that Delilah walked into their lives, a tangled mess, rough and sarcastic, and now Iris couldn't imagine her life without her. Didn't want to.

Iris had always adored her friends, but these past few months without them, she'd realized just how much she needed them, how vital they were to her well-being and happiness, just as vital as Stevie herself.

If not more so.

She looked at Astrid and Claire, her ride or die since they were ten years old, and her eyes welled up again.

"Jesus," Delilah said, wiping Iris's tears away with her thumb. "You're a fucking mess."

Iris laughed. "Here for all your chaotic needs."

"Don't know what I'd do without all the chaos, to be honest," Delilah said, winking at her.

Iris winked back.

And then she started crying again.

———

TWO HOURS LATER, Iris stood on the Everwood's back patio, the green backyard dappled with white folding chairs now filled with Claire and Delilah's closest friends and family. Down front, Josh Foster—Claire's ex, friend, and co-parent—stood in a gray suit underneath an arch of wildflowers, awaiting the brides, to join them together. Iris also spotted Isabel Parker-Green, Astrid's mother, sitting next to Brianne, Claire's pink-haired manager for River Wild, deep in conversation about Iris couldn't even imagine what. Isabel's hair was cut into a new shorter style, the color definitely veering more silver these days as opposed to her ritualistic dyed blond.

Most importantly, Stevie and Jordan sat together with Simon, the three of them talking and laughing. Iris watched them for a while, the sheer happiness of seeing Stevie getting along so well with all of her favorite people like a drug she never wanted to stop taking.

Iris forced herself to suck up all of her overwhelming emotions and turned back to face the wedding party, where Claire and Delilah were already whispering sweet nothings to each other before they even walked down the aisle. Ruby stood with Katherine, Claire's mother, adorable in her baby queer black suit and light pink dress shirt, which complemented Delilah's ivory suit nearly perfectly. Claire's dress was vintage, lacey and off-white, falling to just below her knees and showing off her strappy heels. Astrid and Iris were both dressed in their own choices—Astrid in a black bandage dress, Iris in a dove-gray maxi.

Everyone looked perfect.

"Okay, you two," Astrid said, tapping Claire on the shoulder to get her and her future wife to stop making out. "It's showtime."

Claire nodded, kissed Delilah once more before turning to her daughter. They hugged, Claire pressing a kiss to the top of the girl's head, and then Delilah joined their embrace before Katherine and Ruby walked down the aisle to soft guitar music.

Now it was just the four of them, Claire and Delilah in the middle, Iris and Astrid on either side of them.

"Are we ready for this?" Astrid asked.

"I think we are," Claire said, gazing at Delilah then winking over at Iris.

"Let's do this," Delilah said, squeezing Iris's waist.

"I'm ready," Iris said. And she was. "As long as you all remember this blessed union started because I'm a nosy bitch who wants all of her friends to be happy and have regular access to great sex."

"How could we ever forget?" Claire said, laughing.

They all laughed too then fell silent. Katherine and Ruby reached the front, turning to face the brides. The music shifted, and everyone stood up, their eyes lighting when they saw Claire and Delilah.

Then they looped their arms around one another and the four of them walked down the aisle. Together.

ACKNOWLEDGMENTS

It's not an overstatement to say that when I wrote *Delilah Green Doesn't Care* and sent it out into the world, my entire life changed. Not only because I fell in love with romance writing, but because I also fell in love with its readers. As Iris's story—as all of Bright Falls—comes to a close, I am so grateful to the readers who read, loved, requested, bought, and posted about these stories. *You* brought Bright Falls and all the characters within the pages of these three books to life, and I am so honored to be part of your reading lives.

As always, thank you to Becca Podos, my agent and friend. We've been at this for nine years, and there is no one else with whom I'd rather be on this roller-coaster ride of publishing!

Thank you to my editor, Angela Kim, who knows exactly how to fine-tune these stories and make them really shine. Thank you to my whole team at Berkley, including Kristin Cipolla and Elisha Katz. Thank you, Katie Anderson, whose book designs are some of my favorites in the business. And thank you, Hannah Gramson, for your excellent copyediting skills.

Leni Kauffman, who has brought all the characters of Bright Falls to life, there are no words to express how much I love your work and how you've interpreted my characters. Thank you!

My writing crew—Meryl, Zabe, Emma, Christina, Mary, and Mary—thanks for the joy of your faces, your humor, your weirdness, and weathering all the blaring smoke alarms with me.

Thank you, Brooke, for being my first reader once again, and for so much more. Here's to many more first reads.

Meryl, thank you for always believing in me, for being my confidant, my friend. Stars and skies and galaxies.

Thank you, Craig, Benjamin, and William, for giving me time, space, and support, always.

IRIS KELLY DOESN'T DATE

Ashley Herring Blake

READERS GUIDE

QUESTIONS FOR DISCUSSION

1. Iris and Stevie are quite different in personality, but connect in a way they haven't with anyone else—why do you think they work?

2. Stevie struggles with an anxiety disorder. Can you identify ways that her anxiety debilitates parts of her day-to-day life as well as big-picture things? Is there any part that you can relate to?

3. Iris tries something new to get out of her funk and find inspiration. How do you gain inspiration, and what's the last new thing you've tried?

4. Do you have a favorite Shakespeare play? Would you ever want to try acting in a play?

5. Would you move across the country for someone?

6. Do you think Adri was still in love with Stevie?

7. Iris insisted she didn't need love to be happy—is she right? In what ways does love enhance our lives? Are there situations in which we really do need love—or some form of it—to be happy?

8. Stevie was worried about moving far away from her friends and community, but she's able to maintain her friendships and also make new ones. Do you have long-distance friends? How do you stay connected?

Keep reading for an excerpt of

MAKE THE SEASON BRIGHT

the next romantic comedy by Ashley Herring Blake

BRIGHTON FAIRBROOK WIPED down the lacquered bar, glaring as that night's live musician crooned a twangy version of "Silver Bells" into the tiny stage's microphone. The singer was a woman, with a jean skirt and cowboy boots, long dark hair, fingers plucking deftly at her Taylor guitar—three hundred series by the looks of it—while she sang about city sidewalks.

"She's not bad, huh?" Adele said, nudging her shoulder. Adele folded her brown arms, the sleeves of her button-up rolled to the elbow, a deep green vest cutting the perfect fit just like always. Her braids fell over her shoulder, black glasses perched on her nose as she listened to the act she herself had booked. Adele was Brighton's boss, owner of Ampersand—the bar where Brighton worked—and her only friend in this godforsaken city.

"Mesmerizing," Brighton said flatly, nodding at a customer lifting up their empty gin and tonic glass for another.

"Oh, come on," Adele said. "She's good."

"And hot," Brighton said, grabbing a new bottle of Beefeater gin from the amber-lit shelves behind the bar.

Adele smirked. "Aren't they all?"

Brighton had to laugh. Adele, a passionate lesbian, had yet to meet a female form—cis or trans—she didn't appreciate. Although, wisely, she never "slept with the talent," as she put it, the myriad singer-songwriters who came through here each month, searching for any stage that would have them and a willing audience. This was Nashville—stages abounded, as did audiences, but finding listeners who actually gave two shits . . . well, that was the real challenge. Everyone was a musician here, which meant everyone was good, everyone was competition, and no one was ever, ever impressed.

Brighton placed the fresh gin and tonic in front of her customer, telling herself she was glad to be free of Nashville's hamster wheel. She was glad to have steady work and good tips at Ampersand. She was glad she didn't have to constantly restring her guitar anymore, worry about humidity and the wood of her own Taylor getting warped. Didn't have to chase gigs, emailing bookers who would never email her back, and spend hours every night pouring out her heart and soul and blood into her songwriting notebook, only to be told she wasn't good enough, didn't have what it took, and face betrayal by the very fuckers she brought together as a band.

"You've got that look on your face again," Adele said. She was now sitting on a stool at the corner of the bar, the light from her iPad a blue glow reflecting on her glasses.

"What look?" Brighton said, slapping down a towel and wiping a spot that wasn't even dirty.

"That look that means you don't give a shit about tips."

Brighton lifted a brow. "Are you telling me to *smile*?"

"I would never. But maybe, you know, try to at least look like you're not out for blood."

Adele had a point. Brighton was barely making ends meet with her tips as it was—she couldn't afford to be grumpy. Her roommate,

Leah, had been pretty flexible on the rent lately, but it came with caveats. Last week, Brighton found herself at an ornament exchange party for the singles group at Leah's church. After being late with the rent three months in a row, Brighton hadn't felt like she could say no to the invite, so she ended up with a plastic Christmas pickle ornament and fake smiling for an hour at a guy in khakis and boat shoes while he talked about the album he just released, a folked-up version of sacred Christmas music, because of-fucking-course he was a musician too.

Leah had asked her about Boat Shoes for the next three days, but Brighton couldn't even remember his face, to be honest. Brighton liked cis men sometimes, but it took a lot to catch her attention, and Boat Shoes did nothing but bore her, despite Leah's insistence he was *the nicest guy.* Leah was twenty-four and a conservative Christian, a tiny detail she'd neglected to include on her Craigslist ad six months ago. The resulting partnership had made for an interesting living situation, considering Brighton was not only a flaming liberal, but also very, very queer.

Suffice it to say, Brighton was desperate to make the rent on time this month. Leah was perfectly nice, but whenever Brighton got roped into some church event, she ended up stuck in a conversation that was, essentially, some version of "hate the sin, love the sinner," and Brighton preferred to leave the word *sin* out of her identity altogether, thanks very much.

So she put on a smile, rolled her shoulders back, and fluffed her dark bangs so they fell over her forehead just so. At least she'd get out of this town in a few days, heading home to Michigan for Christmas. Her parents went all out for the holiday and, to be quite honest, Brighton couldn't wait. She wanted her mom's cinnamon hot chocolate and her family's traditional lineup of Christmas movies playing every night, always starting with *Home Alone.* She wanted to walk all bundled up through the snowy sand on the shore of Lake Michigan, waves frozen in mid-crest so that the whole world looked like another planet.

She and Lola used to—

She froze mid-stir of a dirty martini, shook her head to clear it. She and Lola . . . there was no she and Lola. Not anymore. Not for six years now, but Lola still crept into so many of her memories, like a habit, especially at Christmastime. Six years was nothing to the ten before that. Still, Lola might as well be a ghost, might as well not even exist at all, and Brighton didn't care to think too deeply about why.

About how it was all her fault.

She plopped an olive into the drink and handed it over to a girl with brown curls and green eyes. Their fingers brushed, just for a second. The girl smiled, her gaze slipping down from Brighton's own dark eyes and pale face to the tattoo of the Moon tarot card surrounded by peonies on her upper right arm.

"I love that," the girl said, eyes back on Brighton's.

"Thank you," Brighton said, feeling her cheeks warm and leaning her forearms onto the bar. She rightly sucked at dating, but hookups she could do. She looked at the girl through her lashes, smiled with one corner of her mouth. "It's—"

But she froze as Cowboy Boots shifted from "Silver Bells" into a song that most definitely was *not* a Christmas tune, the familiar, catchy melody like a splash of ice water on Brighton's face.

Rain is gone and I'm feeling light
Your ripped jeans like silk and wine
Cherry lipstick still on my mind
Can't blame me, darling, I'm back in line

Brighton closed her eyes, tried to block out the lyrics she'd heard on *Saturday Night Live* a month ago and now couldn't seem to escape even sitting in her own bar. The song, "Cherry Lipstick," was everywhere—Instagram, TikTok, YouTube, Spotify, covered at least twice a week in Ampersand. In the last six months, the band, a trio of queer women called the Katies, had rocketed from near nothingness to the hottest thing to hit millennial and Gen Z ears since Halsey.

To most people, "Cherry Lipstick" was just a song—a damn good indie pop song that many a gal would probably attach to their queer awakening, but a song nonetheless—and the Katies were just a band finding some success. Good on them. So this ubiquitous song playing in all corners of the world was fine and dandy . . . except for the fact that a mere nine months ago, Brighton had been the Katies' lead singer.

And now she most definitely was not.

Cowboy Boots came to the chorus, belting out the lyrics with such gusto, Brighton was nearly positive this woman was in the middle of her own awakening.

"Oh, I love this song." The girl was still standing in front of Brighton, martini in hand. "Don't you?"

"Ah, Christ," Adele said under her breath. "Here we go."

Brighton glared at her friend, then turned a saccharine smile on the girl. "It's a fucking masterpiece."

At Brighton's tone, the girl's smile dimmed and she drifted away back to her friends. Just as well. Brighton was clearly in no mood to be accommodating, and anyone who loved "Cherry Lipstick" was bound to be horrible in bed. Granted, Brighton knew her logic there made absolutely zero sense, but it made her feel better in the moment, so she went with it.

"Isn't it time for your break?" Adele asked.

Brighton sighed, pressed her fingers into her eyes. "Yeah."

"Then by all means, please." Adele waved her hand toward the back room, but her expression was soft. Adele knew all about the

Katies and Brighton, knew the whole affair was still an open wound. Knew Brighton hadn't touched her guitar or sung a single note since Alice and Emily's betrayal nine months ago.

Adele reached over and squeezed Brighton's hand, then gave her shoulder a little shove. "Go. Jake's got this."

Brighton obeyed, nodding to Jake, the other evening bartender, before pouring herself a large glass of water. She disappeared into the back, passing through the bustling kitchen making fries and Monte Cristos to get to Adele's office space, the song still trailing after her like a ghost.

I can't, I can't forget the taste
Your cherry lips, your swaying hips . . .

She kept moving, passing by Adele's desk and big leather couch to the back door. She burst outside into the cold December air, breathing it into her lungs like a new form of oxygen. She leaned against the building's red brick and closed her eyes, which were starting to feel annoyingly tight and watery. On Demonbreun Street, she could hear the bustle of the Saturday night crowd—laughter, even more live music, all the sounds she used to love.

The sounds she used to be a part of.

Because she clearly loved being miserable, she took out her phone and opened up the Katies' Instagram page. One hundred and ninety thousand followers. And counting, no doubt. Emily's dark curls haloed around her lovely face, falling nearly to her shoulders. She favored crop tops and plaid pants, and Brighton even spotted the pink-and-green pair Brighton herself had found at that thrift store in the Gulch last winter. Alice was brooding, as always. A tiny dark-haired pixie with huge butch energy.

Brighton and Emily met first at the Sunset Grill, where Brighton had gotten a job as a server when she first moved to Nashville six years ago. They bonded quickly over music, melancholy queers like Phoebe Bridgers and Brandi Carlile. They started playing together on their days off, messing around on Brighton's guitar and Emily's keyboard in Emily's tiny East Nashville apartment that she shared with three roommates, but they soon started writing. Writing turned into whole songs, which turned into small gigs at coffee shops, just to try it out.

That's how they met Alice.

They'd just finished playing a late afternoon set at JJ's Market, a quirky coffee shop slash convenience store on Broadway that also hosted live music, and Alice walked up to them afterward, declaring they needed a drummer.

"And you're just such a drummer?" Emily had asked.

Alice grinned. "I sure as hell am."

And she was—brilliant and passionate and driven. Soon, the three of them were sharing an apartment in Germantown, and when they discovered they all shared the same middle name, same spelling and everything—Katherine—the Katies were born.

That was four years ago. Four years of struggle, gigs that paid nothing, tiny regional tours to audiences of ten or less. Still, it was the best time in Brighton's life, the *reason* she'd blown up everything she ever thought her life would look like. It had been worth it . . . at least she thought so at the time, dreams still possible. Still alive.

Now Brighton couldn't help but smile at a photo of Alice smirking at a topless Emily, Emily's bare back to the viewer. They always had chemistry, though they'd never officially gotten together. She wondered if they were now, this silly photo evidence that they might have taken the leap.

Then she read the post's caption—a shoot for NME Magazine.

And on Emily's other side, there she was.

Sylvia.

Even her name sounded musical. Red hair like a Siren, feathery bangs like a rock star. Emily and Alice had discovered her in some bar in East Nashville nearly a year ago while Brighton had been home for Christmas. Emily wanted to bring her into the group as another singer and songwriter, a suggestion Brighton did not take very well. The three of them had been clashing lately, Emily and Alice wanting to go more King Princess–style pop, while Brighton clung to Phoebe Bridgers and Lizzy McAlpine as her inspirations.

Sylvia, of course, was pop all the way, funky and fresh and sexy as hell. Even Brighton could admit that. Then, this past March, it all came to a head when Emily invited Sylvia to a Katies practice without even running it by Brighton first. Sylvia played a new song on her guitar—"Cherry Lipstick"—and Brighton hated it. Said as much, which Sylvia took with an annoying amount of grace.

"This is the direction we're going, Brighton," Emily had said. "If you don't like it, maybe this isn't the best fit for you anymore."

Brighton had left before she really started crying, then went home to Michigan for a week, figuring everyone would calm down with some time off. But the day before she flew back, Emily called her, told her she was out.

And that was it.

Nearly four years of friendship and struggle and creative work, all finished in a single phone call, and for a redhead with a talent for writing bops.

Brighton knew she should swipe out of Instagram—her own account was currently set to private, with all of four followers, so there were no notifications for her to check. For Brighton, social media was now nothing more than a catalog of her failures, everything she was missing out on. Still, she couldn't help but type another name into the search bar, another account she didn't dare follow, but couldn't seem to leave alone either.

@RosalindQuartet

The grid was much different than the Katies—muted colors and the deep wood of stringed instruments, four beautiful, very clearly queer musicians in the throes of their art in various auditoriums and theaters.

One woman in particular drew Brighton's eye, always did. Salt-and-pepper-haired and gorgeous, quintessential red lipstick, black attire. Lola's style never changed, not that Brighton ever expected it to. She started going gray at twenty-one, and Brighton was glad to see she'd just let her hair silver, never dyeing once as far as Brighton could tell. It looked beautiful—regal and ethereal, just like Lola.

"What the hell are you doing out here?" Adele's voice piped up from behind her. Brighton clicked her phone dark. Adele knew about Lola . . . well, she knew that Brighton had been engaged, that the wedding was called off at the last minute, but that was about it. Brighton left out the smaller story points, as well as the fact that Lola was pretty much a world-famous violinist now.

No, Brighton kept that little tidbit for her own private musings, as well as any and all details about Brighton and Lola's disastrous wedding day.

"Just getting some air," she said to Adele now.

"It's freezing," Adele said, rubbing her arms.

Brighton nodded, goose bumps texturing her own bare arms. She hadn't even noticed, honestly. Too busy being a sad sack.

"Hey," Adele said, nudging her shoulder, "you need to go home?"

"Do you want me to?" Brighton asked. God, she really was a sad sack—her own boss was pretty much begging her not to work.

Adele pressed her mouth flat. "You've got to move on at some point, baby girl."

She said it so softly, so gently, Brighton nearly started crying right there. Trouble was, she felt like she'd been *moving on* for the last six years, and she hadn't gotten anywhere.

Before she could say anything else, her phone vibrated in her hand with a call. Only one person ever called her, so her heart already felt ten times lighter when she saw *Mom* flashing across the screen.

"Mama, hey," she said, her throat thickening as she pressed the phone to her ear. *Mama* only slipped out when she was feeling really sorry for herself.

Adele gestured to the door, but Brighton shook her head, grabbed onto Adele's arm. She didn't want to stand out here alone anymore, even with her mom on the phone.

"Hi, darling," her mother said. "I've got Dad on the line here too. You're on speaker!"

"Hey, Rainbow," her dad said, employing his name for her ever since she was four and latched onto a Rainbow Brite doll. The nickname became even more fitting when she came out as bisexual when she was thirteen. "How are you?"

"I'm good," she said, her voice nearly fluorescent. Adele rolled her eyes. "Can't wait to be home in a few days." She stuck her tongue out at Adele.

"Oh, honey," her mom said. "I know. That's actually why we're calling."

Brighton's back snapped straight, all her senses on alert. Her mom's tone had gone a bit saccharine, almost song-like, the way it always did when she had to deliver bad news.

"What's wrong?" Brighton asked. "Are you both okay? Is Grandma all right?"

"Fine, Rainbow," her dad said. "Everyone's fine. Fit as fiddles."

Brighton exhaled. "Okay. Then . . ."

Her parents were quiet for a second before her mom said it all in one rushed breath. "The magazine is sending me to Provence to review a new winery, so your dad and I are going to be in France for the rest of the year. I'm so sorry, baby."

It took Brighton a second to register her mother's words. But when they hit, they hit hard. "What?" was all she could get out, her voice a pathetic squeak.

"I know," her mom said. "The timing is so horrible, but the magazine just landed a spot at the winery's opening last week and we're the only American publication invited, so it's a pretty huge deal."

Brighton felt dizzy and slunk down on the wall a bit more. The rough brick scratched her back and Adele grabbed her arm.

You okay? Adele mouthed.

Brighton couldn't answer. Didn't *know* the answer. Her mom had been the head chef at Simone's, a fancy restaurant in Grand Haven, for all of Brighton's childhood. Five years ago, she retired—arthritis making it too hard for her to continue working in a kitchen—and started writing for *Food & Wine* magazine, traveling the country and reviewing restaurants and bistros. She loved it, and Brighton knew going to France to do nothing but eat and drink wine and write about all the eating and drinking was a dream come true for her.

"That's great," she managed to say.

"I wish we could bring you with us, honey," her mom said. "I asked the magazine, but—"

"No, it's okay," Brighton said carefully. "It's fine. I'll be fine." Her brain whirled, trying to think just how she'd be *fine*. Her only grandmother lived in Florida, near her mom's oldest sister, Brighton's aunt Rebecca. She supposed she could go there, but the idea of spending Christmas in swampy Tampa, her uncle Jim drinking Bud Light Lime in his pleather La-Z-Boy and watching Fox News twenty-four hours a day made Brighton literally nauseous.

"You sure?" her mom said. "We don't have to go."

That sobered Brighton up a little. "Mom. Of course you have to go."

"That's my Rainbow," her dad said, and Brighton could tell he was smiling. "I told her you'd be fine. You're a grown woman."

"A grown woman," Brighton repeated, as though saying it out loud would make it true. She felt anything but her two-years-shy-of-thirty right now. Still, a lie rolled off her tongue, easy as pie. "Yeah. I . . . I have some friends here who are getting together on Christmas Day."

Adele's brow lifted.

Brighton ignored her.

"I'll spend the day with them," Brighton continued. "It'll be fun."

"Oh good," her mom said, exhaling so loudly her breath buzzed into the phone. "I'm so glad to hear that, baby."

Brighton nodded, even though her mother couldn't see her, and proceeded to ask all the right questions about her parents' trip—when they were leaving, the name of the winery, etcetera and so forth.

By the time she hung up ten minutes later, her chest felt tight enough to burst.

"Aren't you a smooth liar," Adele said, pocketing her own phone and leaning one shoulder against the brick wall, facing Brighton with her arms folded.

Brighton leaned her head against the building, looked up at the inky black sky. "My parents are going to France for the holidays, I had to say something."

Just like she'd said so many somethings to her parents since the Katies booted her out—*I'm doing awesome! Things are going great! Of course I'm still playing! I've got a gig this weekend! And the next! I'm a star!*

Okay, she hadn't exactly said that last one, but the spirit was the same. Her parents believed she was a fully-functioning adult in Nashville, paying her rent dutifully and living her musical dream as a solo artist. They didn't even know how to access Instagram or

TikTok, much less search for their own daughter among the accounts. The lies were easy, harmless, and made Brighton feel like someday, they might actually cease to be lies if she just kept at it. Kept at . . . what?

All she was doing was slinging martinis and grinding her teeth at every musician who stepped onto the Ampersand's stage.

"Fuck," she said, dropping her head into her hands. She just wanted to go home. Maybe she still could. She had a plane ticket. She loved Grand Haven more than any other place in the world. She'd be fine spending Christmas . . . all alone.

But without her parents, she'd have no buffer. No traditions to fall back on. Every shop and restaurant, every bike path and snow-covered sand dune, every rise and fall of the lake already reminded her of Lola, every time she went home, but she always had her parents to distract her. Her mom, only twenty-one years old when she had Brighton, was her best friend, and without her . . .

Brighton would drown under all the memories. She'd absolutely drown by herself. She knew she would.

Before she could stop them, tears streamed down her cheeks. She tried to wipe them away—Adele was her friend, sure, but Brighton hated crying in front of people—but Adele saw them anyway.

"Baby girl," Adele said, pulling Brighton into her arms, which really set Brighton's tears loose. Adele patted her back and let her cry, which Brighton took full advantage of. She couldn't even remember the last time someone hugged her—probably her mother, back in March, right before her entire life blew up.

Again.

"All right," Adele said, rubbing Brighton's cold arms. "Okay, here's what we're going to do." She pulled back and looked Brighton in the eyes. "You're coming home with me for Christmas."

Brighton blinked. Sniffed some snot back up her nose. "What?"

"You heard me," Adele said. "You're not going home by yourself, and I know I'm your only fucking friend in the world, so you're coming to Colorado with me. You can tell all your woes to my mom over a nice cup of cocoa—she'll love it, my sister and I never tell her anything."

Brighton prepared herself to refuse, but who the hell was she kidding? Adele *was* her only friend, and she was desperate enough right now that the idea of crying into a strange woman's lap actually sounded pretty nice.

So she nodded, dried her eyes with her shirt, and then she and Adele went back to work. The next day, she got on her airline's website and then went to a potluck dinner with Leah, complete with a five-minute blessing over the green bean casserole, having spent her rent money on the exorbitant fee to change her plane ticket from Grand Rapids to Colorado Springs.

ASHLEY HERRING BLAKE is an award-winning author. She loves coffee, cats, melancholy songs, and happy books. She is the author of the adult romance novels *Delilah Green Doesn't Care*, *Astrid Parker Doesn't Fail*, and *Iris Kelly Doesn't Date*, the young adult novels *Suffer Love*, *How to Make a Wish*, and *Girl Made of Stars*, and the middle grade novels *Ivy Aberdeen's Letter to the World*, *The Mighty Heart of Sunny St. James*, and *Hazel Bly and the Deep Blue Sea*. She's also a coeditor on the young adult romance anthology *Fools in Love*. She lives on a very tiny island off the coast of Georgia with her family.

VISIT ASHLEY HERRING BLAKE ONLINE

AshleyHerringBlake.com
🐦 AshleyHBlake
📷 AshleyHBlake
📌 AEHBlake